ALISTAIR'S KISSES WERE
RARE AS DIAMONDS

Pen was surprised, hopeful, when he bent his mouth to her own. Cool and firm, his lips took hers, while one hand caressed the small of her back and the other came up to cup her breast. A thousand times since he had kissed her weeks ago, she had dreamed of this. Her body responded deliriously. Pressed so close against him, she nearly forgot to breathe. It could have been a single heartbeat that shook them both.

Finally he freed her, looking down at her now with intense blue eyes the color of searing flame.

"Go," he said, "before I throw propriety to the winds."

She went—not knowing the day would come when Alistair would beg her to stay...

D1602582

AND NOW...

 # SUPERROMANCES

As the world's No. 1 publisher of best-selling romance fiction, we are proud to present a sensational new series of modern love stories— SUPERROMANCES.

Written by masters of the genre, these longer, sensual and dramatic novels are truly in keeping with today's changing life-styles. Full of intriguing conflicts, the heartaches and delights of true love, SUPERROMANCES are absorbing stories— satisfying and sophisticated reading that lovers of romance fiction have long been waiting for.

 # SUPERROMANCES
Contemporary love stories for the woman of today!

JOCELYN GRIFFIN

BELOVED INTRUDER

Harlequin Books

TORONTO • LONDON • LOS ANGELES • AMSTERDAM
SYDNEY • HAMBURG • PARIS • STOCKHOLM • ATHENS • TOKYO

Harlequin first edition, October 1981

ISBN 0-373-70008-3

CHAPTER ONE

PEN'S EYES WIDENED for a moment as she stifled a
yawn. It was only, manners, however, and not
interest that made her bother, she admitted to
herself. All of these conversations about casting
calls, rehearsals and new productions might be
important to Nigel's theater friends, but the un-
varnished truth was that they bored her. With a
polite murmur she doubted anyone even heard,
Pen turned away from the fringes of the group
nearest her.

Other voices and loud music swirled around
her, while a thick haze of smoke drifted overhead.
In the press of bodies someone bumped against
her and disappeared into the mob again without
even noticing—or caring—that he'd jostled the
last of her drink onto her dress. She patted at it in-
effectually, then resigned herself to sending it out
for cleaning the following morning. In the meantime, if she didn't get at least a whiff of breathable
air she'd probably suffocate right here—and go
unnoticed for hours, she added to herself hollow-
ly.

One of Nigel's caterers went by, and she managed to leave her now empty glass on his tray, then concentrated on getting across the room to the long windows that opened onto a minute balcony. If she could just get out there, she could escape this lunacy for a few minutes at least! Using a combination of sweet smiles and sharp elbows, tried in desperation when nothing else worked, she struggled across the crowded room through the voices that rose and fell around her.

"The casting call is tomorrow morning at nine, you know."

"...Lady Macbeth, and just as I reached, 'Here's the smell of blood still,' I began *sneezing*!"

"I'd do absolutely anything to get a part in that one."

"Yes, I know."

"Tony did a perfectly dreadful job with that production and the critics were merciless, don't you remember?" That voice spoke with a sort of malicious enjoyment.

Another one purred, "Of course he's witty, but he hasn't written a play worth staging in five years, darling."

"He just gave me one of those martyred looks and sighed, 'Next, please.'"

"The real problem is that he drinks."

"...it all depends on who you know. That's how you have to break in."

As the sounds beat through the smoky air, Pen felt as though she were searching the dial of a radio, hearing individual voices come and go like different stations. But this radio played only theater "programs," and all the stations sounded the same—strident, artificial or even catty. Finally, though, she reached the far side of the room; a little fumbling with the catch, and she was through the windows, pulling them to behind her so that they shut off the radio abruptly.

Outside in the early March night, she leaned on the balcony railing and drew in deep thankful breaths of air that was sweet even here in the city, too hot and flustered to care that it was also still a bit chilly. Maybe she had claustrophobia, she speculated wryly, and had just never noticed before. Come to think of it, she had loathed Nigel's last two parties, too, and they had been just as crowded and noisy as this one. Nigel, of course, must be loving them. He had worked tirelessly to earn all this recognition for his set designs, and now that he'd finally made a name for himself as one of London's most talented newcomers to the theater scene, he seemed to revel in the attention.

Just as she thought that, however, the windows opened and closed again, and Nigel squeezed in beside her on the tiny balcony. Pen had swung around in dismay at having her retreat invaded, but her expression changed to amusement as he looked at her with a comically relieved face.

"Whew!" He mopped his brow with an over-sized gesture. "Sanctuary!"

"Refuge from your enemies?" Pen questioned. "Oh, come now! You know you love every minute of these parties, when all these people come to lionize you."

"Do I?" She'd been teasing, but for a moment as he looked back at her the usual bright satirical gleam was entirely gone from his black eyes. "I wonder. I'm beginning to have a faint niggling suspicion, my Penelope, that they come not to see me but simply to be seen by each other. London's 'brilliant new young set designer'—" his voice gave the quoted words an almost bitter twist "—is really just running an employment agency, and that's all his hard work has achieved."

Startled, Pen could only gaze at him, wondering what to say. If Nigel was right, then his "triumph" must be tasting like ashes, and what could she possibly say to make it more palatable? Before she could think of anything, however, he seemed to erase the hard unfamiliar look from his face with an effort of will, and when he spoke again it was to complain lightly, "Pretty crowded refuge you have out here anyway, my girl."

Back on more solid ground now, Pen responded spiritedly, "It wasn't until you came out here, too!"

"Well, since I'm here now, we'll clearly have to make better use of what little space is available. Come here so I can put my arms around you. That way we'll take up less space, you see."

Agreeably Pen shifted so that she was pressed

against Nigel's chest, and when he linked his arms around her she leaned her head on his shoulder with the ease of old habit. For a few minutes they just looked companionably down at the street-lamps glowing quietly in the narrow road three stories below them, while the noise of the party went on unabated behind the windows. Then Nigel murmured hopefully in Pen's ear, "I've had an idea how we can take up even less space."

"Oh?" She looked up laughing, guessing what his drift might be. "And what was that?"

"This," he replied promptly, holding her more tightly so that he could cover her lips with his own. Idly she wondered how many times they'd kissed each other—certainly it was no small number; they'd been going out together ever since those first few chaotic months of art school four years ago. Then she stopped thinking about the past, because right now, in spite of all those other kisses, there was something unusual about this one. This wasn't the familiar casual embrace she knew so well. Instead, this time Nigel seemed to be kissing her with a sort of desperate thoroughness. Increasingly breathless, she tried to respond but was almost relieved when he lifted his mouth from hers and held her at arm's length to look into her puzzled face.

"I have another idea, too, Penelope," he said, his own face shadowed against the windows' light so that she couldn't read it.

"What's that?" she asked, totally at sea now.

"Come and share my tiny apartment as well as my even tinier balcony."

"What?" she repeated blankly.

He dropped his arms from around her and flung his head back, putting one hand on his heart to declaim, " 'Come live with me, and be my love, and we will all the pleasures prove.' "

She didn't respond immediately, so he went on more mundanely, "Move in with me, Pen, and then when I'm lionized—for whatever that's worth—you can be lionessed."

No, this wasn't a proposal, as she'd almost thought for a moment; it was a proposition. Startled, Pen tried to collect her wits and respond matter-of-factly. On the few occasions when she had taken a little time from the present to wonder about the future, she had assumed vaguely that someday Nigel would probably propose and she'd probably accept his proposal. She hadn't ever considered his propositioning her, but now that he had, she realized the possibility should have occurred to her. For a lot of people it seemed to be more the style—at least these days. The question was, was it hers?

"Nigel," she began tentatively, "I'm awfully fond of you, of course—"

"Then move in," he interrupted, "and you can fondly protect me from those theater people who are in there right now parading for each other, pouring drinks on my plants, dribbling ashes on my rugs and eating me out of house and home."

In spite of Pen's surprise, laughter bubbled up in her, but she said, "No, seriously—"

"Not seriously. Just fondly, say yes."

She reached up and turned his head so that the light fell across his face, revealing the familiar satyr look that was the product of his slanting black brows and thick dark hair. One lock of it fell over his forehead, and she pushed it back absently, letting her hand fall to his shoulder afterward. "But I already have a roommate," she evaded. "What about Bree?"

"She can move in with her Sam, and we'll all prove the pleasures," Nigel returned without hesitation. "So that's taken care of. Now say yes."

"I honestly don't know if I can."

"Think about it and then say yes."

"I'll think about it, anyway."

"Think fast. I definitely need you to come protect me." His eyes were in the shadows again. "I sometimes have an uneasy feeling that if I see too much of these theater people I could turn into one of them, and then I'd be lost without redemption."

"No, never that." She smiled up at him. "But for now, at any rate, I have to go home. I'm afraid I've had about as much of your party as I can manage."

"Deserter! So have I, and I can't leave."

"And *this* is what he's generously offering to share with me," Pen observed to the street below, and then ducked aside laughing as Nigel reached for her threateningly. She blew him an unrepentant kiss and fled through the windows, leaving him to brave the mob inside or not as he chose. For herself, she braved it temporarily, working her way back across Nigel's small living room to the little bedroom studio where she'd left her coat. Then it took only one more brief struggle for her to get to the outer door, and she was free at last.

Half an hour later she reached the welcome peace of her own tiny apartment, which she'd shared with Bree Davis since art-school days. Bree was still out when Pen arrived, so she set her dress aside to go for cleaning and washed the odor of smoke out of her hair. That done, she combed her hair dry in front of the electric fire, thinking about Nigel and his startling proposition.

Somehow, even though other people shared apartments, it really had never occurred to her that he might calmly suggest they live together— although by now she ought to be used to his doing the unexpected! Willingly distracted, Pen turned away from the immediate problem with a reminiscent little smile as she remembered how she had first met Nigel Burnett.

Already friends with Bree and Sam, she had been working hard to keep up in art school when she noticed Nigel and realized that at least one person apparently took his work far less seriously. He had been in her life-drawing class, and she first became aware of him when he solicitously helped that day's model onto a metal chair that was icy cold because he had just brought it in from outdoors, where the temperature was nearly freezing. Not surprisingly, when she felt the cold metal on her bare skin the model had leaped to her feet, shrieking—and in the resulting uproar Pen had taken her first good look at the laughing faunlike face that was to become so familiar.

In spite of that zany debut, when she got to know him well, Nigel had proved to be full of contradictions. On one hand he was capable of such nonsense as attending classes for a month dressed in a full-length burlap sack, instead of the more "artistic" clothes nearly everyone else affected. But on the other hand he was already so seriously interested in set design for the theater that he dragged her to nearly every play opening in London.

Together they had found inexpensive seats "up in the gods" for musicals in the West End, waited in line to get standing room for serious drama at the Old Vic, explored smaller theaters like the Mermaid and the Roundhouse and investigated theater-in-the-round at the Royal Court. Occasionally they even managed to go out to Stratford to see one of the Royal Shakespeare Company's productions. And everywhere they went Nigel made sketches and notes, copying sets, redesigning sets and inventing sets. Pen, meanwhile, had simply enjoyed the plays and being with Nigel; all of this was a welcome break from classes, but she

developed no abiding passion for the theater—or
for theater people!

Her hair dry at last, lulled by the fire's warmth
and too tired to think anymore, Pen crawled
thankfully into bed, promising herself that no
matter what she decided to do about Nigel's suggestion, she was *never* going to another one of
those awful parties. He might as well entertain by
staging a little riot! She knew full well that Nigel
wasn't likely to let the issue of his proposition rest.
She might prefer to, but he would insist on an
answer.

Right now, though, sleep seemed more urgent
than answers. She burrowed into the bedclothes
and admitted wryly to herself that at any rate, illustrating children's books wasn't likely ever to
bring her rewards as mixed as the ones Nigel was
getting.

She was fathoms deep in slumber when Bree
bounced mercilessly on her bed, demanding that
she wake up *immediately*.

"Why?" Pen inquired sleepily, her eyes still
resolutely closed. "What could possibly be so important it can't wait until a civilized hour in the
morning?"

"This could!" Bree's laughing voice had a
triumphant note that was new, and it finally
opened Pen's eyes. The elfin face above her was
alight, the feathery hair ruffled—and on the hand
Bree extended for inspection, a small diamond
glowed.

"Bree!" Satisfactorily awake at last, Pen flung her arms around her friend. "I thought you were going to a new Chinese restaurant, not a jeweler's!" she teased.

"We did," Bree chuckled happily. "Sam took me to the restaurant, and at the end of the meal they brought us fortune cookies. When I opened mine, this fell out—" she cast the ring another delighted look "—along with a fortune that said, 'You will marry the lovable man sitting at your table—please?' And when I turned to him, he was looking so scared and hopeful I didn't see what else I could do but say yes!"

Pen hugged her again and asked, "Well, when do you say it again in front of the witnesses?"

"In two weeks! Sam's just been notified he was awarded that teaching post in New Zealand he wanted so badly, and they asked him to go out there immediately. He says he won't go without me, though...." Her color rose again, and she put her hands up to cool her hot cheeks, finishing in a rush, "So I'll be getting married and emigrating all at once. Oh, Pen, you've got to help! There's so much to do!"

The last was almost a wail, so Pen put on a grave face and said sympathetically, "I know, love. It's so bad you just don't want to get married at all."

"Well..." Bree began to disclaim, but then she looked suspiciously at Pen, whose gravity collapsed into giggles, and rational discussion gave way to a session of jokes about weddings and brides.

It lasted long enough for both of them to be completely exhausted by laughter, but finally they pulled themselves together again and began to draw up lists and make Bree's plans. That kept them both awake for another hour until at last Bree took the lists and stretched out on her bed to look them over in comfort, "for just a minute." But a minute later she was asleep, with a faint smile on her face and her cheek pillowed on her left hand so that the new ring was near her lips.

Pen, somehow still wide awake, looked affectionately at her sleeping friend. Bree was a dear, and so was her Sam. In the four years since they'd all met at school, those two had quietly but steadily fallen deeper and deeper in love. It had been obvious for nearly a year now that they would eventually marry, but Sam had stubbornly held off proposing until he could offer Bree more of a future than his present job doing commercial lettering afforded. Now they'd have that secure future; Sam loved to teach, and Bree could work free-lance at home in the house that came with Sam's position. It was a perfect opportunity for them, and Pen was delighted—she only wished it weren't going to take them half a world away, for she'd miss them badly and so would Nigel.

And there was another thing. Pen frowned a little to herself as she gently draped a quilt over the sleeping Bree and switched off the overhead light.

Slipping back into her own tumbled bed, she bunched her pillow against the headboard and leaned back into it, staring thoughtfully around the little room she'd shared with Bree for nearly four years. With Bree gone she would have to look for another roommate—or accept Nigel's proposition that she move in with him. Certainly her handy objection that she couldn't abandon Bree was useless now! That problem was solved, but somehow it didn't make Pen feel any more eager to go and live with Nigel; much as she cared about him, she just couldn't see herself in that kind of situation.

Then what kind would be better, a practical little voice in her mind asked, and she tried to answer the question honestly, making herself think seriously about a relationship she had been taking for granted. Marriage was what she had always vaguely expected her relationship with Nigel would lead to; she supposed she had been assuming that after Bree and Sam were married, she and Nigel would follow suit. But a wedding wasn't what he had suggested tonight.

Pen rolled onto her side and propped her head on one hand, gazing at the nearby figure that was Bree—Bree, whose feelings for her Sam lighted her whole small face with candles. Sam looked about the same way, too, and Pen had teased them gently about it but had known it meant they were well armored for any battles they might have to fight side by side. But she and Nigel didn't look at each other that way, and now Pen realized it consciously for the first time. They loved each other; was it perhaps that they weren't "in love" with each other? At any rate, whatever tender magic glowed between Bree and Sam, it didn't seem to exist yet between herself and Nigel. Had he been aware of that when he suggested living together instead of marrying?

Lying in her quiet room with only Bree's soft breathing for company, Pen admitted to herself that she couldn't imagine marrying Nigel unless she felt the way Bree did. She didn't, so clearly marriage *wasn't* right for them—at least not now. But perhaps their relationship was just slower to develop than Bree's and Sam's; sharing an apartment might bring them closer, so that marriage would be the next natural step. Maybe Nigel had the right idea after all, and she was just being old-fashioned in hesitating to accept it. Maybe if she could just put her doubts aside, she and Nigel would eventually find the same magic as Bree and Sam. Longingly, Pen knew she hoped so, but she still felt undecided.

At any rate, for the next two weeks she would be so busy helping Bree prepare for the wedding and pack for New Zealand that she wouldn't have much time to think about Nigel's suggestion. Pen realized this with a sense of relief that was the measure of her confusion. With a last wistful look at Bree, dreaming so happily nearby, Pen curled into her bedclothes and fled from her problem into sleep at last.

LONG AFTER Pen had finally dozed off, Nigel saw the last of his guests out the door with profound relief and then turned back to the wreckage of his apartment. The three musicians he'd hired had long since gone, but the caterers were still dimly visible through the haze as they quietly collected half-empty plates of wilting hors d'oeuvres and lipstick-stained glasses from every horizontal surface. Going to the windows, he swung them wide open to the cool night air and tiredly watched it wash into the smoky room. A glass rolled away from his foot, and he resisted the urge to kick it childishly, folding his arms grimly across his chest instead.

One of the caterers, a graying motherly woman with humorous eyes, retrieved the errant glass and said to him understandingly, "'Old on, ducks. We'll 'ave it set to right in 'arf a mo'."

Nigel glanced over at her quickly, then gave her a sudden sweet smile that softened the sardonic lines into which his face had fallen. "I know that, and I'm devoutly thankful to you for it."

"If you'd be wantin' to lie low for a bit, like, we could be off without disturbin' you when we're through," she offered.

"Done," he agreed readily, remembering that the room that served as both studio and bedroom for him had been left relatively undisturbed because the guests, except for Pen, had simply flung their wraps in a heap on a chair by the door. That one room ought to be a haven of peace in all this mess. "I'll bid you a good-night right now, then, and thank you again." And with a last smile he beat a quick retreat.

But not to solitude. His room was as orderly as he'd hoped, with almost everything in its accustomed place, but stretched out on his bed was a woman who was certainly *not* in her accustomed place. He was sure he'd never seen her before, but paradoxically she seemed faintly familiar anyway.

He didn't realize she was there until he'd closed the door rather noisily and she sat up at the sound, blinking as if she'd been asleep and patting vaguely at tendrils of chestnut hair that had escaped from a sophisticated knot at the top of her head.

Already tired and irritated, Nigel could only think that his last remaining refuge had been invaded. The slanting black brows dropped as his usual suavity deserted him, and he barked, "Who the hell are you?"

She swung long slim legs in very sheer hose to the edge of his bed and then adjusted the neckline of her low-cut amber dress before answering with surprising composure, "Elise Robbins." Her voice was low and musical, and entirely free of the slight hoarse unsteadiness common to most newly awakened people.

Its beauty didn't pacify him, however, and he stayed where he was, looming over her. When she spoke again, her voice had taken on a more placatory tone. "I'm sorry. I came in here to lie down for a bit, because I had the most beastly headache, and I must have fallen asleep. I wonder if I've been here very long?"

"Long enough so that everyone else has gone," Nigel answered unpromisingly, and at that she stood up with a suddenness that still managed to be graceful.

"Oh, no! Really? But I was to have a lift home with the people who brought me!" Her voice became a soft tremulous wail, and she turned to him with widened appealing eyes.

"Since it's well past three o'clock in the morning, they seem to have given up on you and left," he answered, but more gently.

"But how can I get home? I'll never be able to find a cab at this hour."

The lovely voice trailed off forlornly, and somewhat to his surprise Nigel found himself saying with only the least trace of resignation, "Never mind. I can give you a lift myself; I have an old Volvo down on the street."

Her face cleared as if by magic, and she said warmly, "Thank you! Oh, I do appreciate your going out again in the middle of the night like this for me."

Good thing she did, Nigel thought wearily, because his tired mind and body certainly wouldn't appreciate it; so much for the quiet solitude he'd been craving. He motioned her politely ahead of him, however, and turned resolutely away from his bed. In the living room the woman ahead of him waved cheerily to the surprised caterers and extracted some sort of soft gold wrap from behind the chair his other guests had used as makeshift coatrack, and in a few moments she sat beside him in the Volvo, chatting lightly in that pleasant voice.

In a surprisingly short time she had directed him to a handsome block of new apartments. Switching off the car's engine, he walked around to let her out, but when she stood beside him on the sidewalk, she hesitated.

"We've never even been properly introduced—I just came along to your party with some other people who know you—and yet you were kind enough to bring me home like this. Couldn't I fix you a drink or something, please, just to repay you a little bit?"

She looked pleadingly at Nigel with eyes that were wide and shadowy, and intending to say no, he found himself saying yes instead. Oh, well, he thought, riding up in the elevator with her, at this hour of the night what did a few minutes more matter?

It was longer than a few minutes, however. When he awoke in the morning he was in a strange bedroom and Elise lay sleeping beside him. His past had not been monkish, and he had awakened in other women's rooms before, but the odd thing was that this time he couldn't at first recall how he came to be there. Then gradually, frowning in concentration, he remembered the strong drink she'd fixed him, this stranger who lay beside him in a tangle of satin sheets. And at one point, while he was cautiously sipping it, she'd vanished, reappearing in some sort of negligee that had revealed more than it covered. He remembered also that she'd offered to massage his aching neck and shoulders, and that, too, had all been part of her "thanks." Apparently her gratitude for a small favor had even reached this far. He glanced around the luxurious room again, and when his eyes had finished their tour, Elise was watching him from the other pillow, completely awake.

Her hair had come down from last night's knot, tumbling loosely over her shoulders this morning, and now, appalled, he knew why he'd thought when he first saw her that she looked faintly familiar. She did indeed; except for the fact that her features were sharper and her eyes green instead of gray, she looked enough like Pen to be her sister. Oh, Lord, he groaned to himself, what weird ideas had that damn drink put into his head? "All cats are gray in the dark." The cynical old saying popped into his mind, and he scowled at applying it to Pen. To deflect the thought, he spoke.

"Good morning," he said rather gruffly to the woman beside him, wondering how she felt about him this morning and whether she was as unsure of her ground as he felt of his.

"Good morning to you," she returned calmly, and that answered one of his questions. However it had happened, this woman obviously had no regrets about whatever had happened last night. But why this interest in a perfect stranger? Or a not-so-perfect one, he amended mentally.

"Would you like breakfast?" she asked, and the beautiful voice was rather more businesslike than it had been last night.

"Yes, thank you. If it's not too much trouble," he accepted cautiously.

"No, of course not. I'll be fixing something for myself anyway," she returned briskly, and that answered another question. This woman wasn't the least bit uncertain about anything. Swinging gracefully from the oversize bed, she collected her negligee from the floor and pulled it on in one smooth gesture, then disappeared. In a few minutes he was dressed and following the aroma of coffee into a tiny kitchenette he hadn't even noticed the night before.

Leaning casually against a small fridge, she was sipping from a steaming mug, and another sat beside a plate of toast on a narrow counter between them. She gestured an invitation, and he applied himself to the breakfast she provided while she watched him with unrevealing green eyes.

Just as he reluctantly admitted to himself that his chewing seemed abnormally loud, and that each movement of his jaws seemed to be setting up jackhammers in his brain, she finally broke the long silence to say, "I'll be finished with this in a moment, and then it will take me about twenty minutes to dress. Would you mind waiting?"

"Of course not," he answered briefly, becoming unpleasantly aware that the demolition work in his head was apparently going to include his stomach, as well. When she left to dress he pushed the rest of the plate of toast away and concentrated on drinking as much coffee as he could stand, thinking irritably that last night's party had been even more of a disaster than he'd realized at the time. Not only had it left his apartment a shambles, but it had also landed him here, with the world's worst hangover and some sort of relationship with a woman he'd never even met twelve hours ago.

When she came back half an hour later he was feeling somewhat more in control of his rebellious body but only minimally civil. The fact that she was now immaculate in a dress of some soft green material didn't make him any sunnier, either, and he looked at her rather sourly as he fingered the stubble on his chin.

"Thank you for waiting," she said, and he nodded shortly. "Now if I could beg a lift from you, as well, please...?"

She let the request trail off charmingly, but he wasn't charmed. "Fine," he said flatly. "Where would you like to go?"

"To the theater, of course," she answered, and he raised his eyebrows stiffly at the "of course." "For the casting call this morning," she explained patiently, as if to a slow child, and painfully his thumping brain reminded him that he'd known all along the newest play he was designing sets for was to be cast this week. Then he laboriously worked out the corollary of her remark: this Elise Robbins hadn't just happened to come to his party by chance; she was an actress. Just what he needed, he thought bitterly.

"I'll drop you at the door, then," he suggested testily. "That way you needn't be embarrassed by coming in with me."

Her laughter was a lovely sound, but it knifed through his ears, and her words were worse. "Embarrassed? Not likely, my dear. Coming in with Nigel Burnett could only be a recommendation for any ambitious actress."

And that answered the last question he'd awakened with: now he knew why she'd been interested in him in the first place. For a long minute he simply looked at her, then he spun on his heel and left. The outer door slammed behind him, but Elise only shrugged and followed, too practical to miss her lift.

CHAPTER TWO

HAVING DECIDED that Sam *was*, in fact, worth all the confusion, Bree managed with Pen's help to finish everything she needed to do in the next two weeks; right on schedule she said her yes again in front of the registrar, with Pen and Nigel as witnesses. Then she tossed her bouquet neatly into Pen's hands, and she and Sam were off—their honeymoon would be en route to New Zealand and a new life.

Pen and Nigel stood side by side to wave goodbye to the other two as they climbed into the cab that would take them to Victoria Station, and after they had disappeared from view Nigel dropped his hand and turned to look at Pen, whose own hand was falling to her side much more slowly.

"Very nice," he commented, raising one eyebrow quizzically and surveying the picture she made in a pale green spring suit that set off the ivory of Bree's flowers. "A bit damp—" he shook out a large handkerchief and mopped her eyes "—but otherwise quite lovely."

Pen managed a watery chuckle at this qualified

compliment, and he brushed a brief kiss across the top of her head before releasing her and saying very practically, "However, in spite of your very evident attractions, my Penelope, I'm due back at the theater yet this afternoon for a meeting with the playwright and the director. Before I have to be there, can I give you a lift? Preferably to my apartment, of course."

"Oh, Nigel—" Pen began, but he cut in smoothly.

"However, I won't insist on that just yet. Where would you like to go instead, to flee from my clutches?"

She hesitated, thinking of the empty spaces where Bree's things had been and all too conscious of how large a two-person apartment could be when only one was left. On the other hand, somehow she still wasn't ready to tell Nigel she would move into his little one-person apartment and make it far littler with two, either.

"Home, please, Nigel," she said finally. "Home to Dulwich."

He slanted a satiric look at her and murmured sweetly, "Hiding from the wolf where there's safety in numbers? Yes, my little lamb, whatever you desire."

His little lamb recovered herself sufficiently to make a face at him and counter, "Baa, humbug!" and they walked to his car laughing. Half an hour later the Volvo deposited her in front of a comfortable red-brick house on the southern edge of

London, where her professor father searched endlessly for the answers to profound philosophical questions—and for peace and quiet in the midst of his vociferous family. There Pen was welcomed with the usual affectionate uproar that left her no more time to miss Bree or wonder what to do about Nigel's proposition.

"Hello, love," her mother greeted her while her father gave her a vague but loving smile. "How was the wedding?"

"Pen!" Fifteen-year-old Sally pounced before her sister had a chance to answer. "You caught the bouquet! Are you going to marry Nigel, then? Can I be your bridesmaid? When's it going to be?"

"A wedding—ugh!" Twelve-year-old Evan cut across Sally's raptures. "Pen, you wouldn't!"

At the same time Margery—at ten the baby of the family—breathed, "Ooh, Pen, you look so nice!" With no apparent guile she added wistfully, "And your flowers are so pretty."

"Yes, pet," Pen confirmed, responding to everyone in reverse order with the ease of long practice, "and you may have them." She handed Bree's bouquet to her youngest sibling, and Margery bore it off triumphantly, away from Sally's envious gaze. "Yes, I would, Evan, but not right now, so you're safe for the time being. And yes, Sal, you may be my bridesmaid whenever I get married, but no, it won't be anytime in the immediate future because no one's asked me to marry him." She didn't mention what Nigel *had* asked and didn't let herself wonder again, either, whether she and Nigel would ever be ready to marry. "You'll just have to hold off on the wedding plans for now."

All of that said, she took a deep breath and turned laughing to her parents. "Hello, dears." She kissed them both and finally answered her mother's question, too. "Thoroughly satisfactory, and bound to be the beginning of a thoroughly satisfactory life for them both. Now, tell me what I can do to make myself useful."

Nell Bryce smiled fondly at her oldest daughter and then suggested pragmatically, "Anything you can think of, love, provided it gets these three hooligans out from under my feet long enough for me to discover what's on hand for tea."

THE LETTER CAME the next day while Pen was in the garden reading the manuscript of the next children's story she was to illustrate. She'd looked for Margery, hoping to read the story to a sample audience as she often did, but her younger sister had vanished. So, in fact, had Evan and Sally, but since there were no audible cries of distress, Pen forbore any further hunting for them. Instead she gave up and read the story aloud to herself, with considerable relish.

"Penelope." Her mother was crossing the sun-striped lawn with a long white envelope in hand, and Pen looked up in immediate attention, knowing that the use of her full name meant her mother was concerned about something.

"Yes, dear. What's the problem?" She pulled a second garden chair over, and Nell sank into it with an absentminded murmur of thanks.

"This is, although I'm not sure that 'problem' is precisely the word. Pen, do you remember your father's Uncle Andrew? You haven't seen him in years, but when you were just a little girl and his wife was still alive, we spent a month's holiday with them, staying at their cottage in the Lake District."

Pen wrinkled up her forehead in thought. "Yes," she said slowly, "I think I do remember— at least Uncle Andrew. Wasn't he a very tall old man with thick white hair? And he carried peppermints and smelled of pipe tobacco?"

Her mother smiled at the things that had impressed a very young Penelope enough to be still remembered. "And he was very taken with you. You were a beautiful child, of course—" Nell's glance lightened for a moment as it rested on the rich chestnut hair and fair smooth skin of the tall girl beside her, and Pen grinned at this maternal interpolation "—and he and Aunt Hannah had never been able to have children of their own.

"Well, we kept in touch after that visit, but then several years ago Hannah died and Andrew stopped answering our letters. Even your father finally noticed and became worried, so he contacted Andrew's solicitor and old friend, an Edward Bannister whom we had met when we were there. Mr. Bannister replied that after Hannah's death Andrew seemed to have lost heart. He cut his contacts with nearly everyone, and even his old friend was able to keep an eye on him only by intruding every so often on his solitude. Mr. Bannister promised to let us know periodically how Andrew was, but he warned us not to expect any letters from Andrew himself.''

Here her eyes dropped to the envelope her fingers had been smoothing absently, and she paused.

''But if the letter is from Uncle Andrew after all,'' Pen prodded gently when her mother didn't continue, ''why are you looking distressed? Is he ill?''

''He's dead, Pen,'' Nell answered quietly, and Pen slipped a cool soft hand over those restless fingers. ''He had been ill and then was doing rather better, but he died in his sleep ten days ago, and this letter was somehow delayed.''

She fell silent again, and Pen's eyes lifted, but instead of seeing her mother's garden around her she saw Uncle Andrew's, as more memories of that long-ago visit came into focus. Underneath the looming fells of Lakeland, Uncle Andrew's garden had been a friendly and enchanted place to a child of five. In damp green corners, ferns and mosses thrived, and she remembered her efforts to fashion herself a hat of green ''velvet'' with long green ''plumes.'' In the late-summer sunshine hydrangeas and roses, dahlias and delphiniums blossomed riotously, and masses of daisies let a small girl make endless daisy chains. Inside again on a warm afternoon there were glasses of cool lemonade in a white cottage kitchen—and always a feeling of love and welcome.

"Penelope." Her mother's voice recalled her, and Pen turned gray eyes filled with remembered joys. "Andrew left you his cottage."

A WEEK LATER Pen sat in her car in the driveway of her parents' house and buckled up her seat belt, listening for the decisive click that meant it was firmly engaged. Then she reached forward and switched on the ignition of the elderly Cortina she'd bought the year before. As usual, the little green car came to life only reluctantly, and while she waited for its initial coughs to subside into wheezes she looked a loving and amused farewell at her family, gathered in the pale spring sunshine to say goodbye but momentarily silenced by an engine even louder than they were.

Standing side by side, her parents were nevertheless a study in contrasts. Her father, much though she knew he loved her, looked as usual several thousand miles away—lost again, Pen guessed, in some complex philosophical problem. Her mother, on the other hand, was very much concerned with the immediate practical problem of Pen's trip. She wore a determinedly optimistic smile, but Pen knew full well that Nell suspected her oldest child was acting far too impulsively. At any rate, her other children had no such fears. Sally looked wistful, regarding Pen's trip as an adventure into the unknown; Evan, standing out of their mother's line of sight, had one hand raised and the other occupied with the sweet bun he'd managed to filch from this morning's baking; and Margery was busily spinning mad pirouettes around her abstracted father.

Pen blew them all a final kiss and then—the Cortina's coughing having settled into an asthmatic but steady hum—reversed the car neatly onto the quiet street, turning downhill and away from home as her family's last shouts of advice and encouragement rang behind her.

"Bye, Pen!"

"Drive carefully, and don't feel you have to stay there."

"I wish I could go, too!"

She tooted the horn and a minute later passed with a resident's wave of the hand through the Dulwich tollgate, the last one remaining in London. Soon she was merging into the northbound traffic on the highway that would take her to the Lake District and—as Sally insisted—the unknown.

Pen loved driving and did it well, and even though the high speeds of the expressway demanded her attention, she was still able to take a mental inventory of the past few days, reassuring herself that she really had tended to everything that needed doing before she left.

Her relief at inheriting a property that would need looking after had been clear proof that she still wasn't eager to move in with Nigel—not now. So that first day she had wired Edward Bannister both her regret upon learning of Uncle Andrew's death and her pleasure that he had left her his cottage. She had also told the solicitor she'd be coming up to see the cottage in a week, and in return he had immediately written back a brief courtly note of welcome, promising to have the house provisioned for her and enclosing a key.

That key now reposed in a pocket of the comfortable navy trench coat she wore over a trim red suit, and she patted her pocket to double-check the key's presence. The key to her apartment, on the other hand, was gone. She had subleased the place, easily and without regret, packing up her own things and resolutely ignoring the empty spots where Bree's had been. Now the Cortina's trunk bulged with her clothes and, more importantly, her art supplies for a working holiday.

She'd visited the publisher of children's books for whom she did free-lance illustrating, explaining about her inheritance, and found the company perfectly willing to give her several stories to take north with her. These lay in a fat folder on the seat beside her, and she checked them, too, with a quick glance.

She had also, of course, paid one more visit before she left the city. Although she'd simply phoned most of her London friends to tell them she would be out of town for a bit, she felt that she had to see Nigel in person. After all, she might be avoiding his proposition, but she wasn't avoiding Nigel himself; besides, she'd told herself, he did deserve an answer, even if it wasn't going to be the one he wanted.

She had found him at the theater, where rehearsals were beginning for the new play, and during a short break she'd dragged him away to a nearby café for a hasty meal while she told him about her legacy. As she poured out her news, he ate with the efficiency of a man who is equally hungry and hurried, and she fiddled with a sandwich of some indeterminate filling. He finished long before she did and then folded long graceful hands on the table in front of him and waited with exaggerated patience for her to run down.

When she finally did, and noticed the folded hands and the cocked eyebrows in his satyr face, she chuckled penitently. "I'm sorry! Have I completely deafened you? Why didn't you stop me?"

"Interrupt an heiress?" he asked in tones of mock horror. "Never! I'm learning that in the theater world it's a cardinal rule that you take pains to stay in favor with the rich."

His voice was light, but Pen also heard again that harsh note he'd used when he escaped with her the night of the party. Still uncertain of how to respond to his tone, because this seemed so unlike the Nigel she'd always known, she shied away from his comment with a perfunctory little laugh.

"But seriously, isn't it all amazing, Nigel? I barely knew Uncle Andrew, and here he's left me his house." Then everything else faded for a moment, and she looked away in sudden wistfulness. She was quiet for a bit while he simply watched her in silence, and when she spoke again it was to murmur, "He's given me so much, and I hardly even remember him. I'm sorry about that."

"Tardy but creditable sentiments," Nigel commented in a tone that was perhaps deliberately dry, and Pen turned an indignant face back to him. He regarded it briefly and then, before she could frame a defense, added, "You'll sell out, of course."

Still off balance, she floundered. "Well, no, I—"

"Oh, come, Pen!" The usual slanting lines of his clever face became more pronounced. "You can't honestly mean you're thinking of keeping property way up in Cumbria. Renting is a nuisance, and as for ever living there yourself—I can hardly picture you up there among the sheep, cavorting with quaint country types amid the pastoral scenery!"

"Well, I'm going to live there anyway!" Pen reacted hotly to a gibe that had perhaps been unwise. "And quaint country types can't be any worse than the city ones—better, in fact, than those theater people of yours!"

His eyes were suddenly the flat black of pebbles. "I see."

Oh, no! She hadn't meant to tell him like that. She slid forward in her seat and laid placating fingers on his arm.

"I'm sorry, Nigel; I didn't mean to put it that way. I probably will sell the cottage eventually, but first I feel as though I owe it to Uncle Andrew at least to visit his house, so I thought I'd have a working holiday up there and then decide."

"A holiday is all very well, but your work and your life are here in London," he said, still expressionlessly.

"I know," she agreed, "and you are, too."

"I was going to mention that next," he concurred, his tone becoming more normal. "But since you've said it for me, I'll just add, 'and so is my lonely apartment.'"

Her eyes fell, and she pulled her hand away from him to draw small circles on the table between them. "I know that, too," she nodded, "but I just don't seem to be quite ready to move in with you."

He reached over and tilted her chin with one long forefinger so that he could meet her unhappy eyes for a silent moment. His own had lost their opaque look, but she couldn't read his thoughts in them. Then they crinkled slightly at the corners, and his lips bent slowly into a smile. "Then go and have your holiday among the sheep first. And who knows—I might even come up from the metropolis occasionally to visit you. That way, when I need to design stage sets that represent bucolic bliss, I'll know what it looks like."

Her eyes filled suddenly, and he kissed her lightly across the table before releasing her and saying matter-of-factly, "Meanwhile I have to get back to the theater, and you probably need to get your shepherdess outfit ready."

Blinking away the tears, she smiled back at him and assented, "Yes, I still have to pack my sheep shears. I'm leaving in two days, and I've just remembered I left them in my sewing basket."

She stood up on the words, and he saluted her with his raised coffee cup before draining it and setting it aside to follow her from their table. Outside the café he caught up with her and then hesitated uncharacteristically, staying her with a hand on her shoulder.

"Pen, don't—" he began, but the rush of London's noonday traffic pressed around them, and he gave up on whatever he had been meaning to say. Instead he pulled her into his arms for a brief hard kiss and then left her, striding away as if he were already forgetting her for the demands of his theater work. She looked after him for a minute or two, relieved that he was letting her go so easily, but at the same time paradoxically almost disappointed. She couldn't see that as he walked away, his usual merry pagan expression was entirely gone.

It had been the next evening, when she was spending her last night at home in Dulwich, that the doorbell's strident summons had temporarily quieted the younger Bryces' usual squabbles.

Quickest and most inquisitive, Evan had opened the door—and a moment later pranced back into the living room caroling, "Delivery for Miss Penelope Bryce!" and brandishing a large shepherd's crook decorated with an enormous pink bow.

For Pen comprehension was instant, but not so for her mystified family.

"Pen, what on earth—" her mother asked, and even her father roused himself from his usual abstraction to look mildly inquiring.

When she could control her laughter, Pen explained, "It's from Nigel. He thinks I'll need it if I'm going to be so reckless as to go traipsing off to the wilds of the Lake District!"

Then, while the others were hilariously occupied with Evan's flailing version of penning up the stock, she captured the waving crook long enough to extract a small white envelope that was tucked under its ribbon.

In Nigel's neat angular handwriting, the note began, "Bo Peep," and Pen chuckled softly. Then she read on, her lips still curved in a smile. "Farewell for the moment," the note continued. "Enjoy your springtime revels, but when you tire of your pastoral idyll come back to me, here in civilization. My apartment and I will be waiting. Your Nigel."

Her smile deepened as she read the note over a second time and then slipped it back into its minute envelope. He wasn't letting her go quite so easily after all. This was the nearest thing to a love letter she'd ever had from him, and characteristically it wasn't a missive of moonlight and roses but instead of silly pink bows and a flippant nickname. In a moment's intuition she guessed suddenly that this might be as near as he would ever allow himself to come to the traditional trappings of romance; they weren't at all his sort of thing.

For herself, those trappings had their charms; it was one of the differences between them that while she delighted in tradition, he distrusted it. Still, whether or not she ever fell really in love with him, and whether or not she ever did move into that apartment of his, Nigel was dear to her. Carefully, then, Pen had tucked his note deep into the pocket of her canvas skirt.

Now, as she drove north, the crook, still bedecked in its absurd bow, reposed at an elegant angle across the Cortina's rear seat. When she turned her head slightly, the glow of pink satin caught her eye, and with a sudden grin Pen decided that, whatever might finally become of their relationship, when she saw Nigel next she really ought to make a point of appearing as a Dresden shepherdess, with crook, bonnet, ruffles and all.

Another turn of her head showed her that the red brick of the Midlands was giving way to the gray stone of the north, and as Pen drove smoothly on along the route she had memorized at home, her thoughts inevitably left their inventory of the recent past and hurried ahead of her wheels into the immediate future, to the Lake District and the generous inheritance that awaited her there.

Most of Edward Bannister's original letter about that inheritance had been couched in legal terms that concealed all emotions, but in the last paragraph it was as if the lawyer had been replaced by the man. There he had expressed both his regret at Andrew McKenzie's death and his hope that Andrew's cottage would bring her pleasure. Then, begging her indulgence in an old-fashioned way, he had closed with a few lines of verse by William Wordsworth, the poet who had lived most of his life in the Lake District and loved it all of his life. Pen had never been especially fond of Wordsworth, but two of those beautiful lines had caught in her memory, and she said them over softly to herself now, the artist in her enchanted by the vivid pictures they drew.

The solid mountains shone, bright as the clouds,
Grain-tinctured, drenched in empyrean light....

Like the happy memories of her childhood visit there, those lovely words led her on to the lakes.

CHAPTER THREE

As IT HAPPENED, however, by the time Pen reached Kendal—traditionally gateway to the lakes—the clouds were far from bright. The pale sun that had shone in London that morning was gone now, and here in the north the skies were dark. Still, they had a monochrome beauty, and Pen appreciated that, too. As she drove on, the landmarks of England's greatest park appeared around her, and she scanned them eagerly, sometimes indeed feeling an echo of recognition, while the weather continued to deteriorate.

Windermere, longest of the lakes, was only a broad band of silver under a pewter sky when she occasionally glimpsed it from the road, and at the far end of the lake the fells at Waterhead were melting into mist. In the village of Ambleside, tiny Apple House caught her eye as it stood atop a little arched bridge over Stony Beck, but heavy mist was alloyed with rain now, and switching on her windshield wipers Pen drove reluctantly past. Along the River Rothay she glimpsed a chain of large round stepping-stones set across the river, but today no holidaymakers perched or teetered along them, and the river was hammered metal under the raindrops. Rydal Water, too, seemed to show the silversmith's marks, and the reeds etched along its shore bent under the force of the rain.

Last of the lakes along Pen's way was Grasmere, its grassy shores empty of strollers today. Beside the lake the village also seemed nearly deserted as most of its occupants waited out the rain, and Pen picked her way carefully through its winding streets, peering through the downpour. Nevertheless, she didn't see the pedestrian who dodged across the road until he was directly in front of her car, and then she jammed on the poor Cortina's brakes and sounded the horn simultaneously as the little car came to a shrieking halt.

Pen was shrieking, too. Although usually the calmest of drivers, she was horribly shaken by the near miss, and she wound down her window furiously in the aftermath of fear.

"You could have been killed, you idiot!" she shouted to the tall mackintosh-clad man who now stood safely on the curb.

His head turned toward her, but a dripping hat brim hid his face as he answered with infuriating composure. "No, probably not. My reflexes are faster than yours appear to be. At worst I might have got a broken leg."

"A broken neck would have been more what you deserved!" she raged. "Why did you have to practically throw yourself under my wheels like that?"

"For the same reason that the legendary chicken had to cross the road," he replied dryly. "Because I wanted to get to the other side. And I did not throw myself under your wheels, as you so colorfully put it. I simply crossed a quiet village street the way I've been doing for months now."

She wasn't pacified by his oddly attractive voice or by an impression of lean masculine grace in the figure on the curb. "If that's the way you've been crossing the street for months, I'm surprised you're still alive to do it!" she fumed.

"But it's no less surprising than the apparent fact that someone who drives the way you do hasn't yet killed herself on the road."

"There's absolutely nothing wrong with the way I drive!" she protested indignantly.

"Oh?" he inquired in a sweetly skeptical tone that set her teeth even more on edge. "Then it must be with the way you see."

The only response she could make to that was a strangled sound of fury, all the more enraged because there seemed to be just the tiniest grain of truth in his claim—she simply hadn't seen him through the rain. Further conversation with this annoying lunatic, however, was obviously going to be unrewarding, so she put the car into gear again, clenching her jaws at the deplorable sound that proved she hadn't done it smoothly, and crept on up the road with exaggerated caution.

Though she wondered if her near victim was watching, she refused to check the mirror to find out. But if he *was* watching, she told herself with a tight little smile, he was probably doing it from the center of the roadway again! She shook her head at the thought and pushed away an errant curiosity—without the mackintosh and hat, did he look as attractive as his voice sounded? Not that it mattered one way or the other, of course; she'd probably never see him again. Driving on through Grasmere, she told herself she hoped she wouldn't.

Past the old village church she turned along a lane that led outward to the encircling fells, and almost in their shadow she found her destination at last, pulling up with a sigh of relief. She switched off the abused and weary Cortina and looked at her cottage.

Of an indeterminate age, it was built of gray native stone, covered in whitewashed plaster and slate roofed. More of the same gray stone made a wall along the lane, and behind it lay the enclosed garden of her childhood memories. Instead of brilliant sunshine and late-summer flowers, however, Pen saw at first only the persistent rain and a few brave early-spring flowers, their bright colors huddled together as if for warmth. Ruefully she recognized memory's selectivity; it must have rained during that long-ago holiday, too, but her mind's eye had preserved only sun-drenched images.

In contrast, the picture presented to her now seemed completely desolate, and her spirits sank.

Coming right on top of her altercation with that character in the village, the cottage at first made her feel thoroughly unwelcome, but then she realized that a soft rosy light gleamed out through the curtains at the front windows of the little house. Puzzled but heartened by the sight, she nerved herself to face the rain, belting her trench coat tightly around her and tucking her hair into its upturned collar. A deep breath then, and she rocketed out of the car, abandoning it in the downpour while she sprinted through the gate and up the stone walk that led toward that encouraging light.

As Pen reached the cottage's green-painted door, shining wetly beneath the tender early leaves on a honeysuckle vine that arched above it, it swung open, and she dashed inside to sanctuary. In a moment the door was shut again, and the energetic tattoo of the rain had faded to a muted drumming.

Breathing quickly, Pen stood in a small cozy parlor, her eyes adjusting slowly to its warm dimness after that cold daylight outside. Just as firelight and gay flowered chintz took shape before her, a brisk voice behind her said, "Well, I'm thankful you're not half-drowned, child, but you are wet. Let me have your coat, and you sit yourself there by the fire to dry out."

A minute later Pen had slipped obediently out of her sodden coat and—suddenly more cold and tired from the long drive than she had realized—

was seated thankfully by the fire's welcoming warmth, with a hot cup of tea clasped in her stiff fingers. Across the hearth from her, in another comfortable chintz-covered chair, sat a little round woman whose abundant white hair capped a rosy wrinkled face lit by bright gentian-blue eyes behind gold-rimmed spectacles. She wore an ageless dress in a soft plaid of subtle hues of brown, and that—with the inquiring tilt of her head—made Pen think of some plump and lively little bird. A shrewd kindliness looked out of her eyes, too, and Pen reacted to it immediately, her own eyes lighting up in a responsive smile. She was still puzzled, however, and her bewilderment showed on her face.

"Och, child, you do look so like Andrew when he was working out something that confused him," the little woman said with a slight catch in her voice, and now Pen recognized a soft burring to her speech. Her eyes filled with shadows for a moment, and then the shadows lifted as she went on. "And well you should, of course; you're Andrew's kin, and you haven't the least idea what I'm doing in your house.

"I'm Ellen Bannister, Penelope. Edward had intended to come over himself and make things ready for you, but his rheumatism is bothering him more than he likes to admit, and today he can barely budge, so he had to let me see to things for him. Even after fifty years of marriage," she added with a twinkle, "he still finds it difficult to believe that I might be responsible enough to manage a few practical things on my own, but today he had no choice. At any rate, I was just going to set the kettle on the back of the stove and leave a fire laid on the hearth, but then the rain came on and I thought I'd sit it out here and keep watch for you, as well."

The comfortable flow of words had given Pen time to collect herself, and she responded warmly, "And it was a lovely welcome to find you here. I'm so glad you stayed, Mrs. Bannister."

"Now, child, let's have none of this 'Mrs. Bannister,' if you please. It's a deal too formal for Andrew's Penelope to be using. You won't remember it, of course, but when you were here as a wee little girl you called me Banny and came down the lane to visit whenever I was baking bannocks—except you called them 'Banny-cakes.'"

She chuckled softly at the memory, and Pen suddenly blurted, "And you had a ginger cat named Maggie!"

"And you dragged her all about the garden with you, her front paws clutched in your little arms and her back ones nearly touching the ground, such a tiny mite of a thing you were. That cat was a marvel of patience."

They shared a look of amusement—the little white-haired woman and the tall girl whose chestnut hair was drying in soft tendrils that curved around the oval of her face—and in this cold wet spring Pen felt again the summertime warmth of that earlier visit. Banny was remembering, too, and they sat a minute more in companionable silence until she stirred and said, "As a matter of fact, child, I've left you some bannocks in the kitchen. Let me show you where they are and a bit about Andrew's temperamental old cooker, and then I'll be leaving you before Edward gets to worrying about me."

She came to her feet and bustled from the rosy parlor to the white kitchen Pen had remembered. In an old cupboard of softly polished wood, blue-and-white plates added a note of color, and a paler blue cloth covered a scrubbed deal table in the center of the room. Along one wall, with a small fridge and a huge old-fashioned double sink, stood the balky cooker Banny had maligned, and Pen had an immediate lesson in dealing with its quirks.

"Above all, treat it firmly, lass, and never let it know if it has you bamboozled," Banny concluded.

"I'll be very strict," Pen promised obediently, but she was chuckling. "Thank you for the warning, and thank you for stocking the fridge, too, Banny. You're very kind to have done it."

"Oh, pshaw," Banny disclaimed with a small ladylike snort. "It was little enough to have done for Andrew's girl. Let me fetch my coat now, and I'll be off."

She disappeared into the stone passage where

her coat hung with Pen's, and Pen herself turned her attention to the rest of the kitchen.

At the far end of the room a massive hearth held logs laid ready for a match, and flanking it stood a pair of deep comfortable old chairs. A reading lamp was near at hand, too, and a long shelf of books whose loose bindings revealed they'd been much read. What most drew Pen's eyes, however, was the large wooden hand loom standing against the outer wall of the room, where it could catch the light from a pair of wide windows. On it was an unfinished length of blue green material in the softest mohair and wool, and Pen was stroking it with gentle wondering fingers when Banny came back into the room, looking rounder than ever in a thick tweed coat. She came to stand beside Pen, and the girl breathed, "It's so beautiful, Banny!"

"Aye, that it is. Andrew always was a bonny weaver," Banny agreed gruffly. "He was making this for Hannah when she died, and he never worked on it again. He left everything just as it had been; it was as if he had stopped living himself and was only waiting until he could die, too."

Her voice was unsteady, its burr suddenly much more pronounced, and she took a deep breath before she went on speaking.

"Seventy years ago Andrew and I were children together among the weavers in Selkirk, but when we grew up we both left Scotland and married other people. I'd lost touch with him by the time Edward brought me here as a bride, but within a year Andrew and Hannah settled here, too, and Andrew began weaving for one of the shops in the village. He was their master weaver for nearly half a century, and his blankets and shawls must have been taken all over the world by people who came here on holiday from all sorts of foreign places.''

A remembered pride echoed in her voice, but then it faded as she said softly, "Edward and I both hoped the weaving would be a comfort to him after Hannah died, but he lost all interest in it and never touched a loom again, either here or down in the village." She sighed but then concluded in a matter-of-fact tone, "It grieves me now to see this lovely blanket unfinished, but the loom is far too big to move and I'd not be running in and out of your cottage to finish weaving it here.''

Pen linked an arm through hers in a quick affectionate gesture and said firmly, "I'd be delighted if you did.''

"Nonsense, child,'' Banny returned briskly, patting Pen's hand to take the edge off her words. "If this blanket is ever to be finished, you'll simply have to learn how to do it yourself. Andrew's weaving books and notes are here somewhere, and you could come to me for a bit of help, but I'll leave this to you otherwise.

"Meanwhile I'll be off home to Edward and leave you to get acquainted with the rest of this house by yourself. You're a nice child, Penelope, and just the sort of daughter Andrew and Hannah would have loved for their own. I'm sure their cottage will make you welcome.''

Wordlessly Pen touched a gentle kiss to the rosy old cheek, and for an instant Banny stroked the soft hair that fell forward over Pen's temple, then she turned away.

Pen reached the green door first and swung it open for Banny, peering up through the dripping vine to see if the rain had indeed stopped; if not, she would drive Banny down the lane. In fact, the downpour had ended, but the small wet shape that slipped in through the open door with a glad cry looked as if the storm had lasted forty days and nights instead of a few hours.

Pen jumped as something cold and soggy brushed past her ankles; then she crouched down to find the culprit. Over against Banny's feet now was a kitten, a little orange rag of fur, and Banny identified it with a resigned smile as Pen chirruped to it and it raced to her caressing fingers.

"There's one of those dratted kittens again. They're some of Maggie's great-grandchildren, and ever since their eyes opened they've been all over everywhere. This one must have followed me over here and sat out the rain among the daffodils, little shelter as they offer."

She looked askance at the small creature nuzzling Pen's hand and added, "I'm going to have to find homes for this lot soon, too, since they've taken to using Edward for tree-climbing practice, and that doesn't do kindly for his rheumatism.''

Pen, by now entranced with a tiny rumbling purr, looked up at that. "Oh, Banny, may I keep this one? That is, if it's ready to leave its mother and you really mean that about finding homes for them—"

"I do mean it, Penelope, and yes, you may have the kitten with my blessing if you'll promise not to drag it around the garden."

Pen glanced up indignantly. "I'd never—" she began, and then caught the teasing look in Banny's eye. "Well, hardly ever," she amended.

She stood up now, the kitten cradled in careful hands that made sure its hind legs didn't dangle. It burrowed into the collar of her soft wool suit with an inquiring pink nose, ridiculously decorated with stubby new whiskers, and then closed its eyes contentedly. Looking over its little head, Pen found Banny surveying her above gold-rimmed spectacles with an expression of tolerant amusement.

"Milk and bread for supper tonight, tinned cat food from the shop tomorrow, and yes, she is housebroken," she said succinctly, anticipating Pen's questions. "And mind, if you let her sleep on your bed tonight, you'll be hard pressed to persuade her to sleep anywhere else in the future."

That last came in an admonitory tone, and Pen tried to look firm, but somehow she only managed to look infatuated and guilty instead, and then she and Banny were both laughing. At the sound, the kitten opened one golden eye and, deciding all was well with its future, closed it again.

When Barny had left with a last wave and a command that Pen come to her with any difficulties, Pen latched the green door and carried Maggie's great-granddaughter back into the kitchen again. There she unearthed a soft old piece of toweling, and wrapping the sleepy kitten in it, she took her purring bundle into the warm parlor. Sitting on the floor in front of the fire and murmuring nonsense, she toweled the kitten gently until it was barely damp and settled it on her knee in the firelight, fluffing its fur until it was completely dry and standing out in a halo. Dry, the kitten was much more prepossessing and exactly the color of marigolds.

"Marigold, that's it, little cat," Pen crooned, christening the kitten, but when informed of her name Marigold only yawned delicately, flexed tiny claws harmlessly against Pen's hand and dozed off. For a long time Pen sat peacefully in the firelight, stroking the soft orange fur beneath her fingers in dreaming contentment.

Bustling London seemed to be on another planet than this quiet place, and she thought of it entirely without homesickness. She had always considered her life there exciting, with her family, work and friends and all their varying demands on her time. But right now that life just seemed frantic, and she couldn't even quite remember what there was about it she had so liked.

Closing her eyes a moment, she tried to picture herself back in London, but the images in her mind slipped away again before they'd even finished forming. Musingly she let them go, and tried instead to picture Nigel's familiar face as it had looked when he told her to enjoy her bucolic bliss for a while. That image formed clearly, and with eyes still closed she smiled at it. Dear Nigel! She *was* fond of him; maybe she really was in love with him after all, in spite of those theater people of his—if by love people meant the warm affection she felt for him. At least, she'd never felt anything more for someone else.... Perhaps, she thought regretfully, she just wasn't the sort of woman who could feel what the novels called a grand passion for some "tall, dark, handsome" man.

On the thought, however, Nigel's well-known face faded away and in its place was the figure of a tall man in a dripping raincoat, his face shadowed mysteriously. He stood there clearly on the screen of her eyelids, and for a moment she just stared blankly at the man she had nearly run down on her way into the village. Then her eyes snapped open, and his image vanished. How odd that she should have thought of him again! She shook her head slightly in bewilderment; the man was a total stranger to her, and not a particularly pleasant one, either. So why should he intrude upon her thoughts like this? With an indignant little toss of her head she put him firmly back out of mind and steered her daydreams in other directions.

THE AFTERNOON was entirely gone when she finally roused herself, tickled Marigold awake and, putting the kitten down, set out to tour the rest of the cottage.

Up a narrow flight of stairs lay an old-fashioned bath and two bedrooms, whitewashed and airy, and Pen chose for her own the spare bedroom looking out to the fells that she had shared with her parents years ago. A deep feather bed, a plain chest of drawers and a trunk made up most of her furnishings, but on the gleaming wooden floor there was a bright rag rug that she guessed Uncle Andrew had woven, and a comfortable-looking chair stood conveniently by the window, its arms polished to a soft patina by years of Aunt Hannah's loving care. Looking around the pleasant room, Pen felt immediately at home, as though it really did welcome her, and Marigold—who had followed her upstairs with some difficulty— scrambled into the chair and settled herself with an expression of relief that made Pen laugh.

She left the kitten there while she fetched her luggage from the Cortina, but when she began unpacking, Marigold revived sufficiently to come down from her perch and attack the tags on Pen's cases. And a minute later, without ever consciously deciding to leave the rest of her unpacking for some other time, Pen found herself stretched full-length along the floor, dragging the tags back and forth while Marigold launched a series of surprise assaults on them in furious combat. Common

sense did finally get the better of Pen, however,
and she admitted to herself with a rueful laugh
that all this warfare, entertaining as it was,
wouldn't get either of them fed. Declaring a truce
at last, she tucked the vanquished tags out of
Marigold's sight and scooped up the victor, carrying her down to the kitchen again.

Supper was simple for them both. As she put
down the dish of bread and milk that Banny had
recommended, Pen slipped easily into the habit of
talking to her only companion, like so many
solitary people before her.

"Well, absurd beastie, let's see if this meets
with your approval."

Evidently it did, because the kitten attacked it
with relish, and Pen dispatched her own supper
with as much pleasure, brewing herself a fresh pot
of tea to go with a boiled egg from the fridge Banny had stocked, and a Banny-cake.

That proved to be as delicious as she had
remembered, and it was as she was finishing the
last delectable crumbs that Pen noticed the light in
her kitchen had changed. The cold white of a rainy
day had become the shimmering gold of a flawless
sunset, and she flung open the wide windows. The
air that drifted in was still damp, but it smelled of
spring instead of winter, and the day's overcast
sky had become the evening's nebulous ocean
where gilt-edged galleons floated. Dazzled, Pen
leaned dreaming against the window frame until
the golden armada had faded into twilight, and a

cuckoo's pensive call broke the silence. The fells by then had become only bulky dark shapes beyond the back garden, the daffodils—upright again after the rain—looked like the gentle ghosts of springs past, blue evening filled the quiet kitchen around her, and Marigold had collapsed again into slumber, a pale ball of fur beside her half-empty dish.

For a moment more Pen gazed around her at the ring of shadowy fells that held this small cottage and its tranquil kitchen so securely. The loving welcome of her childhood was still here somehow, and she knew suddenly that she would be happy in Lakeland. This holiday would refresh her and give her a chance to think about her relationship with Nigel and decide once and for all what to do about his proposition when she went back to London. But between now and then there would be time on her own here in this lovely place. Contentment warmed to a feeling of anticipation.

Without knowing why, she had a sudden irrational fancy that the next weeks would be the most important of her life. Something exciting seemed to lie ahead of her, even though she had no idea what it could be. The image of a wet and irritated stranger flashed before her eyes again, and for a moment she let herself wonder if this feeling of anticipation could have anything to do with him; it seemed as plausible as anything else. But no, it wasn't really—*if* she ever saw that man again, he's probably just run for his life, since he was apparently convinced she had already tried once to end it for him, right there in the middle of the village! With a little breath of rueful laughter, Pen latched the windows and gently gathered up her kitten.

CHAPTER FOUR

PEN WAS AWAKENED all too early the next morning by a small sandpaper tongue working its way over the back of her wrist. It tickled, and she rolled over to catch Marigold up in both hands, holding her high for a brief scolding.

"You and I need to have an agreement, little cat. Either you let me keep the hours I choose in my own bed, or we find you a bed for yourself! While you imitated a dormant earmuff last night, I was awake till all hours hunting up those lines of poetry in Uncle Andrew's copy of Wordsworth's *Prelude*. Therefore I am *not* feeling as alert this morning as you appear to be, and I do think you might have a little regard for a hapless sleepy human!"

Marigold simply blinked unrepentant golden eyes at this, and Pen's lecture ended in a laugh. "Yes, I see. As far as you're concerned, it's morning, and that's that. Well, since I'm obviously not going to be allowed any more sleep just now, I guess I'll have to get up."

With a final pat that was as much affection as admonition, she set the kitten aside and reluctantly swung long graceful legs out of that enticing feather bed. The discovery that the morning was clear and mild, however, did much to reconcile her to losing some sleep, and in a few minutes she faced the day in comfortable gray trousers and a red plaid tunic top, her hair tied back in a bright scarf. Downstairs, breakfast in the sunny kitchen was much like supper the night before for both of them. When it was over and the dishes put away, Pen's first interest was in rediscovering the garden she had so loved as a child.

Only daffodils and narcissus were in full bloom in the delicate April sunlight, but Pen puttered contentedly around the garden anyway, finding favorite nooks again and pulling a few bold weeds. Marigold did her share, too, helping Pen rid the garden of pests by leaping ferociously on the few small insects she could locate. Almost before Pen knew it, half the morning had ambled pleasantly by. No more weeds or pests were visible, and she sat down to admire their handiwork, dozing off in a patch of sunshine while Marigold went exploring, and woke only when a sudden tumult disrupted the quiet of her garden.

She sat up vaguely, just in time to find herself the center of the commotion. Marigold leaped into her arms and spun around, back arched into a little bow, to face the enormous dog who arrived immediately behind her. An instant later two additional small figures hurtled into the fray, and Pen was totally overwhelmed. For a moment more all was total confusion; then she scrambled to her feet, holding Marigold high out of harm's way, and yelped, "Stop!"

Amazingly, everything did. Marigold, feeling herself out of danger, stopped hissing, the dog stopped barking and sat down, and the two voices trying to explain it all stopped, too. Briefly they all made a tableau of suspended motion, and Pen was able to see the new arrivals in her garden. Her first visitor was a huge fawn-colored mastiff with a black-masked face, his forehead wrinkled in attention, ears slightly lifted and long tongue lolling out in a guilty expression. Her other two visitors had clearly been in pursuit of the first, and Pen saw now that they were a young boy and girl, the former about seven years old, the latter maybe five. They were dressed in identical dungarees and blue-and-white-striped sweaters. Matching freckles decorated identical snub noses, and inky hair topped each head, but on one it fell straight in a short silky thatch with the forelock awry, and on the other its riotous curls were confined in stubby braids tied with navy blue yarn. From beneath the dark hair, two pairs of anxious indigo eyes gazed at Pen.

Her breathing almost back to normal, she lowered Marigold into a more comfortable position and smiled into those eyes, and the worried looks vanished. So, however, did the silence, as both children broke into eager explanations and apologies.

"Levvy doesn't usually chase cats, but it was in our garden."

"We're awfully sorry about waking you up."

"We live next door."

"Is that your kitten? What's its name?"

And finally, forthrightly, "Who are you?"

The words rushed out in counterpoint, reminding Pen of the usual racket at home in Dulwich, and she responded as she would have there, answering the questions in reverse order.

"I'm Pen, and I've come to live here for a while. This is Marigold, and when she isn't invading your garden she lives with me."

From the small girl with braids the clearer of the two voices answered, "I'm Megan, and he's Corey. We're sister and brother."

"Yes," Pen agreed gravely, "you do seem to be." The children grinned at her tone, and since the gigantic Levvy hadn't moved again she settled herself back on the lawn. Marigold scrambled nervously higher, perching on Pen's shoulder, but when no one paid her any further attention she inched her way back down to the ground.

The children, too, sat down, and while Megan surveyed Pen intently, Corey asked her, "Do you have a sister or brother?"

"I have a brother and two younger sisters. How's that?"

Corey laughed and nodded, but Megan persisted, "Are they here, too?"

"No, they live in London. I'm here on my own."

"You're living here all by yourself?" Megan's voice sounded uneasy now, and Pen noticed that Corey linked hands with his sister.

"Yes," she answered cheerfully, "but I don't think there's any danger I'll be lonely with you and Levvy and Marigold around!"

"And Uncle Lister," Corey added. "We live with him now." Megan brightened at his words, and then both children suddenly pointed past Pen to the shady spot where Levvy had stretched his massive body.

His huge head rested on his forepaws, and his brown eyes were fixed on Marigold, the explorer, as by a casually roundabout route she worked her way ever closer to him. Finally she reached him and for a moment stood perfectly still, her little nose nearly touching his big one, and her small body poised for flight. He remained completely motionless, and after a pause during which all three watchers held their breath, Marigold sat daintily beside his heavy jowls and began grooming herself. She stopped when he sniffed gently at her, then he shut his eyes, and she went calmly on with her toilet.

Pen let out her breath and smiled at the youngsters' spellbound faces. "I think the war is over. Shall we celebrate the peace with a bannock?"

Blue eyes consulted blue eyes, Corey's eager and

Megan's uneasy again. Then Megan said, speaking rather quickly, "No, thank you, Pen. We should go home because Uncle Lister doesn't know where we are."

Pen smothered a grin at the thought that Uncle Lister must be very old and deaf if all the fuss just next door hadn't told him exactly where the children and their dog were, but she made herself answer seriously, "I understand. Well, thank you for saving my kitten from Levvy's jaws. I'll try to keep her out of his territory if you'll come back and eat bannocks with me some other time?"

Her inquiring tone made Corey, crestfallen a minute ago, nod happily, then both youngsters scrambled to their feet, while Levvy rose majestically nearby.

"Thank you very much," Megan said primly.

Corey blurted, "You're nice, Pen," and then they turned and ran back across the garden, with Levvy galloping hugely behind. In a moment they had clambered over the stone wall that divided Pen's land from Uncle Lister's and disappeared, and Pen was left exchanging looks with Marigold. The kitten yawned, and the girl laughed.

"You're just lucky Levvy didn't swallow you in a single mouthful when you tried that trick," she admonished, but Marigold simply tucked her paws beneath her and went to sleep, so Pen gave up and left her snoozing in the sun. Going back into the cottage, Pen gathered up her change purse and a short list of supplies she wanted to add to those Banny had left her and, leaving her kitten still asleep, walked down into the village.

Half an hour later, her arms laden with purchases, she was backing out of the grocer's shop, calling a farewell to the friendly couple who had served her, when she ran into something hard. She hit it with such a jolt that her grocery bag flew out of her hands, fell and tore, scattering boxes, bundles and cans everywhere. The can that rolled the shortest distance, however, was the one that fell squarely on the foot of the man she'd collided with. He said something pungent that she didn't catch and then bent to retrieve the can and give it to her.

Already on her hands and knees to collect her tumbled supplies, Pen found a large hand, holding a can of cat food, reaching into her line of vision, and she looked up, breaking off the automatic apology she'd been making.

"I believe this weapon is yours," a disturbing voice she had heard before said irritably. "Perhaps you'd like to add it to the car that's already in your arsenal?"

Speechless, her face flaming with embarrassment, Pen took the can from the man she'd nearly run down on her way into the village yesterday. Today he wasn't wearing the mackintosh or hat, and she could see that he had thick black hair that curled with springy vitality back from his forehead, and eyes of a blue so intense they were startling in his tanned face. With that straight nose and those high cheekbones, he looked like an emperor from some old Roman coin. The whole face had a sculpted quality, in fact, with the lean purity of its lines, but an overall impression of severity was contradicted by the long mobile lips that Pen imagined might look quite whimsical if he smiled.

Almost mesmerized by the face of the man who had already intruded twice into her daydreams, Pen had got that far with a thorough inventory before she finally realized those lips were tightly compressed, the straight nose was flaring at the nostrils, and the eyes were sparkling with annoyance. He'd got off unscathed when they met yesterday, but apparently hadn't been so lucky today. Recalled to her circumstances and flushing scarlet, she glanced across the floor at his feet and discovered he was wearing some sort of soft moccasinlike shoes that wouldn't offer much protection from errant cans. And one of his shoes had a visible dent in it.

Finding her voice at last, she mumbled, "Thank you—I really am sorry—"

"Not half as sorry as my foot is," he cut in brusquely. "I suppose the same people who failed to teach you to look where you drive also failed to teach you to do it when you walk?"

Now that really was a bit much! Yesterday at least he'd been just as much at fault as she. She wrenched her eyes away from his, and abruptly the rapt appreciation she'd felt staring at him

faded completely. How could she have thought
him attractive? Her apology died on her lips, and
she became gallingly conscious that she was still
crouched near his shoes. It was an oddly infuriating realization, and clutching the torn bag
with the things she'd already collected she leaped
to her feet and counterattacked.

"Well, at least they taught me not to dash out in
front of moving cars!" she snapped. "And they
also taught me to accept a sincere apology when it
was offered."

An edge of angry color flared along the planes
of his cheekbones at her tone. "In that case I accept your 'sincere'—" he gave the word a twist
"—apology, of course. I suppose I should be impressed anyway that you offered some kind of
apology this time. Yesterday when you attempted
to put a period to my life, you simply shouted in
frustration when the attempt failed."

The way he bit the words off, she couldn't help
but notice the smooth interplay of muscles in his
jaw and lean cheeks, under that tanned skin. But
this time she didn't let herself pause to admire the
artistic effect.

"I did *not* shout because I failed to kill you, but
because that seemed to be the only way to address
a lunatic!" she shot back, and then, without
wondering about her motive, added with deliberate provocation, "I'd heard that every little
village had one, and you were obviously it!"

His thickly fringed blue eyes started to glitter

oddly at that, but Pen didn't care. She glared back into them with angry gray ones, and there was a moment's hiatus in the battle, as if he were weighing his next move. It went on, and she was just beginning to wonder in an appalled sort of way if she had accidentally stumbled on the truth—maybe this man *was* genuinely disturbed, and that was why he walked in front of moving cars and got so upset over a little thing like a can of cat food—when he broke the silence in a totally unexpected way by laughing. Disconcerted, she looked at him uneasily now and found that his eyes had lowered to the torn bag she held, estimating the size of the tear and the number of items still inside the bag.

"Lunatic I may be," he said on an attractive chuckle, "but I still have too much sense to stand here wrangling with you any longer when it's obvious the rest of that collection of food is just about to land on my feet, as well. That being the case, I think discretion is the better part of valor. I'll leave you now and limp on inside to buy my own supplies, and in the future I shall simply stay out of your path, by car and on foot."

On the words he sketched her a mock salute and edged past her; just as he was safely out of range, the bag did let go completely, and the things she was holding joined the others on the floor. Irresistibly, she glanced after him and saw that, although he had been walking normally when he stepped away from her, he suddenly began to limp exaggeratedly. He didn't look back, however, and with a little snort of laughter that was both exasperated and amused she knelt to gather her groceries again. What a pity such an attractive man had to be so impossible, she thought.

Both times they'd met he had reduced her to rage, and as she chased her groceries she wondered at herself. Usually her disposition was placid, but there was something about this man that set her off. Whatever it was, he apparently felt it, too; they obviously rubbed each other the wrong way. So she'd simply have to oust him from her daydreams, Pen concluded, scooping up the last wandering can and brushing off her hands—but that was certainly going to be a waste, because if ever a face was made to star in daydreams, it was his!

The rest of Pen's first day in Grasmere was a great deal more tranquil than the morning had been, at least. Early evening found her strolling along the smooth grassy shores of the lake, after spending the afternoon exploring the village so that now she felt comfortably at home in it.

Like every visitor to Grasmere, she had found her way to Town End and Dove Cottage, the pleasant sturdy little house in which Wordsworth had lived for a time and might even have written those lines of poetry Edward Bannister had sent her. She stopped, too, at the small museum nearby and then walked back to the Churchtown section of the village. There she followed a curving path

through the churchyard and along the bright River
Rothay to the poet's grave. It was still too early
for the usual crowd of holiday pilgrims, so Pen
lingered awhile where Wordsworth lay with his
family and friends among the peaceful yew trees
he had helped to plant.

Beyond the churchyard gates clustered the rest
of the village—the gray stone houses of the
villagers, the bookstalls, hostels and hotels,
studios and shops for the visitors. Pen found per-
fumes and paintings of the area for sale, and
woolens in rainbow colors. She wondered where
Uncle Andrew had worked as a weaver all those
years, but Banny hadn't specified and Pen didn't
ask. As she explored the narrow winding streets,
however, passersby smiled at the pretty girl with
eager eyes and spoke to her in their soft northern
voices, and she began to feel a sense of belonging
that had nothing to do with the few hours she had
been there.

The feeling grew now at the end of her first full
day as she stood by the lake's quiet waters, cupped
in timeless fells; and as it had that morning, London seemed far more distant than the miles she
had driven to come here. Musing again, she
thought of Nigel for the first time in hours and
remembered his skepticism about life here among
the sheep. With a fugitive grin she decided that the
sheep who roamed the fells had a good deal more
independence than the ones who crowded the subway. And as for those theater people—those must

be the goats, she thought whimsically. It might
be difficult to go back to all that when her holiday here came to an end, especially if she did
as Nigel hoped she would and sold the cottage,
going to live with him. At that thought her
eyes clouded a moment, then cleared as she put
it away from her again. She didn't have to
think about that decision now; she had plenty
of time yet before she'd have to go back to London.

Twilight was flowing along the lakeshore when
Pen finally tore herself away from the purling
water and turned up the lane toward her cottage.
Banny's lay before hers, gleaming palely in the
dusk, and as she came to it Banny's voice called to
her from the shadows.

"Penelope, lass, come in from your wanderings
and meet Edward again."

"I'd be delighted to," Pen answered readily,
turning in to a garden much like hers and filled
with the warm earthy scents of a spring evening.
Banny and her husband sat together on an old
wooden bench under an arbor by their cottage,
their hands loosely clasped, and as Pen came up to
them Edward Bannister spoke.

"Forgive me for not standing up to greet you,
my dear, but regrettably my rheumatism curbs my
manners a bit these days."

"Please don't try," Pen returned quickly, settling herself comfortably on the flagstones near
their feet. "I know we met when I was a child, and

you've already greeted me again by letter, as well, so I feel as if we're old friends.''

"Thank you, Penelope. You make necessity sound so fitting," Edward replied, and they smiled at each other in immediate liking.

Edward Bannister was a gentle quiet man with a tendency to think of his wife of fifty years as still the wild Scots hoyden he had married so long ago, drawn by the very differences in their personalities. Tall and now silver haired, he was retired from his work as a solicitor and only managed a few continuing affairs for old friends, spending most of his time these days writing. Banny referred to that now.

"Isn't it a fine evening, lass?" she asked. "It was so nice I hauled Edward away from his manuscript to come enjoy it with me."

Pen looked at Edward inquiringly, and he explained, "I'm working on a biography of Wordsworth's wife, Mary, when Ellen here will let me get on with it."

He patted his wife's hand as he teased her, and Pen—liking him more by the minute and intrigued at finding herself in the poet's own village—asked Edward a dozen questions about the Wordsworths. He answered them all in his quiet voice, his face alight with enthusiasm, and Banny sat uncharacteristically silent with her pride and love clear in her face.

Finally, though, Edward himself smilingly called a halt. "Enough, my dear. You're an excellent audience, Penelope, but this has been a one-man performance long enough. Now tell me—Ellen assures me she made everything ready for you in Andrew's cottage, just as he and Hannah would have wanted it, but are you really certain you're all set?''

Recalling their conversation the day before, Pen shot a laughing look at Banny, who folded her hands and returned the look with one of wry but loving resignation, and answered, ''I have everything I need, thank you, and more than I dreamed of. I remembered being happy here as a child with Uncle Andrew and Aunt Hannah, but I didn't remember how beautiful this valley is. I've spent only one afternoon learning my way, but I can already see there's enough loveliness here for a lifetime.''

Both of her listeners looked pleased at Pen's delight, and Banny agreed, ''Many an artist has found it so. Did Andrew once tell us, Penelope, lass, that you were in art school yourself?''

Surprised and touched to find that Uncle Andrew had known more in recent years about her than she had about him, Pen said, ''Why, yes, I was, but I've been out of school for quite a while now. For the past two years I've been working as an illustrator of children's books and stories. In fact, I brought some of them with me to spend a bit of time on while I get to know Uncle Andrew's cottage. I thought I could have a sort of working holiday here.''

Both Banny and Edward were too tactful to ask how long her holiday would be, and Pen couldn't have told them at this point, but·she knew Banny was itching to do just that. Instead, however, the older woman limited herself to observing a bit tartly, "You're only a bit more than a bairn yourself. Do you still remember the tales of Peter Rabbit and Squirrel Nutkin, Penelope, or is the reading of stories for little ones too far behind you now that you do the drawings for them?"

"As a matter of fact," Pen returned promptly, "even at my present great age I remember them perfectly. It used to be my duty as the oldest child to read aloud to the other three, and since Margery is only ten she didn't outgrow them awfully long ago."

· Edward chuckled quietly at Pen's diplomacy, and Banny, mollified but still determined to pursue her point, sniffed, "Of course. Well, Beatrix Potter made up those stories right here in the lakes, down in Near Sawrey, and her house is always open during the holiday season. If you're still here then, Penelope, you might just want to pay a visit to her farmhouse, whether it's the artist or just the tourist in you that goes."

"Both of us would love it, I'm sure," Pen rejoined equably, refusing to be drawn about the length of her stay but touched that Banny was proffering inducements for her to prolong it. More each minute, she was beginning to suspect that very little would be enough to keep her here much longer than she'd originally planned, but she hadn't really thought about it yet, so for now she simply turned the conversation in another direction.

"Speaking of children," she laughed reminiscently, "I found a pair in my garden this morning, come to save that kitten from the dire consequences of her wandering."

Edward looked amused as Pen told them about her young neighbors' sudden visit, and Banny's first response was to say with a shake of her head, "That kitten was born for mischief, it's clear already, and I'm doubtful if you'll be firm enough with her to train her out of it, Penelope."

She peered over her gold-rimmed spectacles at a face Pen tried to make stern and guessed, "And unless I'm much mistaken, that beast already spent the night on your own bed."

Accused, Pen mimed such guilt that Banny laughed in spite of herself. "Och, well," she said resignedly, pushing the spectacles back up her nose, "she can warm your feet on cold nights."

She still looked somewhat disapproving, however, so Edward stepped in to rescue Pen from any more discussion of her overly soft heart. "The children live at the end of the lane, Penelope, in the cottage beyond yours. They've been there only a few months, though, as their uncle rented the house in February. We understand they are his brother's children, orphaned just after Christmas."

He stopped, and Pen saw the children again
in her mind, holding hands after Megan asked
if she lived alone. Those small hands, Pen
guessed now, must have been holding tightly to
the one stable thing in their lives. Empathetically
her heart contracted, and her eyes showed her
distress.

"Don't look so, child," Banny commanded.
"They're safe now. Their uncle has provided a
home for them and even that monster dog of
theirs. He has Nora Button up from the village
most days to tend to them, and at night he seems
to fare well enough by himself, though I'd not say
he's had much experience at looking after young
ones. He looks a mite dour, but the pair seem
devoted to him, and I've no doubt he's a good
man."

Pen was still haunted by the glimpse of what
Edward's simple words "orphaned just after
Christmas" must have meant to the children, but
as Banny intended, she was comforted by the
reminder that they had someone to care for them
again—their "Uncle Lister," rather deaf but
devoted. Overlooking Banny's use of the word
"dour," Pen had a reassuring picture of a plump
bachelor, snowy haired and bespectacled, retired
from a lifetime of teaching, perhaps, and now for
the first time learning the joys of having a family
of his own. Cheered by this image, Pen let the subject of the children drop for now and in a few
minutes said her good-nights, leaving Banny and

her Edward still sitting close together in the mild darkness.

They faded quickly from her sight but lingered in her mind. As she went on up the lane, Pen couldn't help thinking about the elderly couple. Hadn't Banny said they had been married fifty years? Then for all those years they must have somehow managed to mesh their two contrasting personalities, and now in old age they sat hand in hand, obviously as much in love as when they were young. It was wonderful to see their love endure, but at the same time it made Pen's heart ache a little. Could the affection between her and Nigel weather life with that warmth and grace?

The small pain at the base of her throat hinted that she didn't really believe so, and Pen sighed softly. What she felt for Nigel suddenly seemed pale and colorless; was that the most she would ever be able to experience? Wistfully she remembered how at about Sally's age she had lain awake at night dreaming in delicious detail of the man she would someday love, utterly and endlessly. Her soul mate and the other half of herself, he would have thick dark hair and eyes that were both piercing and passionate; his chin would be firm and his lips sensual. For a moment the hero of her girlish fantasies materialized again in her memory, and she smiled to herself a little sadly— without recognizing that the dream figure looked distinctly like the man she'd run into so disruptively for the second time that morning.

When Pen's slow footsteps finally reached her own cottage, Marigold was sitting primly on the doorstep, waiting for her mistress and dinner in a posture of such innocence and virtue that it was hard to believe she was the same abominable creature who had ruined Pen's sleep twice in a single day. At the sight of her, Pen's brief melancholy fled, and laughing softly she picked up the feline actress and carried her inside for a supper from the offending can of cat food that had caused so much commotion.

CHAPTER FIVE

IT WAS FULL DARK that same night in London when Nigel heard the insistent sound of the bell at his door.

"Damn!" he muttered energetically, throwing down his pen and leaving his drawing board to answer the summons. And if he was irritated at the interruption, he was infuriated when he found its source. Standing at the door of his apartment, with an assortment of cases, boxes and bags around her, was Elise Robbins.

Whatever else she might be, she wasn't stupid, and when he saw her the black expression on his mobile face was clear evidence of the way he felt about her. Rather than pretend ignorance of those feelings, she simply said dryly, "I was going to say, 'Good evening,' but obviously yours just became a bad one."

He didn't deny it. Instead, equally blunt, he demanded flatly, "What do you want?"

Now she hedged, as if she couldn't keep up this openness. "Why do you assume I want something?"

"Because, as you told me the last time we spoke

to each other, you're an ambitious actress. You used me that time, and it seems probable you're hoping to do the same thing this time, even though there's no play being cast. Except this time I know what to expect from you, so I'm forewarned. You got your part; what do you want now?"

"A place to put all this."

"What?"

"Someplace for my possessions and me to go."

"How about the street?" he suggested nastily.

"I might consider that, of course," she agreed, apparently unperturbed, sitting down gracefully on top of the largest case. "I could set up in the street just outside your building, and then when the police came I could spin them quite a tale of a lovers' quarrel."

"You wouldn't!" In spite of the theater's influence, he was still essentially a private person, and at the thought of a public display he gave her an appalled look.

She returned the look calmly. "No? Of course I could. After all, you've decided what sort of woman I am, and I wouldn't want to disappoint you by being anything less than the bitch you think me."

A measuring glance, and he yielded a little ground to ask, "Why don't you simply stay at that apartment you were in when—"

He broke off, and she finished the sentence in that beautiful voice of hers. "When I seduced you? Because its owner came home from a run in

New York and wanted it back. And since he brought a mistress with him, there's obviously no room for me there.''

He considered her a moment, wondering whether she had been the previous mistress in that apartment, but only asked, "Then why not rent a place of your own?"

She countered that with another question. "Have you tried to rent an inexpensive place recently?"

He didn't answer because the question had been rhetorical; obviously he already had an inexpensive apartment in which he was perfectly comfortable.

She answered for him. "No, of course not. Well, I searched this city for a week, while I ran out of money to pay my hotel bill, and there's absolutely nothing to be had."

"Not for love or money?" he asked sardonically.

She gazed at him coolly and then said, "Not for as little money as I have, anyway, and love seems to be rather scarce in the circles we move in."

She folded her hands and sat there looking at him again. Because her last remark had been painfully true, he grew uncomfortable under her stare. "Well?" he barked. "What do you expect me to do about it?"

"Just for a few days, until something else turns up, let me stay here."

"Absolutely not!" He folded his arms over his

chest and leaned across the doorway, as if to block her physically. "I don't want you, and there isn't room anyway." The apartment that was easily large enough for him and Pen was far too small for him and this woman.

She ignored the first part of his remark and pointed out, "I could sleep on the sofa."

"You could if I let you," he conceded, "but why in hell should I do that?"

"To avoid having me set up housekeeping in the street, remember? That would be embarrassing to me, too, of course," she admitted, "but at least it might get me a little valuable publicity—you know, 'Starving Actress Ousted by Successful Boyfriend.' Who knows, headlines like that might get me a few more parts. I don't think they'd be as useful for you, though."

He stared at her with an expression of concentrated disgust that would have made most people quail; Elise Robbins didn't, but she added with sudden simplicity, "The truth is, I really am desperate enough to make a public spectacle if you don't take me in. That part you unwittingly helped me get is the first thing I've had in months, and what money I've earned with it so far has gone to paying off my debts. I have absolutely nothing else to fall back on, so it's either you or the street."

There was a thick silence between them. Still leaning across the door in her way, he studied her. She sat on the corner of one case as though she were perfectly at ease, slim legs crossed and one foot swinging gently, but now he noticed a slight tremor in the foot. She had unclasped her hands, too, and one of them was abstractedly tweaking apart the luggage tag that dangled from the case. The silence went on, and she noticed the direction of his eyes, stilling the nervous hand.

I'm a certifiable lunatic, he thought. "Then, for a few days, it's me and the sofa," he said.

PEN'S NEXT FEW DAYS in Grasmere only strengthened the love for the area she'd felt beginning that first day. Waking the next morning she had resolved to try keeping Nigel and the decision he was waiting for out of her thoughts for now. She didn't seem to know her own heart very well yet, but maybe she would learn in time if she just didn't struggle with it. One small clear voice in her mind had observed that she was simply hiding from the problem, but she allowed herself that escape with a feeling of relief she didn't analyze. And having decided not to decide, she found that her life in the cottage quickly fell into a comfortable routine, and she relished everything about it, even though it was completely different from the city life she was used to.

Here in the Lake District the spring weather was changeable, and occasional sunny days were separated by soft mists and more drenching showers. An old scarlet parka had been among the clothes Pen brought north with her, and she soon learned to cope with the unpredictable climate. On all but the very wettest days she was outdoors as much as possible, and she became a familiar sight around the village and along the neighboring fells and sales, a brilliant figure whose vivid parka echoed the color in her cheeks while her gray eyes sparkled like lake water on a brightly hazy day. She generally took a small rucksack with her, loaded with art supplies, and if a corner was left she stuffed it with a sandwich and thermos and ate her lunch wherever hunger found her.

Walking, and sometimes driving the old Cortina on longer journeys, she explored all the well-known Lakeland sights that had so tantalized her by appearing dimly through the rain that first day, and then found others to delight her, too, returning to the cottage most days with quick sketches overflowing her rucksack.

As for the solitude of living by herself, it bothered her not at all. Raised in that loving but noisy family of hers, Pen had since then only shared the tiny apartment with Bree, and now she was discovering the pleasures of being on her own. Completely independent, she was free to come and go as she pleased and to choose human company only when she felt sociable. Nearly every day she saw Banny and Edward, falling into the habit of bringing their mail up from the village when she went down to call for her own letters, and she had occasional glimpses of Megan and Corey. But they stayed close to their own garden, and Marigold didn't venture to trespass on Levvy's territory again. For the rest, then, in these early days the kitten herself supplied most of Pen's companionship, and sometimes the girl smiled to think how her beleaguered father would relish a housemate so quiet. Only occasionally did she catch herself longing to look across the teapot and see another face, an intruder upon her solitude but beloved nonetheless.

In the lengthening spring evenings Pen and Marigold usually settled themselves in the kitchen, its blue-and-white serenity making it Pen's favorite room. After supper the kitten would stretch out along the sill of the open window, so she would be ready to watch night stalk the fells, and Pen would spread her work on an easel she'd set nearby. Later, when the daylight failed, she would call Marigold inside and latch the window, moving herself to the deal table or Uncle Andrew's comfortable chair so that she could write long newsy letters home, filled with her adventures and illustrated with tiny sketches down the margins, or read her way through the collection on Uncle Andrew's bookshelf.

It was on one of those quiet evenings, however, that Pen's routine began to change. Wearing a paint-stained smock over her long green fuzzy robe, her hair tied back out of her way at the nape of her neck, she had just begun working on the first sketch for an unusual story about a prince who was bewitched into a snowman when a frantic tattoo sent her hastening to answer her front door.

Under the wisteria vine stood a gaunt gray-haired woman with distress on her long face and Corey and Megan by each hand. The instant the door opened, she rushed into speech.

"Oh, so you're Pen," she blurted, and then hurried disjointedly on. "I'm Nora Button. The children said you lived here, and I brought them to you because I'm at my wits' end. Ellen and Edward Bannister seem to be out, and I can't leave these two alone, but my sister's had an accident—given herself concussion falling down the stairs, her hubby said, and he needs me desperately to tend their four little ones while he's off at the hospital with her. Mr. Heath isn't back yet, and I just couldn't imagine what to do...."

She ran out of breath at last and stood looking pleadingly at the startled Pen, but Pen herself was looking at the children. Dressed for bed in identical striped pajamas and navy blue robes, their small feet encased in slippers made to look like rabbits, they seemed terribly young and vulnerable. There was a lost expression on Megan's face, too, that made Pen say warmly without even looking up again, "I'd be happy to have Corey and Megan here with me until their uncle gets home. They promised to come and visit me again sometime anyway, and Marigold and I would love to have company tonight."

She ran gentle fingers through Corey's glossy thatch as she spoke, then curved an arm around

Megan's small sharp shoulders as Nora Button sighed gustily, "Oh, thank you so much! I'll run back and leave a note for Mr. Heath and then be on my way."

She was hurrying off as she spoke, and Pen led the children inside without a further glance after her, silently fuming that the woman had let her own trouble blind her to the little girl's obvious distress. No matter that Megan and her brother now had a home again or that this was only a hired housekeeper leaving them temporarily; losing her parents a few months ago must have felt like abandonment to the child, and now it would seem to be happening again.

Corey, too, was looking anxiously at Megan, and Pen guessed that, being older than his sister, he had adjusted more quickly to the loss of his parents. She made him an ally immediately, and between them they swept Megan back into Pen's friendly kitchen. Once there, Pen hastily tore off her smock and flung it aside, stooping to build up a cheerful fire on the hearth while Corey fetched an agreeable Marigold for Megan to hold.

Even when the fire had caught, however, and the room was filled with its warm glow, Megan only stroked the kitten mechanically, and the lost look still shadowed her blue eyes. Corey shot Pen a worried glance that was oddly mature, and on a quick intuition she said brightly, "There, that's a good fire for company to toast themselves beside on a short visit. And now, if you two don't mind,

I'm going to ask you a favor. I make my living by drawing, and I was just about to start on some new pictures for a story, but I could use a bit of advice. I usually read most stories aloud to my sister Margery to get some ideas of what to draw, and since you're here I'd like to read this one to you and have you tell me what you think.''

Corey nodded enthusiastically, and even Megan managed a wooden little bob of her head, so Pen gathered up the story of the Winter Prince and settled herself in Uncle Andrew's old chair.

As it happened, it was only a little while later that Alistair Heath found a hastily scrawled note pinned to his front door and with a smothered exclamation came striding over to Pen's. He tapped at it briskly, but Pen, engrossed in her reading, didn't hear him. After an impatient moment's wait, he let himself in and followed the sound of a musical voice back to the kitchen.

Pen's chair by the hearth was partly turned away from the door, so she was unaware of her latest visitor, and he surveyed the room in silence. Soft shadows filled most of it except where vivid childlike sketches done in a swift breezy style were pinned to walls and cupboards, making bright touches of color. Over by the hearth, too, the shadows had been pushed aside by a rosy glow, and there he saw a girl in green with a drift of chestnut hair caught at the nape of her neck by a soft scarf, and a firelit face on which this time neither anger nor embarrassment showed, but only tranquillity. An orange kitten lay blinking at the girl's feet, and Megan's tousled head nestled against her shoulder, while Corey sat on the floor by her chair, leaning up against her knees and staring into the fire with the remains of his last smile or the beginning of his next lingering on his absorbed face. It was a serene and charming scene, but the watcher didn't seem charmed by it. In fact, the look he wore could almost have been one of anger.

Ignorant of her increased audience, Pen read on in a soft expressive voice. "So the princess had found him at last, and she leaned forward to kiss his cold white lips. And just as she touched him— plink! An icicle dropped from his chin and two more from his ears, splintering as they hit the ground. A snow cap slipped from his head, and snow melted from his shoulders, sliding into slush...."

Corey's gleeful chuckle and Megan's murmured giggle blended with an explosive little snort from the far side of the room, and all three gathered by the fire turned startled eyes toward the doorway. Then Corey shouted, "Uncle Lister!" and Megan scrambled out of Pen's arms and flew across the room to the tall man in the dimness by the door.

Her lap abruptly emptied, Pen rose and watched as he stepped forward out of the shadows and coped efficiently with the onslaught of small bodies, while her heart unaccountably seemed to pause and then rush on at a quicker pace to make

up for lost time. Megan was swung high for a hug
and then seated on a broad shoulder, her arms
wrapped around her uncle's head, and Corey's
hand tugged happily at the larger one that held it.

"Uncle Lister, Uncle Lister! We were helping
Pen with her story about the prince who was
turned into a snowman by the wicked witch!"

"Pen was reading it to us, but Marigold
listened, too."

"She's the one we saved from Levvy."

"He could have gobbled her right up!" There
was, perhaps, a note of relish in Corey's tone at
this.

"But Pen said we saved her," Megan insisted.

"Mrs. Button brought us here, Uncle Lister."

"I know, I know!" Cutting across the chidren's
chatter, a deep voice Pen had already heard twice
set the seal on her appalled recognition—even
though when she had heard that voice before, it
hadn't had this gentle teasing tone. Anything but,
she thought tartly, listening with a sort of horrified fascination as the voice amended, "At least,
I know about Mrs. Button. She left me a note on
the front door."

"We thought you might not know where we
were," Megan said, abruptly sounding small
again, as her hold on her uncle tightened.

"I knew exactly where you were," he responded
immediately, "and now I've come to fetch you
back where you belong."

Megan brightened at the matter-of-fact tone of

this and informed him, "Pen lives in her uncle's house, too."

"Oh, really?" the little girl's uncle answered in an entirely different voice, and all three of them looked over at Pen—who shut her mouth with a snap as she met the eyes of the man she'd last seen limping into the grocer's after she'd dropped her supplies on his feet.

He'd been irritated with her then, but now he looked downright angry at finding the children there with her, and under the almost accusing force of his stare her heartbeat seemed to accelerate again. But why on earth should he be so provoked that she'd helped out in an emergency? She could hardly have let Nora Button leave the youngsters alone. Even if she had known their uncle was the same man she'd already crossed swords with twice, she couldn't have done that. Maybe he was afraid she was accident-prone and the children would get hurt staying with her, she speculated on a tiny hiccup of nervous laughter. No, he was looking at her more as though he thought she'd broken a promise. Certainly he'd said that he meant to stay away from her in the future, and at the time she had thought it was a good idea, too, but how was she to know then that *he* was Megan's and Corey's Uncle Lister?

She should have guessed, though, she thought hastily as she finally made herself move toward him. Her knowing the children must be the reason their uncle's face had seemed more familiar to her that second time, outside the grocer's, than a face she'd seen only once before. Was it really only once? Now, anyway, eyes of the same shade of blue gazed out of all three of the faces turned to her, and Megan's inky hair matched the head she clung to so tightly. But while the children looked at her with quick affection, the face under the headband of Megan's arms had become a polite mask.

"You seem to be Miss Bryce," its owner said coolly when she reached him, and Pen knew he'd decided to ignore their first two catastrophic meetings for now, rather than explain them to the children. "I'd heard you were coming. I'm Alistair Heath, little though you might suspect it from the kids' version of my name. I have to thank you for taking care of my family."

Attuned to his voice, Pen heard the slight twist in that last sentence, but the youngsters seemed unaware of it. Corey echoed, "Thank you, Pen," while Megan nodded from her high perch.

Pen made herself answer blandly but gracefully, "It was a pleasure to have their company and a help to have their advice."

The children looked pleased at this, and out of their sight their uncle looked rather skeptical, but he just went on smoothly, as if she hadn't spoken, "And now, if you'll excuse me, I'll be taking this pair home to bed before Leviathan decides we've all gone missing and comes looking for us."

This was accompanied by a polite and noncommittal nod, but Pen, entertained by the discovery of Levvy's full name, forgot the peculiar animosity that seemed to be vibrating between herself and Alistair Heath and gave him a laughing look that made him gaze at her oddly for an instant. Then his lips tightened again, and he turned to stride out of her kitchen, tossing back a curt goodnight. Over his wide shoulder Megan waved goodbye, but Corey lingered a minute to say, "I liked the story, Pen. Can I see what the Winter Prince looks like when you draw him?"

"Of course you may," Pen assured him. "You can check for me to see that he looks the way we agreed he should."

"I'd like that," Corey nodded. "Good night." And he held out a small hand, which Pen shook gravely. "Good night, Marigold."

Although her eyes remained closed, one of the kitten's ears twitched, and Corey said delightedly, "She waved goodbye!" And with a broad grin he trotted after his uncle.

A moment later Pen heard her front door close and sagged bemusedly onto Uncle Andrew's weaving bench. So *that* was Uncle Lister! Her image of him as a retired schoolmaster, with white hair and gold-rimmed spectacles, popped back into her mind and stood beside the image of the man who had just left. Instead of the portly little figure she'd expected, benevolent and ineffectual, Alistair Heath had proved to be a lean powerful man, dark and vital—and disturbing. So much for preconceptions, she thought wryly. And wouldn't you know that, of all the people in the village the children's uncle *could* have been, he'd turn out to be that irritating and unpredictable man she had already had two skirmishes with!

Banny's "dour but good" might be pretty near the mark when it came to describing this man. Certainly the children thought he was good, and if "dour" referred to that icicle politeness he'd just treated her to—and when she was doing him a favor this time instead of running into him—then he was that, too. Alistair Heath evidently hadn't enjoyed any of their three meetings—in fact, he seemed to like each one less than the last—and she had to admit she knew the reason why in the first two cases, but this time his irritation puzzled her. Whether his annoyance was directed at herself, or at Nora Button, or at uncooperative fate, she didn't really know. Any more than she knew why she had thought about him after those first two encounters—or why she was doing so now.

At any rate, Pen decided, in the future she would be perfectly happy to see the children—and even Levvy, if he agreed not to dine on Marigold—but she'd just as soon their difficult uncle found somewhere else to vent his inexplicable displeasure in that coldly polite way. It was a good thing Grasmere wasn't any smaller a village; even as it was, she and the dour Mr. Heath ran the risk of meeting each other in the lane sometimes. As infrequently as possible, she hoped. Just as he'd suggested the second time they met, they might as well simply stay out of each other's paths from now on, and that would be perfectly fine with her. She'd keep him out of her thoughts, too, she vowed. After all, if she'd managed to banish Nigel from her mind for the time being, then how much easier it would be to keep out the infuriating Alistair Heath. He had intruded into her daydreams for the last time—she thought.

CHAPTER SIX

WHILE SHE WAS SUMMING UP and disposing of Alistair Heath, Pen had been setting her kitchen to rights for the evening. That done, she put the annoying man firmly out of her thoughts with a final unladylike little sniff, swept a book at random from Uncle Andrew's shelf of favorites and curled back into his chair by the fireside, giving herself determinedly to her reading.

If the truth be told, however, she had read the first page of the book in her hands three times before she finally succeeded in blotting out that dark handsome face between her eyes and the page, so that she could register that she held a very old and shabby introductory text on weaving. Finally realizing that, her attention focused, and she flipped back to the flyleaf; sure enough, there in a round and unrefined hand was the name Andrew McKenzie.

Her annoyance at the children's uncle forgotten at last, Pen ran careful fingers down the yellowed page, smoothing it thoughtfully as she tried to picture her own great-uncle as a child in Selkirk, learning his first formal lessons about weaving from this book. She wasn't very successful at seeing the child Andrew in her mind, but there across the kitchen, where the shadows deepened at the windows, stood the adult Andrew's loom, and on it lay the soft length of his unfinished sea-green blanket.

Remembering Banny's regret that the blanket had never been completed, Pen gazed at it for a long minute. Then she put the old book aside carefully and rose to cross the quiet kitchen and seat herself at the bench in front of the loom. This side of the room was quite dim now, but the long fibers of mohair yarn running across the loom caught what little light there was and gleamed like fine silver wires.

Pen touched the soft fabric gently and suddenly found herself washed by emotions. Remembering Banny and her Edward as they sat hand in hand in the evening, she felt Uncle Andrew's sorrow that had made him refuse to finish this lovely thing after Aunt Hannah died; at the same time she also felt again her own delight when as a little girl she had sat on Andrew McKenzie's lap in front of this loom and thrown the shuttle through another warp while the loom's owner—then a kindly peppermint-scented giant—patiently gave her instructions and pressed the loom's treadles, which her own short legs couldn't reach.

She hadn't thought of those lessons in years, but now they came flooding back, and Pen slipped forward on the bench, reaching legs grown long

and slim enough for the treadles. Cautiously she
pressed first one, then another, trying all six in
turn, both singly and in combinations. As she ex-
perimented, she watched to see how the treadles
controlled the long wool threads running down
the loom toward her in the warp. Alternately or
in regular groups, threads of the warp lifted in
response to her actions, while other threads remained in place, opening up a narrow space
across the loom between them.

Pen surveyed that space for a minute and then,
guided by memory, she leaned slightly forward
and tentatively passed the wooden shuttle full of
mohair yarn through it. Behind the shuttle the
silvery mohair thread lay loosely in the warp, and
almost instinctively now she reached for the
loom's beater and pulled it toward her so that its
comblike teeth packed her new thread evenly
against those Uncle Andrew had woven.

That done, Pen sat motionless again for a
long time, staring at her thread lying neatly
with the others in the length of finished fabric
that flowed toward her to coil smoothly around
the beam at the front of the loom. It was
beautiful, this unfinished blanket of Uncle
Andrew's, and with a sudden feeling of ob-
ligation, his grand-niece promised herself that
she would finish it for him. She had those
faint and far-off memories to guide her a bit, and
Uncle Andrew's book would certainly help.
Banny had promised assistance if she needed

it. Oddly confident, Pen knew she could do it.

Marigold yawned and stretched, arching her orange body into a half hoop, then came over to the loom where Pen still sat so late at night, twining around her ankles with a throaty inquiring mew. Pen jumped at the sound and then, recalled to the present, laughingly agreed, "Yes, cat, it *is* past bedtime."

Setting the shuttle aside at last and gathering up both the kitten and Uncle Andrew's book, she climbed the narrow stairs to bed.

ALTHOUGH OLD-FASHIONED, the weaving book was clear and comprehensive in its instructions, and over the next few days weaving became a new part of Pen's routine. As before, she spent most of her time exploring and painting. Her sketchbook filled with impressions of the tumbled beauty she discovered around Grasmere, and daily more drawings of the bewitched prince and the beguiling princess leaned brightly against the walls of her cheerful kitchen. When she wasn't painting, however, in the evenings or on those days when the rain fell heavily enough to discourage even her, Pen sat at Uncle Andrew's loom for long contented hours.

She hadn't told Banny about working on the blue green blanket after all, somehow reluctant to mention it on her visits to the cottage down the lane, and instead of asking the older woman for help, she went to Andrew McKenzie's old book for answers to the problems that cropped up frequently at first. The book, with Uncle Andrew's schoolboy notes in its margins, was an excellent introduction to weaving, and as she used it Pen's problems began to come less and less often.

In fact, though she wasn't conscious of it, she had a natural talent for weaving and quickly learned what she didn't remember from those long-ago lessons. The forward beam of the loom grew fatter and fatter as Pen added to the lovely length of sea-green cloth wrapped around it, and her eagerly critical eyes found only the slightest indication in the material that a new weaver had taken over.

Like other weavers, she found the look and feel of her growing coil of cloth enormously satisfying; also like other weavers, she found the rhythm of throwing the shuttle and beating in the new threads a comfortable one that left the mind free to dream while the body rocked to and fro. When she no longer needed to concentrate on the work her hands were doing, her thoughts were at liberty to wander. She kept them away from Nigel and London still, but if she occasionally forgot her resolve and let herself wonder about the dark man in the cottage up the lane, it was, of course, only an idle and momentary thing!

Now that her annoyance with him had cooled, she was simply curious about him—as anyone would be—because she wondered about his guardianship of Corey and Megan. They seemed well cared for, and they clearly loved their uncle, so apparently he was never "dour" with them. Perhaps he'd only picked up that trait at the time of the tragedy that brought the children to him. Or perhaps only she brought out that glacially polite side of him; somehow that possibility was a bit lowering.

Whatever her thoughts might be, however, she enjoyed the timeless serenity of her hours at the loom, and even the wayward Marigold seemed content while Pen wove, generally choosing, after a few strenuous scoldings when she tried to chase the shuttle through the warp, to sleep in a fuzzy ball at the end of Pen's bench.

Indirectly, it had been that annoying Alistair Heath who first sent Pen to Uncle Andrew's weaving book and the resulting contentment; ironically, it was he again who interrupted Pen's tranquillity as she sat at the loom one night about a week after his first compulsory visit. He tapped at her front door in the twilight, but Pen, daydreaming to the rhythmic thumps of her loom, didn't notice the sharper but more distant sound.

When she didn't answer the door, her caller hesitated, his slashing eyebrows lowered in a scowl. The sounds of the loom came clearly to him, and when a second knock also failed to produce a response, he finally opened the door for himself and followed Pen's thumping to the kitchen with an expression on his face that betrayed his opinion of people who were oblivious to the social amenities.

Pen didn't become aware of him until finally a mocking voice murmured into her daydreams:

"Sweet mother, I can weave no more today
For thoughts of him come thronging,
Him for whom my heart is longing—
And I know not where my fingers stray."

At the sound Marigold shot off across the room, and with a startled yelp, Pen, too, leaped to her feet, swinging around to find Alistair Heath in her doorway, hands casually in his pockets and an old navy blue fisherman's sweater emphasizing the color of his eyes. He was undeniably a darkly attractive figure, and her senses noted that traitorously, but strangely the observation only made Pen more annoyed to be caught off guard. All the irritation she'd felt the last time she saw him flooded back, and she snapped with unusual asperity, "My fingers are likely to stray around your neck! Couldn't you knock?"

"I did," he returned smoothly, refusing to be properly abashed by her attack on his manners. "But evidently either your weaving or your thinking was too loud for you to hear me."

"My weaving, of course," Pen retorted, and added, suddenly determined to make sure he didn't imagine she ever thought of him, "And thoughts of 'him' don't come thronging—who-ever 'him' is.''

Somehow that hadn't come out sounding as crushing as she'd intended, or even as clear, and the irritating man still stood in her doorway, his black eyebrows now raised in polite inquiry. Why, oh, *why* did he unhinge her so? And right now he was doing it without even saying a word! Desperate to regain her usual composure in front of this self-possessed creature, Pen retreated to simple fact.

"Anyway," she snapped, "my mother doesn't even know I've started weaving; I haven't written about it to my family."

That said, she sat down again at her bench and picked up her shuttle dismissingly. Marigold, too, climbed up on one of the chairs by the hearth and settled herself with her back to him.

"I doubt, however, that they'll be very much surprised by the news," Pen's unwelcome visitor commented blandly, ignoring their joint displeasure. "They seem to have guessed you'd show an interest in looms someday."

In spite of herself, Pen looked around again, and he continued, "The children call you Pen—" she nodded "—which I presume is from Penelope?"

She nodded again, intrigued and unaware that her curiosity thawed the cold composure she'd been trying for. She pushed a curl behind her ear.

"Then your parents gave you the name of

mythology's famous weaver and left the rest to fate. And now may I come in, if I promise not to keep you from your destiny much longer?''

Disarmed now, Pen felt her annoyance and dislike slip away. "If it's my destiny, then I guess it will wait," she laughed. "Do come in, of course. The chair without the cat is very comfortable, and I'd be happy to fix you a cup of coffee."

He had crossed the kitchen as she spoke, folding himself into the chair she offered with a long-limbed grace that was surprising in a man so tall, and now to her questioning tone he returned a brief, "Thank you, but no." Then he fell silent a moment, as if gathering his thoughts.

Pen gradually became aware that it was as if their positions had been reversed now. At her loom still, she threw the shuttle neatly through the warp in front of her, completely composed at last, while a few feet away her uninvited guest seemed uncomfortable for the first time. Finally, however, with a sound that might have been an exasperated sigh he leaned forward, elbows on his knees and hands clasped loosely in front of him, and spoke abruptly.

"I have to ask you a favor."

Intuitively Pen knew he hated that. Whatever the reason for it, this man would prefer to ask for nothing, from the world in general and her in particular. That had been perfectly clear when he'd come and retrieved the children from her care with such cool politeness last week. Her moment of liking for him evaporated, and she sat up rather straighter but continued to throw the shuttle across her loom without comment. In the brief interval before he spoke again, the only noticeable sound in the room was Pen's beater.

"It's the children. I have to leave them, and I can't."

Suddenly restless, he stood up again and prowled over to the far side of the windows above the loom. Staring through them at the dim fells, his angular face turned partly away from her, he said, "The day after tomorrow I've got to go north on business for about three days, and it's too far to make coming home each night feasible. Nora Button still hasn't come back from her sister's, so I can't leave the kids in her charge, and I can't take them with me."

Pen stopped weaving. "Well, why not?" she demanded, seeing again Megan's urgent little hands clinging to her uncle. "They're perfecty well behaved children, and for some reason they seem to love being with you."

Concern for Corey and Megan made her tone sharp, and when he looked at her now his eyes glittered for a moment. Then he seemed to make an effort to check his reaction.

"I suppose I owe you an explanation," he admitted with evident reluctance, "since I'm asking for your help."

By way of agreement Pen thumped the beater of her loom into the fabric with considerable energy, and one of his eyebrows shot up, but he said only, "How much do you know about the kids?"

"Just that they are your brother's children and were orphaned this past winter," Pen answered briefly. "Edward Bannister told me that."

She didn't add what Banny had said about their uncle's being dour but good, because right now she was sure only of the former. Nor did she add that the children's uncle had for some reason been occupying her thoughts for an inordinate amount of time. The uncle, at any rate, turned back to the view of the fells, seeming to prefer to speak to them rather than to her, and Pen wove more quietly while he talked.

"My brother, Peter, was killed in January in a senseless crash on an icy road. The other driver had been drinking, and when his car began to skid he couldn't control it. Peter died a few hours later."

His words were quiet, but loss and bitterness echoed through them, and Pen's hands faltered for a moment before resuming their steady rhythm. Then they worked automatically again while she listened intently.

"Peter's wife had left him and the children six months earlier to pursue a stage career, and our parents both died years ago, so with Peter's death the children had no one left but me. Circumstances prevent their living with their mother...."

Alistair Heath's tone was now completely expressionless, but the lines of his profile had turned to granite, and the hand that he had laid along the windowsill was clenched. Pen didn't voice her shock and dismay, contenting herself with using the beater violently again, and after a brief pause the hand unclenched with slow deliberation. Its owner jammed it back into his pocket and went on, pacing around Pen's kitchen.

"They were too distraught to be sent back to school, so after the funeral I took them with me back to my apartment in Carlisle. They had visited me there with their parents in the past, and Megan especially seemed to remember it. But night after night she woke crying for her father and mother."

Pen heard a slight change in his voice now and guessed perceptively how that must have wrung his heart. She completely forgot that only a few minutes ago she would have said he didn't have one.

"I thought that perhaps a complete change of scene would help, so I rented the cottage. I was able to bring most of my work down here, and this is a beautiful place for children to run free—certainly Leviathan is happier here than he was when cooped up in my apartment."

For a moment rueful amusement lightened his tone, but then his voice faded into concern again, and he dropped back into Uncle Andrew's chair. He looked briefly at Pen but without really seeing her, then his gaze fell on Marigold, and he reached over to stroke her with absentminded but gentle fingers. She tolerated his touch for a minute, then jumped off the other chair and padded silently from the room. Abstracted, he barely noticed her departure.

"It hasn't worked, though," he continued. "At least not with Megan. Lately the nightmares have stopped, but she's still nothing like the adventurous imp she used to be, leading Corey astray at every turn. He's more resilient, apparently, being older, and seems to feel reasonably secure in his new life, but Megan can't believe she won't lose me, too. Except for that first time here with you, she's never voluntarily gone farther than the garden. In fact, I think she'd keep within sight of me all the time if she could.

"And there's the problem. I can do nearly all my work here, but periodically I've got to go as far as the wall about something, and this is one of those times."

He fell silent at last, and Pen, who had maintained a receptive stillness and questioned nothing else, questioned that. "The wall?" she asked quietly.

"Hadrian's Wall," he expanded, adding by way of explanation, "I'm an archaeologist, specializing in Romano-British ruins in the north of England. Right now I'm trying to finish a book on the subject that's meant to revive the public's interest, so that the government gets a bit more support for its work in preserving the sites that we do have and checking to see what else might still be undiscovered."

He sighed and rubbed the back of his neck unconsciously. "Among other things, all of this means that periodically I've got to go as far as the wall about something, but the weather's still unpredictable up there at this time of year, and in a storm it's no place for young children if they don't have to be there. And if I can't keep the kids with me, they're better off in familiar surroundings than in some strange hotel up there. Besides," he added parenthetically, "they haven't been separated from Leviathan since Peter gave him to them a year ago, and he isn't the sort of guest to set an innkeeper's mind at rest."

With his words Pen got a sudden wry smile that transformed his dark face, and irresistibly she answered it with a twinkle of her own, seeing all too clearly the havoc giant Levvy would probably wreak in a genteel hotel. A brief current of understanding flowed between Pen and Levvy's reluctant keeper, and then Alistair asked abruptly, "Could Corey and Megan stay here with you?"

As directly, she answered, "Of course. And Levvy, too, if you leave me plenty of dog food for him."

His smile deepened, and the contact held an instant longer. Then suddenly he withdrew. With a sharp movement he stood up, becoming again a distantly polite stranger.

"Thank you. Then I'll bid you a good-night now, and go home to see that those two are really asleep and weren't just shamming it when I left."

This was accompanied by a precise nod, and Pen, jolted by his complete withdrawal of the momentary liking she had felt between them, managed to murmur only a startled good-night in response before he was gone, letting himself out as he had let himself in.

She heard the front door close and echoed it with a ferocious thump of her beater. When they'd met before, he had put her in the wrong twice and treated her like an enemy the third time, and now he'd reached new lows with this performance. Of all the infuriating men! He'd begun it by startling her and then had played on her sympathies, appealed to her liking for the children and even touched on her sense of humor; the whole conversation had probably been calculated from the start, even that smile, to make her agree to rescue him by tending Corey and Megan. And when she had fallen for it and promised to do what he wanted, he'd turned off the charm and gone back to being the icicle she had disliked the last time he was here. Oh, the next time he leaped out in front of her car...! Meanwhile it would serve him right, she fumed, if she changed her mind. She could send him a chilly note in the morning, informing him that she had remembered other commitments.

With considerable relish she was wording the note in her mind when she traitorously recalled the lost expression on the children's faces as Nora Button deposited them so unceremoniously on her doorstep. Now even their beloved uncle was trying to be rid of them—that was unfair, but Pen refused to admit it at the moment—and it was really only they who would be hurt if she did change her mind. That obnoxious man would probably just dump them on someone else without any regard for their happiness while he was gone. At least with her they could be reasonably happy, Pen vowed, giving up on her mental letter writing. But she would be just as coldly polite as Alistair Heath himself from now on; he should at least know that she was doing this for the children's sake and not his.

On that final resolve, Pen's kindling eyes fell on the mohair web in front of her, and she let out an explosive little squawk of rage and dismay as she caught sight of the fabric she had woven since she was first interrupted by that man and his poetry. Her fingers hadn't exactly strayed, but her attention certainly had, and looking back along the material she could tell precisely what her emotions had been as she wove each shot of yarn.

Sympathy over Peter Heath's death had made her tap the beater so lightly and quietly that some shots lay loose in the web; irritation at his brother's behavior had made her yank it so energetically that other shots lay bunched together through the web in matted clumps of mohair. Her cheeks as pink with fury as her jersey was with wild-rose color, Pen bent to unweave the last several inches of blanket, murmuring something brief and pungent to herself as she did so.

Had he still been there, Alistair Heath could have pointed out the parallel in ancient mythology in which the other Penelope had undone her weaving every night; but in her present mood such a reference—and from him—would probably have moved Pen to violence. Loyalty and sympathy were excellent traits for the faithful wife of Odysseus, but to Pen right now they seemed a great deal more trouble than they were worth. Utterly infuriated, she went on with her bothersome task.

CHAPTER SEVEN

WHEN THEIR UNCLE brought the children to her
two mornings later, Pen was as frigidly polite to
him as she'd planned to be. Rummaging among
the clothes she'd brought to Lakeland with her,
she had unearthed a rather unfashionable old
white dress that for a long time she'd been meaning to remake. Instead she wore it now, topped
with a much loved but deplorably stretched white
cardigan, and she tied her heavy mass of chestnut
curls back with a severe black ribbon. Without actually being a nursemaid's costume, her outfit
somehow suggested one, and as she stood at the
green door and said a bright hello to the
youngsters, Pen watched their uncle's reaction
from the corner of one eye, hoping to annoy him.
But as he registered her appearance, only a quick
look of distaste crossed his dark face, followed
almost instantly by a gleam of something else and
then complete blankness.

Marigold meantime had followed Pen to the
door, and while the children greeted the kitten
enthusiastically and Levvy watched tolerantly—
lying nearby with a huge sack of dog food beside

him—Pen listened with polite attention to Alistair Heath. Face and voice impersonal, he gave her quick instructions about rituals and bedtimes, wrote down a telephone number at which he could be reached and then handed over a case of small clothing, a very large dog leash and a key he said would let them in if the children found they had to go home for anything forgotten.

Pen guessed this was a safety measure, to be used if Corey and Megan seemed to need the reassurance of being able to run back to their own cottage, but not by the flicker of an eyelash did she let their uncle know she appreciated his affectionate foresight. Nor, to her chagrin, did he give any sign at all that he realized her appearance and manner were out of character. Instead as soon as the requirements were taken care of he turned away from her.

"All right, you two. I know I'll not be gone long enough to be worth much of a goodbye, but see if you can tear yourselves away from that cat for just a minute to give your uncle a hug for good luck."

It was a completely different voice from the one Pen had just been listening to, and a different man from the expressionless stranger held out his arms for the laughing children to scramble into. Face alight and almost ridiculously like theirs, he held one child high on each strong arm, whispering to each one in turn words Pen didn't catch. Then with a final squeeze for Corey and a nuzzle for Megan that mingled black hair with black hair, he set them down.

"Corey, if Leviathan runs out of dog food, scat on home and bring some more back. And Megan, if the food's running low, see that he does it before the dog eats that cat," he admonished in mock-serious tones, and the small faces turned to grin impishly at Pen, who pantomimed exaggerated worry by wringing her hands.

"Goodbye, urchins; see that you behave yourselves. Goodbye, Miss Bryce, and thank you." He looked over the youngsters' heads at Pen one more time, and now he let expression into his eyes as he swept them over her outfit again. But—drat the man—it wasn't annoyance; it was amusement! "Don't weave any tangled webs before I get back Friday evening."

And he was off down her walk before Pen could frame an adequate retort. A minute later he drove past her cottage in a sleekly elegant silver Rover and disappeared with a final wave and fanfare from his horn.

Megan picked up Marigold and held her rather tightly, the kitten's hind legs trailing in a way Pen recognized, but didn't discourage at the moment. Corey looked up at her to ask, "What did Uncle Lister mean, Pen, about not weaving any tangled webs?"

Pen, torn between fury and mirth, was herself trying to decide whether he had been referring to the disaster he must have seen her weaving the

other night or to the "deceit" of the pose offered
by her clothes and behavior. He could have meant
either, or both, with some justice, and she was
rather at a loss to explain to Corey.

Luckily, perhaps, the Lake District's recurrent
rain began to fall, and she was able to buy time
before answering while she collected both children
and their possessions, both animals and their
food, into the cottage. Once in the kitchen,
though, while Levvy and Megan settled themselves
near the friendly flames on the hearth, Corey
returned to the issue with the persistence of his
age.

"What did he mean, Pen?" he asked again, but
Pen dodged the question by explaining weaving in
general and demonstrating her loom to the
children. Corey was successfully deflected by that,
and Megan was distracted enough to let the cat go.
With a little help from Pen, in fact, both children
were able to weave a few shots, and then they
sprawled contentedly on the floor with Pen's
rough sketches of the Winter Prince, using her
tablets and pens to concoct their own versions.
Meanwhile Pen herself went back to the loom,
Uncle Andrew's lovely blanket nearly finished.

The rest of the children's stay was as tranquil as
that first morning. Heavy rains kept all three indoors much of the time, as spring retreated for a
while, but none of them really minded. Oddly
enough, with his charges in her keeping Pen found
her wayward thoughts wandering less often to

Alistair Heath, so that only occasionally was she disconcerted by the memory of the teasing laughter in his voice on that last rallying comment as he left; wasn't that the voice he used with Corey and Megan? And as for the children themselves, happy with Pen by day and perhaps reassured by Marigold's and Levvy's presences on their bed by night, both seemed contented. Even Megan made only one excuse to fetch a sweater from home, and the brief errand to her uncle's cottage seemed to convince her that no real changes were occurring to disrupt her young life again. Afterward she was bolder, and Pen caught a few glimpses of the imp Alistair said she had been before the loss of her parents.

Pen finished the sea-green blanket that first day; the next afternoon, with the book nearby for instructions and the children offering encouragement, she cut it free of the loom. They spread it across the deal table, and Pen brushed it with a bristly little teasel to fluff up the mohair. Then Megan and Corey helped her fold it, and they all pulled on their parkas. The weather had lightened so that only a soft mist filled the air, and they ran together through the cool dampness down the lane to Banny's cottage, Pen carrying the blanket in paper under one arm and holding Megan by the other, while Corey scampered beside them.

As Pen had guessed it would, the damp weather was keeping Edward at home, and his wife was with him. Banny found the three of them breathless and laughing on her doorstep, and only a quick glance at Pen indicated her surprise and pleasure at seeing the children so far afield without their uncle. Then she said calmly, "Come in, lass, and welcome. What a good thing you've brought us company. I just realized I've made far too many bannocks for only the two of us, and we can't possibly eat them all before they go stale."

From a settle by the fire Edward seconded the invitation smoothly, saying with a teasing glance at his wife, "Yes, do come in, and save Ellen's thrifty Scottish soul from the shock of having food go to waste."

Not proof against appeals like those, Corey hurried his sister across the doorstep, and in a minute both children were eating Banny-cakes with sticky-fingered joy. Pen indulged, too, but after her first bannock she dusted off her fingers and left the young ones to empty the heaped plate Banny had provided while she unwrapped her bundle and spread the blanket's soft folds across Banny's lap as she sat with her Edward. "I've brought you a present from Uncle Andrew," Pen said, trying to sound matter-of-fact.

For a long time Banny's head stayed bent and her gnarled fingers stroked the shimmering fabric, while Edward glanced across her at Pen with affectionate approval but said nothing. When Banny finally looked up again, her shrewd old eyes were wet and for once she seemed at a loss for words.

Pen explained gently, "It did seem a shame to leave it unfinished, and Uncle Andrew's old weaving text was very clear. I thought he and Aunt Hannah would be happy if you had this."

Banny cleared her throat, and when she found her voice it was even more burred than usual. "Och, lass, they'd be gladder still to see you here and such a bonny weaver. You've clearly a gift for the loom, and it's a fine thing to see it discovered."

Cheeks pink from the praise, Pen nevertheless felt bound to point out that only part of the work was hers. "But all I did was finish what Uncle Andrew started, Banny. It has to be much harder to start something than just to finish it."

"That may be true, child, but it doesn't alter the fact that you did a neat bit of work," Banny countered, her tone firmer. Then she added with a twinkle, "And the next thing you weave will be entirely your own. I'll give you a wee bit of help with the warping up if you're in need of it, but all the work will be yours."

Pen grinned at Banny's assumption—a correct one—that she wanted to go on weaving, and the children, just dispatching the last of the Bannycakes, looked up at that, white powder encircling their mouths and their faces bright with interest.

"Oh, Pen, could you weave a blanket for me, too? Maybe one just my size?" Megan begged. "I'd help, too, and so would Corey."

Corey nodded dutifully, and both children fixed

Pen with hopeful gazes. Had their uncle ever looked at anyone with an expression so trusting, she wondered for an instant with an inexplicable little pang. Had he been like these two who wore his face in miniature? And if so, what had changed him to the coolly guarded man he almost always appeared to be now? Then with a mental shake she flung off the thought and concentrated on the youngsters.

Megan's deep blue eyes were eager, her smooth black braids ruffled and her sky-blue T-shirt liberally decked with crumbs, and she looked so happy and excited it hardly seemed possible that she could be the same waif in rabbit slippers who had stood so forlornly at Pen's door only a few days earlier. Delighted by the change, Pen felt as though she'd willingly promise anything to keep that glowing childlike look on Megan's expressive little face. Without making any deliberate decision, she heard herself saying, "If you'll choose your yarn from Uncle Andrew's supply, and if Banny will come and supervise, we'll warp up the loom tomorrow for your blanket."

Banny was nodding agreement to the part of that addressed to her, and while Corey shouted, "Hurrah!" Megan flung herself into Pen's arms.

"Oh, Pen, thank you!"

Already amply rewarded by the little girl's joy, Pen swung the small body full circle and then sank down at Edward's feet to catch her breath again, while Megan chattered happily about colors, leaning confidingly against Pen's shoulder, and Edward and Banny watched with smiling eyes.

THE NEXT AFTERNOON found all the activity moved over to Pen's cottage. That morning she had quickly woven off the last fifteen inches of the blue green warp into a scarf for Nigel and posted it with a brief note that read, "Spring is a bit chillier now for my sheep, but this will keep *you* warm while I'm gone. Love, Bo Peep." As she signed the absurd nickname he'd given her, London and their last conversation seemed incredibly remote, but she noticed that only fleetingly as she hurried to gather up the materials and equipment that might be needed for Megan's blanket; weaving was a more immediate problem than Nigel.

Soon after lunch Banny came as promised to help with the warping up, and even Edward, his rheumatism somewhat improved, left his manuscript and came to supervise and offer encouragement. Levvy was exiled to the far side of the kitchen and Marigold betook herself to a high corner of the china cupboard, where she was out of the way and able to survey the goings-on between naps.

Pen brought out all the varied skeins of wools and mohairs that Uncle Andrew had kept on hand, and their rainbow colors were draped around the room as Megan danced from one to the next, trying to make up her mind. Corey meanwhile sat cross-legged on the floor by the hearth, chatting companionably with Edward in Uncle Andrew's chair and occasionally looking up to offer his sister contradictory advice—to which Megan paid scant attention.

Finally, when Pen and Banny were both exhausted from holding up different groups of colors, Megan decided what she wanted at last and collected skeins of pale pink wool and of rose and ivory mohair in a fluffy pile. Heaping them together, she gathered them up and hung them around her neck, skipping over to the weaver's bench where Pen had sat down.

"These, Pen, please. Are they all right?" she asked excitedly.

In fact, they were better than all right. The bundle of soft colors around her neck set off the glowing face of the little girl in a way Megan herself couldn't possibly see, but the others smiled at the picture she made, and Corey said in tones of some surprise, "Why, those are nice, Megan."

Pen seconded his opinion. "They *are* nice. They're perfect for your blanket, Megan, and that's what you shall have."

Face alight, Megan gave Pen a joyous woolly kiss, then danced to Banny and gave her an unselfconscious hug, too, before settling beside Corey at Edward's feet while Pen and Banny consulted. They worked out the size that Megan's blanket should be, and then while Banny diagrammed the weaver's draft they would use to tie up the loom in the right pattern, Pen reached out quietly for her sketchbook and dashed off a drawing of Megan as she had looked carrying her yarn.

It was only a series of quick lines, with a few hasty touches of color, but Pen's accurate eyes had memorized what she saw, and her lines recaptured the eternal quality of the child's delight. When she was finished, she tucked the drawing away in her sketchbook, thinking she might someday make a portrait from it. Perhaps Megan's impossible uncle would like to have it.

Banny was through figuring by then, so Pen dragged out Uncle Andrew's warping reel, a hollow wooden framework with pegs set on it so that yarn could be measured out evenly by being wound around them; each thread would then be exactly the same length as all the others. Together she and Banny wound the many loops of yarn that Megan's blanket would need, taking turns as Banny provided experience and Pen energy.

They worked as quietly as possible, too, after Pen heard Edward asking the children, "Have you two ever heard the story of the Crier of Claife?"

Two small heads shook in unison, and dropping his voice into a rich, almost singsong rhythm, he began to tell them the tale of the ghostly ferryman who haunted Lake Windermere after he was lost there. At the beginning of the story, Megan was relieved to find that the poor man hadn't met his fate as close by as Grasmere, and at the end Corey wanted to rush right down to Windermere that night to look for the ferryman—but all the way through Pen was simply fascinated. Edward, for all his usual quiet reserve, was a born storyteller.

As a result, it seemed only a few minutes until Pen and Banny were ready to lift the warp carefully from the reel, gathering the soft colorful mass into a loose loop so that it wouldn't tangle. Then they cut the long loop at one end and painstakingly "dressed" the loom in its new warp—a process that took all too many minutes.

While Edward used more eerie local legends to occupy the children at the far side of the room, Banny supplied Pen with extra hands and careful instructions at the loom. Departing from the traditional methods of Uncle Andrew's book, they worked from the front of the loom to the back, with Pen beginning by passing each end of yarn through the fine teeth of the beater.

When that was done—and Pen had stretched her cramped muscles—she went on and threaded each end through one of the delicate heddles on the loom; attached to the treadles below, they would lift different threads as she pressed the treadles, opening a space for her shuttle to pass through. Finally, then, the long warp threads reached the back of the loom, and there the two weavers tied them firmly to the back beam.

The only thing left to be done was to wind the whole warp gently through the loom and onto the back beam, tying off the other ends of the yarn loops—cut open, too, at the very last—to the front beam. The dressing finished then, Pen would be able to begin weaving whenever she chose, slowly winding the warp forward again as she worked and rolling the finished fabric onto the front beam.

With so little left to do, Banny decreed a rest break. "That's enough for now, Penelope. As new to this as you are, lass, you're likely to be feeling a bit bent out of true."

To test that prediction, Pen tried to straighten up. "Oof!" she exclaimed, and made a show of opening herself out slowly like a pocketknife.

The children loved it, and while she stretched and groaned comically for them, Banny fixed tea, including in the meal the fresh Banny-cakes that had mysteriously appeared in Pen's cupboard. Corey and Megan, recognizing them immediately, turned to fall on them with delight; and Pen, under Banny's amused eyes, abandoned her routine to rescue one for herself.

It was just as the children began a heated discussion about the fate of the last bannock that a knock at the front door was—for once—audible. Two pairs of blue eyes flew to meet Pen's gray ones, and all three spoke simultaneously.

"Uncle Lister!" shrieked two voices.

"Alistair!" echoed a third, whose oddly breathless owner didn't realize she had forgotten Mr. Heath's surname.

In response to their voices, the knock was followed by the noise of the door opening, prompting Pen to gather up her scattered wits and call, "Come in! We're all in the kitchen!"

The sight that met Alistair Heath's eyes when he

reached the kitchen was one of friendly confusion. Coming in from three cold and solitary days along the wall, he was momentarily dazzled by the warmth and brightness of Pen's kitchen, and Corey and Megan heaped themselves upon him joyously before he had time to sort things out properly. Still, the impression created in the yarn-draped room by tea things and firelight, welcoming voices and small loving arms, gave him an odd sense of completeness. He felt it without recognizing it, and the deep lines etched into his brown skin smoothed and faded. As he set the children down again his eyes held for once an unguarded pleasure that only deepened as he realized Megan had willingly released her hold on him to dart across the room and scoop up the free end of the rosy warp for his inspection.

"Uncle Lister, look! It's my blanket—at least, it's going to be. Pen's making it, and Banny's showing her how to start!"

"It's very pretty, moppet. You'll look like a rosebud wrapped in that. And is Corey to have one that will make him to look like another flower for my garden?"

The deep voice teased lovingly, and Corey's protesting, "Uncle Lister!" was met with a blandly puzzled stare that crumbled into laughter as the boy tried to explain. "I'd rather look like a...like a...caterpillar or something!"

"What do you think, Penelope?" Alistair's eyes, filled with amusement and perhaps even gratitude instead of their usual cool challenge, looked over the children's heads at a completely astonished Pen, and he asked, "Can we persuade you to weave him something long and furry, and maybe even striped?"

Suddenly mute as she met the unfamiliar expression in his eyes, she pushed her ruffled hair distractedly behind one ear and nodded, and Banny, watching them with a tiny smile neither of them noticed, suggested, "What about a jacket, lass?"

Thankful for the interpolation, Pen snatched up her suggestion. "That's it, a jacket. I'll make you one to keep you as warm as a caterpillar, Corey, when Megan's blanket is done."

"Good," Corey agreed in a pleased tone. "And in the meantime I'll study caterpillars and see which one I want to look like."

He was a bit indignant when this provoked more laughter from the others, but unintentionally Marigold saved him from any further notice for the time being. Finally deciding to leave her perch on the china cupboard, she had climbed cautiously down and was working her way toward Levvy, still stretched out obediently in the far corner of the room. At the same time Alistair, in response to Banny's inquiring lift of the teapot, was moving thankfully toward the table. Inevitably their paths crossed, and tired as he was Alistair overlooked the scrap of orange fur at his feet. He tripped over Marigold, and with an indignant howl she shot away into the pink warp while he crashed sideways into Pen's angular old cooker.

Unthinkingly, Pen reacted according to noise. Marigold had made her woes known far and wide, but Alistair hit the cooker without a sound, so Pen hurried into the tangled warp and unwrapped Marigold, unfastening her sharp little claws from the rosy wool and smoothing her ruffled fur.

"There, Marigold, there, love," she crooned to the outraged kitten. "It's all right."

It wasn't really, however. Banny at least realized that Alistair had fallen heavily, and while Edward kept the children out of the way at his side, she helped the younger man into her chair by the fire. He was silent but white-faced, and the vibrancy that had filled the room while he teased the youngsters was entirely gone now. And so, of course, was the look that had so bedazzled Pen.

Eyes closed, he only nodded to Banny's murmured, "Are you all right, lad?" But Pen caught the words and thrust Marigold at Corey, only now learning that Alistair, too, was a casualty of their collision.

To her anxious, "Oh, Alistair, are you hurt?" he returned no response except a quirk of his long mobile mouth, and Pen rushed on, "I'm so sorry! I heard Marigold shriek, but I didn't know you were hurt, too."

Still without opening his eyes, he gritted through set teeth, "And must one wail like a banshee for you to know it?"

Pen flushed the same color as her scarlet sweater, but he went on sardonically, "If I might make a suggestion for your next weaving project, I'd recommend—rather than a blanket for Megan or a jacket for Corey—that you first make a nice little noose for that cat."

"Thank you," Pen snapped back through the children's shocked protests, "for relieving my fears about your injury. Your fall has left you as nasty as ever, so obviously I need be concerned only for Marigold!" And she stalked over to Corey again, making a great show of checking the kitten he held protectively away from his uncle's wrath.

Alistair finally opened his eyes again to see Pen and his niece and nephew glaring at him over Marigold's furry head with assorted expressions of scorn, distress and shock, while Banny stood near him wordlessly proffering a restorative cup of tea and Edward regarded him with a look of quiet sympathy. For a moment he met that look and a tacit understanding flowed between the two men, then Alistair shook his head to Banny and made an attempt to lever himself out of the chair.

It was clearly a very uncomfortable process, and his lips tightened again into a thin white line, but Pen resolutely stayed on the other side of the room and made no move to aid him. It was Banny instead who set aside the teacup and with an encouraging murmur helped him back onto his feet.

When he stood there finally, he seemed to

gather himself for a moment, while a little color inched into his face again, and then with a slightly apologetic look at the children—though not at Pen—he said, "If I swear not to make mittens out of that cat, will you two agree to come home with me and nurse your poor decrepit uncle?"

Megan, won over immediately by this devious appeal to her sympathies, flew to his side, and even Corey was pacified by his promise and walked gravely to stand beside him.

"You could lean on me on the way home if you like, Uncle Lister," he offered solemnly.

For an instant Alistair's eyes measured Corey with a glance that might almost have been hopeful, but then the look faded, and he said only, "Thank you, Corey. I think I can make it, but I'll use your shoulder as a stick if I need to."

His fences mended with the children, Alistair then turned stiffly back to Banny and Edward. "Forgive me, please, Mr. and Mrs. Bannister, for making so noisy an entrance and so calamitous an exit. I'm not usually this disruptive of people's teatime."

Edward made a slight dismissing gesture and smiled, while Banny replied maternally, "Our teatime will recover nicely, lad; you just see to it that you do likewise. Mind that you don't do any gallivanting around for a day or two."

Alistair responded to these strictures with an obedient little salute, and Pen noted with set teeth than even when he was supposedly racked with pain, he was still able to scheme his way back into the children's good graces and even mislead shrewd Banny into thinking he was just a nice boy who needed mothering. She should have expected that, of course, after the canny way he'd used sympathy and a charming smile to maneuver her into agreeing to keep Corey and Megan while he was gone. At any rate, he didn't try charm on her this time. The face he finally turned to her was blank again, and when he spoke, his voice was as coolly distant as ever. The surprisingly altered man of a little while ago, relaxing gratefully after a hard journey, might never have been.

"I thank you for your care of my young charges, Miss Bryce," he said meticulously. "With your permission I'll take them home with me now and send them back sometime tomorrow to collect their things."

One black eyebrow rose in polite inquiry, and Pen nodded an equally polite and frosty agreement.

While their uncle watched impassively, she gave each of the children a quick good-night hug and then stepped back. Megan looked uncertainly from one rigid face to the other, and some of her sparkle seemed to dim, but Corey said calmly, "Good night, Pen. We'll be back tomorrow," and at that his sister brightened again.

"When we come over tomorrow, Pen, will my blanket be ready for you to start weaving?" she asked hopefully.

"Yes, love, I promise," Pen vowed. "Banny and I can finish getting it ready this evening if we spend a little more time on it—" Banny was nodding agreement "—and then when you come we'll get started right away." She was anxious to reassure Megan lest the child's new excitement fade into her old fearfulness.

She gave Alistair a smile that managed somehow to be simultaneously reassurance to Megan and reproof to her uncle, and he returned it with one that was equally forced. Megan, however, was satisfied by this show of goodwill, and after patting Marigold one last time she and Corey flanked Alistair on either side and helped him out of Pen's kitchen with well-meaning if somewhat clumsy solicitude, while Levvy paced watchfully behind them. Momentarily Pen considered running ahead of them to open the outside door, but then she decided that since Alistair was getting so darn good at letting himself in and out of her house he could jolly well do it again this time.

When he and his devoted attendants were gone, Banny said briskly, "Well, now, Penelope, let me give you a hand with winding up this warp, and then Edward and I will be leaving you, as well."

Given no opening to say what she thought of Alistair Heath, Pen had to content herself with thinking some unkind thoughts about his erratic disposition, calculated charm and too perfect manners as she joined Banny by the tangled warp. While Edward surreptitiously fed Marigold the last crumbs from tea, Banny shook the snarls from the warp with expert deftness. Then she held it evenly stretched out in front of the loom, and Pen cranked it through onto the back beam. Perhaps, thinking about the children's infuriating uncle, she cranked more vigorously than was strictly necessary, but Banny said nothing about it.

In a little while they were finished, and the loom was dressed in its new warp, standing ready to give Pen more tranquil hours of weaving. Certainly she was feeling in need of them! Putting black thoughts of Alistair aside as best she could, however, she came out from behind the loom to take one of Banny's hands in both of hers.

"Banny, thank you!" she exclaimed. "I'd never have figured out all that without your help. Thank you for giving me your whole afternoon. And Uncle Edward—you, too. The children loved having you here to talk to them, and I loved being able to listen in. After all, now if I ever take up ferrying on Windermere, I'll know to avoid the Crier of Claife!"

Banny patted her hands and said, "Well, lass, we both enjoyed ourselves this afternoon. Those two are an engaging pair, and they seem to be doing well with their uncle. He's a better hand with bairns than I'd guessed. And to think I called him dour," she marveled. "A fine lad like that...."

She turned away to help Edward lever himself to his feet after he handed Pen her cat. Pen, stroking Marigold's ears, had her own opinion of that "fine lad"!

A few minutes later Banny and Edward had gone, too, and for the first time in three days Pen had her cottage to herself again. With no company left but her kitten, she tried not to feel oddly bereft as she cleared away the tea things and gave Marigold a proper supper—wondering absentmindedly why the kitten didn't seem more hungry.

Then she stood still for a moment, staring at the loom and Megan's warp but seeing instead the unfamiliar look on Alistair Heath's face in those first few minutes of his return. It had been like the look of a man who had found a haven when he'd given up searching for one, and it drew Pen unconsciously toward her sketchbook again. On the page after her drawing of Megan another series of lines took shape, and then Alistair's dark face looked up at her from the paper.

She stared at it for an instant before she realized that not only had she been thinking about the wretched man yet again, but now she'd also gone and drawn his face. "Oh, damn that man!" she muttered feelingly, and tossed the sketchbook away, stalking from the room to air her irritation on a solitary walk.

Behind her, Marigold, left to her own devices, looked after her usually even-tempered mistress with an inquiring golden gaze, but when the front door had shut rather firmly she leaped into Uncle Andrew's chair and curled up to wait for Pen's return. It was a long wait, too, as Pen tramped favorite paths until full darkness, brooding about her inability to keep Alistair Heath from intruding on her thoughts. She'd generally been able to keep from thinking about Nigel these past few weeks, even though he was important to her; so why on earth couldn't she do the same with Alistair, who was so totally unimportant to her? When he was present, why did she listen for every different inflection of his voice, even when she was quarreling with him? And when he was absent, why did his face materialize in her mind and on her sketch pad? Why did she wonder how he managed when he was alone with the children, or care that he had lost their eager expression?

No answers to her questions presented themselves, but at least by the time she finally reached home Pen was too tired to think more about much of anything—or anyone.

CHAPTER EIGHT

WITH THE FAITHFUL LEVVY IN ATTENDANCE, the children came back to Pen's cottage the next day for their possessions, and she helped them pack up their small belongings. Afterward with Pen's help Megan herself wove the first two inches of the rosebud blanket while Corey and Marigold entertained themselves with a small piece of cellophane and Levvy supervised with dignified detachment. Pen's visitors didn't stay long, however, and there was no mention of their uncle.

In fact, there was no sign of Alistair all that week, although the youngsters scrambled over the wall from their own garden nearly every day, and Pen learned from Banny that they visited her house, too—particularly when they guessed she might be baking. Pen was delighted that the children's horizons seemed to be expanding, so that even Megan no longer seemed perpetually afraid to leave home lest home should vanish. But Pen was oddly perturbed by their uncle's invisibility. The children said only that he was working, and Pen never saw his sleek silver car go down the lane.

When she realized she'd been watching for it, she

BELOVED INTRUDER 139

took herself severely to task, but even the sternest
of self-scoldings didn't alter the fact that she was
aware of his absence, irritating though his presence
usually was. She was also, however, far too conscious of the way they'd parted this past time to
make any attempt to find out what had become of
him. Besides, it was about time she admitted that
any encounter between them led sooner or later to
disaster. She might as well accept that, because it
was certainly true, but what did it matter anyway?
In fact, she told herself that she cared about him at
all only because he was important to the children.

At any rate, Pen was working, too. She finished
the drawings for the Winter Prince and with
Corey's enthusiastic approval sent them off to
London, starting to work on another story almost
immediately. Nearly every day she had drawings or
at least letters to post, and so like the children she,
too, stopped in at the Bannisters', whether or not
Banny was baking. On her way down to the village
Pen picked up whatever letters they might have to
post, and then on her way back she dropped off
whatever mail had come for the elderly couple of
whom she'd grown so fond.

The Wednesday after Alistair Heath's disastrous
return, Pen found the children at the Bannisters'
house ahead of her. Coming up the path to the
door, she heard their voices laughing and clamoring, and Banny opened to her knock to greet her
with a twinkle.

"Och, lass, it's glad I am that you're here,

because now you can settle a wee disagreement we're having. Come along in.''

Mystified, Pen followed her into the kitchen and discovered the youngsters busy in a debate over the one piece remaining of ravaged sponge cake.

"But you started before I did," Megan was pointing out.

"Maybe," Corey admitted, "but you eat faster than I do, so you've had more."

At that he whisked the plate out of his sister's reach—but right into Banny's. She extracted it neatly from his clutches and turned to present it with a flourish to Pen. "There, Penelope, help yourself, do. And isn't it providential that the bairns remembered to save a slice for you?"

Corey opened his mouth to disavow any such plan, but then he caught Banny's eye and subsided while Megan gave a little triumphant crow of laughter. More tactful, Pen hid her grin behind the cake and used only her eyes to salute Banny's mastery of tactics.

When she'd finished eating, Corey was still looking slightly crestfallen, so on an impulse Pen said, "Kids, I'm just off to the village to post my letters and Banny's; what would you think of coming with me?"

What Corey thought of the idea was obvious immediately. "Yes!" he shouted, but then he paused and looked at his sister. "Megan?"

Pen and Banny looked at her, too, and all of them wondered in the moment's silence whether or not she would be willing to go so far. Granted, her world had expanded to include all three cottages at the end of the lane now, but she'd never gone as far as the village without Alistair.

Megan, however—perhaps still buoyant over Corey's defeat—simply looked down her snub nose at her brother and said, "Of course, silly." Then her superior pose collapsed and she hastened to assure Pen, "I meant Corey's the silly, not you, Pen. We'd like to go, please."

Pen and Banny exchanged laughing looks of silent congratulation, and a minute later, before Megan could think better of her decision, the three were off down the sunny lane to the village, one child on either side of Pen. As they passed out of sight of Banny's white apron raised in farewell, Pen casually linked hands with both children, and they strolled on together chatting and swinging hands.

Occasionally during their travels Megan's grip on Pen's fingers tightened for a moment, but the little girl never looked back or faltered. Proud of her courage, Pen nevertheless made certain their visit to the village was a brief one, and in less than half an hour they were headed back up the lane again. The letters in Pen's little rucksack had been exchanged for a sheaf that Corey now carried, having appointed himself postman for the day. Striding along, he made much of checking each one for the correct address and return.

"Here's two for you, Pen, both from London, and three for Banny and Uncle Edward. Oh, and look—this one's got an American stamp on it! I can't read the return, but it looks as if it might be New York. Pen, do you think Banny would let me have the stamp?''

"I think she might just, pet, but you'll have to ask her for yourself."

Pen smiled at his enthusiasm, and pulling free of her he ran on ahead shouting, "Come on, Megan, let's go ask!"

"Yes, love," Pen agreed in answer to Megan's questioning look. "You go ahead, and I'll trudge wearily along behind you on my ancient flat feet."

This nonsense earned a little gurgle of laughter from Megan, and then she flew up the lane after Corey—and closer to Alistair—on winged feet. Pen meanwhile followed more slowly as she investigated her own letters. The one from Dulwich she pocketed to read later, but the one from Nigel she opened immediately.

He had written only twice before since she'd left London, but the sight of his angular black handwriting made her smile automatically as she slipped her thumbnail under the flap of the envelope. Both of the other letters had brought him vividly before her. Deftly satirical and wickedly descriptive about the people he worked with, the letters had been as entertaining as a conversation with him, but not as demanding because they couldn't press her so insistently for a decision about sharing his apartment. In fact, both letters had simply ended with a flippant reminder that the apartment was ready and waiting for her—and so was he—so she'd been able to leave the problem in the back of her mind. This letter was a bit different, however.

Bo Peep,
Apologize for me to your denuded sheep, and tell them their sacrifice is appreciated. Spring has come on too fast here for me to be needing borrowed warmth, but a borrowed glimpse of your bucolic bliss is more than welcome. It can serve to remind that there *is* a world off the stage and outside London. Until you come back it can remind me of you.

Nigel

Pen read the brief message twice, then folded it and slipped it back into its envelope, her forehead a little creased and her feet slowing to a complete stop. What was there about this letter that was so different from the other two? It was shorter, of course, hardly a letter at all, but there was something else about it, too: it didn't sound like the Nigel she knew, somehow. In fact—how peculiar—she couldn't seem to picture Nigel at all.

When she had read the other two letters, she had seen him clearly in her mind, almost as if he were standing in front of her, but now she could only glimpse bits and pieces. His dark eyes and slanting eyebrows formed in her memory, but then they slipped away again before the rest of that familiar face could appear. Disconcerted, Pen tried again to picture her old friend, and again it didn't work.

With a little snort of exasperation she remembered how easily Alistair Heath's dark features kept appearing in her mind—and on the thought, they did it again instantly, but she shook them away impatiently. If she could see Alistair's provoking face so clearly, why couldn't she see Nigel's pleasant one? Why should she be able to visualize the man she disliked and not the one who'd been her friend for years? Pen had an uneasy intuition that the answers to those questions were probably important ones, but somehow they eluded her; no reasonable explanations came to mind, and finally she slipped Nigel's envelope into her pocket with the letter from home and went on up the lane.

By the time she arrived at Banny's gate, the children had already come and gone, and the sound of their young voices drifted back from the direction of their own cottage. Banny, however, was still standing at the gate, absently smoothing a thin blue envelope with no stamp in her old fingers. She didn't seem at first to be aware Pen was there, but stood gazing fixedly after the children. Indeed, she seemed so uncharacteristically withdrawn that Pen hesitated to speak to her, but then she finally turned back and looked at the girl with eyes that were awash.

"Banny?" Pen asked urgently, her own concerns completely forgotten. "It's not bad news, is it?"

Banny sniffed determinedly and fished a handkerchief from her apron pocket. She cleared her throat and answered at last, "No, lass. This is just a letter from my son's wife."

"Why, Banny, I suppose I should have guessed it from the way you manage Corey and Megan, but I didn't know you and Edward had a son."

"We don't... now." Banny's answer was muffled by the handkerchief at her eyes, but Pen caught it.

"Oh, Banny, I'm so sorry!" She reached out and touched the little round figure in front of her with a quick sympathetic hand. "I wish I hadn't said anything to remind you of him."

"It's all right, lass." Banny tucked away the handkerchief again resolutely and patted Pen's fingers resting on her arm. "Everything reminds us of him, but after all these years we accept it. It's just that occasionally Jenny's letters remind us a bit too much of what we've lost."

With an understanding little murmur, Pen slipped through the gate and put an arm along Banny's rounded shoulders, walking slowly up the path with her. And as if the movement of her feet freed her mind to remember without too much pain, Banny began speaking again.

"Jenny's the lass from the village here that Jamie loved from the time he was a wee bairn. When they were grown up, Harry Halford fell in love with her, too, but she had eyes only for Jamie and they were wed here in the village church eighteen years ago."

She paused a moment, and Pen knew by her

slight smile that she was remembering that wedding day. Then the smile faded, and Banny went on. "Only a few months after the wedding, though, Jamie got restless; he kept saying there was nothing for a young man to do here if he hadn't a talent for weaving or with sheep. Finally he decided to emigrate to the States with Jenny, and Harry went, too.

"Both of the lads found work in New York, and everything seemed to be going well. Their letters were so happy, and we were so proud when Jenny wrote that she was going to have a baby. When she was about eight months along in her term, Harry came by for a visit, and when he was leaving, Jamie and Jenny both decided to go downtown with him on the subway train. They were waiting at the edge of the platform and laughing and talking...."

Now the words came thickly again, and Pen pulled Banny closer to her own warm vitality. Banny spoke on, however, as if she couldn't stop anymore.

"Jamie'd been having some trouble with a cold in his ears, and it must have affected his sense of balance. They were all laughing at some foolishness of Harry's that made Jenny blush, and when Jamie turned away from her to say goodbye to Harry he lost his balance. Harry caught at his arm but missed and he fell—and then the train was there, before anyone else could move."

A ragged breath, then Banny added, "They managed to lift him clear afterward, but there wasn't anything else they could do. He died in Jenny's arms, and the last thing he said to Harry was, 'Take care of Jenny for me.' ''

Like a scene from some sad old movie, that far-away accident appeared in Pen's mind, and she winced away from it, tightening her hold on Banny. The old woman finished briefly, ''The baby was born that night, and Harry did as Jamie'd asked. A year later he married Jenny and took her child as his own, and he's loved and cared for them all these years.''

With her free hand Pen reached up to brush away tears; Banny saw the gesture and straightened, patting Pen's damp fingers. ''There, lass. You're a nice sympathetic child, Penelope, but I didn't mean to grieve you, too. Most of the time Edward and I don't think of anything but the happy times we had while Jamie was growing up, and I suppose what set me going today was just seeing yon bairns and remembering that Jamie's boy is growing up, too, and we've never yet seen him.''

Pen steadied her voice to ask in a practical tone, ''But couldn't he come here for a visit? Or could you go to the States?''

''Jenny's tried twice to send him over for a summer, but the first time he got sick just before the trip, and the second year he had to stay home to take some sort of classes. He's thinking now of coming here to university, but we're just impatient to see him sooner. It's an awful expense, though, to think of going over there ourselves.''

She smiled determinedly, becoming again the cheery person Pen was accustomed to, and concluded lightly, "So we'll just possess our souls in patience for a bit yet—or win the Irish Sweepstakes!"

Pen answered the smile and promised, "I'll start buying tickets for you, too!"

Banny's usual twinkle came back. "That's a kindly thought, lass, though it would have shocked a proper straitlaced Scot like your Uncle Andrew to the depths of his Calvinist soul!" Pen grinned, with an unrepentant little shrug, and Banny rose, saying, "Now be off with you, Penelope; you've given enough of your time today to a silly old woman. I'll take this letter in to Edward, and you go back to work on those drawings of yours—I've not forgotten you said this was to be a working holiday."

She shooed Pen away smilingly, and with a laugh and a wave Pen accepted her dismissal. Half an hour later she was obediently seated in front of her easel, roughing out preliminary sketches for a sad octopus with only four arms. Banny's story of her son lingered poignantly in her mind, though, and Pen knew she wouldn't forget it. As Banny had said, it was an old sorrow and one that she and Edward had generally come to terms with, but Pen still felt their loss and knew now how they had understood Uncle Andrew's grief so well. Halfconsciously she realized that her own life had been blessedly unscathed so far and felt both grateful and faintly worried by it, but that was a formless fear and it slipped away as she sank into the familiar routine of her work.

She worked all that afternoon and then treated herself to a long walk over the fells after tea, stretching her cramped muscles and easing the restlessness that seemed to be stirring her as spring came on more boldly. She made a point, however, of not letting her ramble take her past the last cottage at the end of the lane. Whatever was occupying Alistair Heath was none of her business—as he'd probably be the first to tell her!

Home again in the second cottage, she worked on Megan's blanket, knowing how eager the little girl was for it to be finished. Pen herself was content to relax into the rhythm of the loom. When the light from her wide windows failed and the long spring twilight faded from blue to black, she pulled the windows to and called Marigold in from stalking shadows. Then girl and kitten settled in the chairs by the hearth, and Pen busied herself with her plan to read her way through every book on Uncle Andrew's shelf.

As she lived in his cottage and read his books, she was getting to know Andrew McKenzie better and better. The peppermint-scented giant of her childhood was becoming a real person to her now, and she guessed regretfully that she would have liked her great-uncle as much as an adult as when she had been a child.

Although he'd lived most of his life here in this quiet valley—and perhaps been as straitlaced as

Banny claimed—his interests had been far-ranging, and Pen found on his shelf books on a variety of topics. The ones that dealt with the Lake District, though, showed the most use, and as her own love of the region grew, Pen herself turned to them most often.

This particular time, however, the book she reached down from the shelf was not an old friend but one she hadn't looked at before. On its worn green spine she spelled out in faint gold letters the title *Roman Britain*, and then the old volume fell open in her hands to a chapter headed, in flowery nineteenth-century script, "The Eagle in the North." Below that on the page lay a map, and by the time Pen had located Grasmere on it, she was hooked.

A fascination with history had almost taken her to university instead of art school, and as she settled deeper into Uncle Andrew's chair she began to explore a period she had never paid much attention to. Like most people, she knew little more about the Romans in Britain than the fact that they had left famous ruins at Bath and Hadrian's Wall. No wonder that irritating Alistair Heath was writing a new book to popularize the subject, her mind observed waywardly, but she insisted to herself that her interest now was due only to Uncle Andrew, and Alistair and his archaeology had nothing whatsoever to do with it.

Whether or not that was true, Pen soon was completely absorbed in this old book, discovering to her surprise that in the Lake Counties alone were the ruins of nearly twenty Roman forts. She read that those forts had been built in the early years of the Christian era, when Rome held Britain for some four centuries with varying degrees of security. Best of all, she learned about the men who had occupied the forts, and the purple Victorian prose of the book in her hands brought those long-dead auxiliary troops to stand before her, setting the seal now on her interest in the period because the part of history she'd always liked best was the personalities of the people who'd made it.

Some of those personalities came alive for her as the hours slipped by unnoticed, and she read on about men who had come to this remote place, trying to live in a wild northern country they had never been able to subdue entirely. A newcomer to Lakeland herself, she guessed how alien and vulnerable they must have felt, these soldiers of the empire. So far the fells surrounding her cottage seemed to offer her only protection and permanence, but she was already wise enough about the region's variable weather to guess how ominous those fells could be, especially to a raw young recruit who might have come all the way from the mild Mediterranean.

It was well past midnight when Marigold finally came and sat on top of Pen's page to indicate that she thought enough of this was enough. Recalled to the present at last, Pen chuckled, then set aside the book to stretch and yawn. In a few minutes she had tumbled into bed, but before she drifted off she vowed to visit the nearest ruined fort, the one at Ambleside, in the morning.

Morning, however, came all too soon. Without regard to the late hours of the night before, Marigold woke Pen promptly at dawn—to find a gray misty morning.

"Little cat, how could you?" Pen groaned after a jaundiced peek out the window. "Just this once, couldn't I sleep past the hour you think suitable?"

Having done her job, the kitten simply jumped down and padded away, leaving Pen to burrow into her bedclothes. It didn't work, though; sleep eluded her, and after thrashing fruitlessly for half an hour, she gave up and crawled from her bed.

That inauspicious beginning set the pattern for the day. When Pen reached the fort at midmorning, she found it lying in a low grassy meadow, swathed in mist and poorly marked. For an hour or so she paced around the site, trying patiently to make it come to life the way the pages of that old book had the night before. She wasn't able to orient herself inside the basic rectangular plan that all standard forts shared, however, and not being able to visualize what had happened where defeated her. Disheartened finally, she gave up and clambered back into her old Cortina.

That wasn't the end of the day's frustrations. In Ambleside itself she stopped to fill up with gasoline, and while she waited a voice from the next car hailed her.

"It's Pen, isn't it? Corey's and Megan's friend?"

Turning at the sound of her name, Pen found a gray-haired woman with a long thin face smiling at her from the next car.

"Why, yes," she answered politely, wondering why the face turned to her seemed familiar.

Reading her evident confusion, the woman explained, "I'm Nora Button. We met when I brought the little ones to stay with you while my sister was in the hospital and her family needed me."

"Oh, yes," Pen replied, remembering now the anxious face at her door. "Is your sister better?"

Nora Button's face clouded, so that she looked still more like the worried woman who had dumped the children so unceremoniously with Pen. "She's back from the hospital now, poor thing, but she still has these terrible headaches nearly every day. That's why I told Mr. Heath I wouldn't be able to tend Corey and Megan anymore at all. Bessie still needs me too much."

"Yes, of course," Pen murmured agreeably, wondering why the children hadn't mentioned Nora's departure to her. Apparently even Megan hadn't been distressed by it this time. Perhaps they'd got used to doing without Nora, so that her official resignation hadn't made much difference to them. Whether or not it would make a difference to their uncle was another question. Pen remembered with a private grin that Banny had decided he was surprisingly good with children; this ought to put it to the test!

Nora was speaking again. "Anyway, I didn't think it mattered all that much anymore, now that you're here."

"I beg your pardon?" Pen asked blankly. Had she missed something?

"Well—" Nora smiled archly "—everything just seems right now, what with your being a bachelor girl and the children so fond of you and all. And there's Mr. Heath, single and handsome, and so good with children."

There it was again! Alistair Heath was good with children—and "single and handsome," and a "fine lad"! Nora Button was as infatuated with the man as Banny was. Well, *she* wasn't! The man was an arrogant, cold, supercilious—*fish*! And she certainly wasn't going to sit there any longer listening to Nora Button matchmake with all the delicacy of a cricket bat.

Mumbling something that was incomprehensible even to her, but which Nora apparently took for agreement, Pen thrust money for her gasoline into the attendant's hands, ground her gears and shot away. All the way back to Grasmere she fumed, muttering to the patient Cortina about sweet little old ladies who hadn't any better sense than to be taken in by surface charm that could be switched on and off like a light bulb, and about Alistair Heath's perfidy in deceiving them so. At home she pulled the little car up with a jerk, charged inside to fetch her rucksack and then marched up into the fells at a furious pace to work off her temper—a process that took until teatime, even longer than the last time he'd irritated her into storming out for a walk. All in all, it was not a successful day.

In London Nigel's day had been nearly as bad. Although he'd meant to be at the theater early to work out a change in the first set for act two, he had overslept. When he finally woke and dressed hastily, coming to the kitchen for the toast and coffee Elise silently supplied each morning, he found breakfast but no sign of her. The sofa had been made up for the day and she was gone, although her cases still stood neatly in the corner.

For a moment he was unaccountably disquieted. Then he remembered she had had an early rehearsal call; apparently she had simply gone without him, which was the sensible thing to do, of course. Drinking his rather stewed coffee with distaste, he decided that it would be pleasant for a change to drive over to the theater alone. As it happened, however, his oversleeping meant that he found himself caught in the traffic congestion he had hoped to avoid, and when he finally arrived at the theater he was abominably late.

That didn't sweeten his mood, and it went from bad to worse throughout the day as he barked at everyone, tore up three different set designs for act two and decided the play was going to be a disaster anyway. Ironically, Elise was the only decent actress in the thing; even his dislike for her didn't blind him to that fact.

He stayed late at the theater, working on replacements for the shredded designs, and then stopped for a sandwich on his way home, so that when he reached the apartment it was past eleven. Elise, with another early call for the morning, had already gone to bed, and he crossed the lounge quietly, shutting the door to his bedroom before he switched on the light.

It was after midnight, and he was sitting reading in a robe and slippers, when he heard the sound. Setting aside his magazine, he listened for a minute, finally realizing it was the sound of weeping and it came from the other room. With a little snort of disgust he picked up the magazine again and tried to read.

That didn't work, though, and he threw it down in exasperation. So Elise was crying—it was probably just another ploy. In the first week she'd been there she had tried a number of them to break down the hostility between them, but none of her charming little tricks had worked because he had no intention of forgetting again what a consummate actress she was. Her feigned sleep, her widened eyes and plaintive voice had all been put on the night of his party, and tonight he knew even those racking muffled sobs obviously weren't outside the range of her talents. *Well, let her cry,* he thought cynically.

She did. The sound went on and on, and finally he couldn't ignore it any longer. If she kept this up, she'd probably make herself sick, and then he'd have that to deal with as well as the irritation of her very presence. Angrily he strode into the other room and switched on the light at the end of the sofa, revealing her.

She lay crumpled up on her side, with a fine coral negligee knotted around her, pulled away from long shapely legs. Her hands were both squeezed into fists, and her hair was tangled across a damp pillow she had burrowed into. There was a look of pathos about her he'd never seen before, but he ignored it and spoke her name sharply.

"Elise!"

She reacted to his voice, turning her head on the pillow, but her eyes didn't open and the sobs went on. Through them he began to hear disjointed words and phrases.

"I didn't mean it. . . I never meant it to end like that! It's better. . .they're better off without me. . . ." Then the words were lost in a fresh storm of weeping.

As if of its own accord, Nigel's hand went out and brushed away the hot heavy hair from her forehead, and she moved into his touch while the sobs abated.

"I'm sorry, I'm sorry," she breathed, and with a sudden motion reached up and caught his fingers in a tight anxious clasp. He tried to pull them away—it *was* all a trick—but she clung, and her next words made him change his mind.

"I had to leave—I would have died, too!" she

said, and flung herself away from him to twist restlessly while her words disintegrated into frantic sobs again.

Instinctively he sat down and gathered her into his arms, holding her tightly and murmuring soothing little sounds as if she were a desperate child, and finally the sobs that had racked her body against his faded. Afraid she might start again, though, he went on holding her close against him, and at last she was completely quiet. Still he stayed as he was, and some time later—a few minutes, an hour—she turned her head and looked at him with eyes that were fully awake and aware.

"Good evening," she said calmly. "Have I missed something?"

He flushed suddenly to the roots of his hair and went to stand up, but she was still lying half across his lap and half on the sofa, and she didn't move.

"You were having a nightmare," he muttered, all of his usual mocking sangfroid deserting him. "I heard you crying and came in."

She looked away from him now, and the mask she'd just put on slipped again. Underneath it, as she recognized the nightmare, he saw her misery; whatever she had been dreaming, it was an old dream and one that made her wretched.

They were both silent for a minute or two, and then she faced him again. "Thank you," she said softly, leaving the mask down deliberately for the first time, and leaned forward against his chest to kiss him gratefully.

Her lips were warm and steady; a lock of her hair fell down along her cheek and he put up his hand to smooth it away. Then, again as if of its own accord, his hand curved around behind to cup her head to his, and his other hand clasped her shoulder under the filmy negligee. Beneath his, her lips parted on a little murmur, and he shifted to lean back along the sofa, drawing her in on top of him so that her legs intertwined with his. The rumpled negligee slipped sideways, and he moved his mouth to the creamy breast it released. A small tremor shook her whole body, then she relaxed, and he reached up to switch off the lamp.

CHAPTER NINE

DESPITE THE FACT that her first attempt had been a disaster, Pen still wanted to visit a Roman fort. Although her large-scale map of the area had somehow vanished, the less-detailed map she had brought with her from London seemed to show that another fort, one called Hardknott, lay only about fifteen miles west of Ambleside. Probably she could make the trip and return in a few hours, and Uncle Andrew's book said that this fort was better preserved than the other. Pen decided to try again.

Three days later Marigold's alarm-clock tongue woke her to the loveliest morning she had seen in the Lake District. The early sun lighted her bedroom with a new radiance, and Pen, who had been preparing a sleepy protest against the kitten's tactics, opened delighted eyes all the way instead of letting them droop into a last little nap. Then while Marigold sat on the end of her bed, looking as pleased as if she'd created the day especially for her mistress, Pen rushed to the open window to rejoice in the fresh-washed air and gulp in its soft scent.

Across the stone wall between her garden and Alistair Heath's, she could see the children throwing sticks that the huge Levvy would gallop loose-limbed to retrieve, and she leaned from her window to call to them.

"Megan, Corey! Isn't it a beautiful morning?"

Following the sound of her voice, they looked up and waved and then scrambled over the wall to answer in chorus.

"Hello, Pen," Corey said.

Simultaneously Megan asked, "Are you just getting up? We've been up for hours," she added virtuously.

"Blame Marigold whenever I'm up at an odd hour," Pen laughed down to them, "since it's her responsibility to wake me every morning when she wants her breakfast. This morning must have been so beautiful that she couldn't think of food."

Corey looked skeptical at that—nothing would make him lose interest in food—but Pen didn't notice because she was moved by a sudden impulse. She spoke without considering. "I'm going out for a drive this morning; would you two like to come along? It looks like a grand day to see a bit of the countryside...."

She trailed off, suddenly wondering if it had been a mistake to suggest a trip this long to Megan. Her world—and Corey's with it, of course—now included all three cottages at the end of the lane and even a bit of the village, as well; she'd gone with Pen again to post letters and seemed comfortable enough with it. Here in this small area, then, she was secure and happy at last, but could she go farther still and be confident that nothing would change before she came back?

From her high perch at the window, Pen watched intently as Corey, too, looked as usual to Megan for an answer. For a long minute the little girl hesitated, and the old fearful expression reappeared briefly, but then the sunlit garden around her and the presence of her brother and Pen seemed to banish it. In a clear little voice Megan said, "We'd like to go, please, Pen, if Uncle Lister doesn't mind," and Corey broke into a triumphant dance.

"I'll go ask Uncle Lister if it's all right," he shouted, and dashed toward the wall, stopping with comic suddenness when he thought to ask, "Where shall I tell him we're going?"

"To Hardknott Fort," Pen called back, and Corey rapidly disappeared, followed more slowly by Megan and Levvy. Turning back from her window when they were all gone, Pen was conscious of a devout hope that Alistair Heath would be too pleased with Megan's decision to go out—or at least too sleepy—to take note of their destination. If he noticed it, the arrogant man would probably assume that her interest in Roman forts had something to do with him, when in fact that was totally untrue. Oh, well, it was still so early that she was probably safe; even if he was already awake, Alistair would probably just give his permission without paying much attention to their exact destination.

She was wrong. Pen was just coming downstairs, dressed for her outing in a pair of neat navy trousers and a scarlet sweater, her hair braided like Megan's for convenience and tied with scarlet yarn, when a brisk tap at the door announced that Alistair had reappeared at last and that this time he was not going to let himself in. With a quick twinge of something that felt unreasonably like guilt, Pen walked slowly to the door, questioning herself along the way. Why on earth should she feel guilty? After all, Alistair couldn't possibly be anything but pleased that Megan dared to go out, no matter what her destination was.

As soon as she opened the door, however, Pen knew that he could be, and was, considerably less than pleased. He stood in her doorway wearing a turtleneck sweater in a pale shade of cream that made his dark face look swarthier than ever, and his black brows were lowered over changeable eyes that had turned ice blue. His whole face was taut, too, but he said nothing immediately, and after a short uncomfortable silence Pen ventured a neutral, "Good morning."

That did it. Apparently he had needed nothing more to set off the explosion.

"It *was* a good morning," he rasped through set teeth, "until Corey came charging in and woke me out of a sound sleep to inform me that you had conceived the harebrained notion of visiting Hardknott and—worse yet—wanted to take him and Megan with you."

The hint of red in her absurd chestnut braids wasn't there for nothing, and Pen's temper flared to meet Alistair's.

"Obviously you are one of those unfortunate people who wake up in a disgusting mood, but is that any reason for you to take it out on everyone else?" she snapped. "Hardknott is a major Roman fort, as you of all people should know, and there's nothing whatsoever harebrained about wanting to see it. Besides, you should be happy that Megan wants to go somewhere. Instead you probably roared at her like a bear with a sore head before you came over here to tear strips off me."

"I do not roar at children—" he grated.

Pen cut in swiftly, "Oh, only at adults?"

Then she stepped hastily backward as he went on, glittering eyes fixed on the braids that made her look little older than Megan, "I spank them."

For an appalled moment Pen thought he might genuinely carry out his threat, but he seemed to conquer the impulse. He changed the direction of his attack, firing a series of questions at her at machine-gun speed.

"You did intend to drive the kids up to Hardknott yourself?" Pen nodded, and he added parenthetically, "That is, of course, assuming that you *are* a licensed driver?"

She looked at him disdainfully, not dignifying his question with an answer, and he went on sarcastically, "All right, so by some miracle—or perhaps a bureaucratic mix-up—you have a license, and occasionally you use it to take a brief drive and liven things up for unwary pedestrians?"

Outraged, Pen spluttered furiously, "I'm at least as good a driver as you are a walker! I've driven thousands of miles, on expressways and in city traffic where people know better than to jump out in front of moving cars! And I drove all the way up here from London."

"Yes, and since then you've probably taken a few pleasant jaunts to Lakeland's more accessible tourist attractions, but have you ever driven up into the fells?"

"No, but—"

"There is no 'but' about the difference," he interrupted her decisively, and went right on with his next question. "And that venerable Cortina is the car you intended to drive today?"

Pen confined herself at first to an angry nod, but then realized it made the silly braids bob ridiculously and muttered gracelessly, "I've got no other."

"And you won't have that one after a trip to Hardknott! Good Lord, girl, didn't you look at a map?"

"Of course I did," she said furiously, omitting mention that her local map was lost and she'd been going by the less-detailed one from the automobile association in London.

"Then how could you possibly be ignorant of the fact that the road to Hardknott lies over two of the most challenging passes in Lakeland? *When* they're even open, the most experienced drivers find them difficult going in powerful cars."

Remembering uneasily now that Uncle Andrew's book *had* mentioned that Hardknott was inaccessible part of the year, Pen began to have a niggling suspicion that Alistair just might be gallingly right. Certainly that would be exactly like the infuriating man, she thought irritably, glaring at him in frustrated silence. For a minute he simply returned the glare, and angry gray eyes locked with implacable blue ones, but then the blue ones suddenly crinkled at the corners. An instant later, to Pen's utter amazement, Alistair Heath was laughing—just as unexpectedly as that time at the grocer's shop—and his face had again lost its usual harsh look.

"I cry your pardon, Penelope," he chuckled penitently. "I said I don't roar at children, and here I've been shouting at you when you look just the same age as Megan."

Wildly Pen flung up her hands and, snatching off the red yarn, began to undo her braids. She was just starting on the second one when her sense of humor finally reasserted itself and she had a fleeting thought of what she must look like. For a moment more she trembled between anger and amusement, then the latter won. A reluctant giggle escaped her, and she dropped her hands, letting the chestnut hair hang half-braided while she laughed aloud, unaware what an enchanting sight she was now, embodying both child and woman.

Alistair saw what Pen was blind to, however, and surprised himself by saying suddenly, "Let me drive you and the children to Hardknott. That way Megan can have her outing and none of you will be risking life and limb."

He was still slandering her driving ability, but now his tone had switched from that of adversary to that of coconspirator. Pen was baffled by his unexpected amiability, but she nodded agreement. After all, she thought wryly, Megan *would* still be going out, although now with her beloved Uncle Lister rather than away from him, and she herself would still have her opportunity to look at the fort, which had been the starting point of this whole uproar. Certainly the aged Cortina wouldn't mind being spared this trip, if it really was as strenuous as Alistair maintained. Perhaps a truce had its advantages. And who knew—they might even manage for once to spend time together without the usual disaster! At the possibility, she felt an odd little leap of excitement.

Nevertheless, when he said, "I'll go chase those two into sensible clothing for this jaunt; meantime, would you mind throwing together some sort of lunch for us to take along?" she started to protest. "Lunch? But we'll be back—"

One of his eyebrows rose again, like the black

flag on a pirate ship, and she said nothing further. Then he was striding away down her walk, and she turned inside to sift through her kitchen to see what she could assemble for a picnic.

Half an hour later, when Corey scrambled over the wall again and shouted from her garden, "Pen, we're all ready—come on!" she had packed a spacious hamper of Aunt Hannah's with assorted sandwiches and fruit and the latest installment of Banny-cakes, a couple of bottles of juice for the children and a thermos of tea for Alistair and herself. She had also tucked in her sketchbook, added an old blue duffel coat to her ensemble for the day and after consultation with her mirror rebraided her hair, this time looping the childish braids up behind each small ear in a way that gave her an odd gamine sophistication.

In response to her call out the kitchen window, Corey came willingly in, and together they carried the picnic basket out into the lane, just as Alistair and Megan glided up in his beautiful Rover. In a few minutes their lunch was stowed in the trunk, the youngsters ensconced in the rear seat, and Pen was relaxing luxuriously in the front passenger seat, discovering plenty of room for her long legs. Settled, she made a few desultory remarks and then fell silent, suddenly content to enjoy the car and the day and let Alistair concentrate on his driving.

At first it didn't require undue concentration. He followed the main road down to Ambleside and there swung west onto more good road. It wasn't until they had turned off toward the villages of Colwith and Little Langdale that they found themselves on very minor roads, and Pen's respect for Alistair's driving began to develop. A ninety-degree turn left around the corner of a barn brought them nearly within touching distance of both the barn on their left and a high stone wall on their right, and then once out of the second village they began climbing—past a sign that laconically informed them, This Road Unfit for Trailers.

Pen read the sign silently, very much aware that she had never seen one like it before, but while she admitted to herself that trailers couldn't possibly navigate this road, she still thought that her Cortina probably could have. The first of the rocky passes Alistair had warned her about was Wrynose Pass, and the silver car climbed it with the neat grace of a mountain goat, winding its way upward along the zigzags that made the going somewhat easier. It was still a challenging climb, however, and Pen kept quiet while Alistair negotiated it. She maintained her private belief that she could have driven her car over this pass, but perhaps it was just as well she wasn't trying.

Anyway, the fact that Alistair was the driver left her free to study his profile surreptitiously, with her head angled as though she were keeping track of the children. And it *was* a profile worth studying, she admitted to herself. Temperamental and unpredictable as he might be, Alistair still had features any artist would admire. Under the curving lines of his hair, the smooth straight line of his forehead led down to a classical nose. His upper lip was strong and his mouth finely molded. His firm chin added balance above the column of his throat—and brilliant blue eyes glancing her way caught her off guard, surprising her analytical gaze. Flustered, she hastily went back to observing the road.

If Pen could have driven the first pass, the second was an entirely different matter. On the west side of Wrynose Pass the road dropped down again and for a time followed the headwaters of the River Duddon along a rocky bottom. At a last remote farmhouse, however, the narrow track that was their road went through a gate and crossed the river on a humpbacked little bridge that delighted Corey and Megan, and then it began climbing again.

Soon the Rover was edging its way up a one-in-three grade, between boulders and around hairpin turns, where for a while, each time they changed direction, they headed directly uphill so steeply that Pen wondered nervously if the car might topple over backward down the mountainside. She thought that driving her own car she might well have done just that, but Alistair held his to the road with steady hands. Pen's own fingers were unconsciously gripping the edge of her seat until they were white, and behind her the children, too, fell silent with their eyes wide and their small hands linked.

The climb over Hardknott Pass probably didn't take too long, but to Pen it seemed hours. When they finally reached the top of the pass without mishap and Alistair pulled off the road onto a lay-by so that they could look around them, she discovered her stiffened fingers and with some effort released her grip on the seat, letting out her breath with an explosive little sound.

At that, Alistair turned in her direction. He said nothing, however, only meeting her eyes with a quietly speculative look, and Pen murmured repentantly, "I'm sorry, Alistair; I hadn't any idea it was so, er, spectacular."

The rare smile lighted his face, and he replied dryly, "That, my good Penelope, is undoubtedly why the Romans chose to put a fort up here. Now take the kids and go have a look around if you like," he suggested, "while I let this one have a bit of a rest." He tapped the steering wheel with an affectionate finger, and Pen, delighted with the idea, flashed him a hasty smile and sprang out of the car, the children piling out behind her.

They were unusually quiet as they gazed around them, and Pen, too, had little to say. It seemed as if they were at the top of the world, up here among these empty fells. All about them were long reaches of bare brown rock, climbing, tumbling, cascading—all unmarked by spring's softening touch. In the vale of Grasmere it might be May, but here March still seemed to reign. Winter had barely receded, and instead of spring's gentle

grace there was a hard and heady glory. The air
was sharp and they drank it in, taking in with it a
spacious and timeless sense of freedom.

For a long while they reveled in the lonely beauty of the place, and both children glowed with excitement. Then by silent agreement they walked
together back to the lay-by where Alistair waited
for them, his long frame leaning against the
Rover's fender. He noted their elated faces with
an understanding glance and simply motioned
them back into the car for the short drive down
from the summit of the pass to the spur where the
fort stood. A few minutes later he had parked the
car again—much to the annoyance of the sheep
grazing nearby, who clearly considered the sleek
car an intruder.

Their unnaturally quiet mood passing quickly
now, the children clambered from the car and ran
shouting to the fort.

"Look, I'm a Roman soldier!" Megan called,
strutting stiffly.

Corey scrambled onto a ruined wall and announced, "I claim this spot for the empire!"

Meantime Pen followed more decorously with
Alistair up the slight slope from the car to the
fort's three-acre site.

It had been called "an enchanted fortress in the
air," and here in its high solitude she found it just
that. Rejoicing in the windswept grandeur of its
setting, she prowled through it, recognizing its
main features from her reading, although she

hadn't been able to do that at the Ambleside fort.
With Alistair strolling quietly behind her now, she
passed the bathhouse first, with its heated rooms
offering three different temperatures, and marveled at the comfort it would have offered to
weary and work-strained soldiers. Then she came
to the walls of the fort itself.

Inside the hollow rectangle they formed lay the
foundations of the commandant's unfinished
house, the headquarters building and the vital
granary for the fort's food supply in this nearly
empty land. The site of the long narrow barracks
buildings, however, which would have housed the
common soldiers and their officers, lay overgrown
with thick silky grass. Now only the sheep stepped
where the soldiers once strode, and Pen herself
walked lightly as she passed through the ruins of
the east gate to their long-abandoned parade
ground, carved from the mountainside itself.

Even there she found little that could still speak
to her of the men, the human personalities that so
fascinated her, and she turned back to the fort. If
today really was a sort of truce for Megan's sake,
then perhaps she could ask Alistair about the
soldiers; somehow their usual guarded behavior
with each other seemed silly in this clear air.
Anyway, she felt too uplifted by all this to worry
about how he'd react to such a request from her.

He had seated himself on a block of stone at the
gate, and when she reached him again she sank
cross-legged in the grass at his feet and pleaded,

"Tell me about it, Alistair, please, so it comes to life. I've read about it in one of Uncle Andrew's books, but I'd like to see it alive again in front of me. Tell me what it would have been like if we'd come here in the early years, when the men were first building the fort."

Her request was almost a command, but her interest was compelling to Alistair, and there was a childlike confidence in her assumption that indeed he could and would bring it all to life for her. So with only the slightest quizzical lift of those expressive eyebrows, he obeyed.

His eyes looking absentmindedly over the fort and westward toward the sea at Ravenglass, he made Pen see the troops coming up the Roman road that had been built past Hardknott. She saw the laden ox wagons creaking toward the pass and heard the shouts of their drivers. She saw the soldiers of the Fourth Cohort of Dalmatia, come from their own mountainous Yugoslavia to this rugged countryside to build and man a small fort. The sun seemed to catch here and there on shields of leather and metal as their shoes paced up the steep slopes, and then she saw them cutting stones and shaping walls, leveling the parade ground and raising their altars to the gods.

Spellbound by the beautiful voice that had been the first thing she ever noticed about him, Pen sat motionless as Alistair spoke, catching the excitement of a time when everything had been new and challenging. The children, too, tired of their own imaginings, crept close beside her, drawn by the magic of that sound as he made the past live again. Finally, though, he fell silent, and the magic faded.

Hating to let it go, Pen breathed, "What ended it all?"

"The Brigantes," Alistair answered, but now his tone was matter-of-fact again and his eyes had come back from their faraway focus. "They were the tribesmen of this region that the fort was built to control. In 197 they managed to sack it anyway, and it was never reoccupied, although most of the other forts in Lakeland continued to exist for more than a century longer. This one was allowed to fall into ruins here on the heights, like an abandoned eagles' nest."

Megan suddenly shivered and crowded against his long legs, and Alistair scooped her up into his lap, saying with a deliberate change of mood, "And this omnivorous pair is probably as hungry as baby eagles, Penelope. What do you say about the picnic basket in the trunk?"

"I say we should probably empty it quickly, before it attracts ants," Pen agreed, smoothly following his lead.

Corey chimed in, "And caterpillars! Can I go get it, Pen?"

"You may indeed," she laughed. "Especially if you give me a hand up so I can go with you to help fight off the hungry caterpillars and carry things back."

Rather dusty little hands clasped hers, and Pen got to her feet—with Corey's help or in spite of it—and the two of them went off to fetch the lunch, leaving Megan still on Alistair's lap. When they returned, with picnic basket and without caterpillars, the shadows were gone again from Megan's small face. As Pen and Corey approached, the little girl danced down to them and lightened the basket by taking out the two juice bottles. Alistair, meanwhile, maintained his position on his rock and watched with amused eyes as the food-bearing procession neared him.

"Now that," he said sweetly, "is the way I like to see people walking toward me—properly burdened with offerings of food."

Pen made a mock gesture of throwing the basket at him, and he ducked aside, laughing, his face more boyish than she had ever seen it. It stayed that way throughout the whole merry meal, too, as they all emptied the basket and talked nonsense, looking for imaginary caterpillars and inventing supposedly "Roman" names for the soldiers who might have garrisoned the fort.

When everything had been eaten, Alistair lowered himself cautiously to the ground beside the picnic cloth Pen had spread and stretching out announced his intention of having a brief nap. For a time the children tormented him with tickly blades of grass, but somehow, in spite of their best efforts, he managed to escape into sleep, and only

a little later they, too, were asleep, heaped
trustingly against their uncle's long body.

Left to her own devices, Pen cleared away the
remains of their picnic as stealthily as possible,
then carried the basket quietly back to the car,
leaving out only her sketchbook. When she came
back up to the fort from the road, her first
sketches were of the valley below it on the opposite side, where the Esk River ran gently
through patchwork fields, their green tranquillity
in sharp contrast to the exciting brown heights
above them. But those breezy heights kept attrac-
ting Pen's artistic eye, and her next sketches were
of the stones, rough and finished, that speckled
their shoulders. And last of all she drew the
sleepers.

Sitting quietly nearby, she sketched Corey's
face, freckled nose to the sky, eyes tightly compressed against the sun and the lock of hair that
fell across them. Next she drew Megan, curled like
a kitten into Alistair's side, one small hand pillow-
ing her cheek and a dark braid flung across his
shoulder. Then finally she drew Alistair himself.

Full length in the wild grasses, he lay with his
hands folded under his head, elbows akimbo and
his face turned into the shadow. Pen simply
studied him for a time, safe now that he was asleep
and couldn't catch her at it, noting how the mobile
face—usually harsh or mocking when awake—
relaxed when asleep into an expression of curious
sweetness. Her eyes traced the clean angle of his

jaw, the smooth plane of high cheekbone and the firm line of his lips. A fan of ridiculously long lashes hid his usual piercing gaze—what a waste to give those lashes to a man, she thought briefly—and the ordinarily smooth black hair was ruffled. She quelled a peculiar impulse to stroke it back into place and picked up her pen again instead.

First she drew just his sleeping face, and then she sketched his body, adding the children, as well—and for a fleeting instant imagined to herself that they all belonged to her. Next, for some reason, she went on and drew Alistair again from memory, in profile as he had looked that morning intent on his driving; as he had looked when he'd just come back from the cold solitude of the wall to her warm and lively kitchen; as he had looked that first time he had come to her cottage, with that politely remote expression on his face and Megan's arms wrapped around his forehead.

Engrossed in her work, Pen sketched rapidly, lost to time and place as she captured Alistair's changing expressions in neat deft strokes. In fact, she wasn't recalled to her surroundings until a drop of water fell on her page, and she looked up blankly. Her beautiful morning had become an overcast afternoon, and now it was starting to rain. And just as she made that unpleasant discovery, Alistair's eyes opened and he sat up, dislodging Megan and Corey, who murmured sleepy protests.

He was obviously one of those people who can

wake up instantly when need be, and a quick glance around produced complete comprehension. It also produced one of Pen's less favorite of his facial expressions: annoyed incredulity. The truce was clearly over, and the disaster rule still held.

"Even if you hadn't the sense to get in out of the rain yourself, Miss Bryce," he said bitingly, "didn't it occur to you that the rest of us might like to be offered that option?"

He was waking the children as he spoke and didn't see the embarrassed flush on her cheeks. With an incoherent little apology she hastily closed her sketchbook and leaped to her feet, to pull Corey up beside her and then encourage Megan up, as well. Standing, the children came quickly awake, looking around with wide eyes at the low clouds rushing over the fells. Below them Eskdale had disappeared.

"A storm in the mountains—super!" Corey enthused.

But Megan said unequivocally, "Rain—ugh!" and Pen sent them scampering to the car.

Alistair meantime was getting to his feet rather stiffly. Wordlessly and without meeting his eyes, Pen held out her hand again; he took it and the contact sent a sudden tremor through her, but he freed himself the instant he'd hauled himself upright. And wordlessly still, she followed him to the car, slipping quickly into her seat while he levered himself more slowly into his, started the engine and switched on the windshield wipers as the rain began to fall in earnest.

CHAPTER TEN

IF THE DRIVE out over Hardknott Pass by sunlight had been long and difficult, the drive back in a slashing rainstorm was infinitely more so. The rain lulled the children back to sleep quite soon, but Pen, far more conscious than they of how treacherous the road was becoming and how white Alistair's knuckles were getting, huddled in her seat unhappily wide awake. She knew better than to talk to Alistair when he needed all his attention for the narrow precipitous road; and anyway, she didn't know what she could have said to excuse her carelessness.

She knew full well he assumed that, having stayed awake, she would be watching for one of Lakeland's sudden changes in weather. And the fact that technically she had been awake didn't excuse her for having become so involved in something else that she'd ignored the changing conditions around her. Now through her negligence she had condemned them all to an unnecessarily dangerous trip home, and had additionally condemned Alistair to a drive that would tax even his obvious skill to its very limits.

Even with the windshield wipers working at full speed, visibility was nearly zero, and Alistair could only inch the car forward through the drumming obscurity. Around them the steep fells were topless heaps of stone, and under them the rainwater ran down the roadway in bubbling sheets, making their passage all the more risky. But the Rover managed to hold the road, guided by a grip on its steering wheel that was both sensitive and unyielding, and slowly they crept on.

Thinking back on it later, Pen was never able to separate the different stages of that horrible trip home. Somehow they navigated Hardknott Pass, certain they were over it only when the tilt of the car changed; traversed Wrynose Bottom, where the water was rising in the river; and crossed Wrynose Pass. The turn at the edge of Little Langdale was so obscured by a curtain of rain that Alistair lowered his window and inched cautiously forward with his head out in the downpour to see the corner of the barn. Behind him Megan woke and squealed in the rear seat as some of the stinging drops caught her, too, and when Alistair finally raised the window again he looked as if he had been swimming, with his black hair plastered wetly to his forehead. He said nothing about it, however, merely raking the streaming locks out of his straining eyes with hasty fingers. In fact, he said absolutely nothing all the way home. Even after they reached good road again, he was still silent, his lips compressed into a thin white line.

When they finally reached Grasmere he turned up the lane and drove straight to his own cottage, switching off the engine at last with a gesture of such unutterable weariness that sharp little claws of regret sank into Pen. Little though she'd liked him at first, much though she might resent having him thrown at her by matchmaking ladies, today Alistair had shown her warmth and humor. He had been the kind of companion every girl dreams of, and she had repaid him with selfish unconcern. He didn't move from his seat immediately, so she opened her own door and stepped out, sending the children on a dash for the cottage. When she turned back to the Rover he was finally opening his door, and gathering her courage Pen walked resolutely around the hood to tell him how sorry she was to have let him in for that horrifying drive and how thankful she was to be home safely.

"Alistair. . ." she began, and then hesitated as her courage ebbed away without warning.

While she paused, he unfolded himself from his low seat and stood up very slowly, but before she could nerve herself again to begin her heartfelt apology, he seemed to lose his balance and lurched into the door of the car. With a muffled groan he caught at it to save himself from falling and then stood there unsteadily, swaying a little. For the first time Pen noticed that an ashen pallor had seeped under the usual golden brown of his face, giving his skin an unhealthy translucency.

"Alistair!" Like a cold flame, fear seared

through her, and now hesitation turned to urgency in her voice. "What is it?"

He made a dismissive little gesture with one stiff hand but didn't seem to have the energy to answer. Nor did he seem able to protest when she said anxiously, "Let me help you into the house."

On the words she slipped around the door, and setting her shoulder under his, she let him shift his weight from the car to her. There was an odd sweetness to the feel of his tired body resting against her, but only one tiny corner of her mind had time to notice that with a little flare of exultation. Then she nudged the door shut with her foot and reached her arm around to steady him. As she did so, under his jacket, rapidly soaking through in the rain, her fingers brushed past something flat and unyielding.

Startled, she let her hand fall, and her involuntary movement jolted him. Beads of sweat suddenly joined the raindrops on his pale face, and he said through set teeth, "Just a brace—it's all right—put your arm back, please, Penelope."

She did as he asked but echoed as they turned cautiously toward the cottage, "Brace?"

"Back," he said briefly. "Thought it was mending nicely, but seem to have been mistaken."

He said nothing else, concentrating instead on the seemingly endless path that lay ahead of him to the cottage, but Pen said a great deal to herself in a furious inner diatribe. If his back was injured, it was obviously the result of that fall he had taken

over Marigold—when she herself had paid more
attention to the kitten's hurts than to his—and she
had supplied both the initial damage and the
strenuous drive that had aggravated it. Entirely
forgetting how angry with him she had been that
night he'd fallen against the cooker, or even this
morning when he'd insisted on driving them to
Hardknott, Pen raged on silently about her own
carelessness, stupidity and general lack of consideration, blaming herself with a violence she had
never felt before.

She was still castigating herself when they
reached Alistair's door, which the children had
left ajar in their hasty passage, and with her free
hand Pen pushed it open. Inside, a quick glance
showed her that his cottage, probably built about
the same time as hers, was much like it in plan.
Then with a tight little nod of his head he said, "In
there, please," and she helped him through the
doorway on their right.

In Pen's cottage the corresponding room was
her seldom used parlor, but here Alistair had
made it into a much used study. Ready-made
bookshelves covered one entire wall, with books
crammed into every available inch of space. More
books bulged out of open cartons that blocked the
hearth, while still others perched on the two chairs
and on the corners of the wide desk under the window, where a typewriter reigned beside untidy
piles of blank and finished pages. Rejected pages
overflowed from the battered rubbish basket near-

by, and charts and maps spread themselves across the walls or draped themselves over the long broken-down sofa. This was clearly a working room, and Pen guessed hastily that the children seldom ventured inside. In fact, Nora Button had probably never been allowed inside to straighten up, either.

Pen herself was interested not in the room's condition but only in Alistair's. As her eyes finished their rapid survey of the study, they swung back to its owner, and she looked at him with a dubious expression. He read it with a faint trace of his usual asperity and said succinctly, "The floor, Penelope."

Forced to leave him propped exhaustedly in the doorway, she picked her way into the room and hurriedly pushed aside the clutter in front of the sofa to clear a space on the floor, then returned to his side to help him over to the patch of bare carpet. A little sound of relief escaped him as he lowered himself gingerly and then stretched full length, closing his eyes immediately.

For a full minute Pen hovered worriedly nearby, but he didn't move again or speak, so she murmured a little unsteadily, "I'll go see to the kids." A flicker of eyelids was the only response she got, and she left the room quietly, finding her way to the kitchen.

There she found the children having a reunion with the joyous Levvy and still wearing their damp clothes. Pulling herself together, she chased them upstairs for a hot bath, and after helping them into their warm woolen robes and rabbit slippers she made an omelet for their supper. She made one for Alistair, too, but found herself suddenly hesitant to take it in to him.

"Corey, love, run this in to your uncle, would you, and then come back for your own," she dodged the problem. A minute later the little boy came back, and the three of them had a quiet meal, Corey and Megan worn out by the day's adventures and Pen busy thinking about Alistair.

Supper finished, she hied the children upstairs again, promising to say their good-nights to their uncle and ignoring Corey's valiant protests that it was far too early for bed. Instead she judged by his drooping eyelids rather than his brave words and tucked both youngsters snugly into their small beds. While they settled down, she lingered, in no hurry to leave them. She joined in their chatter for a few minutes, and when they finally fell silent, she stopped on her way to the door for a moment at each bed. At Corey's she paused to stroke the silky forelock back with caressing fingers, and at Megan's she smoothed the bedclothes where they'd already been kicked into a tangled heap. At her touch Megan stirred slightly, and Pen dropped a butterfly kiss onto a cheek as soft and cool as flower petals. Then she slipped from the room, leaving the door open a few inches.

Outside it she hesitated at the top of the stairs. Marigold must be waiting hungrily at home, but

Pen was oddly loath to leave for the cottage next door. There was a quiet peace to the presence of the sleeping children in their dim bedroom, and down below Alistair had probably just finished the supper she'd prepared for him.

For a moment she savored that thought with an unconscious little smile of satisfaction; then the smile altered as her common sense pointed out that, once refreshed by her hot meal, he was very likely feeling better enough now to revert to his usual nasty self and give her the full-fledged dressing down that the need to get home through the rain had spared her earlier. He would probably tell her, in that cool and immaculately polite tone he used so effectively, exactly what he thought of her intelligence, character and judgment. That being the case, it must have been just sheer contrariety that now sent her downstairs to another round of combat with no further trace of reluctance in her step.

She did walk quietly into Alistair's study, though—and found him in precisely the same position she had left him in. He hadn't moved at all, and on the worn carpet beside him, just where Corey must have left it, the tray that she had fixed so carefully sat untouched. On it the omelet had cooled forlornly, while the salad had warmed limply, Pen noted ruefully.

She whispered his name, but Alistair made no response, not even the earlier flicker of lashes. Apparently he needed rest more than food, she con-

cluded, and in a few minutes Levvy was enjoying
the cold omelet and she had replaced the wasted
supper with a tin of biscuits and a thermos of fresh
tea, in case Alistair woke hungry later on. She
covered the sleeping man with a blanket she found
on the sofa. Then, after a moment's thought, she
slipped away to the Rover and brought back the
sketch she had made that afternoon of the fort's
massive stones. Across the corner of the drawing
she wrote quickly, "Another offering of food,
and with it my thanks and my apologies. P." She
leaned it against the biscuit tin.

There was nothing more to keep her now; she
had done what she could. Washed and fed, the
children lay sleeping safely upstairs, and if they
called, Alistair would surely wake to hear them.
Meanwhile he had both food and the rest that was
evidently far more important to him, and he
would find her note eventually. There was no further reason for her to stay, but still she delayed,
standing by the biscuit tin to study Alistair's sleeping face for the third time that day.

The boyish relaxation with which he had slept at
the fort was gone now, she noticed with remorse,
but at least the drawn look that had so frightened
her earlier was going, too. The sharp lines that had
been etched at the corners of his eyes and mouth
were blurring, and there was a hint of natural col-
or again along the planes of his high cheekbones.
His hair had dried, as well, and now it fell across
his forehead just the way Corey's did, and without

thinking Pen knelt down to brush it back gently, just as she had Corey's.

The gesture was the same, but its effect on her was far different this time. Even though he himself was deep in exhausted sleep, Alistair's thick dark hair seemed to spring against her fingers with all the vitality he normally had when awake, and still touching it she stopped as though a current of electricity held her there. Motionless, she saw herself lying down beside him on the worn rug and melding her body to his, so that she could gather him into her arms and cradle his head on her breast, stroking away with tender fingers all the pain and tiredness that still remained. And when she had done that, he would stir against her breast and his breath would be warm on her skin before his lips and hands touched her.

Mesmerized, she stayed where she was for a few more heartbeats, and then with a little choking gasp she leaped to her feet, looking down at Alistair now in panic as she realized she had just imagined herself behaving as if he were the man she loved. She *couldn't* love him! If she loved anybody, it was Nigel, waiting patiently back in London. But as for Alistair, she'd seen him only a handful of times, each of which had ended disastrously; she'd spent perhaps a grand total of nine hours in his company. And in that time he had made it perfectly plain on several occasions that he had no use whatsoever for her except where the children were concerned. Even today's brief truce

for the trip to Hardknott had been for their sake
alone, because he agreed they should go out a bit
more but didn't trust her driving. Otherwise that
coldly polite tone he used said clearly that he
wanted nothing else to do with her.

Had Alistair not been so lost in sleep, he might
have heard Pen's flying footsteps as she rushed
now from the house where she had lingered
earlier. As it was, however, he slept on and woke
in the morning as refreshed as if he had slept for
two. He might have, in fact; if sleep is allotted in
portions, he probably had Pen's share as well as
his own. Certainly she passed a wretched night,
prowling sleeplessly from room to room next
door, while Marigold followed her curiously, and
her thoughts were as unsettled as her feet.

The first traces of dawn found her exhausted
but resolute. There might be some holes in her
logic, but she was finally too tired to care; she had
explained things to her own satisfaction anyway.
Last night's fancy had been just that and nothing
more. She wasn't in love with Alistair Heath
because she simply couldn't be. She didn't even
know him well enough for that, and he clearly
preferred that she not get to know him well
enough. The only man she knew that well was
Nigel, waiting for her back in London in that lonely apartment of his. With him she had years of ex-
periences and friends and interests in common,
and she was very fond of him. *That* was a sound
basis for real love and would probably blossom

into it if she gave it a chance. What she felt for Alistair, on the other hand, was usually just annoyance, and last night's aberration had been simply mindless chemistry, operating only because they'd been thrown together.

Just to be on the safe side, though, she'd avoid that chemistry in the future; in fact, she'd avoid it right now by going away. She needed to collect from her publisher a new set of stories to illustrate, and if she went to London to do that in person rather than by mail, she could see Nigel, as well. Once she saw him again there'd be no more odd fancies about Alistair, and at a safe distance from her disturbing neighbor she could decide what to do about Uncle Andrew's cottage. She hated the idea of giving it up. Maybe she could come back for a bit more working holiday after she'd seen Nigel and proved to herself that he was the man she really cared about. He'd probably badger her again for a decision about sharing his apartment, but perhaps he'd let her have a little more time to think about it first. Or perhaps seeing him again would be so wonderful that she'd be able to agree then and there. At any rate, a visit to Nigel would remind her of their feelings for each other and armor her against any more impossible notions about Alistair. With that plan in mind, Pen began to pack.

Alistair and the children found her three hours later, when she'd had a hasty nap and was loading her portfolio and a small case of clothes into the

Cortina. She heard their voices laughing in the garden next door and unconsciously hurried what she was doing, but a minute later this they all came over the stone wall together and found her with the trunk still revealingly open. She had time to notice with a flash of relief that Alistair seemed to be moving relatively easily today. At least she wouldn't be going away with it on her conscience that her carelessness yesterday had somehow crippled him permanently.

But when he reached the car and stood towering over her, all traces of laughter had gone from his face and voice, and he growled, "What in hell do you think you're doing?"

As always, his temper was a goad to her own, and all dangerous fancies forgotten for the moment, she put her hands angrily on her hips and snarled back at him, "I don't *think*—I *know* what I'm doing. I'm going away, that's what."

"You can't go away—we need you here!"

The words could have been a plea, but since they were said at a roar, Pen simply snorted her disbelief in a most unladylike way and went on trying to cram the large flat rectangle of her portfolio into the trunk. It utterly refused to fit, however, and with a muttered remark she wrenched it free and stomped past Alistair to the side of the car, flinging the unwieldy thing onto the rear seat. There it came to rest on Nigel's absurd shepherd's crook, forgotten in the back of the car since her arrival, and now Pen finally tugged it free.

Swinging impatiently around with it, she came face to face with the children, whose steps had slowed when they caught sight of the partly loaded car and who only now came up to stand pressed close against Alistair. Corey was looking surprised and puzzled, and on Megan's face was that old look of anguish. It gave Pen a sudden sharp pang of remorse that cut through her irritation with Alistair. How could she have let herself concentrate on escaping him to the point where she forgot how Megan would be likely to feel about having her go?

Corey, the direct, broke the momentary silence. "Where are you going, Pen?" he asked, and still holding the ridiculous crook she crouched down to answer his words and Megan's expression, giving them the answer she hadn't given their uncle.

"I'm just off to London for a few days, Corey. I need to pick up some more stories to illustrate."

She shot a quick look from Corey to Megan, but the little girl's face still wore that tremulously fearful look, and to erase it Pen rushed recklessly on, making a change in her plans, "I'll be back soon, though, and in the meantime I'd be grateful if you two would help me out by keeping Marigold with you. Her food is in that bag by the wheel."

She ended on an inquiring note, and Corey nodded readily.

"Sure, we'd be glad to." He looked to Megan for confirmation, and she gave her head a bob of agreement, beginning to look a little less frozen as she stepped slightly away from her now silent uncle.

"Really, Pen? Really just a few days?" she asked hesitantly.

"Yes, poppet, just a few days—really." Pen threw caution to the winds and was rewarded when Megan rushed forward to give her a strangling hug. The crook that Pen was still absentmindedly holding got in the way, and with a determinedly light chuckle she added, "And take care of this foolish thing, too, would you, love?" She handed the shepherd's crook to Megan and suggested wickedly, "You can use it to herd Marigold and Levvy around the garden."

Instantly entranced with the prospect, Corey gave a whoop of delight. He grabbed up the bag of cat food with one hand and caught his sister's arm with the other, yanking her away as he shouted over one shoulder, "Bye, Pen! We'll go practice."

Megan let herself be dragged away, and the two of them thundered off. Marigold, who had been sunning herself on the walk, watched their noisy approach uneasily for a moment and then fled across the wall with the young twosome in gleeful pursuit. Pen, confident of the cat's ability to vanish when need be, rose laughing to her feet and found Alistair still standing by, his arms folded, watching her intently from under those dark eyebrows. He didn't say anything at first, and she flushed, her laughter gone, turning away from him to lean into the car and rearrange her portfolio unnecessarily on the seat.

From the far garden came the children's laughter, and then Alistair's voice said gravely behind her, "Thank you, Penelope, for understanding the way they need you."

He paused, and without turning she acknowledged and dismissed his thanks with a wave of her hand. Then, however, he went on speaking, and this time his words brought her around, after a breathless instant's pause, to face him again.

"But what about me? I need you, too."

She backed out of the car so fast that she cracked the back of her head on the door frame. "You do?" she asked, looking at him with sudden elation, while Nigel and the protection his love would offer vanished from her mind.

"Yes," Alistair answered, "indeed I do." That sounded promising, but he wasn't looking at her as he said it. Instead he was gazing down at something he now held in his hands, and dropping her own eyes Pen discovered it was her drawing of Hardknott, left beside the biscuit tin last night.

Suddenly he looked up from it and demanded, "Penelope, why in heaven's name didn't you tell me you could draw like this?"

His eyes had gone the deep blue they turned when he was excited about something, and fatuously she loved it. "Tell you I could..." she repeated absently, and then collected her battered wits. "Well, you never asked me."

He gave her a disgusted look, accompanied by an exasperated sigh. Neither the look nor the sigh seemed very promising, and she began to suspect that something was amiss here. What could her drawing possibly have to do with his declaration that he needed her? "Anyway, why should I have?" she inquired, rubbing the back of her head carefully while the rapid rhythm of her pulse began to slow.

"Because I've been looking all over the north for weeks, trying to find an artist of your caliber, while you sat right here under my nose wasting your talent on nursery rhymes, that's why."

Pen shut her eyes tightly, her fingers still at the nape of her neck, and Alistair interrupted himself to ask, "Penelope, did you really hurt yourself? Is your head all right?"

Yes, she thought wildly, in an unconscious confession to herself, *but not my heart! I should have guessed he just "needed" me for something practical. I've got to get away from this man.*

Letting her hand fall and taking refuge in anger, she opened her eyes and ignored his questions to snap, "They aren't nursery rhymes; they're mostly fairy tales, and I enjoy doing them."

"But you can't do them all the time!"

"And why not?" she demanded perversely, realizing that although he would have seen plenty of her childlike illustrations pinned up around her kitchen, he knew nothing of the thick sheaf of serious drawings she'd done since she came to the lakes. Those she had kept in her sketch-books.

"Why not?" he repeated her words, nearly bellowing, and she heard him with an ostentatious look of pain, putting her hand to her head again. Flushing slightly, he lowered his voice a little but went on forcefully still, "Because doing those sketches exclusively would be just about as sensible as eating only those bannocks you and the kids seem so fond of—they're fine occasionally, but hardly satisfying enough for a steady diet."

Pen glared at him, determined out of misery to argue, but diverted by his mention of Banny-cakes. Should she disagree with him about them or about her fairy-tale sketches?

Before she had made up her mind, he took advantage of her pause to alter his tactics. Somehow this whole discussion wasn't going the way he had meant it to, so instead of arguing with her—since that only seemed to encourage this impossible girl to argue right back anyway—he turned to simple persuasion.

"Penelope," he went on much more quietly, "all I'm trying to say is that you're a very fine artist, and I need one to illustrate my book. This drawing of Hardknott—" he gave it a look of surprise and appreciation that Pen couldn't miss and that mollified her a little in spite of herself "—is so good I can almost feel the texture of the stones and smell the air around them. I've finally found out that you have enough knowledge and more than enough talent to make technically perfect drawings, and besides that you seem to have an empathy that gives your work life and immediacy. Since those are just the qualities my book is supposed to convey, I want your help in doing it."

He flashed her a quick look, but she had lowered her own eyes and didn't meet it. He made a little shrugging gesture, switching to another strategy. "I can't promise you a fortune in commission on it, unfortunately, since I've got no guarantee we'll succeed in firing the public's imagination, but please say you'll do the illustrations anyway, Penelope. I really do need you."

There they were again—those wretchedly misleading words. Pen shook herself free of the spell his quiet persuasion had been spinning around her and without a word slipped away from him into the driver's seat of her car. With deliberate motions she buckled her seat belt and switched on the ignition, looking at Alistair only as the engine coughed into life. He still stood beside the car, one hand in the pocket of his trousers and the other holding her drawing, and his eyes—those beautiful eyes, she thought involuntarily—were fixed on her steadily.

When he could be heard again over the old car's splutters, he said, "Penelope?"

It was a question but not a plea, and Pen hesitated. The reasons against saying either yes or no were all too obvious, and she put the little car into gear while her mind worked frantically. Alistair stepped closer to her window to hear her answer, and reflexively she let in the clutch to escape him. "I'll think about it," she said breathlessly, and pulled away without looking back.

CHAPTER ELEVEN

SHE FLED DOWN THE LANE at considerably more than her usual speed, and as the familiar little green car shot past the window where he was drinking his morning tea, Edward Bannister murmured mildly, "Our Penelope seems to be in a great hurry. Is she running away from us?"

Coming to stand behind him with one gnarled hand on his shoulder, Banny, too, looked after Pen and said on a quiet chuckle, "If she is, it will be only for a little while, love. She'll be back."

Pen herself didn't dare contemplate that prospect, despite her words to Megan. She hastened out of the Lake District as if she were being pursued and only stopped when she reached the Midlands to phone home and let her family know she was coming.

"That's nice, dear," Nell's calm voice came down the line. After years of coping with her absentminded husband, little surprised her. "It will be lovely to see you."

In fact, though, she didn't see a great deal of her oldest child. Reaching home, Pen kissed her parents and accepted Evan's casual hello and a whirlwind hug from Margery, fending off Sally's eager questions.

"What's it like in the Lake District, Pen? Is it really as romantic as the books all say? Are there handsome shepherds and dark brooding hills, and have you fallen in love with anybody yet?"

"Now, Sally," Nell intervened gently, stemming the tide of interrogation.

Pen flung her mother a grateful look before saying, "Later, Sal—let me have a rest before you grill me. For right now just lend me a hand with my things, please, and after I've had a nap you can have a chance at me."

Sally opened her mouth to protest this delay in satisfying her rampant curiosity, but Nell caught her eye and she subsided regretfully. "Oh, all right," she pouted, and followed her older sister out to the car, where she scooped up the little case and left Pen to take in the much larger portfolio.

Pen was too exhausted to quibble about this distribution of labor, and a few minutes later she slid thankfully into a deep and dreamless sleep. She didn't wake until evening, either, because Nell stepped in firmly when she found Sally exhibiting a sudden and uncharacteristic desire to run the vacuum cleaner outside Pen's door. Once Pen finally awoke, however, she was fair game, and she spent her first evening home visiting with the family in general and Sally in particular, answering all but the last of Sally's earlier questions— and a great many more, as well.

Finally, though, even Sally ran down and sat in silent thought for a minute before she said, "Well, if it's really that gorgeous, Pen, I think you must be wasting your chances. That sounds like a super place for getting carried off by an impoverished lord or going back to nature with a rustic shepherd or *something*!" Or falling in love with an impossible archaeologist, Pen's thoughts offered, but she squelched them firmly and offered no defense other than to throw a cushion at her younger sister. It missed her completely, striking Evan instead, and after a startled yelp he returned it enthusiastically, ending all quiet conversation for the evening.

The following morning Pen sat alone in front of the telephone for half an hour, hesitating. She should ring up Nigel; after all, he was a major part of the reason she had fled back to London. With him she could slip back into old familiar patterns and forget the threat to her peace of mind that Alistair Heath represented. Once she saw Nigel again she'd be safe—so why was she just sitting there, weaving the telephone cord through her fingers? She took a deep breath and dialed Nigel to ask if he could have lunch with her.

For a moment the voice on the other end of the line sounded nonplussed, then the crisp tones Nigel had answered in warmed and he said, "It would be good to see you, Bo Peep. I'm tied up with theater business the entire day, but I'm giving a party at my new apartment tonight. Why don't you at least come there?''

"All right," Pen agreed, forgetting that she had once vowed never to attend another of his parties and relieved that he'd said nothing about her decision. The new apartment would presumably still be too large and lonely for one, of course, but between now and the party she could think about the whole problem and decide at last what to do. A few minutes later he had given her the address and hung up, and Pen was left to wait until evening to see him.

Part of the intervening time she did spend thinking seriously about the question of living with Nigel, but she still didn't reach a decision. On one hand, she knew perfectly well that lots of people shared apartments, and apparently without all her doubts and hesitations. Maybe she was just being hopelessly old-fashioned. After all, surely it *would* put Alistair out of her mind for good. But on the other hand, she kept finding a surprising number of reasons for not moving into that apartment. She wasn't completely sure she was ready to leave Grasmere for good yet—and if she did, she'd be breaking her promise to Megan and Corey. She'd be abandoning Marigold, too, and leaving Uncle Andrew's cottage untended. Besides, her parents wouldn't be happy about a living arrangement like that. She honestly wasn't very comfortable with the prospect of it, either. Around and around Pen went until finally she gave up in despair. Oh, well, maybe it would be easier to know what to say when she was actually with Nigel tonight. Exhausted, she put the whole problem determinedly out of her mind with a sigh.

An hour and a half later she was in the offices of Standish Publishing, in the huge airy room that was the heart of the art department.

"Pen, these are really excellent." Fred had got out her sketches for the Winter Prince and spread them on the long table in front of him, his kindly middle-aged face enthusiastic. "I've never seen you do a better job of catching the essence of a story. This one's a funny, touching sort of a thing, the way it reverses the usual fairy-tale roles, and you've caught it exactly. In fact, everything you've sent in since you left town has been particularly good, but these are the best of the lot."

Happily distracted from everything else, Pen dimpled in pleasure at the praise. "Thank you for the bouquet, kind sir!" she smiled, adding, "But I have to admit I had help."

Fred let his glasses slip down his nose and looked over them at her inquiringly. "I've had two young critics living next door," she explained, blocking any thought of the critics' uncle, "and they helped with the preliminary drawings, then approved the final ones."

"Ah, I see—a workshop," Fred grinned.

She added, "But, Fred, it isn't just the three of us. That's such a marvelous story, I couldn't help doing a good job. Who wrote it? I couldn't find a name anywhere on my copy.''

''It's a girl named Ann Osborne, Pen—just a little slip of a thing who looks as if a single good gust of wind would blow her away.'' His face grew concerned as he added, ''And as a matter of fact, I'm beginning to think one has. She was sending us things regularly—and all of them as good as the Winter Prince story—but we haven't heard from her in weeks now. I'm getting a bit worried about the child, frankly, because she doesn't look to me as though she has much to fall back on.''

He rubbed the bridge of his nose and pushed the wandering glasses back up. ''I tell myself I'll just go out to the address she gave us and see that she's all right, but somehow I never get it done,'' he said ruefully. ''Each day I mean to go there on my way home, and each day some new problem crops up and I don't do it.''

Pen nodded understandingly and then on an impulse asked, ''Fred, could I do it for you? I enjoyed her story so much I'd really like to meet her anyway, and if she's fine I could just let her think that was the only reason I came.'' She ended on a questioning note, and Fred looked at her thoughtfully, his light blue eyes intent.

''Yes,'' he said finally, ''you could indeed, Pen. I don't want her to think we're invading her privacy, and if you went it would be a bit more casual—but we'd still know then that she really was all right. It's an excellent idea, my dear, and thank you."

Relief made him look younger, and he put down her drawings to stride away energetically. "I'll just get you that address right now while we're thinking about it," he said over his shoulder.

The address proved to be that of a women's hostel on a quiet street with a tired air of poverty, and when Pen tapped at the door she was directed to a room at the back of the top floor. When she reached it, three flights of steps later, she was a bit breathless, but even so she wasn't breathing as noisily as the girl who opened the door of room 3G.

Pen saw instantly what Fred had meant about Ann Osborne's fragile air. In fact, this girl looked as if only a tiny puff of wind would be enough to blow her away to some far country from which there would be no returning.

"Yes?" she greeted Pen, and then coughed before asking, "May I help you?"

"Well, not exactly." Pen floundered a little, torn with sympathy for this thin girl whose face was all bones and blue shadows. Then she gathered enough presence of mind to say, "But I did want to meet you." She smiled reassuringly into Ann's puzzled eyes and explained, "I'm Pen Bryce, and I do illustrating for Standish Publishing."

"Oh," Ann said hoarsely, "then won't you come in?" She stepped aside and Pen walked past her into a room that was completely out of character with the gray, run-down air of the house. Once it had obviously been a garret, but now its walls were painted a brilliant white, and bright inexpensive fabric fluttered at the windows and covered a narrow metal bed frame. The floor was bare, and the only other furnishings were a plain chair, an old wardrobe and a table with a hot plate. Still, it was a pleasant room, and Pen liked it, just as she already liked the girl who hesitated in front of her now.

"Please sit," Ann was saying, with a little gesture toward the chair, and as Pen sat she asked, "May I make you a cup of tea?"

Pen debated an instant, wondering whether she should use up any of Ann's supply, but then she guessed Ann would be happier if she accepted.

"Yes, I'd love it, please," she said gratefully. While Ann set the kettle on the hot plate, Pen explained, "I didn't mean to disturb you, but I did the drawings for your story of the Winter Prince, and ever since then I've wanted to meet you. I was in at the office this morning, and Fred gave me your address so I could."

"Oh, Fred," Ann said smilingly. "He is kind, isn't he?" Pen nodded with an answering smile, but then Ann broke into a paroxysm of coughing.

When it was past, she apologized breathlessly, and Pen made a decision. "Yes, Fred's a dear, and he's worried about you." Startled, Ann peered at her over the handkerchief she held. "He hasn't heard from you in weeks, and he's afraid something dreadful has happened to you." Pen had decided to tell the truth that far, but now she hedged a bit. "When I told him this morning that I wanted to meet you, he asked if I'd check to make sure you were all right."

Far from being offended, as Fred had feared she would be, Ann seemed touched. "That was kind of you both, then," she said, and smiled with real warmth at Pen's anxious face. "But I *am* fine—or almost, anyway." She corrected herself as she caught Pen's skeptical look. "I had pneumonia for a bit last month, but that's over with now. I just have this cough left, and I suppose it will go away eventually. But I do appreciate your caring, both you and Fred. If you see him again before I do, would you thank him for me and tell him I mean to get back to work in a few more days?"

"Yes, of course, if you want me to," Pen nodded, but she wondered if Ann would be able to work anytime in the near future—and what she would live on in the meantime.

Ann herself didn't seem to want to talk anymore about it; instead she deliberately changed the direction of the conversation. "Now tell me, Pen, did you really like the Winter Prince?" she asked eagerly, and admitted, "I probably shouldn't have any favorites, but I'm afraid he's one!"

Perforce, Pen followed her lead, and for another twenty minutes they chatted over tea in heavy white mugs about that story and others they both remembered enjoying in childhood. Pen told Ann about Corey and Megan—although little else about Grasmere—and the other girl laughed at her description of the two small children and their giant dog. Even her laughter, though, didn't cover up her exhausted pallor. Pen said an affectionate goodbye, promising to watch for more of Ann's work that she could illustrate.

Back outside again after the airy Spartan comfort of Ann's room, Pen found the street unseasonably hot and grayer and noisier than ever. For a while she tried to distract herself with shopping, but nothing pleased her and London seemed more frantic than she remembered. Everywhere she went in the city, she felt as caged and breathless as she had before she fled that last party of Nigel's. Tall buildings made soot-stained caverns of the streets, and through them cars raced loudly past like shrieking and demented bats. Stepping absently off a curb, she was nearly run down by a red-faced and choleric cabby, who shook a furious fist at her and shouted something she was fortunate not to catch.

Shaken, Pen retreated to the slightly cooler depths of the subway, but it seemed completely airless. When her train finally came, a surprising number of people were already aboard, and they crowded around her so closely that she had no need to look for a strap to cling to—even if one had been available—because the press of bodies wouldn't have let her fall. By the time she reached home, she was limp and bedraggled.

After that, the house beyond the tollgate in Dulwich was a cool haven. But even at home the time remaining until Nigel's party passed slowly. After a long bath, Pen drifted restlessly, thinking about Ann, thinking about Nigel, and not thinking about Alistair—a process that Nell watched quietly but forbore commenting on.

Finally Pen arranged her hair on top of her head and slipped on a favorite emerald green chiffon dress, forgetting her old plan to appear as a Dresden shepherdess the next time she saw Nigel, and when she was ready she phoned for the luxury of a cab. The address she gave the driver proved to be that of a sleekly handsome and very expensive-looking block of modern apartments, and after she had swept elegantly past the doorman, Pen masked her nervousness by commenting to herself with a disrespectful but soundless little whistle. Clearly, Nigel's set designs were still very successful; this was a far cry from the old apartment he'd had since art-school days. She'd been rather fond of that one, actually. When she had tried to imagine herself moving in with him, that was what she'd seen—although not very clearly. Living here in this luxurious setting seemed even more unlikely.

The new apartment proved to be near the top of the building, and it offered a superb view of the river, but otherwise Pen didn't find much to recommend it. Nigel seemed to have disposed of all his old possessions and replaced them with new. The place was decorated with furniture that was modern and starkly handsome but seemed cold. The apartment itself was anything but cold, though. Pen had come quite early, hoping to see Nigel alone, but the place was already hot and smoky and full of people. They were all talking animatedly and they were all complete strangers to her; it was as if no one else from Nigel's past life had been invited.

She left her lacy stole in a large and much mirrored bedroom, where in the middle of a chatting throng of women some girl seemed to have constituted herself wardrobe mistress for their wraps. Then Pen braved the crowded lounge again, sounding its smoky depths. Someone put a glass in her hand and Pen thanked him abstractedly, slipping from group to group around the room with a casual remark here and there, but always looking for Nigel. Finally she found him—in the midst of the largest and noisiest group of all, gathered around an elderly but famous actress.

"...and on opening night the set fell," she was saying dramatically as Pen came up to the group. "But of course it wasn't one of yours, darling," she concluded, patting Nigel's arm, and he raised one of her heavily ringed hands to his lips in a dashing gesture that made her chuckle.

Then he caught sight of Pen and excused himself, bending to whisper something to the actress.

The old eyes, famous on London stages for half a century, flashed to Pen in her bright dress, and the actress lowered her voice to say something that made him look both amused and irritated as he left her side and came to Pen.

"That should take care of that for a little while," he muttered, and she was rather shocked by the harshness of his tone.

Taking her hand, he led her away to a corner at the far side of the room where it was a little quieter, and upon reaching it he turned her around slowly, looking at her intently.

"What is it?" Pen recovered from her surprise of a moment ago to ask, laughing a bit under his stare.

"No wisps of hay," he said finally, "no tufts of wool...." His dark eyes had the familiar satyr look now, and she warmed to it. "Well, Bo Peep, have you lost your sheep or eaten them?"

"Neither," Pen responded, "but I had a sudden urge to lay aside my shepherd's crook and visit the bright lights of the city." His slanting eyebrows rose, and she added honestly, "And you."

For an instant after that he just gazed at her, and his expression was unreadable, even though she thought she knew him so well. Then he reached past her to unlatch a nearby door. It swung open, and he switched on a small lamp as he led her into the room behind it, shutting the door again on the din of the party. This was obviously his workroom, and here at last Pen felt blessedly at home. His old drawing board was here, and several familiar overstuffed chairs, and leaning on almost every available surface were sketches of new sets.

She had little time to study them, though, because he said softly, "I've missed you, Bo Peep," and took her in his arms. Against her lips, so that his breath was warm on them, he said, "Come back and marry me quickly, Pen, and straighten out my life." And then he kissed her before she had time to react to his amazing words.

Although it had most of the elements of passion, the kiss was not a success. He kissed her deeply, hungrily, almost bruising her lips as he searched her mouth with a sort of desperation, while she raised one hand to a cheek that was leaner than she remembered. Then he tore his lips from hers and rained kisses on her eyelids, her cheeks, her forehead, before moving down the side of her neck. Pushing aside the soft chiffon straps of her dress with hasty fingers, he trailed more kisses along her collarbone, moving toward the scented warmth of her breasts.

It was an embrace to set her senses on fire, but it didn't. Clinging to him desperately, she tried to escape the memory of Alistair Heath; under Nigel's hands she tried to forget another man who had never touched her. But she failed. And Nigel had just proposed! Her whirling thoughts fixed on that incredible fact and steadied for a moment. Nigel wanted to marry her. She forgot all her old doubts about the strength of their love, and fixed on only one thought: she could be his wife, rather than just his live-in girl friend. She realized this with relief. And surely married to him she'd forget everyone—anyone—else. She'd love only Nigel, because they had so much in common—art, their years at school together—and she would even grow to like this new life-style of his.

Thinking frantically, she was like clay in Nigel's hands, and he touched her more urgently, but the noise of the party outside seemed to rise and intrude, as did the persistent image of a man other than the one who held her in his arms. And then the commotion rose well and truly, flooding in on them as someone flung their door open. A jovial voice boomed, "Nigel, my boy, there you are— been looking for you everywhere. Come and tell me if you think I should back this new play of Greene's."

Shielded by Nigel in the shadowy room as she struggled to retrieve her lost straps, Pen was invisible to the newcomer, but there was enough light for her to see a plump, florid little man in the doorway. She could see Nigel's face, too, as for a moment he simply held her in rigid arms, while his face changed to an angry mask she'd never seen before and he breathed a single vituperative syllable.

A moment later, however, his face was clear again, as if by some disturbing magic, and he turned from her, striding toward the door as he said smoothly, "Not only should you back his play, but you should also sign me up to do the sets for it." He shut the door quietly behind him, and Pen was alone.

Unhappily, she gave his workroom a last searching look and had a sudden fancy that this room contained all that was left of the Nigel she had known so well. With a strange certainty, she knew that the man who had just gone out that door was not her arrogant, devil-may-care friend but someone new and compromising, whose actions were cold-bloodedly controlled and calculated. And how was she going to marry a man like that?

It looked as if the Nigel she had come home to no longer existed, and a lump rose in Pen's throat, but she swallowed hard and let herself quickly out of the room. Back in the gleaming bedroom she searched the heap of wraps with hasty hands, trying to find her own, but it wasn't there. No one else was in the room now, and she stood alone in the center of it, dashing away the tears with her fingers so that she could see better. Her stole was still missing, and for want of any other idea she opened the door of a large mirrored closet. There was her stole indeed—and through her tears Pen could see that it hung in the midst of another woman's elegant wardrobe.

Nigel might have just proposed to her, but he had someone else living with him. Someone, perhaps a well-meaning third party, had apparently moved Pen's wrap to make sure she found out. In the whirl of emotions surging through her, Pen recognized anger, and surprise, and disillusionment. Then she snatched her stole from the closet, spun on her heel and left.

CHAPTER TWELVE

THAT NIGHT IN DULWICH was nearly as long as the sleepless one Pen had passed in Grasmere forty-eight hours earlier. Barricading herself in her room, she ripped off the green dress and flung it over a chair, then paced furiously around in her slip for hours. She walked quietly, controlling her movements so as not to disturb her family, but she couldn't control her feelings, and they swirled through her like a hurricane.

Part of the storm was directed at herself. After avoiding his proposition for weeks and weeks, she had run home to Nigel like a naive child, never dreaming everything might be different now for him. And part of it was directed at Nigel. How could he propose to her while he was living with another woman?

If things had changed that much between the two of them since she'd left London, she supposed she could eventually accept it. After all, she admitted recklessly to herself, her own feelings had altered enough that for a moment she had thought she was in love with an impossible archaeologist; so she could understand that Nigel's situation might have changed, as well. But she couldn't understand why he hadn't told her about it—especially if he still cared enough about her to propose tonight!

Hadn't they always been honest with each other? He could have written to her—more than that last enigmatic note—or at least told her on the telephone this morning. But instead he had left her entirely in the dark, and she might not have found out about the other woman if she or someone else hadn't chosen to let Pen know by the devious means of hanging Pen's wrap in that closet.

Over and over Pen relived that horrible moment at the closet door, and it did nothing to calm her feelings. On the contrary, it made her feel slightly ill. She might have once had doubts about the strength of her love for Nigel; she might have had doubts about moving in with him, too. But she had never doubted their friendship. Even two months ago, when she had wondered if he ever would—or should—propose to her, she had known that whatever else happened, they would still be dear friends. But, ridiculously, now that he *had* proposed, it seemed as though she would lose even his friendship. Whoever the other woman in his life was, she certainly made it impossible for Pen to marry Nigel or to live with him, and she would probably make it impossible for Pen even to be friends with him. The woman who had moved in with him was likely to be jealous of Nigel's and Pen's old friendship.

A hundred images of Nigel, from all the years they had known each other, flickered through

Pen's memory, and she sank tiredly onto the edge of her bed, her angry storm spent. Picking up her pillow with hands that shook, she cradled it to her and felt utterly bereft. Even though she had managed to go two months without seeing him, she had always felt that Nigel was there. And now he really wasn't. The Nigel Burnett she used to know—who would never have asked one woman to marry him while he was living with another—was apparently gone, and in his place was someone quite different, a calculating and secretive man who belonged to another woman.

So Nigel was gone from her life, as completely as Bree and Sam, living on the other side of the world. A few forlorn tears slipped down Pen's cheeks. Everything else aside—all past doubts and hesitations, all present anger and disillusionment—she had cared about him deeply. And whatever tangled reasoning might have brought her south to him for refuge from Alistair, now that refuge was well and truly gone. At the thought Pen brushed the tears away and stared unseeingly across the room. With an emotion compounded equally of desolation and panic, she realized that her old friend could no longer be used as an emotional shield. Whatever kind of love it was that she had felt for Nigel, it could no longer protect her against the emotion that had swept through her as she knelt beside Alistair two nights ago.

IN THE MORNING a white-faced Pen enlisted Evan to help her load up the Cortina, kissed her parents and sisters and, as she settled into the driver's seat, refused to rise to the bait of Sally's parting remark.

"Pen, why don't you go on up to the Highlands instead? I just *know* they're romantic—think of all those kilted chieftains!"

"And all those knobby knees," Evan chimed in sacrilegiously, and Sally flung herself at him indignantly. The shadows disappeared for a moment from Pen's eyes, and she met her mother's speaking glance while an amused but wordless dialogue flowed between them. Then Nell reached out and deftly settled the two combatants on opposite sides of her long enough to wave as Pen drove off.

She didn't immediately drive far, however; instead she checked in at Standish Publishing, consulted briefly with Fred and then drove herself back to the sad street where Ann Osborne's hostel stood. Pulling up, she left the old Cortina at the curb and a few minutes later she was tapping at Ann's door.

"Pen!" Ann greeted her with puzzled pleasure in her hoarse little voice. "How nice to see you again already!" Then her tone changed as she looked more closely at her visitor. "But are you all right?" she asked with concern. "I'm sorry; I don't mean to pry or be rude, but you don't look very well."

From somewhere Pen scraped up a wry smile and said lightly, "I've been having too much of life in the big city, I think."

Ann nodded understandingly, and Pen went on,

"And that's why I'm here, Ann. I told you I've been living in my uncle's cottage in the Lake District. . . ." She paused, and the other girl agreed.

"Yes, I remember. It sounded lovely."

"It is, and that's why I'm going back up there today. Ann, come with me."

"But—"

"I'd love to have the company, and we could escape London together for a bit," Pen suggested. But Ann turned slowly away and walked to one of the high windows, where she stood with her back to Pen, fiddling with a fold of the bright curtains.

"I'd love that, Pen, but I can't afford to pay you for it," she said with difficulty.

"You wouldn't need to. The cottage is mine now, so I'm not making payments on it myself," Pen explained, adding, "I know you'd have to pay to keep your room here in the meantime, but otherwise you wouldn't have any expenses except for sharing the food with me."

She would gladly have paid for that, too, but before she could say so, swift instinct warned her that Ann would rather feel she was sharing in the costs. She looked at the slight figure silhouetted against the windows and realized that, more and more, she really did want Ann to come with her. She had been drawn to the other girl's quiet gallantry from the start, and besides that had a vague feeling that Ann's presence might make her own return to Grasmere a little easier.

"But my work . . ." Ann protested feebly, turning back to gaze across the room at Pen with eyes in which hesitation and longing struggled. "I do have to get back to work soon."

"So do I," Pen agreed equably, "and we'll both work better when we're somewhere cool and lovely. And besides, think how easy it will be to work with the children next door at hand for a sample audience. They loved the Winter Prince and will be overjoyed at the prospect of more stories like that."

Her tactics were working; Ann's resistance was obviously crumbling fast now. So with a quick cheeky smile Pen added cavalierly, "Anyway, you might as well come peacefully because I've already told Fred I'm kidnapping you!"

At that, Ann finally gave in. With a little laugh of pleasure she resigned herself to her fate. "Then I guess I'm at the mercy of my captor! Oh, Pen, thank you for coming up with such a wonderful idea!" She flung her arms around the older girl in a quick hug, and Pen returned it. An hour later they were on their way north.

Along the road they talked companionably, and Pen was grateful to escape from her own thoughts. She told Ann about the village, the Bannisters, Corey and Megan—everything except the real reasons why she'd left them, and why now she was going back. Desperately Pen refused to let herself think anymore of either Nigel behind her or Alistair ahead.

When they reached Grasmere in midafternoon,

Pen drove Ann on a short tour through the village before following the lane to her own cottage and pulling up there with a flourish. "We're home!" she announced, and Ann looked around her with delighted eyes that were enormous in her thin face.

"Oh, Pen," she breathed, "it's perfect!"

Pen nodded silently as she stepped out of the car, gazing at her house and garden through a sudden mist and thinking that it seemed as if she'd been gone much longer than two days. Corey and Megan apparently thought so, too, because as they scampered over the wall after Marigold, they caught sight of Pen. The cat loped across the garden to twine herself ecstatically around Pen's ankles, and right behind her came the children.

Corey reached them first and skidded to a halt long enough to register Ann's smiling presence and blurt, "Hello! Are you Pen's sister?" Then without waiting for an answer he wrapped Pen in a bear hug, backing away afterward to prance around and shout, "Pen's home, Pen's home!" in case anyone should be in doubt of that fact. Megan, meanwhile, replaced her brother in Pen's arms and clung to her like a limpet, face buried in Pen's blue shirt so that Pen had to bend down to hear the words she mumbled into it.

"You came back."

"Yes, poppet, I did. Didn't you believe I would?" Pen asked gently.

"Ye-es." The syllable was drawn out, and then

other words followed it in a little rush. "But people don't always."

Pen's arms tightened convulsively. How could she have thought of not coming back—even before that horrible moment in Nigel's bedroom? "But usually they do, love," she said. "And I won't ever just go away and leave you—I promise."

"Really?" Megan loosened her hold a little, so that she could look up into Pen's face.

"Really." Pen met the anxious indigo eyes steadily, and in a minute the anxiety faded.

Megan stood on tiptoe to kiss her and then said matter-of-factly, "I guess we'd better go get Marigold's cat food for you, Pen. There's lots of it left, because she ate out of Levvy's dish while you were gone." She flashed Pen an elfin grin and added, "He'll be glad you're back, too."

Surprising herself, Pen laughed at what was probably an understatement and stayed the children. "For Levvy's sake, then, do get it, and we'll make Marigold dine alone again now. But first, this is Ann, kids, and she's come to stay with me for a bit."

Corey had been whirling around them like a satellite, but now he stopped and walked to Ann— only the least bit dizzily—and held out his hand. "I'm Corey, and that's Megan," he said composedly, adding by way of explanation, "She's my sister."

Ann shook the small hand he presented and said the unexpected. Looking intently at both children, she asked gravely, "Is she really? I never would have guessed it if you hadn't said so."

Two astonished pairs of blue eyes locked for a moment, then the youngsters exploded into gales of laughter. "Oh, Pen, she's nice!" Megan said frankly, and they whisked Ann away to see Levvy.

"And for Levvy to see me," her voice floated back. "But who's Levvy?"

"You'll see!" Megan promised gleefully, and they were all gone.

That left the smiling Pen alone with Alistair— she realized only now, with a sudden jolt, that he had followed the children more slowly and stood by quietly.

"Thank you again, Penelope," he said softly, looking in the direction in which Megan had vanished.

"Oh, well. . ." Pen floundered, uncertain how to respond; she had half expected him to resume hostilities right where they had left off. And exhausted as she was by the drive and the miserable night before it, she wasn't sure she could cope if those hostilities did develop.

Alistair spared her the necessity of a coherent answer by bending to pick up her things and motioning her with his eyes to go before him through her green door. Inside, Marigold ran ahead of them into the kitchen, and Pen followed automatically. Coming along behind her, he set the portfolio case down by her loom and then leaned against the doorjamb with his hands in his pockets, watching

without comment as she avoided his eyes by opening a can of milk for the cat.

When she had put the saucer down, however, she
finally had to look at him—and found him gazing
at her with something in his expression that said
plainly he would brook little more delay. He had
asked her before she left if she would illustrate his
book, and he meant to have her answer. He would
hardly plead with her, but inside his pockets his
knuckles made little ridges of tension. Tiredly, Pen
stared at them for a moment as if they were hyp-
notizing her, then took a deep breath and walked
over to the thick sheaf of drawings she had left on
Aunt Hannah's china cupboard.

Carrying them back across the room, still in a
silence that vibrated, she spread them out on the
deal table, one after another—drawings of Hardknott so accurate that Alistair, coming to stand
before the table, felt he could have reconstructed
the entire fort from them.

"When do we start?" she asked simply, in a
voice without expression, and he tore his gaze away
from the drawings to look at her with eyes that had
gone brilliantly blue again.

"Penelope, you are a marvel!" he shouted, and
before she had any idea of what he intended, he had
caught her by the shoulders and was kissing her
soundly, while she forgot her exhaustion as though
it had never been.

It started out as a kiss of sheer thankfulness. Her
mind suddenly moving rapidly again, Pen told her-

self frantically that she had had those before when a difficult class at art school ended or the right team won a match, and she tried desperately at first to accept the kiss as casually as it had begun. But then it changed. Alistair's hands slipped from her shoulders to her waist and gathered her closer to him, so that she could feel his heartbeat against her breast. It seemed to beat faster and harder, shaking her with its rhythm as his lips tightened insistently on hers, coaxing them open, while one hand slid down to clasp the soft flesh over her hip.

For a moment she yielded to him, opening under his touch like a flower to the sun, then panic welled up in her. Not this, her mind shrieked despairingly; not now that she'd just agreed to work with him. If she found herself imagining she loved him when they fought, whatever would she do when he caressed her?

Putting her fists on his chest, she arched her back away from him, murmuring incoherently against his lips, but he followed her movement, shifting one hand so that it tangled in the soft mass of hair at her neck and held her face to him. Again he searched her lips and then moved his own to drop light kisses on her eyelids, while the tendrils of hair along her forehead were ruffled by his warm breath, its pace growing more rapid by the moment. His chin brushed her cheek, too, and she was exquisitely conscious of the slight sandpaper roughness of his beard and the faint spicy smell of his shaving lotion.

As she breathed in the scent of him, his lips moved along the curve of her cheek to trace the smooth line of her jaw, and she felt the feathery touch of his lashes on her skin. Then he reached her lips again, and with a little helpless sigh she gave up and clung to him with eager hands. Catching his face to hers now with fingers that crept into the silky hair at the nape of his neck, she used her other hand to brush back the stray lock on his forehead with butterfly delicacy, and her lips moved softly under his as all rational thought faded into passion that blazed with everything lacking the night before.

And then, just as suddenly as it had begun, the kiss ended. One moment spangled darkness was spread out against her eyelids and her senses were reeling, and the next she was alone, propping herself upright with one shaking hand on the table and looking bewilderedly at Alistair's back, on the far side of the room.

There was a long and very loud silence. Pen's heart had finally stopped pounding before Alistair broke the quiet, still facing away from her.

"I apologize for that, Penelope," he said tightly, and she sagged a little against the table.

"Oh, it's nothing," she managed to choke out in a voice that was totally unfamiliar. "People kiss all the time, and it isn't important."

He wheeled at that and gave her a dark look. "I don't," he said flatly. "I don't consider it part of a working relationship, either, and I promise you won't be subjected to it again."

Almost on the words he was gone, leaving her to stare wretchedly after him until the sound of the outer door closing hard came to her. She winced away from it, and from the uncompromising coldness of his last words, but they kept repeating themselves in her brain. He would never kiss her again. But that one kiss had been enough to teach her that everything she'd felt the last time they touched—when she'd imagined herself lying beside him and then told herself the surge of love she felt was due only to proximity—was real. She was completely and hopelessly in love with Alistair Heath. And he had no use for her except as a friend for the children and an artist for his book! Oh, God, how was she going to work with him now? Dropping onto a bench by the table, Pen dissolved in exhausted, racking tears.

SOMEHOW SHE DID work with him, though, and he kept his promise.

Over the next few weeks Pen often felt as though she were leading a double life, one part full of strains and the other full of pleasures, and the two seldom crossed.

She and Alistair almost always worked alone together, but their solitude wasn't like anything she might have predicted. She had dreaded facing him again the morning after her return to Grasmere, but he behaved so matter-of-factly that it was almost as if the scene in her kitchen had never taken place, and she was gradually able to recover some equilibrium. She couldn't forget what had happened, or what it had taught her, but she knew far better than to let her feelings show.

As for Alistair, he never spoke again of his gratitude for her help on the book, and he certainly never mentioned what had come of that gratitude the day she came back from London, but neither did he go back to being the polite icicle she had so detested. It was as if he'd blotted out both those extremes by a conscious effort of will and replaced them with a more or less happy medium, offering her the same casual friendliness he'd shown when they were at Hardknott that memorable day. They worked together easily, sharing an absorption, but somehow he never let her forget that theirs was only a working relationship.

For Pen the result was that on one hand working together was easier than she'd expected, because they weren't fighting, but on the other it was harder, because she wanted so much more than this from their time spent together. Her dreams gave that away night after night, when she felt his hands, his lips, his breath touch her again. Still, out of necessity she followed his lead as they worked.

Inevitably she felt the strain of this part of her life and escaped from it to the pleasures of the other whenever she could. Ann proved to be a perfect housemate, although Pen saw less of her than she'd expected, since the younger girl seemed to avoid Alistair and he and Pen spent so much time together. When he did see Ann he was always charming to her—in a way that Pen contrasted wryly to his early treatment of herself—but Ann usually found something else to do when he was around, and in Pen a half-conscious hope her new friend could be a buffer between herself and Alistair faded.

In the evenings, though, when Pen was through working for the day, the two girls talked for long contented hours—about every subject except Alistair. Ann was too observant to have missed the traces of Pen's tears that first day, too intelligent not to guess their significance and too kind to ask about them. Other nights Ann worked on new stories while Pen sketched or wove quietly, finishing Megan's rosy blanket and then doing Corey's black-and-gold caterpillar jacket. By daylight, however, Ann spent most of her time with the children, who welcomed her as another boon companion when Pen was busy; anyone who wrote stories like hers was clearly an ally. If it rained the three of them could usually be found indoors talking about short-necked giraffes or salmon who couldn't swim or the Snowflake Ball. If the weather was fair, they walked up onto the fells, following Pen's directions to favorite places she'd discovered, while the youngsters explored more new territory and Ann lost her cough, gaining weight and a bright wild-rose color.

All of that Pen watched delightedly; then she wrote Fred a gleeful note reporting on the success of their experiment in wafting Ann away from the heat of London's summer. Pen wrote home to Dulwich, too, of course, and to Bree and Sam in New Zealand, telling them all the continuing saga of her adventures in Lakeland. She told them about Ann and about the fascinating book she had agreed to illustrate, but she said nothing of the man who was writing it.

Nor did she answer a letter from Nigel that came a few days after her return to Grasmere. In it he made no mention whatsoever of their interrupted kiss or her early exit from his party, and he said nothing of the woman who must own the clothes in his apartment. Instead in a plaintively humorous tone he pleaded with her again to come back and marry him, so that she could protect him in general from theater people and in particular from a voracious flock of would-be performers who apparently hoped to follow his sets on stage.

Those pungent lines sounded like the old Nigel, and Pen smiled over them a minute, all her earlier fiery anger and disillusionment washed away by the flood of her feelings for Alistair. But Nigel's words said too little, and it was too late anyway; her smile turned sad. She folded up the letter—and Nigel's image with it—and put it safely away. When later she carried her letters and Banny's to the village to post, there wasn't one to Nigel.

She did still find time to go to the village most days, and one cloudy afternoon when she and Alistair had quit early, Pen picked up Banny's letters and then asked, "Banny, which of the shops in the village did Uncle Andrew weave for?"

"The older one, of course, lass," Banny answered absentmindedly, her attention on the spikes of purple blue delphiniums she'd begun cutting to add to her basket of roses.

"Why 'of course'?" Pen persisted, and on the second question Banny looked up at the puzzled pretty face in front of her.

"I'm sorry, child, I was forgetting you wouldn't already know that," she smiled apologetically. "The 'of course' was because Andrew would have sold his soul to the devil, proper Calvinist though he was, rather than have anything to do with that new shop and its automated looms."

"Automated?" Pen asked. "But they advertise handmade woolens, like the other shop."

"They may advertise them, but they use those 'infernal machines'—Andrew's phrase," Banny explained parenthetically. "All the operator has to do is yank a lanyard or turn a crank and the shuttle goes across the warp automatically. Andrew always held that turning a crank meant the cloth was crank-made, not handmade, and folk who just turned cranks had no cause to lay claim to the title of weaver."

As she spoke, her tone had deepened and gained force, and now she looked sternly at Pen over her glasses; for a moment the girl almost cowered in front of an uncompromising Calvinist wrath. Then she caught the tiny twinkle at the back of Banny's eyes and realized that, rather than haranguing her personally, Banny had simply given her a perfect portrait of Andrew McKenzie in a righteous rage; it was a side of him the young Penelope wouldn't have seen all those years ago.

"Whew!" Pen breathed. "He did feel strongly about it, didn't he?"

"Indeed, yes, lass," Banny answered in her normal tone, with a remembering smile. "Even after Hannah died and he stopped weaving himself, that was the one topic would still provoke him to a show of feelings, so that for a little while at least he'd be our old Andrew again."

Pen picked up Banny's smile with one of her own, but she was still curious. "But why did the whole question matter so much to him, Banny? He'd never had to work at an automated loom, had he?"

"Never! He would have dismantled it first, and made it back into a hand loom! No, it wasn't that, Penelope; it was two other problems." Banny's voice grew serious again, and she paused a mintue, as if to gather her thoughts.

"First of all, lass," she went on more slowly, "he was afraid that the use of automated looms might someday drive out the last of the hand weavers, so that a time would come when none of them were left. As it was, a century and more ago, when the weaving machines first began to appear, most of the real hand weavers were put out of work. He didn't want that because—as you're finding out for yourself, child—hand weaving has a serenity to it that's good for the human spirit. And only a hand weaver loves the fabric he weaves—that's a love you can see in the beauty of the cloth.''

She bent to set down the shears and basket of flowers she was holding, and when she straightened Pen was nodding silently, remembering the shimmering blue green loveliness of the blanket that had first lured her to Uncle Andrew's loom. With a glance at Pen's wordless gesture of agreement, Banny added, "Aye, lass, you do know what I mean, and Andrew would have loved you all the more for it.''

She patted Pen's hand, resting on the gate between them, and then looked past her, gazing down the lane toward the village.

"And the other problem Andrew saw with such gadgets as automated looms lies down there," she went on, and Pen turned to follow her eyes, mystified. Down the green, sun-dappled lane a fraction of the village was visible from Banny's gate; Pen could see a few of the old houses with their clean whitewashed walls and enduring gray slate roofs.

"But it looks so. . .peaceful," she protested.

"Now—yes," Banny agreed. "But he was afraid all that would be changed or lost."

"How?"

"To progress," Banny answered Pen's sharp question with a twist on the words. She looked back at the concerned face Pen turned to her and explained, "Except for the commotion every August when the games are held, this has always been a quiet place, Penelope, and people have come here for that. Now there's a group in town that says we could bring in a good deal more people if we'd only be a bit less quiet. They'd like to see some modern motor hotels, instead of just the old places, and a cinema or two, maybe even a real nightclub to liven things up a bit, they say.''

"Oh, Banny, no!" Pen whispered, appalled and instantly on Uncle Andrew's side of the issue.

Banny looked at her shocked face with sympathy. "I know, lass; like Andrew, Edward and I have always thought it would be a terrible thing." She sighed and added softly, "It was the only notion we never agreed with Jamie on. Jenny seemed to understand how we felt, but Jamie was always on the side of progress."

"But that's not really progress!" Pen protested vehemently, and coming back to the present, Banny nodded agreement.

"I'd dispute it certainly, child. In fact, we do; whenever some bright young lad comes here with another idea for some fancy new 'attraction,' all the townsfolk get together to talk it over. And there've always been enough of us who hold with keeping the village as it is that we've limited our modernizing to letting in a few such things as yon looms Andrew detested so. The truth is, he just feared they might let 'progress' get its foot in the door.'

She ended on a deliberately lighter note, but Pen still said stoutly, "And he was right! If that's progress, better it should go somewhere else."

She was serious, but Banny's old face suddenly crinkled and she began to laugh, somewhat to Pen's indignation.

"I'm sorry, child," Banny apologized a minute later, straightening her expression. "It's just that since you first asked me about those dratted looms, you've taken on the look of Andrew more and more, and right then you looked exactly like him when he was on one of his rampages about them."

Mollified, Pen smiled, too, and on a last little chuckle Banny asked, "Now tell me, Penelope, why was it you started all this anyway by asking where Andrew wove?"

"I've finished Corey's jacket," Pen explained, "and thought I might get a bit of yarn of my own, instead of just using up all of Uncle Andrew's supply at once. Could the shop sell me any, do you think?"

"I'm certain of it, lass," Banny said, and bent to retrieve her basket and shears. "Just tell them who you are—and don't be too surprised if they try to hire you on the spot!"

They did, too. It was too late for Pen to call at the shop that day, but the next morning she went in, carrying some of her watercolor sketches of Lakeland in the hope that she could match yarns to their glowing colors. Surely the colors that harmonized so beautifully in the fells and lakes would harmonize on her loom.

The shop was clearly a family concern. A young man directed Pen, without asking her name, to a loft filled with yarns in every imaginable color, while a woman and an older man who appeared to be his mother and grandfather served two eager young American students from the youth hostel. And by the time the students had gone, Pen was so engrossed in her yarns that she had no idea she was, for the moment, the only customer in the shop.

She was sitting happily on the floor of the loft with her sketches spread out around her, piling beside each sketch the skeins of rich soft yarn that matched its colors, when a voice spoke behind her.

"And where did you get that canny idea, lass?" it asked, and she swung around, both hands still full of yarn, to look up at the seamed and kindly face of the shop's owner, watching her with a pipe clenched between his teeth and a smile in his eyes.

She answered the smile first, and then the question. "From everywhere!" she said exuberantly. "Everywhere I look here the colors are so beautiful I couldn't resist trying rugs like this."

He nodded and lowered the pipe. "Aye, we all work in the colors we see around us, but none of us ever tried a hand at sketching in those same colors." He moved closer and sank slowly into a crouch to see the sketches better, picking up first one and then another.

"Mmm," was all he said as he studied them, and Pen wondered what he thought. Finally he told her, when he'd finished looking at them all and had stood upright again.

"That's grand work at painting, lass, as well as a

grand idea for weaving. Choose the yarns you want, and I'll just give them to you if when you've finished you'll come back and show me the rugs and the sketches they go with.''

"Of course, if you'd like me to," Pen agreed. "But I could buy the yarns—"

"Nay, lass, we'll do it this way; it's how all our weavers work, and I've a notion we'll be asking you to do some work for us, too. We could sell your rugs and sketches together here, if you prove to be half the weaver you are an artist—and I've reason to believe you will.''

He looked at her intently with the light blue eyes of the northerner and answered her puzzled look. "You're Andrew McKenzie's girl, aren't you, lass? You have just the look of him sitting there in all that yarn.''

Pen swept a glance over the heaps around her and then looked up, laughing. "But I'm sure Uncle Andrew didn't strew your yarns all over for you like this!'' she said apologetically.

"No, he had his own ways of choosing colors," Ian Ballantyne agreed. "But he was our master weaver for half a century, and kin of his will have the weaving knack. Besides, lass, Ellen Bannister's told me how you finished the blanket Andrew left undone, just as Andrew would have done himself in your position. That's sign enough for me.''

He put the pipe back between his teeth and said past it decisively, "Now choose your yarns, Penelope, and take what you like.''

Pen hesitated a moment longer, but Ian Ballantyne motioned her on with that pipe, and an hour later she staggered from the shop, her arms piled high with bundles of yarn, to begin another career as a professional weaver. After all, she told herself breathlessly, she loved to weave, and Uncle Andrew would have been pleased—and besides, it gave her another distraction from the unsatisfactory way things stood between herself and Alistair.

Heaven knew, she needed all she could find of that sort of distraction!

CHAPTER THIRTEEN

ANN FINALLY TOOK A TRAIN for London, and Pen said goodbye regretfully, sending back word for Fred begging to be allowed to illustrate Ann's new stories when they had been accepted. Looking at the lively, glowing face that hung out the window of Ann's compartment to wave a last farewell, Pen felt she'd earned that reward.

Meanwhile, however, she hadn't much time to miss the other girl, or even to weave for Ian Ballantyne. So far Alistair had kept her busy enough just learning the background information she needed to know about Roman England and helping him decide where in his manuscript her illustrations should go, but now he started her on the actual drawings. Under his careful—and carefully impersonal—eyes she drew clear diagrams from his rough jottings and often sketched small artifacts he borrowed from local collections, including such evocatively personal things as brooches and rings, and even two shoes found at Hardknott.

With the children, Pen and Alistair began visiting some of the other Roman sites in the area,

too, but they never went back to the fortress in the
air; only partly, Pen guessed, because Alistair
already had her vivid drawings of it. In other
places she gathered a fat folder of sketches of
Roman forts, marching camps and signal stations.
And finally, of course, there was Hadrian's Wall.
The day they went to see that changed Pen's life
forever.

At the northern edge of the Lake Counties, the
western part of the great wall lay a considerable
way from Grasmere, and they made an early start.
As a result the children slept away most of the
long drive in the rear seat of the Rover, Corey
bundled happily in his new caterpillar jacket and
Megan beside him holding tightly to the picnic
basket that contained their lunch, conscious even
in sleep of the need to keep the food from her
brother's eager clutches. Pen, too, dozed along
the way, but they all awoke refreshed and eager
when Alistair pulled up into the roadside car park
that lay below Housesteads, the most famous of
the ancient forts that measured out the length of
the wall.

Not surprisingly, Corey was the first out of the
car, tumbling clear of it in his eagerness to be first
into Housesteads. "I'll go capture the fort!" he
shouted. Then he stopped dead and looked
around him in comical dismay. "But where is it?"

"Up there, imp," Alistair responded on a smile,
nodding toward the north as he unfolded his long
length from the Rover with considerably more

decorum. "Unfortunately, your transport goes
only this far, so you'll have to manage the last half
mile or so on your own," he added, walking
around the car to open Pen's door while Megan
squirmed out by herself. "In fact, if you'll hold on
for a moment, you can march us all up there
together."

He helped Pen out, and she fought a brief
familiar battle with herself until she squashed the
tiny tremor of her nerves that even those mean-
ingless contacts with Alistair always produced.
Then his hand was gone, and the momentary
warmth she'd felt from it cooled on her skin while
she dragged her attention back to more prosaic
things.

"Thank you," she said in a carefully matter-of-
fact tone, and Alistair just acknowledged their
reciprocal courtesies with an absent nod. Like the
children's, his eyes were looking eagerly north-
ward.

Leaving the Rover behind them then, the four
followed the paved path that curved away from
the road and down a hill, then up to the fort itself
and the wall. At that point, almost dancing with
excitement, the youngsters bounded ahead and
Alistair strolled after them, leaving Pen to savor
and draw at her own speed.

The first thing she found out was that not only
was this fort far larger than Hardknott, it also lay
in far different surroundings. Hardknott had been
cut into the rocky fells of Cumbria, but House-

steads grew out of the grassy ridges of Northumberland. Like sea waves rolling to the north, those ridges swelled slowly upward on the southern side, crested in the fort and the mighty wall it had maintained, then broke into steep drops. And like sea waves they were a clear green near at hand but changed to variable blues in the distance. Overhead the immense sky of the north was dappled with towering clouds, and through them the slanting rays of the sun gave the land infinite variety, so that Pen forgot everything else as she gazed around her with wonder and delight, breathing air that was cool and invigorating even at the height of summer.

For a minute she stood rooted to the path. Then the contrast of the land's variety with the wall's unchanging permanence drew her straight through the fort to the line of massive stones that marked its far boundary. In spite of centuries of neglect and pilfering for newer buildings, the long line still marched boldly east and west. Working rapidly with pastels, she sketched the wall again and again, trying to capture something of its enduring vitality. Finally, though, she gave up in frustration as she realized she could never catch all of the wall's fleeting moods in a slow net of pastels.

Disappointed, she turned away and found Alistair and the children just returning from a foray along the top of the wall. "Pen, guess where we've been!" shouted Corey.

While Alistair swung himself down and then

turned back to lift Megan onto the grass beside him, Corey hopped down on his own and cannoned into Pen. She lost her balance, and the two of them collapsed onto the ground. Laughing, Pen rolled Corey off of her and sat up as he burst out without even getting up, "Pen, we walked along the wall, just the way the Romans did! And we went all the way to another little tower over there where they used to keep watch for the enemy to come sneaking up!"

He pointed westward with a sweeping gesture, and Pen caught the flailing arm in its woolly caterpillar jacket. "Yes, and then you came marching back and attacked me instead of an enemy tribesman!" she scolded with mock seriousness.

Corey gave her a repentant grin. "Sorry, Pen," he said, scrambling to his feet and holding out a hand to her. "It was farther down than I thought."

"Yes," she agreed seriously, "much easier to use my battered body as a stepping-stone." She sighed deeply and made as if to check for broken bones, but then gave up in laughter as Corey started to look genuinely worried.

"I'm all right, goose," she chuckled. "Just sound your battle cry before the next attack so I can at least ready my defenses."

Relieved, Corey joined in her laughter, and Pen clambered to her feet, brushing bits of grass off her trim plaid trousers and as much of her shirt as she could reach before she turned to find Megan and Alistair surveying them both.

"I see we'll have to build a fort around Penelope to protect her from the onslaughts of the infantry," he said resignedly, but instead of being chastened the children greeted this idea with glee.

"Like that little tower," Corey agreed.

Megan added eagerly, "The one through those woods, Pen. We could build it in the garden at home, and then march around to protect you from Levvy."

Immediately she and Corey began to strut practice circles around Pen, and over their bobbing heads Alistair's eyes met hers in a look of amused apology. Then he collared both soldiers as they marched within reach.

"Enough, troops," he said firmly. "As your commanding officer, I order you to cease and desist. New fortifications can be built if and when they become necessary—that's presumably when mild-mannered Levvy turns into a slavering lion," he added in a parenthesis to Pen. "And in the meantime we have some old ones to inspect."

Giggles turned the soldiers back into children, and as Alistair freed them they scampered ahead into the fort. Then he retrieved Pen's sketchbook from the little hummock where Corey's return had sent it, and handed it back to its owner. Pen smiled a brief thank-you, but then she leafed through the new sketches again and her face clouded with disappointment. When she looked up, Alistair was watching her with an understanding smile.

"It takes everyone that way, Penelope. Those old stones resisted most attacks for more than two and a half centuries before the Romans' final withdrawal, and since then they've also resisted capture by further centuries of artists, though I'd guess you've come closer than most. Come away now while I round up those two rowdies, and then I'll try to keep them occupied while you have a crack at the fort. I suspect you'll find it easier to work with."

"Certainly it couldn't be more tantalizingly difficult," Pen agreed ruefully, folding away her earlier sketches. Then while she followed at her own pace, already familiar with the fort's standard Roman plan, Alistair and the children made a tour of Housesteads and its environs. Like eager puppies the active pair scrambled and tumbled among the low walls remaining, and their uncle recreated for them the daily lives of the one thousand auxiliary soldiers who had garrisoned this fort on a frontier so far from home.

He showed them the house for the commandant's family and the partially excavated barracks where the common soldiers slept eight or ten to a room, while their officers had more spacious quarters at one end. Then they saw the hospital where an ailing soldier received treatment from the medical officer for any physical complaint from an earache to a broken leg or a virulent fever, and the great hall of the headquarters building where an angry soldier got a hearing from the commandant for any personal or legal complaint. In that building, too, were the unit's chapel, with its standards and its altars to the soldiers' gods, and the offices where a soldier's pay and savings were recorded. Sheds and stables along the outer edge of the compound housed the carts and draft animals that brought his food to the great granaries, and workshops repaired his equipment and made him new weapons. His other needs were met, too: fresh water was collected in many stone tanks, and at the lowest corner of the fort, one tank supplied a spacious latrine, while outside the walls lay a bathhouse.

Also outside, on terraces that followed the slope of the land, was the village that grew up in the shelter of the fort to house the soldiers' wives and children and the merchants and traders who supplied them. Temples and shrines, shops and cemeteries lay outside the fort but still within reach of its protection.

Her sketchbook nearly filled now, Pen joined Alistair and the children below the fort in the village, just in time to help Alistair referee a heated discussion between Megan and Corey over the question of whether the little girl had to stay in the village with the soldiers' dependants or could go and perform guard duty with her brother in the fort proper.

"You're a girl—you can't possibly do guard

duty,'' Corey insisted, and the conversation was becoming acrimonious when Pen cannily deflected it.

"Megan," she said thoughtfully, "since you're running the only inn in the village while your husband is stationed at the fort, shouldn't you go get fresh supplies to feed your guests? After all, without you they'll go hungry."

With a little whoosh Megan let out the deep breath she'd already inhaled for her next exchange of compliments with Corey and turned to Pen with an arrested expression. Pen raised her eyebrows significantly and looked back toward the distant car park, and quick comprehension lighted Megan's small face. Wordlessly Alistair handed her the keys to the Rover, and with a gleeful laugh she darted away on winged feet.

For a moment the discomfited Corey gazed unhappily after her, but then inspiration struck and he blurted, "I'll go guard the pack train!" before dashing after his sister.

Left alone, Pen and Alistair met each other's eyes, her look compounded of relief and amusement, and his of relief and admiration.

"Penelope," he said gravely, "as commanding officer of this unit, I am awarding you a special commendation for extraordinary services rendered in the cause of peace on the northern frontier."

Drawing his lean body up to its full height, his eyes warm and laughing, he gave her a soldier's salute, clapping his clenched right fist to his chest before relaxing into a more comfortable stance to add ruefully, "I don't know what the Heaths would do without your civilizing influence."

At his casual words the little pain in Pen's heart, dormant while she had sketched, now stirred; she quieted it firmly and made herself say flippantly, "You'd manage very nicely as charming barbarians, then, I'm sure, but right now I'd manage much better myself if I found somewhere to rest my weary feet. Could we choose someplace to have our picnic when the innkeeper and her guard return with lunch?"

She was avoiding Alistair's eyes now and so didn't see the blue gaze sharpen as it lingered on her averted face. A moment later he responded obligingly in her own light tone, "Your wish is my command. We can find ourselves a spot along the banks of the Knag Burn near the bathhouse, if you approve."

Pen nodded briskly and set off in the direction he had indicated; easily Alistair matched her pace with his longer and slower strides. By the time the children arrived, puffing under their burden of picnic basket and thermoses, Pen was settled on the grass near the still-buried bathhouse, and Alistair was poking rather longingly at its ruins.

Lunch was quite silent as they devoured Pen's picnic, she and Alistair only a little less hungry than the ravenous youngsters. Finally everything had been eaten except for the four bannocks that

Pen was hoarding for teatime on the way home. Corey eyed them wistfully, but Pen, catching the look, moved them firmly out of his reach, and with a lugubrious sigh he swept up the last crumbs of the three Banny-cakes he'd already engulfed. Then he lay back on the grass beside Megan and muttered, "I bet a Roman soldier got all he wanted to eat."

Chuckling at his tone, Pen yanked up a handful of turf and tossed it at him, and then while he pretended to eat that in desperation, she looked to Alistair, her active curiosity roused again. Whatever else their relationship lacked, this interest at least they shared, and she turned to it now, saying, "Seriously, Alistair, how did the fort supply itself with food?"

Like the children, he was lying stretched out in the grass, hands clasped behind his head as he watched the clouds hurry across the sky, and he answered her question without moving.

"In several ways, Penelope," he said slowly, and she thought for an instant of how she loved the sound of her name on his lips. Then she let herself relax into the beloved rhythm of his voice as he went on. "Some of it was sent up from the Roman and native farms in the more peaceful lands to the south; some was obtained by trading with the less-hostile tribesmen in this area; and some was probably grown in kitchen gardens on the terraces in the village below the fort. We know they ate cheese, some fruits and vegetables, bread and a kind of porridge—'' Corey had looked up on "cheese," but at "porridge" his interest faded "—and food would usually not have been a problem until the later years of the Roman occupation."

Pen looked across the rolling countryside, dappled by the play of light and shade and dotted with peacefully grazing sheep. The land itself changed so little, and yet the people who moved across it left only mute and scattered traces of themselves. Rome's tossing plumes and glittering armor, her striding armies and proud commanders were all gone, and gone, too, were the road builders and farmers, the merchants and innkeepers who had lived in the service of Rome and trusted in her power. Little was left now of the mighty walls and towering forts, and still less remained of the settlements that had sheltered below them.

The shadow of a racing cloud fell across her, and Pen was swept by a sudden aching pity for the transitoriness of human life. It was that which made her ask in a suddenly urgent voice, "What happened to it all, Alistair? How did so much become so little?"

He heard an age-old cry in her words and gave her a brief compassionate look that unsettled her still further. Like the fine sticky threads of a spiderweb, their glances caught and tangled. It was as if for a moment he forgot his pose as her uninvolved employer and looked at her with a much warmer understanding, and Pen's heart began to race. Her gaze clung to his, and she felt the cool unemotional composure she'd fought so hard to preserve all these weeks now thawing and melting; then she wrenched her eyes away and stared unseeingly at the wall.

There was a small throbbing silence that made Megan turn over restlessly and glance at them. Then Alistair spoke again, and his tone was as matter-of-fact as usual. Megan flopped back down, and listening to him, Pen was gradually able to steady her erratic pulse and even to look at him again with unrevealing eyes. He seemed to answer only the answerable part of her question, telling her about the end of the occupation.

"In the early years after Hadrian's Wall was built, the troubles of the Romans resulted from overexpansion. Hadrian's successor, Antoninus, ordered Roman forces past this first wall and into Scotland to build a second one. Troops were drawn north and away from the fortifications here, so the Brigantes in this area rose in revolt. They were put down, however, and this wall was secured again for a time.

"After that, later troubles were the result of conflicts within the empire itself, between emperors and would-be emperors. Again and again troops would be ordered away from the frontier to fight elsewhere in the empire, and the defenses here on the wall would be left weak and subject to attack. Repeatedly the wall was breached from the north, and the forts and villages below it put to the torch.''

He looked back up toward Housesteads, his eyes darkening, lost now in the past, and Pen was able to watch his clear profile as he spoke musingly. ''Life here must have changed drastically in the later years. The remaining soldiers must have been uneasy at best, and the bold wide gates of the fort were narrowed; some were even blocked completely. In the village, too, the common people must have been fearful as the pattern of their lives broke down with the breakdown of Rome's power, and perhaps Roman law crumbled with Roman peace. At any rate, the frightened tenor of the times may have caused and been reflected by a crime in the village that was hidden for centuries until excavations a generation ago uncovered it.''

Corey had been daydreaming—probably about food again—but at this he rolled over and focused on his uncle's words.

''In the living quarters behind one of the shops that fronted the main street lay the skeletons of a middle-aged man and woman, presumably done to death by the ancient sword whose point was found still between the man's ribs. Their bodies were hidden underneath a new clay floor, and the victims were silenced for the better part of two thousand years. Now, though, we know the place and manner of their deaths, and those facts can tell us of the pervasive fear that might have caused them.''

He paused, seemingly far away in his thoughts, and three pairs of eyes were fixed on him now. Both children lay sprawled on their stomachs, their chins propped in their hands. Pen, her knees drawn up and her hands clasped loosely around them, had forgotten the earlier moment of tension that even Megan had recognized, carried away into the distant past by Alistair's words.

When those words didn't continue immediately, Corey prompted his uncle. "Which house was it, Uncle Lister, where they found the skeletons?" he asked with a small child's morbid curiosity.

Megan scowled at her brother, but Alistair, perhaps understanding his interest better, came back to them and ruffled Corey's hair. "It's the one on the east side of the main street, a little way below the south gate of the fort, ghoul. But disappointingly, there are no old bones on the spot for you to rattle, only the lowest stones of the building's walls and a little sign that proclaims it Murder House. Will you settle for that?"

Corey nodded regretfully, and Megan said, "Ugh! But what happened to everyone else, Uncle Lister?"

"We don't entirely know, little one. We do know that after the last time the village was burned, its people were moved into the fort itself and quarters were made for them in the granaries and headquarters building. One other building seems to have been changed into an internal bath-house, too, as conditions outside the walls became more dangerous. More and more, both the civilians and the soldiers had to rely on the strength of the fort's walls, but even that wasn't enough.''

He paused a moment and then went on quietly, ''We don't know precisely when the end came, but it must have come suddenly. In one of the inner rooms of the headquarters building, where in better times the secretary had kept the fort's records, a smith was still making arrowheads until the last possible moment. Then for one final time the fort was destroyed, and later years saw it either empty or used as a refuge by a succession of hermits who withdrew into solitude, local people who fled from later invasions, and moss-troopers who raided along the border three centuries ago. Since then, though, only farmers in search of stones to build their barns and archaeologists in search of the past have disturbed it.''

He stopped speaking again, and this time, with the spell of his voice lifted, Megan and Corey abruptly changed from attentive students back into restless children. Seeing that with the eyes of experience, their uncle said dryly, ''Your history lesson for the day is over, urchins, and school is out. Why don't you go burn off some of that energy I see simmering inside you before we start the trip home?''

Released, the children galloped off again, no longer Roman soldiers or their dependants but now moss-troopers pillaging the countryside as

they carried off the picnic basket. Pen, however, sat where she was, returning only slowly
to the present. As at Hardknott, Alistair had
taken her completely out of herself with his ability to bring the past to life. The whole long history of Housesteads had been spread out for
her to see, like a length of many-colored tapes-
try, woven in the brilliant hues of conquest
and the somber ones of defeat. And perhaps that
was Alistair's tacit remedy for her hurt at the im-
permanence of life, she guessed suddenly. By
making the long-dead Romans live again, he had
answered as one both of the questions she had
asked.

Conflicting emotions surged through Pen: love
and admiration on the one hand, and panicky
exasperation on the other. Certainly this knowl-
edgeable man was the ideal person to write a
history of all this that would fire the public's
interest—but why, oh, why in heaven couldn't he
just stay in one of the neat pigeonholes her mind
had desperately constructed for him? As long as
he was being the icicle or the cool employer she
could arm her heart against him, but then he had
to go and remind her he was the same man who
was capable of sympathy and understanding—and
of that one passionate embrace she had tried so
hard to forget! Much more of this and her
defenses would be as vulnerable as the fort's had
become, and then she'd have to run from Alistair
again without concern for the unfinished book,

the promise she'd made to Megan or anything else.

Unconsciously she was lacing her fingers together, and she jumped when longer fingers covered them. Would she ever learn to ignore his casual touch, she wondered desperately, longing to feel his hands on her body and not just on her own hands. A wash of betraying color tinted her cheeks. All that Alistair said, however, was, "Come over to the museum with me, Penelope, while those two lively ones exhaust themselves. There are some exhibits I think you'd enjoy, and I need to look up the curator for a brief chat."

He swung her to her feet without waiting for a reply, and Pen went along with him willingly enough, relieved at the return of book concerns. She did enjoy the museum, too, browsing curiously among its models and various artifacts, photographs and diagrams of nearly eighty years of modern excavations. Alistair's chat turned out to be more than just a brief one, though, and by the time he returned from it, Pen was sitting outside the museum with one exhausted child leaning against her on either side.

The three of them were a rather dispirited group, and Alistair, coming to find them at last, surveyed them with amused eyes. "I'm sorry to have kept you waiting so long, Penelope. In the meantime my plan for these other two seems to have worked out all too well. Now it looks as though I'll have to cart the whole lot of you back to the car."

Brightening slightly, all three nodded in unison, and with a resigned chuckle Alistair scooped Megan up and sat her in the crook of one strong arm. He handed her Pen's sketchbook to carry and with his free hand hauled Corey to his feet, keeping hold of the small hand in his so that he could provide its owner with a little extra forward momentum. Corey took the thermoses, but that still left Pen sitting with the picnic basket.

Tilting her head, she looked up at the tall man standing over her to ask in an aggrieved tone, "But where's my ride? Don't tell me I'm going to have to fend for myself—and carry the picnic basket besides!"

Alistair met her look with one of deep concentration, his inky brows knitted in thought, and then he said, in the voice of one struck by inspiration, "Eureka! I have it! I'll take the kids up to the Rover and then come back and carry you up there, too, balancing the picnic basket on my head."

The tone was serious, but there was a gleam of devilment in his eyes, and Pen, weighing tone and gleam, experienced both an unholy impossible desire to make a respectable archaeologist carry her out of an important excavation and a lurking suspicion that he really would do it. He turned away with the children and started toward the distant car park as if it were all settled, and for a mo-

ment more Pen perched indecisively where he'd
left her. Then discretion won out over temptation,
and with a regretful little giggle at lost oppor-
tunities, she picked up the basket and followed
after the others, feeling only a little disappointed.

When she came up to the Rover, Alistair was
shepherding the children into the rear seat of the
car. Without comment Pen extracted the hoarded
Banny-cakes and then set the basket on top of the
trunk; without comment Alistair opened the trunk
and stowed the basket away, but there had been a
slight lift of those piratical eyebrows when he
caught sight of Pen, and it was perfectly clear he
knew exactly how her train of thought had run.
Cheeks pink, she opened her own door, slipped
into her seat and folded her hands demurely; she
couldn't be quite sure whether or not she really
heard him murmur, "Coward."

CHAPTER FOURTEEN

AT ANY RATE, very little else was said on the way
home. As their uncle had intended they should be,
the children were indeed worn out, and the
smooth motion of the car sent them to sleep
almost immediately. They woke up only briefly to
devour the last of the bannocks before dozing off
again, curled up together, and Pen herself did very
little better. She leafed quickly through the day's
drawings and made a few safely desultory remarks
about them, but as Alistair seemed intent on his
driving she soon fell silent. Then for a few minutes
she allowed herself the pleasure of studying him
from under lowered eyelids, admiring the clear
straight profile again and the competent long-
fingered hands. But soon her lashes drooped lower
still, and Pen, too, was asleep.

At some point along their way a bend in the
road that was sharper than most tipped the sleeping Pen sideways, and with a little protesting
murmur she shrugged herself into a comfortable
position again, dreaming of the touch of Alistair's
hands and not waking to know that she was comfortable because she had nuzzled herself into his

shoulder. The shoulder shifted slightly to make a more secure pillow for her, and she rubbed her cheek against it sensuously, then was still again. Tumbling over the collar of her coat, her hair flowed over Alistair's old tweed jacket in soft perfumed wisps that occasionally tickled the hard incisive line of his jaw, but he made no effort to brush it away, and although his lips smiled a little, his eyes were dark with thought.

Pen didn't wake until the Rover had glided quietly up the lane and stopped at Alistair's cottage; then the silence woke her a minute or two after he'd switched off the engine. She sat up slowly, blinking like a baby owl, but didn't realize where she'd been sleeping, and Alistair slid away from her out of the car before she could guess. He came around to her side of the Rover and helped her out, steadying her with one big hand while she gathered her wandering wits. Rather embarrassed, she looked at him with eyes that were alert again and a bit apologetic.

"One way or another, I don't seem to be the ideal driving companion! I'm sorry to have deserted you so, Alistair." A glance into the rear seat showed her the sleeping children, and she smiled. "We weren't much company for you, were we?"

"No matter," he said dismissingly. "I had my thoughts for company. And anyway, you're awake now, which is more than can be said for this sleepy pair. Apparently they mean to sleep clear through to morning, and even Corey's appetite is unconscious.''

He shook his head in wry amazement and then added, ''You'll be wanting to get home yourself, Penelope, so I'll bid you a good evening now before I gird up my loins to wrestle these two out of their clothes and into their night things.''

Pen grinned quickly at his choice of words but guessed that it was probably apt. Having parented Corey and Megan for only half a year—and with Nora Button's help until a few months ago—he couldn't have had a great deal of experience at dressing and undressing sleeping children.

''Would an ally help in the struggle?'' she asked, and he shot her a grateful look before conscience made him protest.

''You've been in the company of my charges since early morning, Penelope, and I'm reluctant to let them be any more of a bother to you than they've already been.''

''It's no bother,'' she responded calmly, ''because I love your charges.''

And without stopping to see the complicated expression that passed over his dark face at her words, she reached into the back seat of the car, gently disentangled the children and lifted Megan out. The little girl muttered something but didn't wake, and Pen was able to gather the small fine-boned body into her arms. Without saying anything more, Alistair followed suit with Corey, and together they carried their sleeping burdens into the cottage. Once inside, he led the way upstairs to the children's room, where he and Pen laid the exhausted youngsters gently on their beds and he switched on the little lamp nearby.

He hesitated then, and Pen flashed him a tolerant smile, whispering, "Pajamas, please."

He produced two pairs of soft flannel pajamas, one with yellow stripes and one with green, and then stepped aside while Pen shucked first one child and then the other neatly out of their small dungarees and jerseys and slipped them into their pajamas. From over her shoulder, she heard Alistair give an exaggerated sigh of admiration, and admitted with a low chuckle, "It's simple when you have two younger sisters and a younger brother."

She held Corey up against her while she pulled back the bedclothes, then slid him down gently into his bed, tucking the blankets in around him. A light kiss on top of his glossy head, and she moved on to Megan. This time, though, when Pen kissed the child she stirred and murmured, "'Night, mummy," before slipping back into her dreams.

Pen swallowed hard past a sudden lump in her throat and brushed the tangled curls from Megan's forehead with tender fingers. Then she stepped quietly out of the room past Alistair, quickly averting her eyes from his ravaged face. She walked softly but hastily down the steps and was nearly at the outer door when his voice said from the stairs, "I'll see you home, Penelope."

Almost reluctant to see him again, she turned slowly, but the anguished expression was gone, and his face was totally empty of anything but control. "There's no need—" she began.

"I'll see you home," he repeated firmly, and for once the conflict of their wills produced in Pen no urge to argue. She simply nodded and stepped outside, and he followed, leaving the door ajar in case the children should wake and call.

Through the cooling air where summer scents lingered like the ghosts of flowers, they walked the short distance to Pen's door in silence, but when she reached it and glanced back to say good-night to Alistair, he said, "May I come in, please?"

"If you like, of course," Pen replied after a second's hesitation. She was puzzled because he had so rarely visited her cottage except to fetch the children, but in his face and voice there was still some undefinable tension that brooked no argument.

She opened the door accordingly, and when Marigold rushed forward for her customary welcome home, winding around Pen's ankles and crooning, she picked up the little orange cat and looked tentatively at Alistair.

"The kids may for once not be hungry, but Marigold certainly is. I'll be fixing her supper and something for myself—would you like something, too?"

He gave the cat in her arms a slightly jaundiced stare and seemed undecided for a moment, but then said, "Yes, please, Penelope—whatever is the least trouble," and followed her into the kitchen.

The room was shadowy and still except for the reassuring tick of the clock, but Pen made her way through the darkness with the ease of familiarity and switched on the lamp by Uncle Andrew's chair. It cast a welcoming glow around it, and the warm golden light caught on the bowl of dianthus Pen had left on the table, the blue-and-white china in the china cupboard, the length of soft green and golden brown fabric on the loom, and one of Uncle Andrew's books lying open on the seat of the old chair.

For a long moment Alistair looked around him at the tranquil scene, while Pen set Marigold down, opened a can of cat food and poured a saucer of milk. Then, in a companionable silence and as easily as if he'd done it a thousand times before, he walked to the hearth and built a brightly blazing fire on it. Investigation of her cupboards and fridge, meanwhile, had shown Pen that her supper menu was going to be limited. Setting the kettle on to boil, she fixed a small green salad and a mushroom omelet, realizing with a little start only as she turned the omelet out of the pan that this was the same meal she had fixed for Alistair the unforgettable night of their return from Hardknott.

The neat movements of her hands stopped, and she glanced irresistibly at the tall man who was now seated in her uncle's chair with his sleek dark head bent over the book she had left there. The expression on his face was remote, but at least he was here in her kitchen, waiting for a meal of her preparing, and there was a sweet intimacy in that fact that quickened her heartbeats. Helpless to stop herself, she remembered again in sudden overwhelming detail the vision she had had of herself lying beside Alistair that other night she had fixed this meal. Feeling as though every inch of her skin ached for his touch to become a reality again, she poured the tea with hands that moved unsteadily and said, "Supper's ready"—the ageless words of a woman to her man, coming out in a cracked little voice Pen barely recognized as her own.

At the tone of her voice he looked over, but she kept her head lowered lest he should somehow read in her eyes the desire in her thoughts. Then he closed the book with an oddly decisive little sound and set it aside, coming to sit at the far side of Pen's small table without comment. Vitality and purpose were back in his face, and she told herself with a rattled attempt at humor that at least he wasn't going to sleep through this meal.

He didn't. What he did instead, however, guaranteed that Pen would barely sleep at all that night. He ate his supper with genuine appreciation first, but when he was finished he set his dishes out of the way and folded his arms on the blue table-cloth. Pen, glancing at him at last to ask if he wanted more tea, forgot the words when she found him looking at her with a light in his sea-blue eyes that she had never seen there before.

"Penelope," he said quietly, "would you marry me, please?"

His words were so astonishing that at first she absorbed only their sound and not their sense. Then, as their meaning began to penetrate, too, she felt as if she were drowning in those seawater eyes. Her senses swam helplessly, as they had when he had kissed her here in this room, drawing from her reactions she had hardly guessed she could feel and making her body clamor for more. Now that clamor could be sweetly stilled.

She felt a slow melting into weakness, and her fingers unconsciously gripped the handle of Aunt Hannah's little teapot as if it were the one piece of flotsam supporting her in a whirlpool of emotions that was drawing her into the dark intent face across the table from her; that face whose every expression over the past weeks and months was beloved. And yet she'd tried so hard to keep her love for him small and secret, controlled and hidden, while all the time that was unnecessary, because he had been falling in love with her, too.

Wanting to share that delicious irony with her love, Pen raised a luminous gray gaze from his lips—lips that could set her skin ablaze and dissolve her bones—to his eyes again, but he was

no longer looking into her face. Instead her taut
fingers held his attention, and the light in his eyes
had vanished as if it had never been.

Without looking at her again, he said in a voice
that was now completely flat and devoid of all
emotion, "Of course, this would be just a business
arrangement of sorts. We don't love each other,
but we both love the children, and together we
could make them a real home. We work well
together, too, and that's a more stable and lasting
tie than the most all-consuming passion could be.
Passion is deceptive, but mutual interests aren't;
long after the fading of passion has revealed all
the ugly realities, shared work and responsibilities
can bind people together."

We don't love each other. His cold words
pounded out a steady and implacable rhythm in
her brain, washing away the warm living passion
that had filled every cell of her—the passion he
said was a liar. Like an icy tide his words flooded
relentlessly over her, and with the tiniest gasp she
loosened her hold on the teapot. Better to drown
than struggle with this pain.

Alistair didn't seem to hear the gasp, and he
didn't notice her despairing little gesture. In the
same empty voice he went on speaking of marriage
in terms of work and responsibilities, and all Pen's
hopes that if she stayed here in Grasmere, if she
worked with him on the book, and if only she was
patient, he might someday come to love her, too—
indeed, her brief blinding joy that he did love

her—died noiselessly. She sat lifelessly still and let his words wash over her bowed head.

"I realize this doesn't sound much like 'Love's Young Dream,'" he was saying when his altered tone finally reached her again. His voice now had a hard cutting edge that jabbed her into awareness again as he continued sardonically, "No moonlight and roses, no waltzes and white dresses, whispered plans and promises of undying fidelity."

Her protective numbness sliced away, Pen turned instinctively to anger for a shield against her hurt. All the old antagonism surged up in her. He was destroying her dreams; must he ridicule them, too?

"You, of course, would never be guilty of such foolishness," she observed in a tightly controlled voice that betrayed her anger by a slight tremor.

Apparently, though, he heard not her tone but only her words. With a sudden sharp thrust away from the table that made the legs of his bench squeal in pain, he stood up and strode across the room to the dark window. His back to her, he said in a voice that was no longer mocking, "I was once, Penelope. I was engaged to a beautiful woman in my last term at university, and my whole life seemed to be full of moonlight and promises. Then three weeks before our wedding date she eloped with someone else."

His words were muffled, but Pen heard the searing agony that they only hinted at. It was as if her own misery sharpened her senses to his, and she felt her anger melt away. She was proof against him if she could hate his cynicism, but not if she grieved for the hurts that had caused it.

"I'm sorry," she said softly, mourning for them both now that she understood why he had nothing left of "Love's Young Dream" to offer her.

For a time they both were silent, then finally he turned back from the shadowy window to the luminous room, and it was as if he'd returned from some far lonely place to ask bluntly, "Can you accept an offer like that, Penelope?"

She didn't answer immediately, and while he waited for her response, he stepped to the graying coals where the fire had gone out and stooped to build it up again. This time, however, he built a smaller fire instead of the earlier leaping blaze. It caught more slowly but then burned with a warm and steady glow; by its light he looked across the room at her again, and she finally responded.

Her heart ached with love and pity and longing, but she answered with the same lack of pretense with which he had asked his question. "I don't know, Alistair," she began, then something in the way he awaited her reply made her add, "Perhaps. May I have some time to give you my decision?"

"All the time you need, Penelope. While we finish the book, we'll go on working together closely and can get to know each other better. That may help you decide."

His words were matter-of-fact now, but as the firelight welled up between them it almost seemed to reflect back into his eyes that earlier unfamiliar light. Before she could be certain, though, he moved, crossing the room to the table where she still sat bonelessly, her hands clasped loosely on the blue cloth.

Taking one of those hands in both of his, he held it and said in a voice that was suddenly gentle, "You must be exhausted; there's nothing left of you but those bottomless gray eyes. You've been too many miles today and felt too many feelings.

"I shouldn't have spoken to you now, but it's done and I'll let it stand. We'll go on as we have, but keep my question in the back of your mind and think about it now and again. I won't press you for an answer, and I'll not mention this to the children at all; I won't have them badgering you into a yes when you're being offered such a poor bargain."

The firelight gleamed on his raven's-wing hair as he bent his head and pressed a light kiss into her palm. "Good night, Penelope," he said, and releasing her hand he walked swiftly out of her kitchen. A moment later the outer door latched quietly behind him, and Pen lowered her head to rest her cheek on the hand he had kissed, trying instinctively to prolong the fleeting warmth of his lips.

For a long time she sat perfectly still—so long

that Marigold, content before to sit with her back to the doorway watching the proceedings from the corner of one golden eye, roused herself, stretched and gave a little tentative call. That didn't get any response, so the cat decided on more direct tactics. Padding delicately across the room, she leaped into Pen's lap and sat down, purring loudly to announce her arrival, and that finally produced a response, but not the one Marigold had expected.

Instead of chuckling and running gentle fingers through the little cat's fur, Pen burst into tears. Her face disappeared into her hands, and her shoulders began to shake as deep sobs racked her body. Eyes wide, Marigold clung to Pen's quivering lap for a minute or two but then jumped down and crouched at her feet unhappily. With her body tense and her ears back, the cat waited, but still the tears went on. At last with a worried wail Marigold stood up on her hind legs, resting one front paw on Pen's leg, and used her other paw to pat at the girl's shin.

Even that didn't work immediately, but the second time she tried it Pen finally reacted. With a last gulping sob she sat upright, mopping her reddened eyes with one hand and reaching down with the other to caress the cat's ears. "Sorry, Marigold," she said in a husky voice. "Were you worried?"

Relieved, the little cat jumped into her lap again, turned twice and settled down with a

rumbling purr, blinking magnanimous eyes in for-
giveness.

"I didn't really mean to ignore you," Pen went
on, scrubbing at her damp cheeks with a handkerchief while she fought to control her ragged
breathing. She added with a watery sigh, "I think
I need to be ignored a bit more myself! Instead,
here I am with two unanswered proposals of marriage and both of them impossible. I can't marry
Nigel because I don't love him enough or even
seem to know him anymore, and besides, it looks
as though someone else *does* love him. And I
shouldn't marry Alistair because I do love him."

Her voice trembled again on the last phrase, but
for the moment she held off further tears, even
though she had reason enough to cry. Alistair had
proposed to her, and if anyone had suggested such
a thing even this morning, she would have said
that nothing in the world would make her happier.
For a moment as he sat there she had been daz-
zlingly, blindingly happy. But then he had told her
his terms for marriage—that it would be a
business arrangement by which she would have his
name and his home but nothing of himself. She
would live with him, work with him, raise the children with him, but never love him—never share
his bed or her body with him. A long shiver swept
over her, and she knew now that his proposal
alone wasn't enough; she would never be happy
again unless she were able to be his wife in every
sense of the word.

His wife. The words trembled in her mind like some rare and beautiful butterfly, and for a few minutes she let herself dream of being Alistair's real wife. She dreamed of days of laughter and nights of love, when he would gather her tightly into his arms so that she lay along the whole length of his body, while he caressed and stroked her into a sweet frenzy and then gave her sweeter release. With his lips he would draw her soul up and out of her, and with his loving give it back. But that would never happen, because he had no love left to give her. With a despairing little cry Pen buried her face in her hands again, and the precious butterfly was gone.

Eventually, somehow, she fell asleep in her chair, and when the first gray light of morning woke her she was stiff and pale but oddly calm. With a sort of detached wonder she remembered how sorrowless she had once thought her life to be; now she felt as though she had joined some silent and timeless fellowship of eternal human grief. Either answer to Alistair's proposal would be intolerable. If she refused, she would have to leave—leave the village and everything here that she loved, so that she could run somewhere so remote in space and time that she might someday forget Alistair. If she accepted, she would spend the rest of her life trying to control her mind and body and make them forget his touch.

She couldn't bear to give him either answer, and so she would give him none. He had said she could have time to make her decision, and so she would take time. For a while, at least, she could postpone a decision that—whichever answer she gave him—meant a part of her would die with the memory of him. Very slowly she levered herself out of Uncle Andrew's chair and shuffled across the kitchen to feed Marigold, moving as though she were a thousand years old.

When she opened the front door a little while later to let the cat out into a pale gold morning, Pen found a white envelope on her doorstep; apparently she had missed it last night in the dark. Bending stiffly, she picked it up and read her name in Nigel's angular hand. With fingers that fumbled a little she opened it and read it numbly, too drained even to realize that it didn't really sound like either her old friend, mocking and merry, or the new Nigel, cold and calculating, whom she had met so disastrously the night of his party.

"Bo Peep," it began, and she read the salutation with the tiniest weary smile, which faded as she read on:

Opening night is tomorrow, and the cast is all home taking a last break, but I wanted to see you and drove up for the day. The little old party in the next cottage told me she had seen you go out early this morning, so I waited and occupied myself like a properly respectful tourist. I have now visited Dove Cottage and

the museum, made the pilgrimage to Wordsworth's grave, and investigated every shop in
town. At the little weaving shop, by the way,
I recognized your watercolors and found myself a few minutes later the owner of a sketch
of Buttermere and a green-and-blue rug I was
given to believe was also your work; you see
how devoted I am. But then I ran out of
things to do, and surely the same ought to
have happened to you long ago. So leave your
sheep (I counted fourteen on that hill behind
your house, but they can obviously manage
without you) and come back to me, because it
isn't obvious that I can. Marry me and
reform me, Pen, before I'm completely un-
redeemable. I miss you.

Nigel

She read the note twice and then folded it carefully, slipping it back into its envelope. In front of
her, Marigold was intently stalking a bug on the
path, and Pen watched without really seeing as she
thought laboriously about Nigel's note. He had
driven all the way from London to see her, and
whatever was the situation with the woman who
shared his apartment, he still wanted to marry her.
The morning air seemed a tiny bit warmer to Pen's
chilled heart, and for a moment she hoped that
perhaps the old Nigel wasn't completely gone.
Then she admitted sadly to herself that it didn't
matter anyway, because the old Pen was gone

forever. The girl Nigel wanted back was heart-whole and could someday love him; the girl who read his letter had already given her heart somewhere else and lost it for good. Whatever it was that Nigel needed from her, she couldn't give; she couldn't help him, and she couldn't even help herself.

A few last weary tears spilled down Pen's cheeks, but she wiped them away; they brought no comfort. What did bring comfort, though, was Uncle Andrew's loom. She knew that from past experience, and for the next few days she spent most of her time losing herself in its ageless rhythm. Perhaps guessing she needed time to think, Alistair left her alone and worked on the book by himself, and even the children seemed to find other companions, so that Pen had long uninterrupted hours of weaving. And as she made the separate threads of yarn into a whole rug of leaf-green and fell-brown beauty, somehow she also gathered up the tangled bits of her emotions and made them into a kind of calm acceptance. She couldn't marry Nigel—instead she wrote him a brief friendly letter explaining only that she thought their lives had grown too different for marriage to be a success. And she might not marry Alistair. She would work with him until the book was done and enjoy whatever he could give her, and if that proved to be unbearably little, then she would refuse his proposal and bid the children goodbye, rent Uncle Andrew's cottage and leave

Grasmere—probably for Tasmania, she decided with the first slight return of her sense of humor.

When the leafy rug was done, Pen cut it free of the loom, brushed its soft mohair fluffy and then carried it upstairs to her own bedroom, laying it across the foot of her bed. And then she went up the lane at last to find Alistair.

In the third cottage the children greeted her with their usual tumult. When she had sorted it out, she went on into Alistair's study and found it in even worse disorder than she'd seen before. Alistair himself sat distractedly at his desk in the middle of the confusion, with both hands full of papers and others piled in slippery stacks all around him.

Catching sight of her, he said nothing about her absence in the past few days but only exclaimed in heartfelt tones, "Thank God you're here, Penelope."

Then with no other salutation and no reference to what lay unanswered between them, he went on, gesturing with one full hand to the far side of the room where Levvy lay dolefully on top of a heap of old newspapers.

"That one there just did his one trick—the one where he brings me in the morning paper all wet and torn," he explained in a disgusted parenthesis, his black brows snapping down as Pen surprised herself by giggling. "Laugh if you like, young woman, but that abominable beast also had in his soggy clutch a letter from my publisher that I had never seen before. It was dated weeks ago and was virtually illegible. Heaven only knows where Leviathan got it or, worse yet, where he's been keeping it, but the important thing is, it informed me that the editing deadline on the book has been moved up to the fifteenth of October, and the finished manuscript is due in the publisher's offices in London no later than the fifteenth of August.''

He cast an appalled look around the untidy room, where pages of typescript covered every horizontal surface, and demanded, "Have you any idea, my girl, what a miracle it's going to take to get this thing *anywhere* by the fifteenth of August?"

CHAPTER FIFTEEN

INCREDIBLY, THEY DID. Pen herself was the miracle, setting aside the stories she'd been working on and cutting back on her weaving so that she could give herself full-time to Alistair's book. She tracked down missing pages, proofread typed ones and even pecked out on the typewriter ones that were still in longhand. Then while Alistair wrestled with notes and references and credits, she produced final versions of her drawings and captioned them, organized the last of his sketchy diagrams and made final copies of them, and inserted both drawings and diagrams into the text in the places they had agreed upon.

It was a painstaking, laborious job, but Pen found she didn't mind. She spent nearly all her waking hours with Alistair, and as they worked they had to share meals and laughter, ideas and arguments. As he had suggested that night in her kitchen, they did get to know each other better, and it felt to Pen as if he had finally lowered his guard and let her past it, so that she worked every day now not with the icicle or the cool employer but with a good companion she'd glimpsed only a

few times before. He said little that was personal,
and he never touched her at all, so that sometimes
she had to move away from him because nearness
made her body clamor for that all too well
remembered sensation—but he was an entertaining companion and a good friend, and as her
spirits rebounded Pen told herself that that was a
great deal. Delicately and cautiously they were at
least building a relationship as partners, and
although Alistair never mentioned his proposal,
Pen thought about it often. Perhaps sharing his
home and his work and Corey and Megan might
be enough satisfaction after all, if she could only
ignore the longings that filled her heart—and her
body.

Ironically, she was spending less time with the
children than ever, in spite of the fact that they
would influence her final decision about whether
or not to marry their uncle. Immersed in the book
as she and Alistair were now, she saw Megan and
Corey only irregularly. The youngsters, apparently content these days to know that Pen and their
uncle were both available in Alistair's littered
study, depended on them less and less for security
or even company. They were still favorite companions, of course, but so were Banny and Edward, so had Ann been, and so were most of the
children in the village.

Pen and Alistair had both been half-aware of
the children's new independence, but they didn't
really register it until St. Oswald's Day came in

early August, and they took a rare day off from work to join the rest of Grasmere for the rush bearing.

It was a day-long ceremony based on the ancient custom of spreading rushes on cold stone floors to help keep out the chill. Every year the old rushes were replaced with new ones cut from the lake, and that tradition had become linked to the memory of the village's patron saint. He had been a Saxon king who once stopped in his feasting to give gold to the poor, and the day the new rushes were laid, that generosity was remembered with a procession in the saint's honor.

Led by the village band, little boys carried images of King Oswald's generous hand made from rushes and flowers, and little girls carried a sheet filled with more flowers. Behind them came the rest of the village, crowding into the church for a service of thanksgiving. In the press of people, Pen and Alistair were separated from Banny and Edward, but they found a space toward the back of the old building, standing side by side in the sweet fresh rushes. Then Pen looked anxiously for the children; they had waved from among the other youngsters, but now she couldn't seem to find them. Lost in the crowd and unable to see her uncle and Pen, would Megan panic and think she'd been abandoned?

Scanning faces, Pen discovered Banny and Edward smiling in the far aisle and caught sight of Ian Ballantyne's kind leathery countenance, but she couldn't locate the children. She tugged worriedly at Alistair's arm to tell him and just then found Megan's small face, surrounded by a group of friends and totally rapt. Corey nearby was intent, too, and neither one seemed to show any need to know where Pen and Alistair were.

Looking down at Pen's insistence, Alistair followed her eyes to the children and realized what she had just seen, too. For a moment he simply studied the two enthralled little faces, then he met the delighted gaze Pen turned up to him and smiled into her eyes. Without turning back to the hymnal he held, they both sang the words of thanksgiving they knew from memory.

Two nights later they took time off from the book again, at Pen's insistence. A village meeting had been called to consider a proposal to build a discotheque. Guessing what Pen would think of that idea, Banny had made sure she knew about the meeting, and in turn Pen had enlisted Alistair, too. Leaving the children in Banny's garden to keep Edward company, since his rheumatism had flared up again, the other three walked down the lane through the chirping evening to the hall where the meeting was being held. Inside virtually all of Grasmere had gathered, and they settled for seats in the back corner.

After the meeting came to order, the young man from Liverpool who wanted to build the discotheque stood up and described his project, speaking in glowing terms of its attractive plan and the

vitality it would add to the town. While most of
the villagers sat silently with their arms folded, he
produced drawings of the building he hoped to
construct and charts of the tourist boom he hoped
it would create among those who wanted some
nightlife with their holidays. As he spoke, faster
and faster, his slicked back hair began to fall
about his forehead a little; he shed the jacket to his
blue-and-white pin-striped suit, and a fine sheen
of perspiration appeared on his upper lip.

In spite of all his energy and enthusiasm, however, Pen found that when he had finished she was
just as horrified by his proposal as she had been
when he started. Looking to either side of her, she
found Banny sitting rigidly upright in her seat with
her lips tightly pursed and Alistair leaning back in
his chair with no expression whatsoever. Knowing
as clearly as if she had spoken what Banny
thought, Pen wondered what Alistair's opinion of
all this would be.

The rest of the village was also hard to read. A
few of the younger women were nodding agreement with the plan, and one thin young man stood
up and spoke in favor of it. Banny looked away
from him, and Pen knew sympathetically that she
was remembering her Jamie, but almost everyone
else sat silently. Just as Pen began to worry that
the proposal might be accepted simply because no
one spoke out against it, Ian Ballantyne rose slowly, removing the ever-present pipe to speak.

"It seems to me," he said thoughtfully, "that

yon lad has a fine set of drawings and charts and
wants to build a grand, glossy sort of a place." A
slight stir spread across the room as people shifted
in their seats and murmured to their neighbors,
turning to look at Ian. Knowing how well re-
spected he was in the village, Pen felt her spirits
plummet. Then Ian went on speaking.

"My only question to us all, however, is
whether or not Grasmere is the right kind of town
for a fine Liverpool dance hall. Granted, it would
probably bring us a few more of the holidaymakers. Is that what we want?" Without answering his own question, he sat down.

And there it was, the issue Banny and Edward
worried about, Uncle Andrew had rampaged
about and Pen herself now fretted about: would
Grasmere stay as it was, or would it risk losing its
old traditions—like the rush bearing—to new
ones? Ian Ballantyne had identified the problem
and made his own feelings clear, but now silence
fell again.

Pen glanced at Banny and found her still sitting
with her head bowed. Alistair, too, made no move
to speak. And so before she realized what she was
doing, Pen was on her own feet, speaking.

As had happened with Ian, everyone swiveled to
look at her, and her first words came out in a
squeak. "I'm Penelope Bryce, and I'm new here,"
she said, stating the obvious, but then she
gathered her wits and went on. "As some of you
know, Andrew McKenzie was my uncle, and he

lived here for fifty years. From him I inherited his cottage and perhaps his love for this village, so I'd like to speak for him and for myself, if I may.''

Several people nodded, so Pen drew a deep breath and continued, gaining strength that steadied her voice. ''I've lived and worked here for only a few months—'' had she once come here meaning to stay only a few weeks, she wondered briefly ''—but I've had enough time to find out that Grasmere is a very special place. Any place can have a discotheque, or cinemas, or glamorous nightclubs, but only a few places have as much beauty and peace and serenity as Grasmere. Since we have something rare and wonderful, shouldn't we keep it?''

More heads nodded, and those who had been in favor of the plan looked away from her eager eyes. ''After all,'' she finished, suddenly breathless, ''we can still go somewhere else to dance!'' And then her knees abruptly gave out beneath her, and she sat, while a little ripple of friendly laughter moved around the room.

''Penelope, lass, you were grand!'' Banny was patting her hand excitedly. ''I just didn't have the heart to speak out myself, but Andrew would have been proud of you.'' She chuckled warmly and added, ''And not just because he didn't much hold with dancing anyway! But, child, you're as white as a sheet. Come along out of here and we'll get you some fresh air.''

She urged Pen to her feet, and around them

people smilingly made room for them to pass. Alistair murmured, "I'll stay a bit and see what they decide," and then they were outside.

"Whew!" Pen gulped in the cool water-scented air gratefully while Banny watched with a sympathetic smile. "I didn't know I was going to speak until it was too late, and then stage fright caught up with me." She leaned back against the whitewashed stones behind her while her knees steadied and added, "I'm afraid I got a bit carried away, Banny, and forgot I haven't much right to talk like that to people who've lived here all their lives."

"Nonsense, child," Banny returned, leading her slowly toward their lane. "We all have the same right to speak about what concerns us, and you certainly spoke like Andrew's kin!" She gave a low delighted laugh. "Och, Penelope, when you got going properly you looked so like Andrew on one of his rampages that it was a joy to see you. I only wish Edward could have seen the show!"

Pen couldn't help laughing, too, and they strolled on up the lane. Before they reached Banny's cottage, though, Alistair caught up with them, and both women turned to look at him with questioning expressions.

He stepped in between them and linked arms with one on each side, answering their faces. "Well, I gather you will both be pleased to hear that Grasmere is going to do its dancing elsewhere for a while yet," he said with a note of amusement in his voice, and Banny gave a little unladylike cheer that made her sound at least as young as the other two. Pen nodded happily, as well, but his casual touch on her arm—the first unnecessary contact in all these long weeks—made a warmth seep through her whole body as disastrously as if she'd been a statue of ice. Coming on top of her stage fright of a little while ago, it undid her completely, and she couldn't have answered aloud if she'd been asked whether she wanted to live or to die. Luckily, it didn't come to that; Alistair simply gave her a long unfamiliar look—it couldn't possibly have been pride, could it—and they all walked on.

At Banny's cottage the children galloped out to meet them, shouting back their farewells to Edward, and Alistair kissed the old hand that had lain in the crook of his left arm; delighted by the gallant gesture and the results of the meeting, Banny went smilingly in to report to Edward. Then, while Megan and Corey raced on home, Alistair and Pen sauntered the few steps to her cottage, and he said good-night with the same graceful gesture before following the youngsters on up the lane. Bemusedly Pen drifted inside, wondering if her kiss had perhaps been longer than Banny's.

The next night they finished the book, working together in Alistair's deplorable study. While he struggled with the final copy, Pen quietly collected and sorted the rough draft so that it could be put away in case it was ever needed for future reference. He sat at his overloaded desk, and she moved unobtrusively around the room, picking pages off the floor, out of books and even from behind the sofa's rumpled cushions—the last being a discovery that, after so much hard work and tension, made a spring of laughter bubble up in her. Trying not to disturb him, she struggled not to let the laughter overflow. She must have made some little sound, however, because he glanced up just as she extracted the last battered page from under a cushion. At his bright inquiring look, she waved the crumpled page with a helpless gesture as she fought to retain some decorum, and then, losing the battle decisively, she gave way at his sheepish expression to a gurgle of laughter that rapidly became a torrent.

He simply watched her for a moment, seeing the way her changeable eyes lightened as the merriment danced in them, so that they nearly matched the smoke blue of her shirt. Then with a precise little motion he set aside the pen he had been holding and straightened the edges of the pages in front of him, stood up and walked over to her with that long easy stride of his. She was still chuckling when he reached her, but her laughter turned to astonishment as he took the thick sheaf of pages from her and with a quick deliberate movement flung them into the air. And while the pages rained down around them both, he swept back her tangled hair, capturing her bewildered face in his hands, and kissed her thoroughly and with deliberation.

"That," he said softly a few inches from her lips, "is for your temerity in laughing at me, and this is for your patience in putting up with me until the book was done."

Another kiss followed his words immediately, but after that Pen lost all notion of the passing of time, sinking blissfully into the rapture of that touch she had longed for, dreamed of and thought she would never feel again. His first kiss had been a swift teasing punishment, but the second was devastating in its gentleness. Slowly and deliberately his lips took hers, cool at first and then warming with the contact. Her own lips quivered a moment before they parted beneath his touch, and gathering her closer to him he began to explore the softness of her mouth. She yielded to him, and a little muffled cry of gladness escaped her as he searched ever deeper and more insistently.

His hands, which had begun by cupping her face to his, now moved slowly to rest a moment on her shoulders, then her waist and next her hips. There they caressed her with a deep rolling motion that made her knees go weak. She clung to him for support, and he gave it to her by holding her still more tightly against the hard male strength of his body, always caressing her hips with one hand so that she gasped a little and her breath was hot on his lips. His other hand at the same time rose to her waist and tugged her shirt free of her belt, then slipped beneath the fabric to rest against her bare skin. Low in her throat she made a tiny moan of assent and turned slightly to free herself to his touch, and his hand rose across the shivering softness of her skin until it reached her breasts. They quivered and then pushed themselves into his fingers, while Pen—delirious with the pleasure so long denied—trembled from head to foot.

After a brief eternity, his hands slipped away and his lips lifted from hers. He still held her in his arms, however; this time he hadn't broken from her hold, and a brief ripple of breathless fear subsided. Even if he didn't repeat this embrace, he wasn't denying it. In fact, when she could look up dizzily she found him gazing down at her with eyes that were the intense blue of a very hot flame. She met that look for an instant, her own eyes ablaze, and the searing contact did nothing whatsoever to steady her ragged breathing. Then, both ecstatic and frightened, she wrenched her eyes away with a delicious little quiver of delight. She discovered she was trembling in the iron arms that supported her, and to distract Alistair from such an absurd— and betraying—reaction, she tried to gather her wits and murmured almost at random in a husky sensual voice that sounded like a stranger's, "Done?"

A rumble of laughter shook the broad expanse of white turtleneck she had hidden her face against, and at that she looked up again indignantly.

"Yes, my gray-eyed Penelope, done—thanks to you," he said exultantly, his eyes still brilliantly blue. "And again thanks to you, better than anything else I've written."

He put both hands on her shoulders and held her away from him, saying into her flushed and upturned face, "And now, my girl, while I chase the kids into bed and ring Banny up to beg for her presence in our absence, you have one half hour to go home and dress for a celebration."

"Half an hour!" she repeated in a voice that was suddenly hers again, simultaneously delighted and horrified.

Laughing, he turned her toward the door, repeating firmly, "Half an hour. And tell that cat you'll be late getting home!" he called after her an instant before the door slammed on the sound of her racing feet.

Back in her own cottage, Pen didn't have time even to relive the ecstasies of Alistair's embrace. Instead she dashed upstairs to her closet and began rummaging desperately for something to wear. Alistair hadn't told her where they were going, but no matter where they went she wanted for some reason to bedazzle him by producing a Penelope he'd never seen before. She wasted no time wondering why that should be one of her reactions to his kisses but flung aside with impatient hands the tunics and trousers, sweaters and jerseys that clad the everyday Pen, burrowing deeper in the closet for the few good clothes she had brought north on her working holiday all those months ago.

There weren't many of the good clothes; she had left most of her sophisticated city things at home and packed for a generally casual outdoor life. Now her rocketing spirits dived as she rejected a beautiful but sedate forest-green suit and even her good black dress, its becoming vee neckline edged with a wide collar of tiny soft pleats. Everything else seemed even worse, until one final trip to the closet produced a last garment that had been crowded into the farthest corner, and she unearthed it with a little crow of triumph.

Goodness only knew why she had brought it, but even creased from several months' residence in the closet it was still a spectacular dress. A long caftan made from fabric she loved, it was a dress she had spent recklessly on after she saw it in the window of a London boutique. It was made of raw silk in varying stripes of aquamarine, turquoise and sea green, and she had known intuitively from the start that it would set off the rich color of her hair and the fairness of her skin. With its plunging neckline and loose flowing sleeves, vertical stripes broken only by a broad aquamarine sash around her waist, the dress also gave her a dramatic willowy grace, but she didn't know that.

Satisfied at last that she had discovered the right dress for celebrating, Pen raced downstairs to iron the caftan, then back in her room hung its soft folds near at hand while she made up her face for the first time since she had come there. She had

just finished dressing when Alistair knocked at the
door below, and with a last glance at the mirror
and a farewell pat for Marigold, who had watched
this whole process curiously, she caught up a
delicate stole and a tiny evening bag, calling him
to come in. Then she swept down the stairs to present herself for his bedazzlement.

Wearing a perfectly tailored blue gray suit with
a crisp pale blue shirt and a darker tie, Alistair
himself was sleekly handsome, and Pen's heart
seemed to do a reckless somersault. Those eyes—
which his suit made almost impossibly blue—were
fixed on her, and the black brows raised, as she
came elegantly and imperiously down the stairs to
meet him, stopping finally on the lowest step for
his inspection.

He took his time about it, noting everything
about her: the little sandals with their narrow
straps crossing at her ankles; the marvelous caftan
and the smooth shadowy hollow its neckline exposed; the pale column of her throat, circled by a
fine gold chain; and the silky chestnut tresses held
high on her head by a tiny flower clip and then
cascading down in artful carelessness.

All this he noticed immediately, and Pen,
watching him eagerly to see if she had succeeded in
astounding him, glimpsed instead a far more complicated expression, as he saw that the ruffled girl
whose breathless pliant body had clung to his half
an hour ago, while she gave him back passionate
kiss for kiss, was now an almost theatrically

beautiful woman, glossy and perfect. Seeing that, he looked almost angry for a moment, and she was reminded of the hostile expression on his face that first night he had come to collect the children from her keeping. But before she could really identify the look in his eyes, it was gone, disappearing as his inspection reached her face. There he found not a cold supercilious beauty but warm, lovely Pen—and a clear gaze that waited for his verdict with both a child's trepidation and a woman's confidence.

For a minute or two he looked deep into that entrancing gaze, and his own eyes warmed now with the appreciation she'd hoped for. Taking her hand to lead her down the final step to his side, he quoted softly, almost more to himself than to her, " 'But still the hands of memory weave the blissful dreams of long ago.' " And when she stood beside him with her bright face lifted to his, he added, "Lovely Penelope, you are a celebration in yourself," lifting the hand he still held to kiss it before he escorted her out to the Rover.

As he seated her in the luxurious car, she asked excitedly, "Where are we going, Alistair?"

But he only smiled a little and said dryly, "Not to the village disco, that's certain." Pink cheeked, she laughed and had to wait and see.

Afterward the details of that first enchanted evening together tended to be lost in a haze of happiness for Pen. In due time she did find out that he was taking her to Windermere. There they dined in a hotel at the water's edge, where they could look out a large window and watch the last brave banners of sunset give way to the soft scarves of night on the water. She knew, too, that the man who sat across the small table from her was warm and witty, charming and attentive. And as their conversation, filled with laughter, ranged over a dozen different topics, she knew one other thing: though she wouldn't have thought it possible, now with every passing minute she loved Alistair Heath even more.

She had no idea what she ate—only that it was delicious—or exactly what they said, but after dinner they strolled along the lakeshore in the summer-scented night, and occasional lights illumined the curves that smiling drew over the usual angles of his face. And as he took her in his arms again in the darkness, she knew a sense of wonder and deep thankfulness. When he had denied their first embrace, and later when he had proposed a loveless marriage, she had thought she would never feel his quickening touch again. But this afternoon he had kissed her passionately, and now his hands were warm on her shoulders again. Trembling a little with joy, she didn't question this change or her happiness.

Instead she dared to reach up and trace those new curves of his face with tender fingers, until he caught her hand and kissed it, pressing his lips to her palm and each fingertip in turn. Then he exchanged her hand for her lips, exploring them slowly, lingeringly, with a deliberate restraint that was far different from his incendiary kisses in the afternoon. Almost unbearably moved by his gentleness, she felt her heart beat thickly in her throat and her breathing caught a little while her lips trembled beneath his.

Eventually, though, his mouth slipped away from hers and down the white column of her neck, following the silken stripes of her caftan down to the warm shadowed valley between her breasts, and she caught fire again. He kissed the scented softness of that hollow and then pushed aside the fabric with his lips until he reached the velvety summit of her breast. And there he tarried while she blazed beneath his touch. His tongue fluttered delicately on her tremulous skin, and she replied with little broken murmurs of delight. Around them the only other sounds were the gentle lapping of water at the shore and the whisper of leaves on the dark trees overhead. They said nothing in words, and she was content to have it so; she was saying everything with her body.

That magical evening was their official celebration of the finishing of the book, but it was only the first of many times they went out together in the next weeks. Nearly every evening at the children's bedtime a smiling Banny appeared at the door of the last cottage in the lane and watched with a pleased expression as the young couple said good-night to Megan and Corey, and then Alistair led a glowing Pen to the silver car.

Together they dined and danced, laughed and argued, learning about the region around them and the common country of their two minds. Although he had proposed a loveless marriage to her, it nevertheless seemed to Pen as though Alistair had decided to court her, and she reveled in it. For her, being with him was always as exciting as that first evening, and she refused to speculate why the rules had changed so much. Still, he never mentioned his proposal and never spoke of loving her, so she, too, said nothing with her voice about her feelings for him.

Instead with her body she learned a whole new language to tell him wordlessly things she had never wanted to tell anyone else. She told him with the gentle touch of her hands, the tender gift of her lips and the aroused quickening of her breath. At the same time she learned the delights of a wealth of new sensations she'd never known before, gradually losing her earlier fear that this lovely intimacy would end as suddenly as their first kiss. It didn't, and she gloried in every encounter between them, discovering in the set of his ears, the shape of his fingernails, the hollow of his shoulder new beauties of human architecture that even her artist's mind had never dreamed of. Rejoicing in them, she came to know them well.

To have Alistair speak of love, of course, would have made her joy complete, but simply to touch and be touched was more happiness than she had ever thought to have. With newfound wisdom, then, she contented herself for now with the wonders of showing her love and didn't try to measure out their relationship in words.

As by night, so, too, by day most of Alistair's time was spent with Pen and usually the children, as well. He shut the door on his disheveled study, saying firmly that he deserved a holiday, and they all joined in the village celebrations as preparations were begun for the climax of the summer season, the annual Grasmere Sports.

CHAPTER SIXTEEN

THE FIRST PALE TINTS of yellow showed in the trees and the bracken was turning gold as bright tents blossomed along the lakeshore and trailers crowded the roads. The youth hostels and hotels were filled, too, and all of Lakeland seemed to have come to celebrate the famous games, invented more than a hundred years earlier to preserve the local style of wrestling. Now at the edge of the village an open field was ringed by a kaleidoscope of cars and trailers with their passengers. Under gay marquees, pork pies and spicy gingerbread were for sale, and everywhere the excitement of the games sounded in laughter and cheers.

Along with the others Pen cheered through the long leap and the high leap, and through the wrestling events in which fair-haired giants from the fells, trained by years of throwing sheep, clasped their hands behind each other's back and tried to throw each other. Even the inescapable rain didn't dampen her spirits, though it wet her clothing clear through, for when Megan and Corey crowded against their Uncle Lister under his old black umbrella, Pen inevitably found herself beyond the edge of its shelter. Uncaring, she shouted herself hoarse during the grueling guides' races up Butter Crags and back, and when the winner returned in what seemed like an impossibly short time she crowed triumphantly to see that he was a middle-aged farmer with a kindly face who had been running in the games for years.

Not surprisingly, when the day's events ended, Pen's voice was virtually gone, and damp tendrils of hair framed an overheated face on which bright color flamed along her cheekbones. Flanked by a child on either side, she walked laughing but weary through the village, and Alistair, who had watched her enthusiasm all day long with amused appreciation, looked at her now with some concern.

Back in his cottage, he sent the children upstairs to undress and wait for their baths while Pen sank exhaustedly on the lowest step, and then said to her, "I'd bundle you into a hot bath, too, my girl, if those two weren't nearby to make sure I observe the proprieties."

The look that came with his words seemed to be both stern and regretful, and Pen's color deepened still further as her wayward imagination immediately produced intriguing images of those proprieties being flouted. An embarrassed little chuckle tried to conceal her thoughts, but it was so husky that it only made Alistair gaze at her more intently, and she was almost grateful when a sneeze interrupted them both.

His automatic, "Bless you," was nearly lost in the volley of sneezes that followed the first prophetic one. When she was able to see clearly again, Pen was clutching an unfamiliar white handkerchief, and Alistair was holding a glass half-full of some dark amber liquid.

"First that one—" a nod to the handkerchief "—and then this—" raising the glass "—and then I'll take you home, draw your bath and hope you have sense enough to get into it as soon as I'm decently out of the way."

Somehow, drawing her bath didn't sound nearly as interesting as bundling her into one had sounded, and regret had given way to simple concern in his expression. Besides, to tell the truth, she still felt a bit addled by so much sneezing. Sadly she mopped her eyes with an obedient hand and reached out the other for Alistair's glass, and when she'd drained that unthinkingly she suddenly felt a good deal more addled. The amber liquid had coursed down her throat like lava, and the coughing that resulted sent her back to her handkerchief for further repairs.

When she could speak again, she croaked indignantly, "What on earth was that?"

"Brandy old enough to be your father, my girl, and a good deal too dignified for you to be choking over."

"Then why—"

"Yours not to reason why; yours but to do and survive," he misquoted unrepentantly. "It might just ward off the attack of that cold you're catching." He left her for what seemed only a moment, but she must have dozed off, only vaguely aware from the sounds upstairs that Alistair was bathing the children and seeing them off to sleep.

When he returned he gently roused her, and without further ado he pulled her to her feet, wrapped her tightly in a heavy old duffel coat he produced from somewhere—rather as if she were Megan's age, Pen thought a bit muzzily but without rancor—and with an arm around her shoulders led her away.

When they reached her cottage, Alistair sat Pen in Uncle Andrew's chair in the kitchen while he set the kettle to boil on the stove and built up a hot cheery fire on the hearth. It seemed only a moment later that he handed her a steaming mug, and she cupped it gratefully in cold fingers as he disappeared.

He was back in a few minutes, and setting her mug aside he picked her neatly up and carried her, duffel coat and all, up the steep stairs to her room.

Taken by surprise again, Pen seriously considered protesting such high-handed actions, but her novel means of transportation was pleasant, so instead she surveyed the firm chin and the rough cheek that her position in Alistair's arms brought so close and announced delightedly, "You've got a dimple!"

The owner of the dimple greeted this observation with an inelegant snort that shook the wool-clad shoulder against which she rested, and attracted by the movement she burrowed her face into his neck, breathing in a scent blended of soap and shaving lotion and warm skin. Her face reappeared reluctantly only as Alistair set her on her own feet beside her bed. He vanished, and the sound of running water stopped, while Pen peered owlishly at the bedclothes turned back invitingly and the orange cat curled at the foot of the bed.

"That cat is imitating a hot-water bottle for your feet, since you don't seem to own one," Alistair said, returning to her side and peeling off the duffel coat. "Your bed is ready and your bath drawn," he continued, "and I expect you to make use of them both immediately, although in reverse order."

He had been removing her sodden jacket, too, as he spoke, and when he finished he looked down into gray eyes that blinked bemusedly at him. So far he had moved and spoken almost methodically, but now the jacket dropped to lie forgotten at their feet, and the big hands that had gone to unbutton the gay plaid flannel shirt she wore stopped on the third button, resting against her hot skin. There was a rather long silence.

"Penelope..." he said at last in a somewhat altered voice. A feathery fringe of lashes had lowered over her eyes, and now it quivered slightly as his thumbs moved gently, as if of their own volition, at the edge of her shirt.

He swallowed loudly but didn't go on speaking,

and after waiting vainly for whatever he meant to say, she politely filled the silence by reminding him helpfully, "Penelope was a weaver."

For a moment more he was still, and the small space between them began to pulsate delicately. Then he drew an audible breath and murmured, "And you've woven a silken web around me of such soft and lovely threads that I'd be a fool to want to escape."

Pen tried to sort that out, hazily conscious that she wanted badly to know what he meant, but her mind seemed to be moving very slowly, and she was still puzzling at it with her forehead creased in concentration when she was distracted by his rueful laugh. She looked up again, and his lips smoothed away the crease with a single gentle kiss. Then his hands dropped slowly to his sides, and he said, "I'll tell you again, my Penelope, when you're a little less muddled."

She nodded carefully, deciding it didn't matter if he thought she was muddled as long as he called her his Penelope and went on looking at her in that unfamiliar way that made her so conscious of her heartbeat. And as long as he held her. Her attention shifted to the sudden cooling of her skin where his hands had been. He'd taken away the touch that was somehow so reassuring and hypnotic, and she gave a little sad murmur of protest, pressing herself wistfully against the warmth of his heavy fisherman's sweater. His hands came up automatically to steady her, and she raised her face hopefully. The look was still in his eyes, and encouraged, she offered him her lips. He hesitated only an instant and then took them.

At the contact she flowered for him as she had never dared to do before. Suddenly it all seemed foolish—why had she ever looked in Nigel's arms for what she could find only here in Alistair's? And why had she ever fought so hard against loving this man, or speaking her love? Perhaps there had once been a reason to control or disguise her emotions, but now she couldn't seem to remember what it was, while the first cool touch of his lips warmed on hers and he searched her mouth with the slow deliberation of a bee drinking nectar.

In fact, she couldn't seem to remember or to think much of anything—all she could do was feel, as the plaid shirt slipped off her shoulders and dropped to join the jacket at her feet, so that those hands she loved could move almost uninterrupted to trace the line of her throat along her shoulders and down her trembling arms. Only a pair of lacy straps limited his freedom, and she raised hands grown clumsy with eagerness to fumble at them until there was a small tearing sound and they were gone.

His fingers followed hers to the boundary she had erased, and there she could feel them hesitate and lose their customary sureness. Somehow his hesitation moved her almost unbearably, filling her with tenderness, and with a sense of wonder at both of them she heard herself croon a little note of encouragement against his lips.

Still he lifted those lips from hers, detached her from him with unsteady hands and set her at arm's length, looking at her with eyes clouded with passion. She met them slumberously, and a tiny smile curved her reddened lips.

"I think," he said rather thickly, "that you had better go have your hot bath before it's too late."

Slowly and carefully Pen shook her head, and the smile grew deeper as their eyes clung. His breathing was ragged, and she knew without thinking it that now, for the first time in all their duels, she was more sure than he. That instinctive knowing was a tender warmth within her, but it didn't stop the gooseflesh that feathered along her skin now that his body heat was gone. Absently she clasped her arms across her ribs, and his eyes fell to her movement as it deepened the silky hollow between her breasts. She stayed as she was, and the distance between them that had pulsated earlier began to throb. Then, with a slow and dreamlike inevitability, he reached for her again.

This time he began with her lips but then trailed his mouth down her neck and along her collarbone, making little rivulets of fire that led him at last with agonizing slowness to the velvety skin of her breasts. There he lingered, describing delicate circles with his tongue. Tenderness was swallowed by desire in her, and she gasped his name, clawing at the thick wool of his sweater with urgent hands.

Finally she found the hem of the sweater and slid her hands beneath it to tug his shirt loose at the waist. Then she could feel the smooth heat of his skin, and for a moment that satisfied the desperate hunger that had begun to gnaw at her. Her fingers clutched at hard muscles, loosened to race over the firm ridges of his ribs and clutched his neck so that his face was pressed against her breasts and she felt the roughness of his beard.

But then, as she loosened her hold again, he turned his bent head against her and took one pink nipple between his lips, kneading it gently with his mouth and then flicking it with the tip of his tongue. The little tugging motions reverberated through her whole body, and she stood motionless for the space of one long shuddering breath, her eyes open wide and fixed on the dark head she cradled to her. Sudden inexplicable tears filled her eyes and a feeling of love welled up in her. Far away, in some remote corner of her brain, she remembered that day at Hardknott when she had looked at Alistair and the sleeping children and imagined they all belonged to her. The next day she had run from them all, never dreaming that even that path could someday bring her here, where his lips beseeched her so sweetly.

She closed her eyes, but his mouth only shifted from one breast to the other, and a hot wild tide rose within her until she tore frantically at the fabric that still separated them from each other. Releasing her for a moment, he shucked off

sweater and shirt together in one rapid gesture and
reached for her again, taking her to him slowly
this time, to prolong anticipation of the first ex-
quisite contact of their skin. That contact came at
last, though, and she didn't know which of them it
was that cried out wordlessly.

She knew, however, that her body was turning
to lava in his arms, and as it flowed into a searing
river of sensation her shaking legs lost the ability
to carry her and she sagged helplessly against him,
now weak and powerless. He caught her as she
slipped down his chest and lifted her up and back
so that she lay across the edge of the bed behind
them. Then he swung her legs onto the bed, as
well, and followed her down so that his weight lay
partly across her, and Marigold leaped from the
bed and disappeared.

Pen was unaware of the cat, just as she was
unaware of everything except the sweet solid
weight that pressed against her. While her hands
roamed ceaselessly over Alistair's broad back, and
he murmured incoherent snatches of endearments,
she hungrily kissed his lips, his cheeks, his chin,
the throbbing hollow of his throat and the tangle
of fine curly hair on his chest. Breathing in the
faintly spicy scent of him, she kissed the arm that
supported part of his weight, feeling the tremors
that ran through it. The arm buckled beneath her
touch, and he descended to catch her busy lips
with his own again, rolling back and pulling her
on top of him while he explored her mouth search-

ingly with a tongue that could no longer be denied.

She couldn't have denied him anyway. Her clamoring body would deny him nothing; she knew it now and gloried in it. Instinctively she slid sideways and settled herself more deeply on the bed, shifting her legs against his so that his hard thigh slipped between hers and she clasped it tightly. But suddenly he lifted himself away from her. Startled, her eyes flew open, and she found him looking at her with a gaze whose lake of blue fire could drown them both. For a moment she swam in it, then she let herself sink into it, relaxing slowly into a feeling of sweet necessity.

She felt rather than saw him turn so that he could reach her feet, and then she felt him tug off the socks she wore. He moved again, and she felt a kiss burn briefly on the inside of her ankle. Then his hands were at her waist, and her own went to help him with the unfamiliar fastenings. They came free at last, and he lifted her with one taut arm while the other hand gently peeled away first her sturdy navy trousers and then the flimsy lace she wore beneath them.

The last of her clothes dropped from his fingers like a discarded chrysalis, and he laid her back tenderly on the bed, moving away from her again afterward. Then he was still, and her eyelids fluttered open. He was leaning on one arm again while his eyes moved with slow delight up the long graceful limbs in front of him. She had a sudden fancy that she lay naked on a giant sun-warmed stone, a willing sacrifice waiting at love's altar. But still a blush spread across her breast, and as his gaze rose lingeringly it followed the crimson glow up her throat and through her cheeks until at last his look met hers. Their eyes clung together, and the hot color ebbed from her skin, while time stopped and even their breathing seemed suspended.

Then abruptly time started again. Without warning, the delicate bridge of their gazes broke as Pen's eyes snapped shut convulsively, and she sneezed once, and three more times in succession. Her eyes still closed, she lay motionless after the last sneeze, and her mind began to function again, slowly and reluctantly. How could she possibly have *sneezed*?

She didn't have long to wonder, however. She heard Alistair let out a deep ragged breath, and then he chuckled hoarsely. "It seems, my beauty, that what you need most is the hot bath I ran for you some time ago."

And before she had time to deny that that was what she needed most, he swung off the bed and for a second time lifted her crossways into his arms, so that she curled kitten fashion against his hard bare chest. She twined her fingers enticingly into the hair on that chest but had no chance to do more before he turned and carried her into the bathroom and dropped her abruptly into the bathtub, without giving her time for more than a squeaked objection.

The bathwater slopped out over the edge of the tub, soaking him thoroughly, and when Pen had wiped more of it out of her eyes she found him nearly as wet as she was, his slacks plastered revealingly to the clean hard lines of his body. He was looking not at her indignant face, however, but at the ripples of bubble bath that lapped gently at her breasts. Seeing that, her expression changed to one of determined mischief, and she slid further into the water so that only rosy nipples parted the bubbles invitingly for his mesmerized stare.

Finally he shut his eyes and swallowed hard, saying, "Minx!" in a voice that croaked. At her little gurgle of delighted laughter his eyes flicked open again and fixed firmly on her face. She lifted shining soapy arms to him, but he shook his head and backed away, muttering hoarsely, "That, my girl, is an invitation I'd rather accept when I'm entirely sure you're not going to catch your death offering it—and that I haven't plied you with too much brandy for you to know what you're offering."

She simply shook her head to that, still pleading with eyes and body, but he refused to come back within her reach, only saying in a thickened voice that struggled to regain control, "That cat is nowhere near enough of a chaperon for you, that's certainly clear."

And a moment later he strode past Marigold— back now and ensconced in Pen's rumpled bed with the infuriating air of one who knows her rights—and down the stairs, leaving damp foot-prints as he went. The door latched firmly behind him, and Alistair vanished wetly into the night; but unlike Pen, he was in absolutely no danger of catching cold.

CHAPTER SEVENTEEN

IN SPITE OF MARIGOLD'S USUAL MINISTRATIONS the next morning, Pen slept late, and when she finally woke she felt so ill that her memory of the evening before was hazy. She knew that Alistair had given her brandy—was that partly why her head felt so like a pumpkin, she wondered—and drawn her bath, and both of those things were surprising enough in themselves, but beyond those facts trembled a memory so much more wonderful that she knew she'd dreamed it. Often enough in these past weeks she had dreamed of Alistair's touch, his kiss, his lovemaking; it must have been the brandy that had made this dream so much more real. Wistfully she tried to relive it, but sneezes kept interrupting her thinking. At any rate, it was all too clear that neither the brandy nor the hot bath had been enough to prevent her from developing a streaming cold.

She had crawled from her bed at last and shrugged her way into the first clothes she found in the closet—yesterday's were still lying crumpled on the floor, but she wasn't alert enough to wonder why—when Alistair and the children, with

Levvy at their sides, knocked at her door. She answered it between sneezes, with a handkerchief to her face, miserably aware of what a sorry sight she must be.

In actual fact, to Alistair this morning even the swimming eyes and the pink nose seemed enchanting, but he had enough sense not to try persuading Pen of that unlikely fact just now. Rather, he just said sympathetically, "Poor Penelope. I was afraid of that," while Megan asked worriedly if Pen was sick.

Pen's nod was interrupted by a bout of sneezing, but when it had passed she pulled herself together and rasped as reassuringly as possible, "Yes, but I'll be fine in a day or two."

At her words Megan looked relieved and Corey fascinated. "You sound interesting, Pen," he announced judiciously.

Alistair laughed at her appalled expression, and at the infectious sound Pen's lips curved in spite of herself. "Well," she growled gruffly at Corey, "I'm glad my sufferings meet with your approval."

They all responded at once.

Corey said guiltily, "I'm sorry, Pen—I didn't mean it that way!"

Megan exclaimed, "Oh, Pen, we don't want you to be sick!"

And beneath the two lighter voices, Pen thought she heard Alistair murmur, "Everything about you meets with my approval."

Her heart missed a beat or two, but then it steadied again as she realized he couldn't possibly have said what she thought she had heard. After all, she was only too conscious that in spite of his proposal all those weeks ago, and in spite of his passionate embraces lately—and her dreams—he had still never spoken of loving her, and there was certainly no reason why he should start this particular morning, when she looked so unromantic and the children were by his side.

She sneezed disconsolately but then roused herself to hearten Megan and Corey. "It's all right, kids. It's really only my dignity that's suffering from the knowledge that I look like a lighthouse."

Holding her aching head very straight, she wheeled the pink nose slowly along the horizon, paused and then swept it back the other way, paused again and repeated the whole process while the children dissolved into giggles and over their heads Alistair, too, grinned like a schoolboy.

Of them all it was Megan who recovered her sobriety first to say penitently, "I didn't mean to laugh at you, Pen, and you really don't look like a lighthouse until you turn your head that funny way. But really, I think you always look nice."

Laughing but touched, Pen gave Megan a quick hug of thanks, and beside his sister Corey nodded, too, as he got his mirth under control. Over his head Pen's eyes flickered without her volition to his uncle. His face was still alight from laughing, but he didn't echo Megan's words or Corey's gesture. He simply looked at her with steady blue eyes, and Pen—careful lest she read in those eyes what she wanted rather than what she saw—knew for certain only that he liked her lighthouse imitation, nothing more.

She gave her bright nose a sad defiant little honk that made it brighter still, then tucked away her handkerchief, missing the brief twitch of Alistair's lips just as she had missed the embroidered *H* on the oversize white handkerchief she pocketed.

"Thank you, Megan, Corey, for such soothing balm on my hurt pride," she said seriously, adding an instant later, "It's nice to know I don't have to go stand by the lakeshore all alone but can come to the village with the rest of you."

It took the children a moment to realize that her grave tone was belied by the gallant twinkle in her watering eyes, but then they bounced laughing to her side and caught her hands to drag her along with them into Grasmere. At that point, though, Alistair finally interrupted them.

"Hold on, urchins," he commanded the children, and over their heads he said to Pen, "The sad truth, my Penelope, is that although you're not going to stand alone by the lakeshore as a lighthouse, you're not going to stand with us as a spectator in that wet field, either."

Three voices rose in immediate protest, although Pen's was a shade slower, because arrested, she was still listening to the sweet sound of "my Penelope."

Megan and Corey said simultaneously, "Oh, Uncle Lister!"

Pen gathered her wits to begin indignantly, "Alistair—" But then she was cut off by an inopportune sneeze, and when she recovered, Alistair was waiting politely for her to continue. One black eyebrow was already raised skeptically higher than the other, however, and it lifted still higher when she protested, "I'll be perfectly fine. A little cold in the head isn't reason enough for me to miss the rest of the festivities."

Even to herself, that sounded a bit lame, since it was punctuated with yet another volley of sneezes. But even if he did call her *his* Penelope, what real right did he have to decide what she could and couldn't do, she wondered heatedly as she groped for that handkerchief again. She didn't find it, but a blessedly cool hand tilted her chin up and a fresh handkerchief mopped her eyes gently, so that she could see Alistair again, now only a few inches away and looking at her with an expression so tender that she stopped sneezing—and stopped breathing, too. He'd looked at her like that last night in her...dream?

"Yes, you will be fine," he was agreeing softly now, "because you are going to stay here and coddle that cold until we get back. You will wrap yourself in warm robes, sleep for several hours and drink tea and juices by the gallon, and by evening you'll be so much better that I won't have to ply you with brandy again.''

His eyes crinkled at the corners, and bemusedly she admired the effect as he went on speaking.

"Tonight, my Penelope, I won't have you getting befuddled—enchanting though you are in that condition—because there's an unanswered question between us, and this evening after I ask the question again I mean to have my answer.''

Mesmerized now by those eyes, Pen gazed at him, and then, as if responding more to his will than to her own, she nodded slowly. This was greeted with a triumphant little laugh as he kissed her hot forehead and let her go before the children's interested eyes.

"You kissed Pen, Uncle Lister,'' Megan observed.

"I did,'' he agreed calmly, "and I intend to do it a lot more.''

"That's nice,'' his niece approved matter-of-factly. And to Pen he murmured, "Yes, it is.''

Pen's eyes dropped in confusion before the loving and purposeful look that accompanied his words, and with a tiny gasp she caught her ragged breath; of course, she sneezed. He grinned and pressed the fresh handkerchief into her fingers, but before he could say anything more Levvy rose to his enormous feet, ears lifted inquiringly as he peered away toward the village and barked.

Pen hadn't been conscious of anything but Alistair for the past few minutes, but now she realized that the sound of many more dogs barking ascended from the village, and looked automatically to Alistair for an explanation.

"We've yet to have the sheep-dog trials and the hound-trailing event," he answered her unspoken question.

Corey repeated excitedly, "Sheep-dog trials! Oh, Uncle Lister, can we enter Levvy?"

"Heaven forbid!" Alistair responded fervently, adding in a dire tone, "He'd probably step on the sheep instead of penning them up."

Megan giggled at this prediction, but Corey looked crestfallen, and with only the hastiest appealing glance at Pen, their uncle went on, "Besides, Corey, he's needed here to play nursemaid to our ailing Penelope while we're gone."

And Pen, without the least hint that she'd caught Alistair's conspiratorial look, said earnestly, "Yes, he can sit on my feet to keep them warm while Marigold sits on my hands."

Corey looked at her suspiciously, but Pen made her face guileless and sincere. A few minutes later, she found herself seated in Uncle Andrew's chair by the hearth, swaddled in blankets from her neck to her ankles, while Levvy obligingly squashed her feet and Marigold settled on her hands.

Alistair was building up a crackling fire on the hearth, and as he finished, Corey stepped back and viewed the scene with satisfaction. "There! Are you nice and warm now, Pen?"

Pen nodded her agreement, afraid to try words lest she sneeze—or laugh. She gave Alistair a speaking look, however, and knew by his answering chuckle that he had interpreted it correctly.

"All right, urchins," he said cheerfully, "I think we have her both torrid and trapped, so she can't get cold or get away while we're gone. She'll be right here when we come home."

INCREDIBLY, THOUGH, SHE WASN'T. She had promised to answer his question when he asked it again, but she wasn't there to hear it. She had promised Megan never to go away and just leave them, but she did it. At the end of the day they came straight to her cottage, but she was gone from Uncle Andrew's chair and she didn't answer when Alistair called, any more than did Marigold or even Levvy. Hasty strides took him up the steep steps to her bedroom, and there he found uncharacteristic disorder, with her closet door ajar and drawers gaping open, but he didn't find Pen.

For a long time he stood stock-still in her abandoned room, where only hours before she had lain in his arms and he had so loved and desired her; slowly his face changed. Glad anticipation gave way to pain and that to emptiness as the warmth that Pen had brought out in him ebbed away, leaving his face cold and hard and dead. For the second time in his life he looked at bitter disillusionment, and its ugliness, like the Gorgons', turned him to stone.

Lifeless and mechanical, he walked down the steps and out of Pen's empty cottage, leaving the distressed and frightened children to follow by themselves. In his own cottage he went straight to his study; leading Levvy from his bed of papers to the door, he locked it behind the puzzled dog, then closed the window and pulled the drapes, shutting out the sunny breeze that had danced merrily in the room. Half a bottle remained of the fine old brandy he had given Pen, and he reached it down from its high shelf, sitting heavily at his desk with the bottle in front of him.

When Megan and Corey knocked timidly at his door a little later, the bottle was empty. At their first knock he didn't move; at the second he rose woodenly and walked to the door, unlocking it with stiff hands.

"Uncle Lister..." Megan had already begun before she caught sight of him. Then she broke off.

After a moment Corey, less sensitive than his sister, finished for her. "Where's Pen, Uncle Lister?" he asked anxiously.

Slowly Alistair raised his bent head. "Gone," he said flatly, and in his face was something that made even Corey back away silently. He stared at them expressionlessly for a minute or two, then turned from them and walked back into the room. And although he went only a few feet, to sit at his desk again with his shoulders hunched and his head in his hands, he might as well have gone to the polar ice cap. For the first time in their lives he was completely oblivious to them, and they both knew it.

IN FACT, Pen had stayed where she was for some time. Nearly immobilized anyway, she was content to lie back in her nest of blankets and dream delicious dreams to the gentle accompaniment of the fire's whisper and Marigold's purr. Even her periodic sneezes were no real distraction as she looked deep into the fire and saw instead Alistair's smiling face, full of warmth and promise as he vowed to ask her a question again.

She knew of only one unanswered question between them now, and if he meant to ask it again before she answered, couldn't that be because he intended to change the terms of his proposal? And if that could happen, could her dream last night perhaps have really happened, as well? Dream or memory, Pen's cheeks went rosy as she relived it, and they stayed rosy as she thought about her answer to Alistair's proposal. Her lips curved, and the hand stroking Marigold fell still.

Happier than she had ever been before, Pen dreamed on in her quiet kitchen as the fire died down—until the telephone's shrill urgent summons made her jump and made Marigold leap from her arms, while Levvy heaved himself upright and released Pen's feet.

Alarmed by the bell's insistence, she hastily extricated herself from her woolly cocoon and hurried into the passage to the telephone while her mind raced still faster than her feet. Could something be wrong? If one of the children, or Alistair—oh, not Alistair—had been hurt, would they ring up from the village?

Her heart was pounding when she reached the telephone and snatched it from its hook, and her "Hello?" was breathless.

"Penelope?"

Not Alistair's voice, and not, thank heaven, the voice of some officially polite and regretful stranger. Relief made Pen sag against the cool whitewashed wall for a moment, and then she registered her mother's use of her full name and stood straight again.

"Yes, dear? Is something wrong?"

"Yes!" Nell Bryce's voice came back along the wire, tremulous and roughened by anxiety. "Oh, Pen, your father's had a heart attack."

Pen's knuckles whitened on the receiver, and her eyes closed, but she said nothing as her mother rushed disjointedly on, "The ambulance has just left to take him to the hospital. They wouldn't tell me how ill he was. But he was just fine at breakfast, and then so suddenly—he stood up at his desk, looking so peculiar, and then fell back...."

For a minute her voice dissolved completely, and tears broke the dam of Pen's eyelids while the distance between them echoed emptily along the open wire.

"Pen, I'm sorry," Nell went on finally in a tone

she tried to steady. "I know I should have prepared you for the news and then broken it gently to you, but I couldn't see how. I'm just off to the hospital myself, but I had to phone and let you know before I went."

"Would you like me there, dear?" Pen asked gently.

Her mother hesitated and then said in a voice that cracked with relief, "Oh, Pen, yes. I'm sorry—I don't mean to be foolish, and I know you have your own life to live up there—"

"Your only foolishness is in forgetting I also have a life down there, especially when you need me," Pen cut in decisively. "I'll leave immediately, but where shall I come?"

Her mother gave her the address of the hospital to which Professor Bryce had been taken, and Pen agreed to drive directly there. Neither of them put into words the desperate hope that there would still be a reason for their presence at the hospital by the time Pen arrived.

Instead all Pen said was, "Bear up, and I'll be with you soon."

"Yes, Pen," Nell responded obediently. "And Penelope...."

"Yes?"

"Thank you, love."

She hung up, and with eyes that had blurred again Pen softly replaced the receiver on its hook. For a moment more she stood beside the telephone, her eyes closed and her head bent, then she sped into action, her cold of necessity forgotten.

In a matter of minutes she had flung a few clothes into her case and thrown it into the Cortina; Marigold, too, she scooped up and deposited in the car, where the startled cat smoothed her ruffled orange fur and then prowled delicately along the seat tops, investigating the car before she settled resignedly down to nap until her mistress should have recovered from whatever sudden madness this was.

Levvy, too, was startled by Pen's incomprehensible actions. Her heart overflowing with fear and love, she snatched up the first bit of paper that came to her frantic hands and scrawled a jumbled note to Alistair. Then she led Levvy across the garden to the cottage next door and into Alistair's study, where the worried dog settled on his bed of papers and gazed at her with mournful dark eyes, convinced that her odd behavior must somehow be all his fault.

Pen meanwhile glanced distractedly around the untidy study. Even without his presence, the room echoed Alistair's personality, and she was momentarily cheered and reassured. More calmly now, she surveyed the study and decided that in such confusion the only place to leave her note was squarely on top of Alistair's desk; surely there he couldn't miss it. She set it down with fingers that lingered an instant, and then caught sight of Levvy's doleful stare.

"It's all right, Levvy." She hurried across the

room and consoled him with a hasty caress. "It isn't your fault—you were guarding me perfectly. Now stay here and guard my note until Alistair and the kids come home."

Heartened, he looked at her with devoted eyes that seemed to understand what she meant, and after a last pat Pen threw open the window to give him some air and sped from the room, leaving the door ajar.

As she hurried across the garden again, a final sweeping glance showed her that the silent fells still stood sentinel over so much she had grown to love, and she drew some comfort from that as she hastened to the Cortina. In a few minutes she was threading her way through the pack of visiting sportsmen and holidaymakers that crowded the village, and as she drove she watched with urgent eyes for Alistair's tall beloved figure or the children's small darting shapes.

None of them came into sight in the milling throng, however, and neither did anyone else she knew, so Pen drove on, leaving the village and then Lakeland itself in a drive even more desperate than her flight from Alistair had been. She hurried south, pushing the old car to its limits, drawn desperately on by anxiety and apprehension.

When she reached London and the hospital at last, she was allowed to see her father briefly, but he was too medicated to know she was there. He remained in grave condition, and the next days were a blur of sleepless worry that Pen was never able either to forget or to remember completely. Her mother seldom left the hospital, and Pen generally stayed there with her, too concerned about her father even to think of her own cold, which continued to run its course.

At home Margery ceased to behave like a whirling dervish and became a still and white-faced child, clinging desperately to the warmth that was Marigold, while Evan and Sally tried to look after their little sister with an uncharacteristic solicitude that was the measure of their distress, meeting Pen at the door whenever she rushed home for a change of clothing or a few snatched hours of sleep. Not allowed in the hospital, they had to rely on her for news.

"Pen, how is he?"

"Is he better?"

"How's daddy?"

The words would tumble excitedly out, but then the youngsters would turn away unhappily when she had to tell them there'd been no improvement in Professor Bryce's condition.

But then finally there was. On the fourth day the professor began to improve—suddenly, as if it had just come to his attention that his will to live was needed. After that he continued to mend quite rapidly, recovering from what his doctors now admitted had been a major heart attack. Pleased with his progress, they set a tentative date for his release from the hospital; he would have a considerable convalescence at home but should, with patience, eventually be able to do again everything he had done before the attack.

With the professor's condition improving, everything else began to change, as well. In the house behind the tollgate, Evan and Sally reverted to their usual bickering selves—a metamorphosis Pen watched with too much relief to be anything but amused—and even Margery seemed to feel that a cloud had lifted: more herself again, she occasionally allowed Marigold to escape from her clutches and vanish into the garden. Pen caught up with her lost sleep, reveling in enchanting dreams of Alistair, whose question would be no less sweet for being delayed. Her mother, who had coped resignedly for years with her absent-minded husband's vagaries but had been shattered by the prospect of losing them, became again her usual serene self. She still spent long hours at the hospital, but at home she made all the decisions and arrangements for the professor's return and no longer looked helplessly to Pen for guidance.

A week after the desperate telephone call that had summoned her home, Pen strolled with her mother in the garden while the setting sun poured across the lawn like a river of gold.

"Penelope." Nell finally broke the comfortable silence between them, and Pen looked around inquiringly. "Thank you, love, for coming home. I don't know what I would have done without you. Before this happened," she added ruefully, "I didn't know that I'd be such a ninny as to go to pieces in a crisis like this.''

"You're never a ninny," Pen contradicted fondly, linking arms companionably with her mother. "You were just distracted with worry about dad because you love him so much—and we all love you for that.''

The arm in hers tightened, and they paced on together until Nell said thoughtfully, "For years your father and I have muddled along from one predicament to another, as we tried to discover the best way to raise our children—''

She was interrupted by a piercing squeal from Sally, followed instantly by Sally herself as she dashed out the French windows that led into the garden and dodged around the corner of the house with Evan in hot pursuit. Their mother glanced after them with a practiced eye that informed her that neither of her offspring was in immediate danger from the other, then calmly finished her sentence.

"—but we must have done some things right." She looked at the laughing graceful figure beside her with fond eyes and continued, "Sometimes I've despaired of surviving their childhood—" a nod indicated the direction of a burst of shouts and giggles "—but it gives me hope for those demons to realize that my firstborn has already become a kind and loving adult.''

Flushing a soft wild-rose pink, Pen dropped a light kiss on her mother's cheek, and for a moment Nell rested gentle fingertips against her daughter's smooth skin. Then they wandered on in perfect accord.

Before them evening flowed slowly across Nell's garden, and noting its quiet beauty with an artist's attention, Pen contrasted this lingering twilight with the swifter shadows of the north, where the western fells quickly swallowed up the sun and only the open sky savored its final rays. In her mind's eye she saw darkness covering up her own garden and across it the lights gleaming in the neighboring cottage. The children cajoled into their beds, Alistair would be in his abominable study, possibly working on some new project and certainly disheveling the room still further. Or perhaps he was even thinking of her, waiting anxiously for her return and missing her as she missed him, longing for the sound of his voice and the touch of his lips and hands. She could have telephoned him, of course, but somehow that would have broken her spell of delicious anticipation. And she knew his beautiful voice would not be the same distorted by the mechanical wizardry of the phone. Perhaps he would call her. Perversely, Pen rather wished he would not.

His face clear before her—infuriating, perceptive, outrageous and totally beloved—Pen rambled on, unaware that her lips had curled into a smile. Nell saw it, though, and knew with a quick pang that she had been more correct than she realized at the moment when she called her daughter a loving adult; the impulsive girl who had left London only six months ago was gone forever, and in her place a tender woman had returned. And that return would be only temporary, too, Nell recognized, as with a mother's swift intuition she now guessed at all that Pen's letters home had left unsaid. Looking at her daughter's dreaming eyes, Nell said a silent goodbye to the child she had loved and a joyous hello to the woman she would love.

"Penelope." She called the woman softly, and at a new tone in her voice Pen returned from her dreams. Releasing her arm, Nell met the clear gray gaze for a moment and said quietly, "You could be back in Grasmere tomorrow night, love."

The gray eyes widened, but Pen began a little gesture of disclaimer, and Nell interrupted it. "We'll be all right now, Pen. Your father will be released from the hospital in a few days, and everything's ready for him here at home."

She glanced across the garden at the brick house that glowed a warm rose in the light of the setting sun, and murmured more to herself than to Pen, "And it will seem like a home again with him here. But if—" she turned back to her tall daughter and went on gently "—home is where the heart is, then I think you don't really live here anymore."

She met Pen's eyes, and mother and daughter shared a long look of love and complete understanding. Then in a voice that quivered between laughter and tears Pen said, "But I'll always reserve a room here if I may."

"Of course," Nell agreed in the same tone, with a smile that was only the least bit tremulous, and linking arms again, they turned back toward the house.

In the morning she ran errands, terminating completely the lease on the apartment she had shared with Bree a lifetime ago and checking in with Fred to collect a sheaf of new stories. These she promised to finish more quickly than the last group, now that Alistair's book was done and she could work full-time again. She phoned Ann, too, for a quick visit, and after some hesitation telephoned Nigel, as well. She wasn't quite sure what to say to the person he had become, but he had never acknowledged her letter refusing his proposal, and she wondered if she had angered as well as disappointed him. She couldn't marry him and she wasn't at all sure she liked the changes in him, but still she hated to think of losing his friendship entirely. At any rate, he wasn't at the new apartment, and when she stopped in at the theater on her way to the hospital, she missed him again. From the stage a girl who said she was the lead actress's understudy told her he had gone out of town the day before.

A bit relieved in spite of herself, Pen went on her way. At the hospital she visited her father, kissing a cheek that was leaner than it had been but showing a healthy color.

"Dad...."

"Mmm?" her father responded absently, jotting notes on the semantics of the conditional in his appalling handwriting.

"Now that you're so much better I'll be going back up to the cottage," Pen began, and paused, not entirely sure he'd noticed she had spoken.

He had, after a fashion. When she had just about given up hope for a reaction, he murmured, "That's nice, dear," in a voice so abstracted that she laughed. He looked up for a moment at that and gave her a sweet smile, but when she left he was already lost in his work again. The hospital was proving to be a far quieter place in which to concentrate than his own boisterous home, and he didn't intend to waste any more of his valuable time there. Pen was chuckling as she walked away, certain that his recovery was proceeding nicely.

A hasty lunch at home and she was ready to go, having kissed the rest of her family goodbye and wheedled Marigold from Margery by promising that the cat would come back again sometime. Unaware of this reckless pledge, Marigold settled into the old green car with a look of relief and accepted this drive as calmly as she had the last.

But for Pen herself this journey was different from any of the others she had made along this route. Before she passed the tollgate she was humming gaily to herself, and when she reached the expressway she began to sing outright in a sweet husky little voice. That didn't last long, because

serenading made her cough, but even enforced
silence couldn't curb her joyous high spirits. This
time she wasn't running away from anything or
anyone; this time she wasn't driven by fear or even
pulled by simple curiosity. This time she was going
home.

Good training made her drive with her usual
careful competence, but her mind was far ahead
of her wheels. A week ago Alistair had said, with
that light in his eyes, that he had a question to ask
her again. Certain she knew both his question and
her answer to it, Pen drove north to her love.

CHAPTER EIGHTEEN

IT WAS LATE AFTERNOON when Pen reached the lakes, and the weather, fair and mild in the south, had turned threatening. According to the calendar two weeks of summer still remained, but here in the north the air had an edge to it already, and storm clouds were gathering around the fell tops. Pen watched undismayed, however; memory pointed out that she had made this drive for the first time in a pelting rainstorm that was no ill omen. It had been followed by a springtime of learning to know Alistair—after those first disastrous encounters—and the later storm of their return from Hardknott had been followed by her discovery that she loved him. Intrigued now by the parallel, she predicted happily that this storm in turn would be followed by his proposal and her acceptance. She smiled to herself at the notion that she could easily become a lover of rainstorms and drove through Grasmere village and up the lane, just as she had done for the first time all those months ago.

This time, though, no Banny awaited her. When she switched off the Cortina's tired engine, her

cottage was dark and still. It looked far less
welcoming than it had that first afternoon—
almost forbidding, in fact—but Pen had no time
for such silly fancies. Collecting Marigold in one
hand and her case in the other, she hurried up the
walk on eager feet.

Once inside her green door, she set the case
down in the passageway and hastened into the
kitchen. It was cold but still familiar and beloved,
and she said a silent hello to it as she switched on
the lamp by Uncle Andrew's chair and then
poured Marigold a saucer of canned milk from the
cupboard. Pen herself was too excited to eat,
however. On the far side of the garden she could
see the lights in Alistair's windows glowing a
welcome and an invitation, and without even
pausing to drag a comb through her windblown
hair or change her wrinkled cotton trousers for
something fresher and warmer, she flew out the
door.

One small voice of vanity in her mind protested
against appearing in front of Alistair looking
rumpled, but she was too eager to appear in front
of him in *any* condition to pay it heed. Breathlessly she skimmed over the wall and across his
garden, and finding his door unlatched, she
pushed it open and stepped inside. Confident of
her welcome, she called joyfully, "Alistair!
Children—I'm home!"

Then without waiting for an answer she sped
into his study to find him.

She was halfway across the room, with
Alistair's name on her lips again, when she realized something was terribly wrong, and her voice
faltered. The atmosphere in the room was strained
and still, and standing motionless at the far side of
the study Alistair was staring at her—not with the
tender, intent expression she'd last seen on his
face, but with a look of such icy distaste that it
froze her at arm's length. Even his early cold
dislike of her seemed like warm friendliness com-
pared to this, and Pen caught her breath in an appalled little gasp.

The tiny sound seemed loud in the silent room;
no one spoke, and in the roaring silence she
gradually realized several other people could have.
By the door through which she'd burst so con-
fidently only seconds ago sat Nigel, and she
recognized him bewilderedly. Automatically her
memory told her she'd learned in London that he
was out of town; apparently he'd come here again
to see her—but then why was he sitting in
Alistair's study, and looking at her with such
naked pain in a face for once unguarded, his satyr
mask gone entirely? Had her letter refusing his
proposal caused him so much misery?

The silence in this full room forbade her asking,
and wretchedly she turned away to see its other
occupants. Near Alistair, huddled together in the
corner of the old sofa, were the children, and Pen
found them when her eyes fled again from their
uncle's implacable face. They offered her no

solace, however; Corey—apparently taking his cue
from Alistair but less skilled at scorn—was looking
at her with open anger in his bright blue eyes and
tightly compressed young mouth, and Megan was
gazing at her in stunned bewilderment.

That began to change into delight, and Megan
stood up, but before Pen could respond and go to
the little girl, Corey had yanked her down beside
him. Megan looked helplessly at Pen, then at her
brother's furious face and her uncle's rigid one,
and burst into desolate tears, hiding her eyes with
her hands. The sound tore at Pen's already aching
heart, and she made a little reaching gesture toward
Megan, but at Corey's glare her hand dropped
empty again to her side, and a moment later he
hauled his tearful sister from the room. She went
blindly, her eyes still hidden from the sight of Pen,
and when the children were gone Pen's own eyes—
missing Nigel as he slipped quietly away after the
youngsters—went despairingly to the one additional person in the room, who remained seated at
the other end of the sofa.

The woman sat gracefully, a picture of calm and
studied elegance. An almost shocking contrast to
the disorder of Alistair's study, she was precisely
and immaculately groomed, from her artfully
casual upswept hair to her expensive leather shoes,
neatly placed so that their angle would show off her
legs to their best advantage. A pale yellow suit of
fine wool gave her an illusion of warmth, but there
was nothing warm about the woman who wore it.

Staring at her, too hurt and baffled to be polite, Pen slowly became aware that there was something familiar about the elegant figure before her, and even now the unhappiness she was feeling didn't stop her from automatically cataloging the resemblance. The woman's smooth broad forehead and rounded chin recalled the children who had been seated only a few feet away; even more noticeably, however, her long reddish brown hair and her eyes—either green or gray, Pen couldn't be sure which—mirrored Pen's own hair and eyes as closely as a sister's.

Struck by the likeness, she felt irrationally for a moment that here at least she would have a friend in this suddenly hostile room. But she was wrong. While she was studying the stranger and noting their similarities, the other had in turn been appraising her as closely, dismissing the similarities she, too, perceived and concentrating on the differences.

With a look that perfectly conveyed fastidious disdain, she surveyed Pen's tumbled hair, energetically escaping from its becoming ivory bandeau, the floral T-shirt that her seat belt had crumpled during the long hours of driving, the wrinkled sky-blue slacks that encased her long legs, and over it all the comfortable old navy blue trench coat she clung to even though she knew full well it was past its prime. Under the stranger's amused appraisal, Pen's cheeks flushed a hot pink as she began to guess that this was no friend.

In a moment her guess was all too amply confirmed, and the color in her cheeks slowly ebbed away entirely as the woman before her finally broke the oppressive silence to speak in a perfectly modulated voice.

"So, Alistair," she drawled smoothly, "this must be the children's little friend, whose disappearance so desolated them that you had to summon me up here as a replacement."

She looked Pen up and down once more, superciliously, and added, "Actually, though, she herself seems to have been an attempt to replace me in their lives—and perhaps in yours, too, my dear? I suppose I should be flattered to see that your taste, although deteriorating, still runs along the same general lines as it did all those aeons ago when we were engaged."

The calculated insult was lost on Pen as involuntarily she caught her breath at the stunning discovery that this coldly immaculate woman was both the mother who had abandoned the chidren for a stage career and the fiancée who had deserted Alistair to marry—his brother. As if her memory were a cinema and the woman's blandly smiling face a screen, Pen saw superimposed on it Alistair's anger and pain when he spoke of her.

The film ended, but Pen's eyes stayed fixed on the face in front of her; her gaze was sightless, however, as with a surge of relief she suddenly guessed the reason for Alistair's present look of distaste. It was directed not at her but at the

necessity that had compelled him to have this
woman under his roof. Apparently, in spite of her
note, Megan and Corey hadn't understood that an
emergency had called Pen away, or that she would
be back as soon as possible. Megan, although seemingly so much more independent and secure lately,
must have been terribly disturbed to have what
looked like the old frightening pattern recur, and
despite his own feelings Alistair had been desperate
enough to contact the children's mother for help
rather than add to Pen's worries when she was already distressed about her father. And that was
why he hadn't rung up or written while she was
gone; she had wondered a little at that, but obviously he'd been afraid he might let slip his
troubles with the children and upset her.

Moved by his understanding and kindness, Pen
turned back to Alistair at last with a tenderly
grateful smile curving her lips. But the smile
wavered as she realized he was still staring at both
women, and his expression of disgust encom-
passed them both equally. She knew he had reason
to loathe the children's mother, but why was he
still looking like that at her, too? Her comforting
certainty that she knew what had happened faded,
and Pen suddenly noticed that her theory didn't
account for Corey's behavior when she'd come in.
Nor did it account for the icy glitter in Alistair's
eyes or the hard ironic edge to his voice when he
finally spoke.

"Why, yes, Elise," he concurred at last, looking beyond Pen's anxious face to the bland one so like it and yet so different. "Apparently my taste is still the same, and so is my naiveté. In spite of your best efforts to train me out of such gullibility, I've let myself be tricked again into believing that a lovely woman can be capable of loyalty and consideration."

As though his words had been the thrust of a sharp-pointed sword, Pen opened her mouth to cry out against the pain of his unjust attack. He went right on, however, still speaking to the other woman but battering Pen with his bitterness, and her own desperate words of protest and defense went unspoken.

"But I think I've finally learned my lesson, thanks to you both, and I'll see to it that the children understand it, as well, just as their father finally did. After all, we Heaths should be careful to retain knowledge gained at such a price—loneliness and disillusionment for us all, and death, as well, for Peter."

His tone changed on that last phrase, and the remembered agony in it cut through the spreading numbness of her own hurt to buffet Pen anew. But Elise simply pushed aside the blue green scarf that lay beside her on the sofa and from the expensive handbag beneath it drew out a cigarette and a small jeweled lighter. Almost blindly Pen stared at the scarf she had woven for Nigel, and very slowly she worked out the corollary of seeing it in Elise's possession. This must be the woman who shared

Nigel's apartment—and whose clothes hung in their shared closet.

Suddenly everything was horribly clear to Pen. Not only had Elise destroyed Alistair's love and trust years ago and come back now to do it again by ruining his relationship with Pen, but she had even begun to ruin Nigel's life, as well. Pen saw his unhappy face again in her mind and laid blame for that, too, at Elise's door; her stomach churned and a sick feeling rose in her throat as she stared at Elise with a mixture of anger and loathing that for a moment consumed every other emotion.

Unconcerned with Pen's feelings, Elise was speaking again. "Oh, come now, Alistair," she was saying mildly, pausing to flick the lighter and draw at her cigarette, then continuing as she exhaled. "You're descending into melodrama."

The smoke wreathed delicately before her face, and she watched it idly while Alistair looked through it at her.

"Yes," he said tightly after a throbbing pause, "you would see it all in those terms."

She gave a little complacent nod that acted on him like a goad, and he went on. "And did you enjoy the roles you played in our lives?" he asked her. "Devoted fiancée, ingenue with a change of heart, young wife and mother, and then finally actress who sacrifices everything for her art?"

Her slight smile faded, and she watched him enigmatically.

"Certainly you played them all superbly—at

least up until that final day, when it seems your grasp of believable characterization failed you at last. When Peter came to see you in London, to plead with you to come back to him and the children, what role were you playing then? What character, no matter how stereotyped and shallow, would have driven him away then by hurling at him the one intolerable fact that would destroy forever his last illusions about his marriage—that he had stolen his brother's promised wife?''

Pen drew her breath in with a small ragged sound of pain, her own hurt and rage consumed by Alistair's, but neither he nor Elise noticed it. With a gesture that was less graceful than her earlier ones, Elise was stubbing out her cigarette in an old teacup on the littered table beside the sofa, and Alistair strode to the window as if to escape from his own remembered fury. It didn't work, and he faced Elise again as the words poured out of him like a flood of bitter waters when the dam breaks.

"For eight years I'd kept that from him. I'd lost you, and Peter was all I had left, but I knew I'd lose him, too, if he ever learned the truth about us. His sense of honor utterly forbade involvement with a brother's fiancée, but when he came back from South America that time he knew nothing about our secret engagement or our plans to elope. And before he could find out, you had decided a wealthy businessman was a better bargain than an unemployed classicist and persuaded him it was love at first sight. So instead of Peter, it was I who heard the happy and romantic news about a run-away marriage, and then faced the choice of giving you up silently or telling Peter what he had unknowingly done. Rather than tell him and watch guilt tear my only brother apart, I held my peace and watched you play the blushing bride to perfection, even to that chaste and innocent kiss I got when you came back from your honeymoon in Vienna. Instead of telling him, I kept quiet."

He stopped as if the bitterness had drained him completely, and then added tiredly, "I wish to God I hadn't."

"So do I!" Elise spat out. Her voice had lost its professional modulation, and an angry red stained her cheekbones as her well-bred poise disintegrated. Pushing her handbag and Nigel's scarf carelessly aside, she jumped to her feet and flung her words at Alistair so violently that Pen unconsciously retreated from them both until she backed into the wall by the door and stood there frozen with her palms pressed flat against the cool plaster.

"My God, so do I!" Elise raged. "He could have divorced me on the spot to save his precious honor, and then I would have been rid of both of you! I was a fool ever to get involved with either of you, but I was young and stupid, and I had some addled notion that having a wealthy and devoted husband in the background would be good protection for an actress trying to break into the theater world. But instead of a nice solid rock I got a millstone!"

Her voice had cracked on the last furious word, and she strode wildly across the room and back, avoiding Alistair. Then she went on in a tone that was only slightly more controlled.

"I had to have his children, and then I had to stay at home with them and listen to him telling them what a beautiful and loving mother they had. He got them convinced of it, too, and I suppose he must have even convinced himself of it, or none of them would have been so shocked when I left."

She took a deep breath now and hunched her shoulders awkwardly, folding her arms tightly across her, and the red-nailed hands plucked at her sleeves like slender talons as she hurried on.

"He wouldn't let me go, either. Somehow he found out where I was staying, and then he called up constantly. I'd answer the telephone, thinking it might be news about a role for me, but instead it would always be Peter, and he'd beg me to come home, or put the children on and have them do it. He sent letters, too, and when I didn't answer them and finally refused to speak to him on the telephone, he drove up to the city that day.

"He wouldn't let me go!" Her voice rose, and Pen's hands whitened on the wall. "I told him again that all my life I'd wanted to be an actress, and now I was finally beginning to get a few little parts that could lead to something important. But he wouldn't listen—he just kept saying that he and the children missed me terribly, and if I came home we could all be happy together again. Happy, for God's sake, trapped like that! He wouldn't listen to anything I had to say, so I got desperate and said the only thing I could think of that he'd have to listen to and that would make him let me go. And when I'd said it he looked at me strangely, then apologized for disturbing me and left.''

The spate of shrill words ceased, and she sat down again abruptly, groping for another cigarette with hands that shook slightly, and Alistair, who had stood like a pillar of salt through her diatribe, looked into the darkness beyond the window over her head and took up the narrative in a quiet flat voice.

''So he started the long drive home, going back to the children with nothing—neither the mother they cried for nor the wife he loved. And when that drunk came roaring out of the darkness on the wrong side of the road, Peter wasn't able to avoid him—or perhaps he didn't try very hard.

''They called me in Carlisle to tell me that he was slipping away, even though his injuries hadn't seemed serious at first, and when I reached the hospital he was nearly gone. He was able to look at me, though, and say, 'Lister, I'm sorry. I never knew until today.' I knew immediately what you must have told him, but before I could make him believe you had simply lied in anger, he turned his face away from me and died.''

He stopped speaking, and his last words hung on the room's silent air. Elise sat with her head bowed, as if intent on the cigarette whose tip glowed brightly between her fingers. Alistair continued to stare sightlessly out of the window, and Pen—her earlier anger and disgust at Elise consumed by pity for them all, and her own aching distress compounded by these old griefs that left her cheeks wet—stood mutely against the wall, feeling as if she had aged by a thousand hopeless years since she'd entered this room so joyfully only a little while ago.

She understood it all now; everything—the children's fear of abandonment, Alistair's initial coldness to her and his proposal that wasn't a proposal—had been explained. Only his unfair accusation—that like the unhappy Elise, Pen was incapable of loyalty—still made no sense. The note she had left him in this very room should have cleared her of that charge before he made it.

For a moment she glanced wearily around the cluttered study, but she saw no trace of the sketch bearing her hasty message. Alistair must have found it, but apparently he hadn't believed her reasons for going were genuine. And so she had lost him; painfully trained in suspicion, he had decided she was faithless and deceitful, and that chilling frost had killed the delicate love and trust that were growing between them. The question he had planned to ask her again would never be repeated now, and numb though she was from the tidal wave of emotions that had pounded this room, Pen felt a few fresh tears scald their way down her white cheeks.

She dashed the tears hastily aside, however, when Corey rushed into the room and past her to Alistair. Catching at his uncle's sleeve, he dragged Alistair's attention back into the confines of the little study and blurted, "She's gone, Uncle Lister— Megan is! I can't find her anywhere!"

Alistair and Pen both focused sharply on him, their joint and separate sorrows giving way before Corey's urgency, and even Elise slowly raised her head to look uncomprehendingly at her son.

"When did she go?"

"How long has she been gone?"

Pen and Alistair spoke simultaneously, and Corey glanced quickly from one to the other before he answered them both.

"I thought she was upstairs. She ran up there after we left here." Now he kept his eyes away from Pen, but color crept into his cheeks. "I let her go because I thought she wanted to be by herself. Nigel came out in the garden with Levvy and me, but when it started to rain we came in and I looked for Megan. That's when I found out she wasn't here."

His voice trailed off huskily, and his listeners became aware for the first time of the dull persistent pounding of the rain. The first storm of autumn had come early, and Megan was somewhere out in it, alone and in the dark. An image of the little girl, lost and bedraggled and terrified, leaped into Pen's mind and so appalled her that for now everything else slipped into the background. Her love for Alistair might be unwanted and useless, but her love for his brother's child could be put to use if she joined in the search for Megan.

Pen was in motion almost as soon as she thought that, and as she fled from the unhappy room, Alistair was delivering Corey into his mother's uncertain hands and bidding the boy to stay with her until Megan was found. Pen carried away with her a picture of Alistair bending down to speak to Elise as she sat on the edge of the sofa with one arm awkwardly encircling Corey.

Driven at first more by instinct than by reason, Pen darted up the narrow stairway and looked into the children's room for herself. It was empty, of course, but she hesitated there a minute. The rose wool blanket lay crumpled across a small chair, as if thrown there in anger or sorrow, and she caught it up and carried it back downstairs with her, speeding out Alistair's front door without checking further in his cottage.

Instead she hurried home to her own, where Marigold greeted her with a sleepily inquiring meow. The cat was alone, as Pen had known she would be, and the girl paused only long enough to snatch up Uncle Andrew's old flashlight from the shelf and fold the small pink blanket inside her trench coat. Then, haunted by her image of Megan alone in the wet and roaring darkness, she raced back out into the rain to look for the child.

Outside, a quick survey showed Pen that her garden was as empty of Megan as was Alistair's, and intuition took her out of it and up the lane to

the fells. Thinking now with a clarity born of love
and desperation, she remembered how Megan had
loved all those walks she took with Ann or with Pen
herself, when the little girl's normal high spirits
had been reasserting themselves after the shock of
losing nearly everything familiar had faded. Then
her sense of adventure had led them all far afield,
and now, as though they were scenes in her sketchbook, Pen tried to picture Megan's favorite places,
forcing herself to slow her frantic steps to a steady
ground-covering stride as she vowed to search them
all.

Even at a sensible pace, however, the going was
difficult. The lane quickly deteriorated into a narrow beaten track as it climbed into the fells, and
heavy rain was making the path slippery. Worse,
lightning had begun to flicker away off to the west,
and in spite of Uncle Andrew's flashlight, the inter-
mittent flashes made it difficult for her to see the
scattered sharp-edged rocks that caught at her feet
or turned slickly under them. Pen surged on nevertheless, floundering sometimes but always moving
on and up, grateful that her own wanderings had
made these near fells so familiar. Megan hated
lightning, she remembered with a shudder.

There was no sign of the little girl at the small
waterfall she loved, where a stream that ran beside
the sheep track for a time dropped chuckling over a
clutch of boulders. Pen flashed her light across the
stones, noting uneasily that the water's voice had
risen to a shout, and she called Megan repeatedly.

Only the stream answered, and she hurried on, panting a little.

Also empty was the slope where Megan had found the newborn lamb, carrying it delightedly to Pen for inspection—"Look, Pen! It really does feel like a stuffed toy!"—before its mother appeared and on Pen's orders the lamb was hastily returned to her.

The large flat rock where they had all picnicked in the sun was vacant now, too, glistening darkly in the rain, and in the shelter of the yew trees Pen found only a startled roe deer that bounded away at her approach. Pen herself was far less light of foot as she plodded on, breathing heavily with lungs that ached and rasped. The rain had plastered her hair wetly to her forehead, and she pushed it back with a tired hand, trying desperately to hold at bay a growing conviction that she wouldn't be able to find Megan.

Only one more favorite spot came to Pen's mind, and it lay farther westward, into the teeth of the oncoming storm. For an instant she considered turning back without going any farther; she looked up past the ubiquitous wet boulders and scattered tossing trees to a tumultuous sky, and her courage failed her. Then her own dismay reminded her of how terrified Megan must be, and she angled her face away from the stinging rain, belted her sodden trench coat tighter and trudged off along a faint sheep track that led westward.

She was almost on top of Megan before she saw

her, and then the sight so startled Pen that she
dropped Uncle Andrew's invaluable flashlight, and
it went clattering away into the darkness. Pen made
no attempt to follow it, however; the sight of
Megan's huddled form seemed burned into her
brain, and she had no further need of a light to see
it. Instead she dropped to her knees and reached
forward in the blackness to gather Megan's wet little body into her arms.

At first the child lay there unresponsive, and a
cold fear crept along Pen's spine, but suddenly
shivering racked Megan, and she burst into weeping as wild as the storm around them, burrowing
frantically closer to Pen. Between gulping sobs and
chattering teeth, most of her words were unin-
telligible, but Pen caught a few of the most vehe-
ment phrases.

"...hate her! She's not my mother—I don't
want her to be! She'll take us away from you and
Uncle Lister...don't let her, Pen!"

There was much more, too, as a week of desolation and confusion poured from Megan, but Pen
just held her tightly and crooned soothing nonsense
until the tempest of feeling inside the child had
spent itself. Then at last Megan lay quietly in Pen's
arms, but around them the first storm of the season
raged ever more noisily as it swept in from the west.

Thunder reverberated around the fells like the
long continuous roll of drums, and lightning
flashed like musketry as invading winter made war
against summer's last retreat. Exhausted now,

Megan seemed too spent to care, but Pen knew that they were dangerously exposed to the storm. A flash of lightning showed her Uncle Andrew's flashlight, fallen into a rocky crevice below the path, but before she could shift Megan to reach for it, the next flash showed her that the old light was broken.

Without that light, she knew, she would not be able to find her way down off the fells. Nor would she be able to signal their position to other searchers out hunting for Megan. Instead she would have to wait there with the little girl, hoping that someone else would follow this sheep track as she had done and find them.

Still, they couldn't remain here in the meantime. By the sporadic brilliance of the lightning, Pen surveyed their position. Just above the track where they crouched, her anxious eyes discovered an outcropping of boulders, leaning crazily together like drinking companions at the end of a night's revelry. Between them was a small hollow, partially screened from the storm's violence, that would offer them some shelter, and Pen knew she had to make use of it.

Shivering had begun to jar Megan again as Pen tugged the wet bandeau from her own drenched hair and laid it across the path, pointing like a white arrow toward the little cave. Then she gathered Megan higher in her arms and, stumbling to her feet, floundered up the slope to the boulders. Gasping, she set the child down at the back of the hollow and then yanked the little rosy blanket, still reasonably dry and warmed by her body, free from her coat and wrapped Megan tightly in its soft folds. In the darkness Megan clasped it in cold fingers that remembered its texture, while Pen seated herself so that her back formed a protective wall across the opening of their small den. She shielded Megan entirely from the storm, and held her close in loving arms.

Huddled against Pen in her woolly cocoon, Megan was soon warm, and the racking shivers stopped. Cozy at last, she asked suddenly, "Will we get rescued, Pen?"

From her reading in Uncle Andrew's books about Lakeland, Pen knew only too well the fate of many unlucky wayfarers, lost on the fells, for whom rescue had come too late. But that had generally been in wintertime, she reminded herself, not in early autumn.

"Yes, but I don't know precisely when," she answered honestly, and the little girl seemed unconcerned.

She simply cuddled closer and said matter-of-factly, "I love you, Pen."

A tide of feeling swept Pen, leaving her speechless for a moment. Dear for her own sake and for Alistair's, this child was doubly precious, but when Pen spoke again she answered Megan quietly in her own tone.

"Yes, I know, poppet. And I love you, too. Now what do you say we pass the time until we're found by telling stories to drown out the storm? I think I have some new ones you haven't heard yet.''

Megan agreed readily, and Pen began, drawing from memory stories she hadn't yet told the children and repeating them in a voice that at first was dramatic but then became smoothly singsong. With a child's ability to forget difficult circumstances, Megan laughed at the improbable adventures of Dan the Gadget Man, then chuckled sleepily at the tragic tale of Myron the Cross-Eyed Moose. And while Pen was embroidering on the story of the Left-Handed House, Megan's breathing changed and Pen knew she was asleep. She let her voice trail huskily off, and Megan only murmured without waking as Pen smiled wearily to herself in the darkness. Warm and secure now, Megan would probably come through her own adventures without ill effect.

For Pen herself, however, that was less likely. The storm had finally passed by overhead, and its sounds of battle came only faintly now from a distance, but a steady chilling rain still fell. Screening Megan, Pen's back was exposed to it, and her light clothes had long since soaked through, clinging icily now to her skin. The heat generated by her urgent pace as she searched for Megan had dissipated, as well, and a numbing cold crept over her as she sat motionless so that Megan could go on sleeping. A few times sneezing shook her, but she stifled the sneezes as best she could, and Megan dreamed on.

Pen, too, finally slipped into an uneasy dreaming

state, somewhere between sleeping and waking. She saw, jumbled together, the events that led up to the death of Peter Heath. She stood on a darkened roadway and heard the screams of metal tearing apart, then the sirens in the distance; she felt in her own body the chilling cold of Elise's revelation to Peter; she saw Alistair's inconsolable grief when Peter turned away from him to die. Then she heard again the cruelty of Elise's broken voice, telling all these months later how she had sent her husband to his death, and she saw Alistair's soul-deep weariness as he finished Elise's story. But worst of all to Pen was reliving again and again that brutal moment when he had bitterly rejected her and she had been voiceless to cry out against it. Over and over she saw it and opened her lips, but no sound came out, and he continued to look at her in icy disgust. The cold silent tears slipped down her cheeks, and Pen drifted ever further from reality as the long chilling hours passed.

CHAPTER NINETEEN

Nor did she return when, sometime toward
dawn, a voice roughened with emotion said,
"Thank God, it's Penelope—and she's got
Megan."

Strong arms lifted Pen's cramped and frozen
body to wrap it in blankets, and Megan slid out of
her stiff fingers as other hands drew the child, safe
and warm, from her clasp. Bright torches lighted
the mountainside, but Pen saw nothing as, conscious only of the necessity to shelter Megan, she
fought to free her arms of the blankets that encased them so that she could gather the little girl
close again.

Instead she herself was held tightly against
another body, warm and firm, and a voice said,
"It's all right, Penelope. Don't fight, darling—
we've got you both safe."

The voice was hoarse, and the wool-clad chest
under her cheek rose and fell unevenly, but Pen
noticed neither of those things. She wasn't even
aware of the meaning of the words, responding
only to their comforting tone. Insensibly reassured, she relaxed into the arms that held her,

and her clouded eyes closed as she slipped away again from the lights and voices around her.

She knew nothing of the long trip by stretcher down the fells and the return to her cottage, where Alistair reluctantly gave her over to a clucking Banny. She was unaware of the deft motherly hands that stripped off her sodden clothes and chafed her clammy skin before easing her into a bed that was warmed by hot-water bottles and heaped with soft bedclothes—among them her own leaf-green and fell-brown rug, woven while her heart healed from its first despair of learning that Alistair would marry her without loving her. Now she lay unaware, plucking at it with busy fingers, oblivious to the long watches he and Banny shared by her bed while Marigold crouched nearby and her cold became pneumonia, aggravated by stress and exposure. Too ill to be moved to the hospital, she knew nothing of the doctor's frequent visits, and nothing of his worried prognosis.

All Pen did know through her fever was that she seemed to be huddled helplessly, small and alone, inside the vast echoing emptiness of her skull. A hot dry wind howled endlessly through the vaulted chamber in which she was imprisoned, and when she cried out in the cracked little voice that was her loudest shout, her frightened, fretful hands were stilled by stronger ones, and blessedly cold liquids moistened her parched throat. Cool cloths soothed her burning cheeks, too, and sometimes she lay quietly under them, grateful for their relief. At other times, however, nothing calmed her, and she tossed hectically until a voice that was somehow beloved cut through the noisy nothingness of her hot prison and comforted her so that she could escape into the healing sanctuary of real sleep.

It was while she was sleeping one of these times that Nigel rapped softly on the door of her room and at Alistair's quiet murmur of acknowledgment let himself in. For a time then he simply looked at Pen, lying with her damp heavy hair pushed back from her forehead and tumbled on her pillows, a hot flush across her high cheekbones, and one thin hand lying loosely in Alistair's.

The bedclothes covering her rose and fell quickly, and the only sound in the room was her noisy breathing until Nigel said, "I'm taking Elise back to London with me."

Alistair stayed where he was and answered quietly, "Thank you."

At that the other man's black eyes lifted at last from Pen's still face, and he asked with something of his old satiric gleam, "For bringing her up here or for taking her back?"

"Both," Alistair returned in the same dry tone, and they exchanged a brief look of complete understanding before Nigel glanced away.

He fell silent again for a moment, and when he next spoke it was in a tone Pen wouldn't have recognized because it sounded nothing at all like either the mocking pagan she used to know or the cold, calculating stranger she had found in his new apartment the night of that wretched party. For a little while he spoke without either the old mask or the new shell.

"Actually, I brought her up here for my own sake, not for yours or hers, although after you phoned she finally told me most of the story about your brother and the kids—I'd known there was something, but not what it was. But I brought her here myself because I wanted to see Pen again, even with Elise nearby. The truth is, I suppose I still hoped I could talk her out of her country idyll and make her change her mind about refusing to marry me before it was too late."

Nothing had changed in the quiet room as he spoke, but somehow Alistair seemed to be sitting even more still. Nigel paused again and jammed both hands deep in his pockets, and then he went on in that same low voice.

"But when she came into that room, calling your name, I knew it was already too late. I hadn't a chance because she loves you, and whatever has gone wrong between you isn't going to alter that fact because she doesn't take back affection once she's given it."

Alistair's dark head was bent over the hot hand lying in his as Nigel continued levelly, "So I'm going back with Elise to that hothouse apartment she talked me into and the sham world where we both belong now. It's time, I guess, that I admitted the past is over, and Pen would be miserable with the kind of life I lead these days. Better she should stay here with you and those engaging kids of yours, to work out your lives as you may, without any interference from the two of us.''

At that Alistair came to his feet, unconsciously still holding Pen's hand in his for a moment, and she stirred slightly at the movement as he said in a voice that rasped, ''What?''

''While you've been standing guard over Pen, your kids have come to accept their mother more on her own terms, but they'll never worship her again the way they apparently once did, and they have no interest whatsoever in living anywhere but here with you and Pen,'' Nigel explained matter-of-factly.

He took a measured breath and went on in a tone he made very bland, ''And as for Elise herself, guilt had been making her say she wanted to take the children to live with her, but I pointed out that it would be a touch awkward, since she's living with me herself and there's no room for her to import a family overnight. Besides,'' he added, still more dryly, ''if her career left her no time for a family before this, things are still likely to be the same way. Somehow that seemed to make her reconsider, and after a proper show of reluctance she let herself be talked out of insisting. She's had a charming farewell scene with them and is now waiting for me in the car. I'll take her back to London and her theater world and see that she has contact with the children but doesn't interfere with their life here.''

As Nigel was talking, a gamut of expressions had chased each other across Alistair's mobile face. A look of deep gratitude, which could have embarrassed them both, was followed by one of wry recognition, almost amused now instead of bitter, at the description of Elise's decision to leave the children with him. It was a decision that meant so much to him, and she had made it so easily, preferring to leave her own children with their uncle rather than keep them herself. Obviously that searing scene in his study had left no permanent scars on her—any more than had all of the tragedy before it that had so marked Alistair. At Nigel's final sentence, however, his wry look yielded to one of skepticism.

Alistair was too tactful to express his doubts, but Nigel answered them anyway. Seeing that last expression on the other man's face, he gave a short bark of laughter, quickly silenced, and added calmly by way of a guarantee, "I'll be able to keep an eye on her because Elise is going to marry me. She doesn't know it yet, but marry me she will, because she'll decide that marriage to a well-known set designer—even more than an affair—could further her acting career. And unlike the first marriage, which she also made for reasons other than romance, this one will work out because we're the same sort now, she and I, and we both know the rules of this game. We'll fare tolerably well together.''

He glanced once more at Pen, and for a last moment his face was unguarded, then the mask came up again, more concealing than ever, and he murmured mockingly, "And so I shall leave Bo Peep and your two young lambs to your ministrations and betake myself back to the goats where I belong."

He looked like Pan himself, utterly pagan and unredeemed, but Alistair gave him a long steady look from eyes that saw clearly the choice Nigel was making, and held out his hand. It was gripped with sudden strength, and then Nigel was gone. The door closed quietly behind him, and Alistair gazed thoughtfully at it before he eased his long length back down onto the small stool by Pen's bed. She moved restlessly and murmured something indistinct, but settled into fitful sleep again when he said softly, "I'm here, Penelope."

BUT HE WASN'T when the day finally came that she opened her eyes and knew herself again. She searched the room in weak bewilderment, certain that he had been there, but only Banny appeared, rustling over from the window where she had been knitting by the last of the daylight.

"Well, lass, welcome home," she greeted Pen, the Scots burr strong in her voice as it always was when she was moved.

"Banny . . ." Pen began uncertainly.

"Aye, child," the other responded when she hesitated. "It's I, but you're in your own warm bed and have been there ever since they brought you down off the fells days ago, all wet and chilled, with your cold turning into pneumonia.''

Hazily Pen remembered the endless hours during which she had struggled to keep Megan warm. ''Megan?'' she asked with an effort.

''Bright as a button,'' Banny answered promptly. ''Thanks to you, the bairn took no harm from running off into the storm as she did. She's asked after you over and over, though, because she knows you made yourself ill by coming after her. In all the time you've been sick, she hasn't let that little pink blanket you wove her out of her sight.''

Pen thought that over slowly and then asked, ''May I see her now?''

''Well, no, lass, I'm afraid not.'' Banny's reply came much less promptly this time, and she seemed suddenly discomfited. ''The truth is, she isn't here just now.''

She paused uneasily now, but Pen didn't question her any further, simply closing her eyes again and lying quiet and wan against her pillows. If Megan was gone, she thought hazily, then Corey must be gone, as well. Alistair had probably sent both children away with Elise because he didn't want them to have any further contact with the faithless person he still believed Pen to be; better they should be with their mother...and Nigel? Weakly Pen wondered how her old friend fitted into all this. Her closed eyelids tightened a moment as she recalled his look of pain in Alistair's

study and her own realization that Elise now
shared his apartment. But how those things fit
together, or what part he had played before she
herself reached the study that night, Pen didn't
know.

Nor did she really have the energy to speculate
long. Instead her mind turned tiredly back to
Alistair. Had he perhaps taken the children down
to London himself, to see them settled there? If
so, her conviction that he had been there beside
her while she was ill, calling her out of her hot
prison in that tender, soothing voice, had been
only a feverish dream.

Helplessly she remembered the last time she'd
seen Alistair; he had been bending concernedly
over Elise, while Corey stood in the circle of his
mother's arm. Intent on Megan's disappearance,
they had all been unaware of the picture they
presented, but they had obviously stood together
like that before, in other places at other times, and
they might again in the future. After all, Alistair
had loved Elise once, and surely nothing—not
even her role in Peter's death—could kill a love
entirely? Unwillingly Pen remembered how
natural the three of them had looked together
before she fled the room, and the image now
seemed etched in her mind. It stayed there, and exhausted tears made silvery lines down her white
cheeks.

Seeing the tears, Banny hurried to wipe them
away. She didn't ask their cause, knowing the easy

tears of convalescence and—more importantly—
knowing Pen. Instead for a moment she seemed
about to say something urgent, but then she
changed her mind and just crooned comfort as
though Pen were a child again. "There, love,
there, lamb; you're all worn out by the fever.
Sleep again and build up your strength, and Banny
will watch over you."

She smoothed the tumbled hair back from Pen's
forehead with a cool hand, and under her loving
touch Pen settled obediently to sleep, still too
weak to endure any further thought of Alistair.
She slept most of the next day, as well, but when
early evening came she finally awoke alert and
hungry. Delighted, Banny helped her into her
warm green dressing gown and settled her into the
chair by the window, then steadied her uncertain
hands as she spooned up a hot Scotch broth.

As she ate, Pen gradually realized Banny was
nearly bursting with some suppressed excitement.
The older woman's round wrinkled cheeks were
even rosier than usual, and behind the gold-
rimmed spectacles her eyes were nearly snapping
with excitement. Feeling as though she'd been
gone from the village for a long time, Pen
wondered what had happened while she was ill to
account for Banny's behavior. Finally newly
reawaking curiosity got the better of her; setting
aside her spoon when she'd finished the broth, she
taxed Banny for an explanation.

"All right, Banny, I've finished every drop.

Now tell me what the news is that you're trying so
hard to keep to yourself—and doing such a bad
job with! Your face looks like a lighted Christmas
tree," she teased gently.

Relieved, perhaps, that Pen was taking an interest in something, Banny made no attempt to
deny that anything had happened. Putting the
bowl on the window ledge instead, she raised both
hands to her red cheeks and laughed like a girl.
"Och, Penelope, lass, am I really that easy to see
through?"

"Yes," Pen said unequivocally. "Now out with
it."

Banny took a deep breath and then obediently
burst out with the truth. "We're going to New
York to see Jamie's boy!" she exclaimed.

"Oh, Banny, how wonderful!" Pen breathed
delightedly. "How? When?"

Her old face wreathed in smiles, Banny explained, "Edward finished that Wordsworth book
of his and took the money from it to buy us
tickets, without even telling me what he was up to.
This afternoon he surprised me with them, the
dear man. We're to be off in a week, lass, after
we're both certain you've mended fine."

"Banny, you didn't delay your trip for me,"
Pen protested.

"Just a few days, child; yon doctor from the
village says you're well past the worst of things,
but we both wanted to keep an eye on you just a
mite longer than he said was necessary."

"Oh, Banny," Pen murmured in a voice that had suddenly grown hoarse again, "I do love you both."

The ready tears came again, but this time Banny simply handed her a checked handkerchief from her own pocket. "Yes, child, we know that," she said gently, "and we love you, too. You're as dear to us as if you were our own kin instead of Andrew's. So mind that you behave yourself properly and get well so we can stop fretting about you!"

That last came out in a much brisker tone, which made Pen laugh a little as she mopped away the tears. "Yes, mum!" she accepted her orders.

With a little smiling nod of approval, Banny patted Pen's hand and then collected the empty broth bowl from the window ledge, promising to return with more in an hour or so. Pen was left with Marigold on her lap to watch how the fells, becoming gold now with autumn, preserved the setting sun's last golden rays until dusk had covered all the rest of the Vale of Grasmere.

As she gazed out the window, the smile Pen had produced for Banny faded, and she began to think ahead. She really *was* beginning to feel stronger now, and soon would be well enough that even Banny and Edward could stop worrying their dear hearts about her and be off to the States. When they had gone, only Ian Ballantyne would be left of the people here she'd grown to love; she could stay and weave for him as Uncle Andrew had done—but to be in Grasmere and imagine for the rest of her life that she saw Alistair's beloved face at every corner? Involuntarily she shrank away from the pain in her heart.

The thought was unbearable, and so she resisted it. Soon she would have to make plans for a life without him, but for now some instinct for healing held the future at bay so that her body could mend itself without being whipsawed by grief. Instead of the future, then, she thought of the past, gazing out at the familiar fells but seeing superimposed on them all that had happened to her here in their shadow since she'd first come to the Lakes.

Absently stroking Marigold, she remembered her first two awkward meetings with Alistair and the chaotic encounter with Megan, Corey and Levvy. She relived Alistair's icy politeness when he discovered where Nora Button had left the children, and then traced the slow thawing in their relationship, his tepid proposal and those few blissfully warm days that had led up to his promise to repeat the question. There, however, she halted the parade of memories to avoid remembering that last ugly scene in Alistair's study that had made her feel as though all warmth had gone forever from the world. To escape that absolute cold, she leaned her cheek against the glass of the window and shut her eyes, reliving instead what she'd dreamed had happened the night he gave her brandy and the tender promise of the next morning, before she'd gone south to her father's bedside.

So it was that she failed to see Alistair himself when the dusty Rover purred quietly up the lane at the end of an equally long trip north. She didn't open her eyes until after the car had pulled up in the shadows by his cottage. Then a step in the passage outside her door made her sit up and turn with a bravely smiling face to reassure Banny that she was indeed behaving herself and getting better.

But it wasn't Banny who met Pen's eyes; it was Alistair, and her smile evaporated as Marigold jumped from her lap and went to wind herself affectionately around his ankles. His own eyes were on the fresh bowl of broth he carried, but the rest of his face was impassive, and her searching look could find no clue to his presence. Why had he come—and why now? Had he just returned from seeing the children settled in with Elise, and perhaps Nigel? Or had he in fact never gone but just sent the children with their mother when she left, confident that they would somehow ultimately be happy with her? But then where had he been these past empty days?

Unconsciously weaving her fingers together, Pen wondered unhappily if he had come to finish the indictment of her character he'd begun in the study; nothing in his face indicated he'd revised his opinion of her since that appalling night, and her heart seemed to grow smaller within her. Then she remembered that although he would apparently never forgive what he saw as her desertion, the truth was that she had no reason whatsoever to feel guilty. Miserable, yes—she allowed herself that—but not guilty. And with a little stubborn lift of her chin she faced Alistair courageously.

He had hooked a stool over near her chair and now lowered himself gingerly onto its narrow seat while Marigold continued to loop herself happily around his feet. Pen had a moment to wonder why the cat had evidently changed her mind about someone she'd previously detested, but then Alistair raised his eyes from the bowl he held and looked at Pen. Their eyes met, and she discovered to her bewilderment that his steady look contained not the scorn she had steeled herself to face again but the leaping blue flame she'd seen there only a few times before. The faintest sense of wonder began to stir in her mind, and her heart, contracted from pain like a flower in the frost, began to unfold.

But all he said was, "I promised Banny I'd have you finish this while she went home to make supper for her Edward."

Dipping the spoon into the broth, he held it toward Pen, and too bemused to do anything else, she opened her mouth like a baby bird and let him slide the spoon in. The angle of his lean cheek changed with something that wasn't quite a smile, but he said nothing more until the bowl was empty and he had set it aside. Then he glanced at her and murmured, "Good thing that wasn't brandy; I don't want your wits addled this time, my love."

Her mouth closed now, Pen looked less like a

baby bird, but at the endearment her eyes opened wide until they were enormous in her thin face. He noted that, and the transparency of her pale skin, with a little frown and paused, but then went on speaking.

"I've tried to ask you this before, but first brandy and then fate prevented me. Decency should prevent me tonight, as well, from taking advantage of your illness by pressing you for an answer when your resistance is low, but I'll use any means now to make you forget the recent past and forgive me enough to tell me yes. I love you with all my heart, Penelope—you took the raveled threads of broken lives and wove them with sure and loving hands into a fabric of happiness that could last us all our days. Would you marry me so that it will?"

He hadn't moved; he still sat on the stool near her chair, with his elbows on his knees and his hands clasped in front of him. But in the silence that followed his words Pen saw that now his fingers were laced together so tightly that the tendons stood out whitely across the backs of his hands—those hands she loved, which could be warm and protective, or caressing and inflammatory. Delicate color rose in Pen's cheeks as she looked up and into his face. He had asked it again, the question whose answer she had known for so long, and as he let her see the naked longing in his eyes, she knew also that this proposal was everything she'd ever dreamed of. This time he had said at last that he loved her, and the words washed away her heartbroken disappointment at his earlier proposal and her hurt at his bitter condemnation the last time they had faced each other. All the pain and grief were gone as though they had never been, and she gazed back at him with luminous delight.

"Yes."

He closed his eyes and his face went very still. Then he took a deep slow breath and said softly, "I thought I'd lost you. I thought I'd driven you away with my bitterness, and then lost you with Megan in the storm. When I found you lying huddled and frozen in that little cave and you didn't even know me. . . ."

His voice broke off, and she reached out with infinite tenderness to lay reassuring fingers along his cheek. At her touch he opened his eyes, and the salty wetness of unfamiliar tears spilled onto her hand. She looked at her hand wonderingly for a moment and leaned forward to brush away the tears with her lips. Until she had finished, he sat motionless; then he turned his head to find her mouth with his own, and the blue flame blazed up to consume them both.

When Pen knew time and place again, it was completely dark outside, but inside in a pool of warm lamplight she was still in her chair. Now, however, she lay across Alistair's lap, and his arms cradled her as she traced the curve of his chin and the long clear line of his lips with one joyous fingertip. He kissed it as it passed, and it came back to linger awhile for more kisses before wandering happily on to smooth his straight dark brows. He raised them under her touch, and she giggled until he caught her closer and kissed her breathless again. When he released her lips again at last, her head dropped back against the scratchy warmth of his old tweed jacket, and something in the pocket rustled.

Gently lifting Pen's head back up, Alistair reached into the pocket and drew out a crumpled piece of paper. He unfolded it on Pen's dressing gown, and her sketch of Megan gazed up at them, preserving in its few deft lines the essence of delight that shone through the child's face, encircled by rosy wool.

They both looked at it, but Alistair spoke first.

"Your magnificent drawing of Megan," he said quietly, "embodying all the love you felt for her. And I thought for a time that you could have abandoned her in spite of your promise, abandoned the children and me, too, and disappeared without a trace."

Pen looked up to speak, but he laid two fingers gently across her lips and silenced her so that he could continue. His words seemed irrelevant at first.

"While you were most ill, the children were terribly upset and restless, prowling around like a pair of caged tigers as they hunted for distractions to keep themselves busy. They washed poor

Leviathan, they weeded your garden—don't be surprised if nothing comes up next spring—'' he interrupted himself to slant a laughing look at her before growing serious again ''—and they even attempted to clean out my study. They brought me this when they found it lying in Leviathan's bed of papers.''

He fell silent a moment, and Pen wondered if he had turned it over then and found her note. He answered her unspoken question rather obliquely.

''All I can say, in feeble defense of my indefensible behavior when you came back from London, is that I had already packed the car when I saw your note.''

''Packed the car?'' Pen echoed blankly.

''Yes, my love, packed the car for a trip to see your family and tell them what I had done to you, before I asked if I might marry you and spend the rest of my life making it up to you. And when I'd told them the whole inexcusable thing, your mother simply smiled her permission, and your father asked if I knew there were seventeen different kinds of 'if.' '' He grinned reminiscently and added, ''I took that as an agreement and thanked him, and the kids nearly deafened the poor man with their noisy glee.''

Pen had been smiling lovingly at his description of her parents, but now she looked up in surprise. ''The kids?'' she asked, repeating his words again.

''Yes, my beautiful parrot, Corey and Megan. I took them with me because this time you weren't well enough to tend them for me while I was gone, and because I thought they deserved to be in on my vital interview with your parents. Also,'' he added more seriously again, ''I thought your parents ought to know what you were in for before they gave their permission for me to saddle you with a ready-made family.''

''But such a loved and loving one,'' Pen qualified quickly. She began to cuddle into Alistair's arms again, but then an unwelcome thought crept into her happiness, and she looked slowly up at the infinitely dear face above her and risked her joy by asking, ''Elise?''

Alistair met her anxious eyes and said with quiet conviction, so that she couldn't ever torment herself by doubting his words, ''Elise won't bother any of us. She made her peace with Corey and Megan, but they agree with her now that it wouldn't be best for them to live with her. She was inclined to insist at first, hoping to ease her conscience, but then she admitted to herself that she had always considered them a hindrance to her career, and nothing's changed that. Also, Nigel reminded her how much time and energy it takes to raise children, and her conscience was suddenly stilled.''

Pen considered carefully the implications of Alistair's comments, but then she focused on one name, wrinkling her forehead in a worried little frown. She was so happy herself, but Nigel's unhappy face as she had last seen it rose before her, and she murmured, ''Oh, Nigel.''

"Elise has the lead in the newest play he's working on," Alistair explained, "and when she told him she was coming up here, he offered to bring her because he wanted to see you again."

"But he didn't really see much of me."

"Enough, because he decided after all that it wouldn't do any good to try making you reconsider his proposal. He saw your feelings for me more clearly than I dared to, and I'll always be grateful to the man."

"Why?"

"He reminded me what a generous and loving person you are," Alistair answered gravely, and Pen's cheeks went pink under his gaze. Then his eyes crinkled slightly at the corners, and he added succinctly, "And he said he's going to marry Elise."

She laughed a little at the relief in his voice, but then her smile faded. The past might be over and done, but even in the present Elise was a woman who had serious problems, selfishness among them. How happy would Nigel ever be with someone like that?

"Penelope." Alistair turned her chin with gentle but firm fingers so that she had to look straight at him. "Will you mind?"

"Oh, no!" she reassured him vehemently. "It's only—"

"Only that you wanted something better for him?" Alistair finished her sentence perceptively.

"Yes," she agreed. "But it's just because he's a very old friend!"

Alistair chuckled at her disclaimer before becoming serious again. "Well, I've got the something better," he said, and kissed her pale forehead with a tender gravity that made the gesture a salute. "But he knows from the start what Elise really is, and that's an advantage neither Peter nor I ever had. And I have an odd hunch they might even make something of it; I suspect that in spite of themselves they'll be good for each other. At least he'll see to it that she invites the children to be with her occasionally. As they grow older they'll benefit from a little town bronze."

"But where are they now?" Pen sat up in his lap to demand, realizing that while her fears of losing the children were groundless now, she still had no idea where they were.

"With your tolerant family, and I hope they don't slow down your father's recovery. I rang Ann up and pleaded with her to take them out occasionally, to give your folks a breather. Meanwhile they're raising cain with your siblings and making more noise than ever to distract your poor father while they wait for me to bring you back for the wedding, as soon as you're well enough to travel."

Suddenly teasing, he slid a hand into his pocket again and brought out another piece of paper, which he unfolded and dangled before Pen's startled eyes. "But for now, my love, here's the special license to let you know you can't escape me anymore."

Unconsciously Pen reached for the paper with eager fingers and an instant later blushed at the revealing movement. He kissed her soundly for it, giving the precious license into her keeping, and then asked, "And while the kids stay in Dulwich, would you and Marigold mind honeymooning in Scotland along the Antonine Wall? My publisher wants me to see if there's another book in the Romans' brief time in Scotland, and of course I'll need my illustrator—" Pen nodded delightedly "—and her cat, since somewhere during all the hours we spent watching over you together she seems to have decided I'm not to be allowed out of her sight in the future."

He gave Marigold, crouched at their feet, a resigned look that made Pen giggle, and then he smiled wickedly into her eyes. "Well," he said consideringly, "that seems to take care of all the things we had to discuss, but for some reason Banny still hasn't come back to defend propriety and send me on my way, so it seems I'll have to stay for a bit yet."

He paused, and the teasing look faded as he rose easily with her in his arms and set her on her feet for a minute, so that she stood close against his heartbeat with her hands linked tightly around his neck. Gazing down at her with passion and tenderness that made her catch her breath, he said softly, "I love you, my gray-eyed weaver. You've woven yourself into the fabric of my life on a loom you made of love, and I'll never be ragged or torn again."

The gentle kiss she gave him was like a promise, and he took it from her, but then he lifted his mouth from hers an instant and added, "But I never did think that cat was much of a chaperon."

Pen had a moment to wonder what he was referring to, and then he bent his head to her again and blotted out all coherent thought with his kiss and his touch. His mouth claimed hers softly and then with rising urgency, while his hands slipped beneath her robe, a sweet intrusion leaving a track of fire as they roamed across the smooth flesh of her hips and up to her breasts. Molten in his arms, she clung to him, pressing desperately against this one solid thing in a reeling world of love and need. A small contented sigh escaped her, her breath warm on his lips.

Behind them Marigold leaped gracefully onto their abandoned chair, turned twice and settled herself neatly in place. She blinked at the two across the room and then closed her amber eyes. Her purring was loud in the quiet room.

For a truly SUPER read, don't miss...

SUPERROMANCE

EVERYTHING YOU'VE ALWAYS WANTED A LOVE STORY TO BE!

Contemporary!
A modern romance for the modern woman—set in the world of today.

Sensual!
A warmly passionate love story that reveals the beautiful feelings between a man and a woman in love.

Dramatic!
An exciting and dramatic plot that will keep you enthralled till the last page is turned.

Exotic!
The thrill of armchair travel—anywhere from the majestic plains of Spain to the towering peaks of the Andes.

Satisfying!
Almost 400 pages of romance reading—a long satisfying journey you'll wish would never end.

SUPERROMANCE
FROM THE PUBLISHER THAT UNDERSTANDS HOW YOU FEEL ABOUT LOV

Available wherever paperback books are sold or through
Harlequin Reader Service

In the U.S.A.
1440 South Priest Drive
Tempe, AZ 85281

In Canada
649 Ontario Street
Stratford, Ontario N5A 6W2